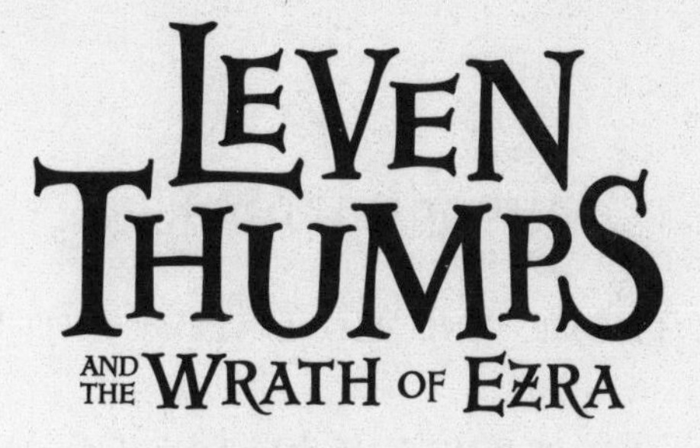
LEVEN
THUMPS
AND THE WRATH OF EZRA

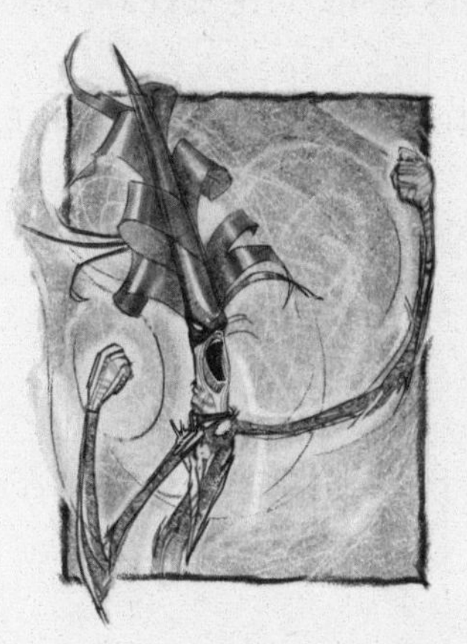

Also by Obert Skye

Leven Thumps and the Gateway to Foo

Leven Thumps and the Eyes of the Want

Leven Thumps and the Whispered Secret

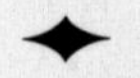

Coming soon:

The Trappings of Comfort

Leven Thumps and the Wrath of Ezra

◆

Obert Skye

Illustrated by Ben Sowards

Aladdin

New York London Toronto Sydney

This book is a work of fiction. Any references to historical events, real people, or real locales are used fictitiously. Other names, characters, places, and incidents are the product of the author's imagination, and any resemblance to actual events or locales or persons, living or dead, is entirely coincidental.

ALADDIN
An imprint of Simon & Schuster Children's Publishing Division
1230 Avenue of the Americas, New York, NY 10020
First Aladdin paperback edition September 2009

Originally published in hardcover by Shadow Mountain
Published by arrangement with Deseret Book Company

For information about special discounts for bulk purchases, please contact Simon & Schuster Special Sales at 1-866-506-1949 or business@simonandschuster.com.
The Simon & Schuster Speakers Bureau can bring authors to your live event. For more information or to book an event contact the Simon & Schuster Speakers Bureau at 1-866-248-3049 or visit our website at www.simonspeakers.com.
The text of this book was set in A Garamond.
Manufactured in the United States of America
2 4 6 8 10 9 7 5 3 1
The Library of Congress has cataloged the hardcover edition as follows:
Skye, Obert.
Leven Thumps and the wrath of Ezra / Obert Skye
p. cm.
Summary: As Leven, Geth, and Winter continue their quest to save Foo from the invading armies of rants, a new threat arrives, the Dearth.
ISBN 978-1-59038-963-8 (hc)
[1. Magic—Fiction. 2. Voyages and travels—Fiction. 3. Fantasy.] I. Title.
PZ7.S62877Ley 2008
[Fic]—dc22
ISBN 978-1-4169-9092-5 (pbk)
ISBN 978-1-4169-9678-1 (eBook)

For Clover

I'm so sorry they now know

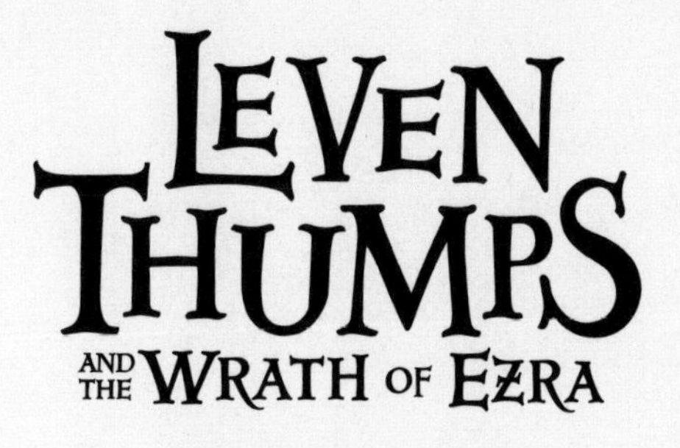
LEVEN THUMPS
AND THE WRATH OF EZRA

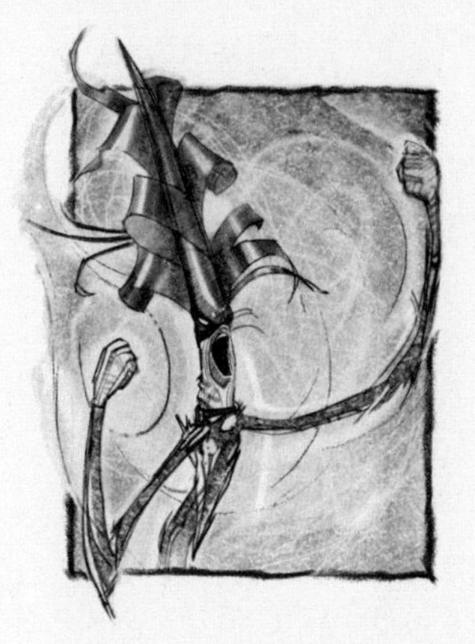

Contents

Contents

Contents

INVISIBLE VILLAGE
RANT ARMIES
FTÉ
CINDER DEPRESSION
RED GROVE
HIDDEN BORDER
VEIL SEA
THE DEVIL'S SPIRAL
CUSP
THIRTEEN STONES
GLOAM
WET BORDER

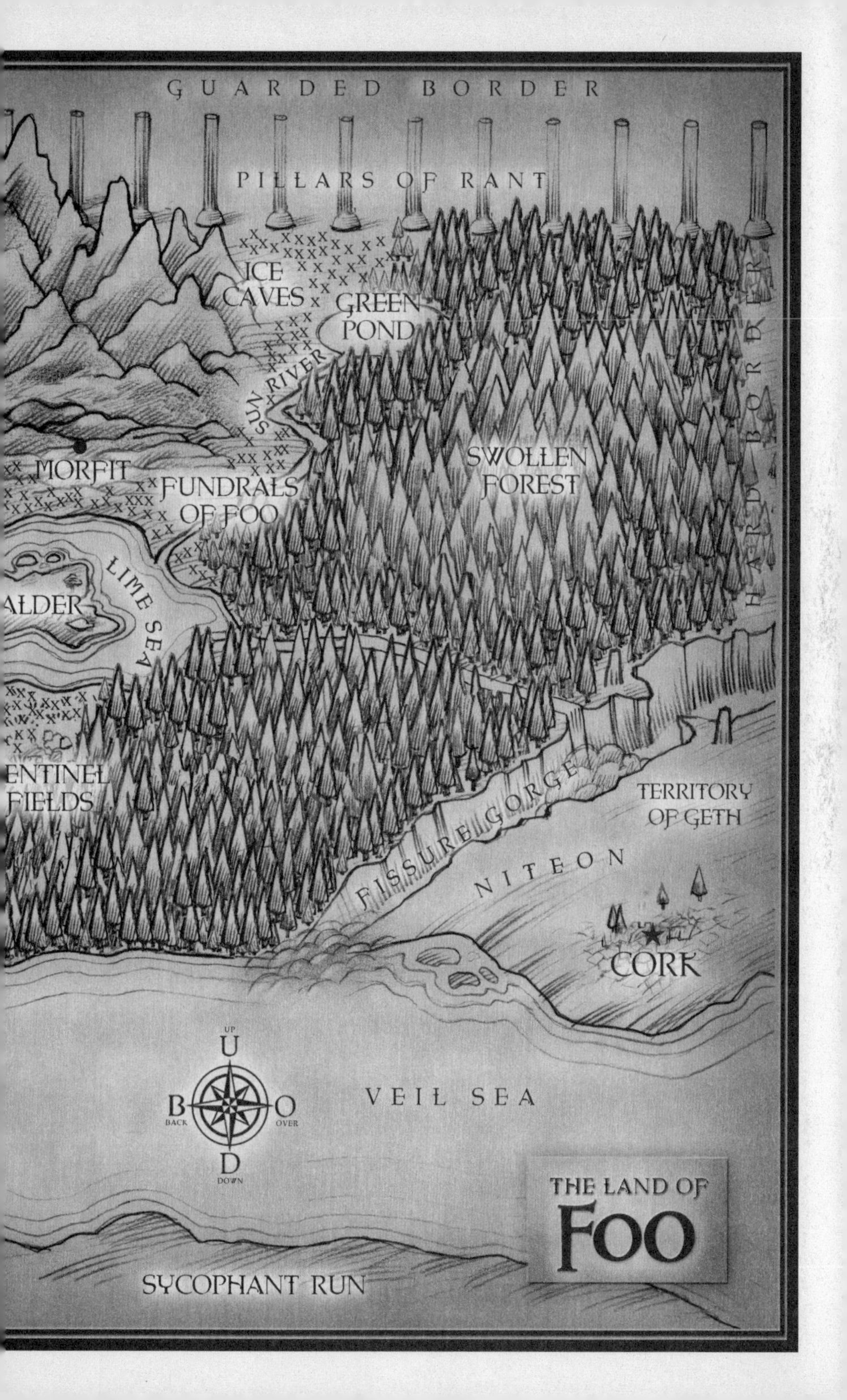
GUARDED BORDER
PILLARS OF RANT
ICE CAVES
GREEN POND
SUN RIVER
HARD BORDER
SWOLLEN FOREST
MORFIT
FUNDRALS OF FOO
LIME SEA
ALDER
ENTINEL FIELDS
FISSURE GORGE
TERRITORY OF GETH
NITEON
CORK
UP
U
B
BACK
O
OVER
D
DOWN
VEIL SEA
THE LAND OF
FOO
SYCOPHANT RUN

FOREWORD

NUTSHELL

I remember it vividly.

It happened years ago as I was innocently eating pie in a small pub in Europe. The pub was called Figamullers, the weather was chilly, and the pie was blueberry. The entire establishment smelled of mint and leather and I remember the waiter was wearing a black wig and spoke with a German accent.

I was sitting there on a bar stool reading the paper when an old man stumbled in and sat next to me. He was a bearded fellow with a ruddy face and dark, honest eyes. He called himself Alder and he looked as if the weight of the world was stapled to his back. Even while sitting he had a difficult time not collapsing under the strain. The old man ordered a cup of potato soup and then proceeded to change my life by sharing a secret about a place, a secret he had been carrying around for years.

I offered to pay for his soup and he thanked me by taking me

into his full confidence. He knew of Foo—but more importantly, he knew that in time Leven Thumps would be called up and the balance of all dreams would be perched on the shoulders of a young boy and his capable friend Winter.

He told me that he himself was trapped in Reality. He told me of a person called the Want and how Leven and Geth and Winter would all be tricked by this selfish man. He told me how sides would gather in Foo and how Reality would slowly be brought into the war. He told me how many would brush the war off as unimportant or unbelievable. How some would find it silly or refuse to acknowledge it despite the fact that signs were everywhere. But what struck me the most was his knowledge of a being called the Dearth and how he believed that the Dearth, if left unchallenged, would destroy all of mankind and force the world back into a state of soil. He told me how if dreams die, mankind would wither and our existence would matter no more. He told me how a person gets to Foo and how fate snatches those it needs. He also ordered a second bowl of soup.

Leven's life before with Terry and Addy was horrible. Leven was lucky Winter got away from her nasty guardian, Janet, and helped him race across the world to find the gateway into Foo. He blew up the gateway believing it was the best thing for Foo. He followed Geth across the realm so that Geth could be restored, and he was tricked into becoming the Want so that Hector could finally rest in peace—leaving Leven in the position of the Want and in control of the entire fate of Foo.

Now the final unfolding has begun. The seven keys of Foo

have been used and the Dearth is rising. The sycophants are in danger and in Reality Terry and Addy are about to join forces with a one-time janitor and the angriest, most confused toothpick alive—Ezra.

I have written many things and hope to write many more. But it is Foo which matters most. There would be little reason to lie down at night without the possibility of seeing things bigger and more amazing than the average day might bring about. Why pick up a pen or type on a keyboard if there's no imagination or wonder left to behold? I would hate to be in the position of hoping for nothing simply because my brain can no longer dream.

Foo is an amazing place. So much is happening there. There are many new creatures and beings; places and powers and confusion abound. But it really comes down to this—good versus evil and hope versus the cold, lonely existence of selfishness.

Believe—it is our best defense.

CHAPTER ONE

Nothing Looks the Same in the Light

The orange sun shifted in the green sky, sending rippling waves of soft yellow warmth down upon the bulk of Foo. The heat hit anyone standing in the open and caused most to wish they hadn't dressed as heavily as they had. The scent of freshly tilled dirt filled the air and gave the sun's rays something to push and twist themselves through. A fat goat waddled across a mossy field, its stomach only inches from the ground. The goat stopped and mewed loudly, bothered by the intensity of the heat.

The mischievous sun shined even brighter.

"Why won't the sun just make up its mind?" a tall cog named Colin complained. "I thought it was supposed to be cold today?"

"I don't think that's gonna happen," a taller cog named Tanner replied.

The two boys were wearing hats that covered their orange foreheads and long work robes that were bound at the ankles so

as to not get in the way. Like most cogs they were at work, doing what needed to be done to keep things moving in Foo. Their blue hands were covered with gloves made from sheepskin.

"Look, we're over halfway finished," Colin said proudly. "This field's gonna be ready for planting early."

"Then let's move slower," Tanner said, looking around. "The sooner we finish the sooner we'll have to do something else."

Colin's diamond-tipped rake pierced the dirt with a satisfying *twitch.* Colin pulled the rake back, turning over the earth slowly. Bright red dirt bubbled up, mixing with the sun-darkened topsoil and bits of green moss.

"I like how that looks," Colin said, pointing to the ground.

"You love the dirt?" Tanner joked.

Colin pushed Tanner. "That's not what I mean."

"You know what?" Tanner said. "We could stop working for a little bit. It's not like anyone's going to see us out here."

The fat goat stared at them.

"Except for that goat," Tanner added. "And guess what, I brought some Spitstick."

Colin stopped working and leaned on his rake. "I thought your mom said she'd freeze you if she caught you with any more candy."

"My mother's not going to catch me," Tanner said, dropping his rake. "Not here."

Tanner reached into his robe and pulled out two short brown tubes. He handed one to Colin.

"You first." Colin looked around nervously.

Tanner popped the top of his off and took a long lick,

swirling the Spitstick around inside his mouth.

"Lemon," he reported.

Colin opened his and did the same.

"Plum," he said, disappointed.

"Well," Tanner said, "it's not like we eat this stuff for the taste."

Both boys' mouths began to bubble.

Tanner gurgled, the sides of his throat fizzing while his mouth filled with saliva. The pressure in his throat built to the point where he had to cock his head back and open his mouth. He thrust backward as a large wad of spit shot from his mouth and out into the air. The giant ball of yellow saliva traveled over three hundred feet and slapped down near the back of the field by a cluster of tall pointed trees.

"Na bad," Colin tried to say. "Wahch dis."

Colin's throat fizzed intensely as his salivary glands excreted massive amounts of spit into his mouth. He struggled to keep his lips closed, letting it build to the maximum amount. His head shook and he stamped his feet as his cheeks expanded to the size of grapefruits. His neck bulged.

"Spit!" Tanner yelled. "Remember what happened to Lark?"

Colin held it two seconds more. Then, right before his mouth exploded, he cocked his head back and opened his mouth. A cannonball-size, plum-colored spitball blew from his mouth. Colin was knocked back onto his rear, his teeth clicking as he fell. The spit arched high into the green air and traveled twice as far as Tanner's. It splashed down out of view, bits of it flinging back up into the air.

"Did you see that?" Colin said proudly.

"You're crazy," Tanner replied. "Lark still can't hear out of his left ear, and he ruined his pants."

"Let's go see where it landed," Colin said, ignoring Tanner. "I bet it was five hundred feet away."

"I bet it wasn't," Tanner argued, taking off running.

They left the fat goat alone, crossed the field, and zigzagged through the trees. They passed the large yellow spot where Tanner's shot had come down and ran a few hundred feet more.

"There!" Tanner shouted.

To their left on the ground was a huge, plum-colored splash mark. It was at least five feet wide and about a foot longer.

"Whoa, that's as big as I've ever seen," Tanner said.

"Let's try it again," Colin said, opening back up his Spitstick.

"Wait," Tanner whispered. "Did you hear something?"

"Only the sound of you chickening out."

"No seriously, listen."

Colin sighed and listened. "It's the wind."

"No," Tanner insisted. "Something's moaning. Over there."

They ran up and over, sliding down a small ditch bank by a dry creek.

"Hhhhaaaahhggg," a dry voice moaned. "Hhhahgg."

"That's not the wind," Colin said, frightened. "We should get back to work."

"Now who's scared?" Tanner whispered.

"Hhhhhhahhhhg."

"That's not a good sound," Colin said.

"Over there," Tanner pointed.

On the edge of the ditch bank there was a short gouge in the soil. A black ooze was moving out of the crack.

"What is it?" Colin said, his heart beating faster.

They walked slowly toward the gouge.

"Is it mud?" Colin asked.

As they got closer they could see the black ooze actually had some form. It was partway out of the ground and not moving. Tanner picked up a stick and reached out to prod it. As he touched it the black form rolled over. It had the shape of a head and arms but it was completely black, as if made from tar. Two dark eyes flashed open, looking directly at the boys, and its mouth relaxed, letting out a long, dry, make-you-never-want-to-be-alone-in-the-dark-ever-again noise.

"Hhhhhhhaaaaaagghhhh."

The boys screamed in harmony and then fell over each other as they scrambled to climb out of the ditch. Once out they ran as fast as they could, never looking back and never fully realizing what they had witnessed.

It had been many hundreds of years since any part of the Dearth had been able to push up out of the soil. The Dearth closed his eyes and moaned again. He lopped onto his stomach and reached his dark arms out. He dug his long fingers into the soil and strained to pull himself farther out of the gouge. Exhausted, the Dearth moaned in agony and frustration and collapsed against the ground.

The sound of footsteps shuffling across the ground could be heard. The shuffling became louder and louder.

"Aaazurrrrre," the Dearth moaned.

"Over here!" one of Azure's rants yelled. "Here."

Azure moved down the ditch bank surrounded by four rants.

He reached his arms forward and parted his way out of those guarding him.

"Aaaazurrre," the Dearth moaned again.

"I'm here," Azure said, falling to his knees. "I've found you."

Azure wrapped his arms around the Dearth and with great effort pulled him all the way from the soil.

The Dearth screamed in pain. He was thin and looked like a pitch-black rubbery mannequin. His body was spongy to the touch and as limp as moist rags.

Azure picked him up and carried him down the ditch and up to a long-abandoned dirt road. There were dozens of rants on the road. They all had kilves and stood by onicks. At the head of the group was a cart with two onicks strapped to the front. On each onick sat a rant. Azure stepped up as if to climb into the cart.

"No," the Dearth hissed. "Drag me, I must feel the soil."

"Of course," Azure said.

Azure laid the Dearth down behind the cart. He retrieved a short length of rope and tied one end around the Dearth's waist. He then tied the other end to the back of the wagon.

"Are you certain?" Azure asked.

"Travel slowly," the Dearth moaned. "My strength will build."

Azure climbed up onto the wagon and hissed at the riders. Slowly the cart began to move, dragging the Dearth behind it.

The remaining rants rode in formation behind as the Dearth whispered softly, "Leeeeven."

CHAPTER TWO

THE TRAPPINGS OF COMFORT

There's some great real estate in Foo—beautiful spots that bring new meaning to the word gorgeous. I love the property above the Sun River and just below the Pillars of Rant. I also wouldn't mind buying a lot near the mountains at the edge of Morfit. But without a doubt the long span of land on the back side of the Devil's Spiral reaching over to the start of the Fté mountains is some of the most beautiful land in all of Foo. There isn't a bad blade of grass to be found growing anywhere on it. For this reason most of the elite and pompous have filled the land with castles and mansions. They have also built many walls in an effort to keep the un-elite from getting too close to them.

It was down from one of those walls that Leven dropped, hitting the ground with a soft thud. The night was dark, but the large house in the distance was well lit. It sat there like a proud mother showing off all her rooms. The land was miles back from

the Devil's Spiral, but the sound of rushing water could still be heard faintly in the distance.

Leven waved and Winter dropped down behind him.

"Looks cozy," she whispered.

Leven pulled his kilve from behind his back and swung it forward. The long wooden staff glowed slightly at its top.

"Geth should be in place by now," he said quietly. "Clover, you here?"

Leven felt something shiver on his right shoulder.

"Good, let's go."

Leven stepped quietly along the wall and down through the brick courtyard. Large stone statues, shaped like roven in various attack positions, lined the path.

"Makes you feel so warm and welcome," Winter said.

Leven looked at Winter and thought of Phoebe. The longing his grandfather had shown him before Lith was destroyed weighed constantly on his mind. He tried to shake off the feeling, but it was so powerful it kept creeping back into his soul. Looking at Winter only reminded him that Phoebe was still trapped.

"I smell mice," Clover whispered, bringing Leven's thoughts back to the situation at hand.

Winter pulled out her kilve.

"I wish I could just freeze them," she said.

"Mice?" Leven asked.

Leven and Winter moved behind two statues and listened carefully. Leven could see a pack of large creatures running

toward them. They were three feet high with long legs and square noses that twitched as they ran. Their round ears and long, rubbery tails gave them a rodentlike silhouette. There were at least a dozen of them.

"Those are the mice?" Leven complained.

Winter didn't answer; she was too busy knocking the wind out of the closest one. The poor beast slid across the stone and up against a far statue.

Leven looked at the creatures. Their faces were expressive and he could see and feel what their small brains were thinking. Leven's heart pumped with confusion and then clarity. Without understanding his own actions he stepped forward and held out his hands. The mice stopped and looked up at him. Their heads twitched and their feet tapped as if being forced to stay in place.

"What are you doing?" Winter whispered.

"I don't have any idea," Leven replied.

The mice folded their legs inward and fell to the ground.

"Wow," Clover said. "That's helpful."

Leven and Winter stepped carefully through the large, resting creatures.

"Seriously," Winter said, hushed. "How did . . ."

"Leeeven," the sky said softly.

"What?" Leven asked, looking around.

"Leeeven," the sky whispered.

"Someone's calling my name," Leven said quietly.

"Well, it's not me," Winter whispered. "I didn't hear anything."

"Me neither," Clover said. "Sometimes the wind can sound like a person humming."

"I don't think it's the wind."

Leven shook his head. They moved closer to the house. Through the large side window they could see someone sitting inside near a huge fire.

"That's him," Winter said. "Knoll."

Knoll was a traitor—a lithen who had turned his back on Geth and Foo. His place was to occupy the sixth stone, but he had given up his responsibility for the opportunity to live lavishly on the mainland of Foo.

Knoll was sitting by the fire, his long braids hanging over the back of a soft chair. The ends of his dark mustache were woven into his braids and he was wearing a long white nightshirt. His cheeks were red from the warmth of the fire and his eyes were halfway closed. All around him large pieces of furniture sat draped in the hides of roven. In his right hand he held a fat wooden cup.

"Are you ready?" Leven asked.

"Of course," Winter said.

"Me too," Clover added. "In case you were wondering."

Leven tilted his head, nudging Clover.

"Good to know."

Leven walked up and gently took hold of the large wooden doorknob that was sticking out of a twelve-foot-high door. The knob was carved into the shape of an eye.

It didn't budge.

Leven motioned for Winter to move back. He lifted his kilve and slammed it down directly onto the knob. The eye cracked in half and Leven kicked the door directly below the knob. The door flew open as Knoll leapt up from his spot.

"Stay where you are," Leven demanded.

Despite the warmth of the room Knoll froze and then coolly relaxed his shoulders.

"How dare you come into my house and tell me what to do?" Knoll said casually. "My mice should have stopped you, but since they didn't, I suggest you leave while the opportunity is still available."

Winter moved in behind Leven.

Knoll saw her and shook his head. "How hard is it to kill one simple girl?"

"I'm not that simple," Winter replied.

"Where is he?" Leven said, ignoring Knoll's obnoxious statement.

"Get out," Knoll insisted.

"Where's Azure?"

"Again," Knoll said, stepping forward. "This is my house and your questions are not welcome."

Knoll sprang forward, grabbing his kilve that lay resting against the edge of his chair. He whipped it up over his head and threw his arms forward.

His hands were empty.

Knoll looked back in confusion. Geth was holding the kilve and smiling as if he had just been invited to test out every ride at

a new amusement park. Knoll tried to shelve his shock, but it was obvious from his twitching that he was unhappy to see his one-time friend Geth.

"How's my timing?" Geth asked.

"Perfect." Winter smiled.

"Where's Azure?" Leven asked again.

"We should sit," Knoll said, shaking. "I see no reason why this—like all problems—can't be talked through."

"You're welcome to sit," Leven said, continuing to stand. "Where's Azure?"

"You bother *me* to find out about another? It's too late." Knoll smiled faintly. "Azure's on to other things. I want nothing to do with him."

"What of the Dearth?" Geth asked.

"That fable?" Knoll laughed. "I know nothing of the Dearth," he insisted. "You must believe me, my part is finished. I am out of the tempest and alone in the lull."

"You're a horrible actor," Geth said, looking around. "You must know what Azure has planned for the Dearth. You seemed awfully close to him last time we saw you. You know, that time when we were bound up and you did nothing."

"My hands were tied," Knoll apologized. "It pained me to leave you."

"I'm sure it did," Winter said.

"Where's Azure?" Leven asked, bringing the conversation back around.

"I don't know," Knoll said. "My part is done. Let me rest."

"Don't tell me you bartered your integrity and sold out all of Foo for this?" Geth motioned to the lavish surroundings.

"I live very comfortably now," Knoll said. "I served Foo for many years with no reward but the health of mankind's dreams. Now I have something to show for myself—a warm place to drink and sleep."

"I don't believe what I'm hearing." Geth was disgusted.

"You always were stubborn," Knoll said.

"Where is he?" Leven insisted.

"Azure fights for more complicated things," Knoll answered. "The meshing of Foo is no concern of mine. So it happens, so it doesn't, I'll sip my ale in front of a warm fire regardless."

Geth looked stricken.

"The Dearth exists," Leven spoke up. "I've heard him."

Knoll looked at Leven. He brushed his mustache and tugged on his braids as if he were milking a cow. His body shook. The warmth of the room was so great everyone began to perspire. Knoll rubbed his forehead and spoke.

"So you're Leven Thumps," Knoll said nervously. "It was quite masterful how the Want played you. Give someone a task and tell him it's important and most anyone will follow. What brings me the most joy is how you, Geth, were strung along."

Geth pushed the sharp end of his kilve up against Knoll's chest. Knoll stepped back up against the wall. He held his drink in his hand and tried not to look as concerned as he really was.

"You can't kill me," Knoll said.

"We could apply some of the dirty tricks you have been

using," Geth said seriously. "Apparently you've become quite good at causing accidents."

"Why fight against us?" Knoll said. "You could have all this. You've done your part and fought hard. Reality must have been a task. So enjoy what you deserve."

Geth still held the kilve up to Knoll but said nothing.

"You could have it all," Knoll said. "Just say the word."

Geth stared at him. "No." He pushed the kilve harder into Knoll.

"Fine," Knoll sighed. "Azure's not here, but I have no reason to keep what I know from you. If it means I can get back to my drink, I'll speak. I am not the calendar by which Azure sets his movements, but it is public knowledge that in three days' time he will be meeting with the Twit of Cusp, cementing Cusp's part in what's to come. Have at him. Of course, you're fools if you think you can deter Azure—fools of the highest caliber. Will you leave me now?"

"I don't think so," Geth said kindly.

"We had a deal," Knoll scolded.

"That was your deal, not ours," Geth replied.

"Azure will kill you," Knoll raged. "You need me to save your lives."

Geth nodded at Winter. "Go ahead."

Knoll looked confused right up until the moment Winter hit him with her kilve on the back of his head. Knoll slouched forward onto his knees and fell facefirst onto the carpet, his drink spilling into the fire. The flames sizzled and snapped.

"Feel better?" Leven asked.

"It's a start," Winter replied, pushing her blond hair out of her face. "That's for the way he talked to Geth and me when we were tied up in the council room."

Leven bound Knoll's hands with rope while Clover rummaged through Knoll's things.

"Do you think he wants this?" Clover asked, holding up a small starfish wrapped around a tube of wood.

"Don't take his things," Winter said. "We're not here to steal."

"But this looks like something he's not going to use."

"Leave it." Leven smiled.

Clover sighed and let go of the object.

Geth bent down and hefted Knoll over his right shoulder. He carried him outside, with Leven and Winter following.

"The onicks are up beyond the road," Geth said. "I didn't want to bring them in and give our presence away."

Leven stood still and clapped like he knew what he was doing. His gold eyes blinked with surprise.

The sound of the onicks' hooves clomping closer could be heard. The three onicks marched up the road and stopped directly in front of Geth. The largest one exhaled, his breath like thin, spiraling spiderwebs.

"Not bad," Geth said with excitement. "Controlling an onick from afar. Nice trick."

"He messed with some mice earlier," Clover said. "Made them lie right down."

"It'll be interesting to see how you end up," Geth said happily.

"Interesting or frightening?" Winter asked.

Geth threw his prisoner onto the back of an onick. Knoll was still unconscious and slumped over the rear of the beast. He looked out of place in his white nightshirt and long braids.

"Leeeven," a voice whispered, rising from the dust.

"Somebody had to have heard that," Leven insisted.

"What?" Geth asked.

"Lev keeps hearing people call him," Winter said. "I think he's getting a little full of himself."

"A little?" Clover laughed. "He can't pass a mirror without stopping."

"That's you," Leven pointed out. "So nobody heard that?"

"The Dearth knows you," Geth said seriously. "Don't stand still for too long. Now, do you want to lead?"

"Of course," Leven replied excitedly.

They all climbed onto their onicks and rode out of the gates toward the direction of Cusp. The wind blew softly.

"Leeeven."

Leven tried to think of other things, like longings, or wishing for a clear head—anything but the fact that the Dearth seemed to know him personally.

CHAPTER THREE

You Scratch My Shell, I'll Scratch Yours

The Devil's Spiral by day was a sight to behold—the deep brown cliffs rose thousands of feet high and spiraled around until they formed a tight circle. It was mesmerizing to view from afar and awe inspiring from anywhere within a hundred feet. Approximately every two hours the water from the Veil Sea would contract and then push out, racing through the Spiral. When the rushing water reached the tight center end it would shoot up hundreds of feet. The water kept the large portions of Cusp well wet.

Of course at night the Devil's Spiral was not quite as cheery. The dark walls, slick cliffs, and the sound of rushing water were unnerving in the blackness. The high canyon walls were pockmarked with small caves that were inhabited by Eggmen. At night the caves lit up as the Eggmen worked their magic making ingenious food and goods for the rest of Foo. The lights and noise and the ever-present danger of accidentally falling from the cliffs

and being sucked into the Spiral were frightening.

The road above the Devil's Spiral was wide and well traveled. It was barren and open, with no bridges that needed talking to. At night the road was littered with flareworms that glowed a variety of colors from the light they had soaked up during the day. The only peril travelers faced on the road was its close proximity to the edge of the Devil's Spiral.

The three onicks were making good time. When they reached the Devil's Spiral, Geth motioned for Leven to take a right turn off of the main road and down into the Spiral.

They slowed their rides as they rode out across dark, wet stone. With no flareworms on the rock, the weak moon was the only light they had.

"Down!" Geth shouted.

They maneuvered the onicks along the edge of the Spiral. The drop on the right side was hundreds of feet. Looking down into the Spiral was dizzying.

"I can see the Eggmen," Clover said with glee. "Look."

"I'd look," Leven said, "but I'm afraid we'll fall and die."

"There's so many of them," Clover shivered, holding onto Leven's neck.

"We're going to die," Leven replied.

"It's so exciting."

There was a narrow opening in the stone and Geth guided his onick into it. Leven and Winter followed. Inside the stone the sound of water was even louder as it echoed through the cave openings. All over the place fires and labs were being tended by

Eggmen. The Eggmen were so consumed with their work they didn't even look up to acknowledge the three onicks that had just wandered in—one of them hauling a bound body.

They slowed and Geth turned down some wide stone stairs. The onicks complained as they descended.

"You know where we're going?" Leven yelled.

"Of course!" Geth yelled back.

"I think one of the Eggmen looked at me," Clover said with unbridled enthusiasm. "Maybe he knows me from some of the ideas I sent in."

"I'm sure that's it," Leven said. "Of course it might be hard to recognize you, seeing how you're invisible."

"Oh yeah," Clover said, materializing. "Maybe there was like an emotional connection."

Tables covered with piles of colorful candy and objects were all over the place. Clover turned invisible so he could better swipe a few pieces.

At the bottom of the stairs was a wide room crammed with all types of unused items. Geth brought his onick to a stop.

"A storage room?" Winter asked.

"Follow me." Geth jumped off of his ride and threw a barely conscious Knoll up over his shoulder. "Grab the leather bag."

"We'll need it?" Leven asked curiously.

"Possibly."

They walked through the clutter and into a poorly lit back room. Inside the room was a desk covered with trinkets and papers that spilled onto the floor. The walls were lined with chalk-

boards and drawings of various objects. An extra-fat Eggman sat behind the desk. He had a round head that sloped into his shoulders. There were some half glasses perched on the end of his fat nose and a few wispy hairs sticking up from the top of his head. He wore a thick robe that appeared brown under the dull light.

The Eggman looked up from his work and smiled.

"Ah, a distraction," he said. "What a welcome relief. But I would be a pale yolk if I didn't think you were here for more than just my relief. Eh, Geth?"

"Wise as always, Durfin," Geth said. "You have offered me a place to store things before. I was hoping that offer might still stand."

"Before was many, many years ago," Durfin said. "But going back on one's word takes so much effort. I take it you're not looking to store a lamp or a couch."

"He might need to be fed occasionally," Geth said, hefting Knoll from his shoulder and standing him up.

Knoll was conscious and unhappy.

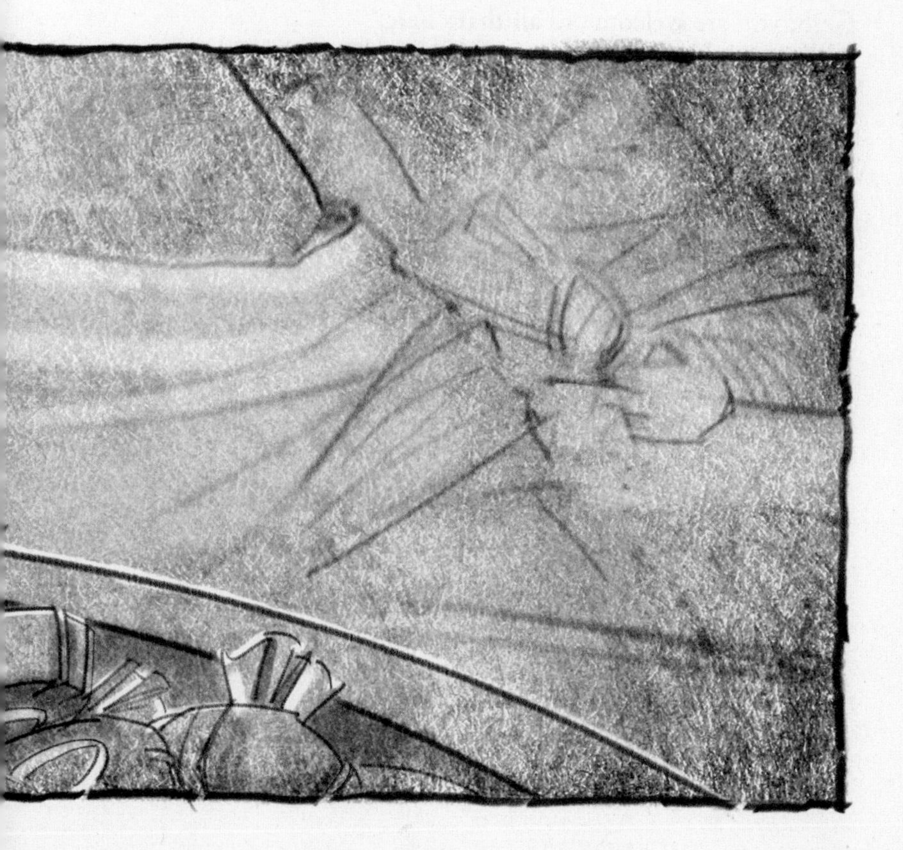

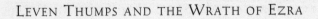

"I am a lithen," Knoll said. "This man's a thief."

"I can see you are a lithen," Durfin said. "I still have my sight, thank the waters. But you are also a liar."

Durfin's face turned red with anger.

"I would welcome Geth as a friend if it were hundreds of years between visits and I had been fed nothing but reports of his dishonesty during that time. I would still believe none of it. You, however, are a different story. From what is said along the shore you are no more lithen than I. We have a spot for you, Knoll, and Geth, you are welcome to all that's here."

Durfin calmed himself and smiled. He pulled on a rope hanging nearby and six heavy Eggmen bounded through the door.

"We have a guest," Durfin said. "Place him where I won't accidentally run into him. Feed him what the goats won't eat and make sure he has at least two pairs of eyes on him at all times."

"You are a fool!" Knoll shouted. "Azure's wrath will be on you. You'll be broken and smeared across Foo."

"Perhaps," Durfin said. "But it is I that will sleep in a bed tonight. Take him."

Knoll yelled Foovian obscenities as he was dragged off.

"So does this favor come with further danger?" Durfin asked.

"No," Geth said. "Nobody knows he's here."

"Who travels with you?" Durfin asked. "I've not seen eyes glow so strong as in this one here."

"This is Leven and the girl is Winter."

"Girl?" Winter said under her breath.

Clover materialized and cleared his throat. He had a couple of pieces of candy in his hands. He stuck the candy behind his back.

"And Clover," Geth added.

"You introduce a sycophant," Durfin said. "How peculiar."

"He's quite a sycophant," Geth said.

"If you say so."

"I've actually sent you some ideas," Clover murmured, awestruck. "I never heard back."

Durfin smiled and his mushy face spread out like dough being stretched.

"I will rest easy," Durfin said, "knowing we have you in our corner."

Clover bowed.

"And this is Leven Thumps," Durfin said, darting a mushy eye toward Leven.

Leven nodded.

"So many stories and myths I've heard about you. I'm surprised you are not twelve feet tall and eight feet wide."

"I'm pretty happy I'm not." Leven smiled.

"You know, Geth," Durfin sighed, "it has been some time since I've seen you. Knoll's not stupid in giving me reason to doubt your intentions."

Geth nodded, his hair falling over his blue eyes.

"You bear the look of one who still fights for Foo," Durfin said.

"And I will till my death," Geth assured him. "But if it makes

you sleep easier, we have brought something for you."

"A gift?" Durfin asked with excitement.

Geth nodded toward Leven and Leven stepped forward holding the long leather bag in his hands. He untied the flap at the end and reached in. As he pulled out the sword, Durfin gasped.

"I'll be scrambled," Durfin whispered.

It was the very same blade that Leven had used to cut the Want. It shined under the low lights and seemed to sizzle in Leven's hand.

"How did you get ahold of this?" Durfin asked in awe.

"Fate placed it in front of us," Geth answered. "And now we must return it to you."

"There were only three shell blades ever crafted," Durfin said with respect. "It has long been rumored that all three were destroyed."

"This one wasn't," Leven said, handing the weapon to Durfin.

"Only a true soul would relinquish something so valuable," Durfin said. "You have my gratitude and hospitality. Do as you wish while you are here."

"Thank you," Geth said.

"But sleep now," Durfin insisted. "It's late and the water will surge soon. I have a few rooms I think you will find most comfortable."

"You are more generous than ever," Geth said sincerely.

"And fat!" Durfin laughed. "Stay as long as you need."

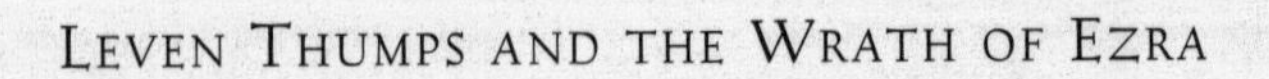

"We need to be in Cusp in two days," Geth said.

"That's not a problem," Durfin said. "Spend tomorrow here; you must be tired. You'll still make it in plenty of time."

Durfin pulled another rope and a single Eggman entered the room.

"Harold, put them in rooms where the water is best seen—the ones on the inner Spiral. Treat them better than you would treat your family."

Harold nodded as well as someone with no neck could, and then led the four of them to their rooms. Geth got the biggest one and Leven and Clover got the room between him and Winter.

"This is cozy," Clover said, as he looked around the room with his hands on his hips.

Leven leaned out the window and glanced down. The window was just a round stone opening on a cliff wall hundreds of feet above dark, surging water. Down on the floor of the room were a dozen tiny holes. Leven leaned back in carefully.

"This is unnerving," he said. "Do you really think this is one of their best rooms?"

"I can't think of a single place I'd rather be," Clover sighed. "Did you hear him say they were happy I was in their corner? They like my ideas."

"I think he was being sarcastic."

"I know," Clover said dreamily.

Through the window Leven could see other lit openings dotting the tall cliff walls that made up a small portion of the gigan-

tic Spiral. Various noises lifted from each room, filling the air with a cacophony of sound. Most rooms had Eggmen in them busily mixing and working over small fires.

The room they were occupying was the size of a small bus. It was lit by stones in the ceiling that glowed like lightbulbs. There was a wooden door at the back, which opened up to a spiral stone stairway and a communal washroom. The only piece of furniture in the room was an enormous round plastic beanbag.

"Looks like a nest," Leven said, pointing to the bed.

"Where's mine?" Clover asked.

"You can sleep on my cloak."

"Thanks," Clover said sincerely. "And I'll share some of the candy I've found."

"Found?"

"Well, it was just sort of sitting there."

Leven looked at Clover. "Just sitting there? On tables where Eggmen were working?"

"Yep." Clover smiled. "Look at this: Lofty Toffee. It's supposed to turn you into wind." He held up an orange tube.

"I don't want any of your candy," Leven insisted. "Especially if it turns me to wind."

"I don't know," Clover said. "It could be a cool way to travel."

"Keep your candy away from me."

"I need to find someone to test . . . try it out on." Clover shivered and disappeared.

"I think you should try it on—"

A noise similar to a fleet of stampeding elephants started to

swell, cutting off Leven. Wind began to howl through the window, blowing Leven's hair back.

Clover held tight to Leven's neck.

The noise increased and Leven reached out to grab onto the wall. The wind grew and grew, spinning around the room and lifting Leven's feet from the ground.

"What . . . ?"

Clover disappeared as Leven flew back into the bed. The sound pounded the walls right up until the point when the water began rushing in. It shot through the hole like a geyser, filling the stone room and pinning Leven up against the ceiling.

Before Leven could even scream the water began to recede. It dropped rapidly out of the window. Leven fell onto the bed as the final foot of water slipped out of the tiny holes at the base of the wall. He bounded to his feet.

"Was that supposed to happen?" Leven asked.

Clover materialized and jumped up to the window.

There was a knock at the door. Leven pulled it open and Winter was standing there soaking wet.

"We're trying to sleep," Clover said sternly.

"So was I," she growled.

"Hold on," Leven said. "I don't think it's over."

Leven pulled Winter into the room as a great vacuum of air began slurping them toward the window.

"It's some sort of after-suckage!" Clover screamed.

"After-suckage?" Winter yelled.

Leven and Winter were pulled to the floor as every last drop

of water was being sucked from the room. The fillings in Leven's teeth rattled and his hair was being pulled out from his scalp. With a brain-shaking pop the suckage stopped.

Things were dry again and the sound of the water lowering outside was comforting. The air had quieted but they kept their heads down while lying on the floor.

"These are the good rooms?" Winter questioned.

"I could do without a view of the water," Leven said.

Clover was at the window looking out. "All the other caves I can see look like nothing even happened. They just use that force to create what they do."

"I hope Geth's okay," Winter said.

"He probably slept right through it."

"Do you think that happens every two hours?" Winter asked.

"I'm sleeping on the stairs," Clover said. "I'll take that cloak."

Leven took off his cloak and handed it to Clover.

"It's wet," Clover complained. He disappeared without taking it.

"I say we get Geth and get out of here," Winter said. "There's no way I can sleep here."

"We've got two hours before it happens again. That's better than nothing. I'll wake you before we drown."

Winter stormed out.

Leven jumped up onto his bed, surprised to find it dry. The lights on the ceiling dimmed.

He lay back and closed his eyes—there was nothing but blackness with a faint light around the edges. Since becoming the

Want, Leven still hadn't seen even a sliver of the future. His eyes burned, but he didn't see anything and his dreams were nothing but dull colors. He thought back to his father's dream. He remembered seeing a man and a boy walking, or doing something by a river. The dream felt hopeful and heavy and impossible.

"Dad," Leven said aloud to the dark ceiling.

"Nope, Clover," Clover whispered back.

"I thought you were sleeping on the stairs."

"They're hard as rock."

"I wonder why."

"Just try not to snore," Clover said.

Leven shifted over and tugged on the beanbag's covering to create a short blanket.

"Don't you ever miss your family?" Leven asked. "I mean, you never talk about your mom or dad."

"I miss them all the time," Clover said. "But as a sycophant, I am part of your family now. I'll see mine again."

"I can't stop thinking about the longing," Leven whispered.

"The girl in the cage?"

"If I'm not thinking about my father, I'm thinking of her."

"I think that's what your grandfather wanted," Clover reminded Leven. "He was messing with you."

"But it's too late," Leven said. "Lith's gone."

"She's not. She's trapped just like she's always been. You could use those special Waves of yours." Clover said the last line with a sneer.

"Are you jealous of the Waves?" Leven said.

"They're just so showy," Clover complained. "I prefer a little tact. But I suppose if anyone could locate her it would be them. Have them find her and then you can swim in to rescue her and be the big hero."

Leven was silent.

"Are you thinking about her?" Clover asked.

"Yes," Leven said.

"Call your Waves. What's the big one called? Gargoyle?"

"Garnock."

"Yeah, call him."

"Maybe I will. Do you wanna come?"

"I think he's chattier when I'm not around," Clover said. "So if it's okay with you, I'll just sleep. In less than two hours we have to get up and take a bath."

"Sure?"

"Yes," Clover said. "Positive."

Leven sat up and worked his way out of the nest. "I'll be right back."

"Try not to wake me," Clover said sleepily.

"You really are the perfect sycophant."

"Thanks," he mumbled.

Leven slipped out the door and stepped quickly down the stone stairs.

CHAPTER FOUR

Look at Me, I'm a Chapter Heading

There are so many impatient people in the world. It seems everyone wants something right this second. We don't want to wait in lines, we get fidgety when our food takes too long to cook, and we have no tolerance whatsoever for anyone who holds us up from doing anything we want to do the moment we want to do it. I'm bothered right now that I'm having to wait till the end of this sentence to see what word I end up on. On, who knew? It's particularly hard to wait for things that are days or weeks or even months away. Calendars mock you, clocks pester you, and the rotation of the Earth seems to slow by at least 40 percent. I suppose, however, that if you were preparing to take over the world and you needed one final piece to fall into place, but that piece had to be slowly dragged over the dirt so that it didn't die, that would be really

hard to wait for. I'd feel sorry for whoever that happened to, but then again they were trying to take over the world and all.

So please, no sympathy for Azure.

The march to Cusp was going slower than Azure would have preferred. The Dearth was weak and required long stretches of time to just lie still on the soil and build his strength. He was weak, and rising above the soil had caused him great strain.

The rank of rants accompanying them sat huddled by the side of the thin dirt road. A small tent was set up in the grass. Inside the tent the Dearth was lying down soaking up the soil and communicating with everything dark that lived below the surface. The Dearth lay on his back with his arms and legs spread out. His features were slowly becoming better defined as he gained strength.

"Can you feel him?" Azure asked.

"My touch is much more sensitive." The Dearth smiled, his tarlike face smearing vertically as he did so. "I can feel and hear so much more from the soil now that I have risen above."

Azure could feel the ground under him vibrating as the Dearth whispered and controlled things beneath the soil. The feeling was not new to Azure. He had long been influenced by the whispering of the Dearth. It was just so much stronger now.

"We're moving slowly," Azure said. "But I can feel your strength growing."

"Yes," the Dearth said weakly. "I'll walk soon. Tell me where we are?"

"We are below the Cinder Depression," Azure said. "I can see the peaks of Morfit from the road."

"But we travel to Cusp."

"Yes," Azure said respectfully.

"There's much stone in Cusp."

"We will travel around it, to the Meadows."

Azure scratched at his infected ear. The Dearth looked at him with his black, foggy eyes and blinked.

"Your ear," he oozed. "It bleeds."

"It's not important," Azure insisted.

"There's still some confusion in you," the Dearth scolded. "Are you not up to the task? Sabine was never infected with doubt."

"Sabine's dead," Azure snapped. "Had he not failed in the first place, we would be much closer to our victory."

"Speak well of him," the Dearth warned. "Sabine was so easy to use, so easy to convince. His influence is not over. Tell me how things look now."

"The whole of Foo is sliding in our direction," Azure reported. "Lith's gone and the Want is no longer a concern. Our armies are gathered on the edge of Cusp. But we rattle no sabers. Those in Cusp believe we are setting the stage to march down the gloam to the stones. There's talk that you have risen above the soil, but for most your existence is a fable too impossible for even Foo to swallow."

The Dearth smiled.

"Cusp is the last stronghold of any forces large enough to deter us. Cork will fall in place. We but need the secret and we will march over the gloam onto Sycophant Run and find the exit. Something Sabine was never able to accomplish."

"Yes, yes," the Dearth hissed. "You, Azure, are three times the mind that Sabine was. What of the keys?"

"The Sochemists have them," Azure said. "Although I see no value to them now that you are unlocked."

"All the keys are there with the Sochemists?"

Azure nodded.

The Dearth closed his eyes and sighed. Small bits of him began to drip from his sides and run along the surface of the ground.

Before Azure could understand what was happening, black strands shot up Azure's legs and coiled around his waist. The Dearth dripped further, sending hundreds of strands of himself whipping up and around Azure. Azure tried to move, but he was bound.

The Dearth lay there, his right side spilling like a puddle of oil and running up around Azure. He choked Azure at the neck, tightening thin strands of black like a tourniquet.

"All the keys?" the Dearth asked again.

Azure pulled at the black strings around his neck, struggling to speak.

"The sycophant key is a copy," Azure admitted. "It's a copy."

Instantly the Dearth retracted himself, leaving Azure gasping for breath.

"How?" the Dearth demanded.

"We stole the image from the key's reflection as Leven looked in a mirror," Azure said. "There is no difference. After all, the key worked and you're free."

"Free." The Dearth released the word like a slow leak. "Free for now, but it would take only one key to lock me back up."

"We'll get the key."

"Of course you will," the Dearth said. "Thank you for being so accommodating. I believe I am ready to travel farther."

Azure picked the Dearth up and carried him out of the tent. Azure's dark heart was pained, but the hatred he felt for the Dearth was greater. Azure knew there would come a time when the allies would have to turn toward each other and fight. It was clear that after they had used each other there would be no friendship.

"I can feel what you're thinking," the Dearth whispered.

"Ignore my thoughts," Azure insisted.

"I will for now," the Dearth answered. "But it would be best for you if *you* ignored them."

"As you wish," Azure said.

Azure carried the Dearth back to the wagon, focusing his thoughts on things far more benign than conquering all of Reality and eventually snuffing out the Dearth.

CHAPTER FIVE

The Devil's Spiral

The Devil's Spiral was even more frightening looking up from the bottom. The lit caves shining in the dark night combined to look like a towering jack-o'-lantern with hundreds of misplaced eyes—and the water sounded like a thousand hoarse voices mumbling something sinister.

Leven had left his room and located Harold, the Eggman who had helped them previously. Leven had persuaded Harold to take him to the base of the Spiral.

Harold was thin and sickly looking. He was taller than he was wide and his white skin was loose and saggy. He wore a striped robe like a dress with various utensils and objects tied to the hem and sleeves. His big wet eyes dripped at the corners.

"The docks are over there," Harold said, objects clattering as he pointed. "Be careful—the water rises in less than an hour.

Bells will toll twice before it does. When the alarm sounds, the water's coming in."

"Thank you, Harold," Leven said. "I'll find my way back."

"It's very late," Harold said.

"I realize that," Leven replied.

"Durfin might find fault with me for leading you here," Harold said. "He said to extend you full hospitality, but he might question this."

"Is this area off-limits?" Leven asked.

"No, but there's much danger at the base of the Spiral," Harold insisted. "And the dark of night makes it even more perilous and concerning."

"I'll be quick."

"Your sycophant is with you?"

"Of course," Leven lied, knowing that Clover was hundreds of feet higher, sleeping on the large purple nest.

Harold looked torn. "I am concerned."

"It'll be fine," Leven insisted.

"The bell will toll twice," Harold said again. "Do not ignore it."

Harold slipped back through the granite door they had just come out of, leaving Leven alone. The water mumbled and surged, splashing up against the shore

Leven ran down the wooden dock. It was so late that night was almost over—morning would be making its first appearance in the next hour or so. Nobody was out or around and the only sound Leven heard was the Veil Sea lapping restlessly against the dock and shore.

Leven ran to the end of the long pier. He stood on its edge as water from the sea misted his face. The horizon was dark and felt thick. Leven wiped his eyes and cupped his hands around his mouth.

"Garnock!" Leven yelled. "Garnock?"

The only reply was the sound of lapping water. Leven sat down on the pier, dangling his legs and wishing he had brought along his wet cloak to keep him halfway dry. His thoughts were with Phoebe and his father. The white streak in Leven's hair shimmered under the tiny bit of light the moon was able to push down.

Water sprayed him again.

Clouds in the night sky blew away and the moon dipped its long beams down onto the sea's surface. Leven could see the choppy waves beating up against the shore.

"Garnock!" Leven yelled again.

"Yes," the water beneath his dangling feet replied.

Leven looked down to see the white, foamy face of the lead Wave bobbing on the surface of the water. Leven pulled his legs up and rolled onto his stomach so he could look straight down.

"Sorry," Leven said. "About calling you out here."

"There's no need for sorrow on my behalf," Garnock said. "We are yours to instruct."

"That's still really hard to believe," Leven said.

"It is the order of things," Garnock replied.

"The remains of Lith," Leven said. "I know the Dearth's moving the soil to the Gloam, but the bulk of Lith, has it been completely dragged apart?"

"It is all beneath the surface, but it will be many days before the Dearth possesses all the soil," Garnock said. "Your concern is curious. Why care for the soil?"

"There's someone who was held captive on Lith," Leven explained. "I need to know if she's still alive and if saving her is possible."

"We can discover that," Garnock gurgled. "But if she lives, the depth will be too great for us Waves to move stone to retrieve the buried."

"We'll come," Leven said. "I'll come with Geth and Winter."

"For whom are we looking?"

"She's a she," Leven said. "A longing kept captive in a metal cage."

"A longing?" Garnock babbled.

Leven nodded, his wet hair hanging down around his face.

"It'll take us most of tomorrow to get there," Leven said.

"If what you say is true," Garnock bubbled, "I'd move with urgency. Longings are quite valuable."

"We will be on our way as soon as I can find a boat."

Leven looked down the dark shoreline. There wasn't a single vessel in sight.

"We will help with that," Garnock said. "A ship will be here at sunrise."

"Thanks, Garnock," Leven said.

"You're most welcome," he replied. "It is an honor to serve one so young."

Hearing that from anyone else, it would have sounded

sarcastic, but from Garnock the sincerity was as apparent as his presence.

Leven nodded.

Garnock disappeared beneath the water. Leven pushed himself up and looked out at the sea. His chest hurt and the compulsion to jump into the water and swim to the longing was very strong. Leven scooted back on the pier to prevent himself from diving in. He looked up at the sky and felt the wet mist from the sea move over him.

The mist that hovered over so much of the Veil Sea was like a blanket to the mind. It made things confusing, but it was a comfortable fog.

A soft bell sounded, signaling the coming surge. Leven looked around but saw no sign of the water rising.

"Leeeven," the scene seemed to whisper.

Leven looked around, expecting to see someone right next to him. There was nobody.

"Leeven."

He stood and slowly walked back to the start of the pier.

"Leeeven."

"What?" Leven shouted to the darkness in frustration.

There was no response. Leven stepped off the pier and walked ten steps in the direction of the granite door.

"Leeeeven."

Leven turned and stepped down the rocky shore. He could see the water receding as the surge grew closer. Mist washed over him and he walked toward the sea as more and more water pulled away.

"Leeven."

Leven closed his eyes and breathed in deep. He took four more steps down toward the receding waterline. The ground was no longer stone but a sandy soil.

Leven stood still.

"Leven."

It was a foolish decision. Leven could hear voices in his head rolling around like wet clothes in a hot dryer. His feet were heavy and dread filled his soul as he continued to watch the water recede.

"Leven," he heard inside his head.

"Who are you?" Leven asked.

"You know," the voice coaxed.

"The Dearth."

"Smart boy."

The second bell rang. Leven wanted to move. He wanted to step back onto the stone and retreat from the danger, but he just stood there.

"How do they die?" the Dearth questioned.

"What?" Leven mumbled.

"Sycophants. How do they die?"

Leven had to fight his own brain to keep from saying it aloud.

"Help me," the Dearth urged.

Leven thought of Clover.

"I can't," Leven said weakly, wishing he hadn't stepped off the pier.

"You already have."

The voice was suddenly gone. Leven stood alone on the sea floor staring into the dark night as the arrival bells started to ring steadily. Leven couldn't move. He grabbed his right leg and strained to pull it up. It broke from the sand with a loud pop.

Leven turned to run just as the water rushed to the shore. The surge had grown hundreds of feet high and was barreling like a locomotive straight toward the opening of the Devil's Spiral.

Leven ran two steps before the water reached him from behind. It pounded his back and then he could feel himself being lifted up and pushed forward.

The water rolled over his head as if it were a great wet whale swallowing him. The force and the noise were so great Leven thought his head would simply thump into mush.

The water jammed into the opening of the Spiral. Fish of all sizes buffered Leven from the cliffs. The fish cycled and circled around Leven, wrapping him like scaly bubble wrap. Leven felt something tugging strongly on his right arm. He turned to see one of the Waves grabbing him by the wrist. Another Wave pushed him to the side, steering him clear of the high cliff walls and keeping him pocketed in the mass of fish.

The water spun through the Spiral at a tremendous speed. Leven became dizzy as they whipped through the concentric circles of the Spiral. One moment before he thought his lungs would burst, the water reached the end of the Spiral, squeezing him up and shooting him hundreds of feet into the sky.

Leven watched the dark sky race up around him and saw

three Waves still clinging to him. The Waves looked odd and out of place with no water around them. Their form was bulky and fluid.

Leven peaked and began to drop, his heart trying to push out through his nose. The spraying water caught the wind and began to blow in the direction of Cusp. Leven might very well have ended up dead on the rooftop of some unsuspecting Cuspinian's house, if it had not been for the Waves grabbing him by the ankles and wrist and puffing up to let the wind steer them like a sail toward the sea.

They separated from the rest of the shooting water and glided softly back over the Veil Sea. Leven wanted to thank his rescuers, but he was still too busy screaming for his life.

They dropped quickly down over the cliffs of the Spiral and then, looking much like the sky had as Leven raced up, the sea now appeared as Leven came down. He and the Waves hit the surface and skimmed the top.

Leven rolled like a log for a hundred feet and then began to settle into the water. The Waves pushed up beneath him, keeping him from sinking too far.

The Waves gently slid Leven onto the shore, where tamer waves with far less personality rolled up and over him until he found the strength to stand.

Leven's legs and arms were like jelly. His heart still had not settled down in his chest and water dripped from his ears and nose. He was relieved to have survived the Spiral, but still felt a nagging sense of dread in his soul.

"I was sad about something," he said to himself.

He looked at the ground and remembered the whispering. Leven shuffled up onto the shore and back over to the pier.

"Thanks!" he shouted to the dark sea.

He walked back to the granite entrance. Harold was there wringing his hands.

"I thought you were in trouble." Harold looked concerned. "You didn't return to your room."

"I'm fine."

"You weren't out there when the water was coming in?" Harold questioned.

"No," Leven lied. "Of course not. I couldn't find my way back so I was looking for you."

Harold exhaled. "Well, I'll see you to your room."

When Leven got back to his room he found Winter sitting on his bed with Clover. The two of them were listing all the reasons why they thought trust was important to a friendship.

Leven halfway explained what had happened, leaving out the part about the longing and the dirt whispering to him. And in the end they halfway forgave him. Only Clover, quite jealous that Leven had gotten to ride the Spiral and live to brag about it, harbored any bad feelings.

CHAPTER SIX

THE *PLUD HAG*

Leven looked out at the blue sky and blinked. He pulled his hood down and scanned the horizon as the temperature dropped. Something was wrong with the weather. One moment it felt like the first day of a welcomed summer, and the next moment cold air would brush across you like paint, wrapping around your body and chilling you to the core.

"What's up with the weather?" Leven asked, rubbing his hands.

"I'm not sure," Geth replied. "I don't remember it being so temperamental."

Leven and Geth were on a boat looking up at a light blue sky, airy as cotton candy. Leven breathed in and could almost taste the day. Every few moments wind would stir across the water, swirling around the sunshine on its surface like cream.

The mist in the distance was thin and almost vacant on the

Veil Sea. And from where the old boat sat there were no immediate clouds to muck up the mind or impede the view. The water, however, was anything but beautiful.

"There's still so much debris," Leven said.

All over the surface of the water were pieces of bobbing foliage and wood—the last remnants of Lith.

"We'll stop here," Angus said, moving down from the bow.

Angus was a tall dark man with huge arms and short, frizzy hair. He wore a leather vest, and the top half of his right ear was missing. He had been the captain of the boat for over twenty years.

"You're the captain," Geth replied, bending to unlatch the stone anchor. "It's amazing to look out and not see anything—a whole island gone."

"The maps will need to be redrawn again," Angus said. "How does a large rock like Lith just sink? Of course, how does a boat sailing in a completely different direction suddenly get pushed hundreds of miles off course and right up to a dock where three outcasts are in need of a ship?"

"Fate's impressive," Geth said.

"Fate, my hindquarters," Angus said, walking away. "But, a fee is a fee and I'm happy to collect it."

Angus went down below on the boat, grumbling.

"It was pretty fortunate to have a boat waiting for us this morning," Geth said.

"I guess I might have had something to do with that," Leven admitted.

"Winter said you all slept with your windows open."

"They close?" Leven asked.

"Of course the stone shuts." Geth laughed. "How else would a person get any sleep? Winter also said you met with Garnock last night."

Leven nodded. Geth remained silent, so Leven began talking again.

"Aren't you curious about what we're doing?"

"If we were heading to Cusp this would be a very long and out-of-the-way route," Geth said. "But I've always been fond of surprises. We could have rested up all day, but where's the fun in that? And I'm assuming this will bring us closer to Azure?"

"Not really," Leven said.

"You know the stakes," Geth said, whistling. "I guess maybe you just wanted to see for yourself that Lith is really gone."

"I witnessed that in person."

"Still, it helps to see things in the light," Geth said calmly.

"I heard the Dearth last night," Leven said.

"While talking to Garnock about getting a boat?"

"After, actually," Leven answered. "The Dearth talked to me."

"You were standing where you shouldn't have," Geth said kindly. "All of us have got to be careful what we say and what we think. Our thoughts may not be our own."

"He felt familiar," Leven admitted. "He asked about the sycophants and then just went away."

"I'm not surprised," Geth said. "They need access to Sycophant Run."

"Why?"

"I'll let that be a surprise for you."

"Thanks," Leven said. "I personally feel like I've had my share of surprises. My grandfather was the Want. That was a surprise—and now I'm the Want."

"It's pretty incredible," Geth agreed.

"I just can't believe that after everything he did I still miss

him," Leven lamented. "He betrayed me—he betrayed us—and I still miss him."

"He was your grandfather," Geth said. "And he was very sick."

"That's not exactly comforting," Leven said. "I mean, is his illness going to be my fate?"

"I don't believe so," Geth said. "But if it is, make the space between now and then remarkable."

"Where do you come up with things like that?"

"I probably read it in a book." Geth smiled.

"Can I ask you something?"

"Of course," Geth answered.

"Do you ever doubt what you believe? You know, about Foo and Reality being kept apart?"

"There are brief moments," Geth said.

"That's not the response I expected. You're supposed to say something like, 'Take a moment to be the best believer so those beliefs can count for something.'"

Geth stared at Leven. "Do I really sound like that?"

"Well, not exactly." Leven smiled. "But if my father's alive, I want to get to him, and the meshing of Foo is the only way to do that."

"That makes sense," Geth said. "But more than anyone I know you have been moved by fate to do extraordinary things. Don't predict disappointment while hope is an option."

"See," Leven said. "That's exactly what you sound like."

Geth shifted the stone anchor to the edge and stood up. He glanced at Leven.

"You know, your eyes really are changing," Geth said quietly. "I hadn't noticed how prominent it was until Durfin said something last night. It only reminds me that you should be hidden away. All those who held your position previously hid for at least the first year."

"Only you and Winter know I'm the Want," Leven whispered.

"It has to stay that way," Geth insisted. "Keep the thought even from your own mind. We are safe out on the water. It is one of the reasons the Waves of the Lime Sea have stayed so faithful."

Geth was taller this morning than he had been yesterday. Of course tomorrow he would probably be a couple of inches shorter. Ever since he had been restored in the flames of the turrets his body had been fluctuating. His eyes, however, were still blue and he wore the same expression he usually did, one of wonder and excitement, with no trace of fear. His long blond hair hung straight down and covered half of his face whenever he turned.

Geth released the stone anchor.

The long line of rope attached to the anchor slipped into the water like a noodle being lustily slurped under.

Leven stepped away from Geth. He walked across the deck and up to the bow of the ship. He was wearing a dark black cloak with the hood pulled back. His dark hair was long and the white streak in it was even whiter. His eyes burned a warm gold, like the hot embers in Midas's campfire. Leven reached out and took hold of the rail as if to steady his heady life.

Something landed in his hair.

"Hey," Clover said, materializing on top of Leven's head. "Do you remember that stuff you used to drink in Reality?"

"Water?" Leven smiled.

"No, no." Clover waved the answer off. "That jumpy stuff in those crinkly containers."

"Soda."

"Yes, soda," Clover said affectionately. "I'd give up a spot in the Chamber of Stars for some strawberry-flavored soda."

Leven reached up and petted Clover on the back of his head. Clover stretched and then twisted around and slid down Leven's arm.

"Well, if you're ever appointed to the Chamber of Stars, I'll know just how to tempt you."

Debris knocked lightly against the side of the boat, mimicking the sound of Winter stepping up from down below.

Winter's blond hair was pulled behind her head and tied off with a green piece of soft twine. Long strands had snaked loose and were waving in front of her face like mischievous sprites. The green in her eyes was as pronounced as the depth of the Veil Sea. She had on a red cloak over her jeans. The color of her cloak made the pink of her lips seem electric.

"I'm surprised this boat even floats," Winter said. "I just found another hole."

The boat they were on was called the *Plud Hag*. It was named after a woman Angus had once been in love with but now had completely different feelings toward. It was a worn ship with a big cabin below and a large open deck up top. The hull was

round and covered with a square canopy of weathered wood.

The *Plud Hag* creaked in the water as it sat tethered to its stone anchor. Leven and Winter looked off into the distance. Leven cleared his throat and glanced at Clover. Clover picked up on the hint perfectly.

"It's the weirdest thing," Clover said. "I suddenly feel—with no prompting from anyone else—like I want to go and see if Geth needs my help."

Leven rubbed his forehead as Clover scurried along the rail toward the stern of the boat.

"Where are we, anyway?" Winter asked.

"Lith," Leven answered. "Can't you tell?"

After Lith had sunk, Leven and Geth had been taken by the Waves to the ninth stone, where they had met up with Winter. Leven had been so glad to find Winter alive and okay.

"Oh yeah, now I can see it," Winter joked.

"Hey, remember that bridge we slept under in Oklahoma?" Leven asked.

"The one the avalands tore up?"

Leven nodded. "I miss that bridge."

"We were cold, and scared to death under there."

"But things were still basically normal."

"Foo will feel that way if we succeed," Winter said.

"And if we don't?"

"I'm not going to think about things like that."

"Okay," Leven said. "Only positive. So we'll win a war that only a few good souls even want to fight, get your gift back, find

my father, put an end to the Dearth, and all live happily ever after?"

"Something like that." Winter smiled.

Two mist eaters flew overhead and screamed as they searched for mist to gorge on.

"So, you're the Want now," Winter said.

Leven looked around to make sure they were alone. "We're not supposed to be talking about that."

"It still freaks me out a little," Winter whispered.

"I know. Just think how I feel."

"So can you see all the dreams coming into Foo?"

"No, not yet, at least," Leven said. "I can't really see any dreams clearly, but the edges of my view are all light and wiggly. I did clearly see that dream my father was dreaming."

"Which is pretty cool," Winter pointed out.

"Yeah, but now I want to know where he's been and what possessed him to leave me to live with Terry and Addy."

"He'll dream again."

"I'm waiting to see it."

"So I guess someday you'll also be able to see my dreams."

"Actually, I've seen a few things already and I think it's time for you to stop dreaming about unicorns and rich boys."

"Nice," Winter said. "Tell me when you really do start seeing mine so I can stop dreaming altogether."

"It'll be a while," Leven said. "My gift has all but stopped working. Geth said that in a while I'll fit my calling and then have the ability to do a ton more things."

Winter smiled. "Are you bragging, Lev?"

"No," Leven said, his face turning red. "I just . . . well . . ."

Winter put her hand on his.

"Bragging about being the Want—how shameless," Winter joked. "You just said you shouldn't even be admitting it. You should be in seclusion. It could be a year before you're safely the Want."

"I'm not going to lock myself up for a year in some remote cave just so I don't get hurt," Leven said hotly. "There's no time for that. I feel more compelled to right Foo now than ever before and I'm not hiding to wait until I'm bulletproof."

Winter put her arm around Leven. "You're tall," she whispered.

"You're . . ."

"What?" Winter asked.

"I don't know, just thanks for sticking around," Leven said.

"I've got nowhere else to go," she pointed out.

"Perfect."

"So do you think that . . ."

Winter stopped talking as Geth drew closer with Clover on his left shoulder. Leven tried not to look too bothered about being interrupted.

"Sorry," Clover said. "Geth started lecturing me and I couldn't take it."

"It wasn't a lecture," Geth insisted. "You were throwing rocks at that poor fish."

"You saw the way he was looking at me," Clover argued.

"He's a fish," Geth countered. "They have large eyes."

"The important thing is, what are we doing out here, anyway?" Clover asked, successfully deflecting the attention from himself.

"We're all wondering that," Winter added.

"When Lith went under, it took something important with it," Leven explained. "We're here to retrieve that something."

"Something?" Geth asked.

"Is it edible?" Clover asked.

"No."

"Oh, I know what it is," Clover remembered. "And . . ."

"Wait," Leven stopped him. "Don't say."

"What could have survived the destruction of Lith?" Geth questioned. "The very soil has been dragged under the water and added to the length of the gloam."

Leven fished for a couple of keys that were tied around his neck and pulled them out from under his shirt. The bigger key had locked up the secret of the sycophants. The smaller key was the one the Want had given Leven before he died. Leven held up the smaller one.

"What does it open?" Winter asked.

"You'll have to wait and see."

"So we just sit here?" Clover sighed, leaping from Geth's shoulder onto Winter's head. "I hate waiting. When I had to wait for Leven all those years it was the worst. Although Reality does have some pretty cool leaves and rocks."

"I always found a good wait to be quite—"

Geth would have gone on and on about the virtues of a good wait, but his discourse was interrupted by the boat being lifted a couple of inches and then dropped back down.

Winter fell and Leven helped her up.

"What was that?" Clover asked excitedly.

The water beneath the boat swelled and then dropped again. Everyone held tightly onto the front rail.

A solid thud sounded.

The boat lifted again and dropped.

"They're here," Leven said.

The water surrounding the boat began to churn and bubble. All four of them peered carefully over the rail. One by one, faces—gaunt, white faces—began to appear on the surface of the sea, hidden within the foam and break of the teeming water. Some of the faces started to moan and chant, sounding like gargling monks.

"That's unsettling," Clover whispered.

A large, thick fist of water rose up twelve feet and towered above them. The water shivered as patches of the liquid ran back down into the sea, chiseling the fist of liquid into the form of a man.

Garnock groaned. His oblong eyes blinked open as he lifted his watery arms from his sides. The Wave had a thick, writhing beard and deep blue eyes. His body was a waterfall with surging water percolating at his feet where he stood on the sea. Next to him two smaller but equally defined waves rose up.

Garnock nodded respectfully in the direction of Leven.

"Any luck?" Leven nodded.

"Yes, she lives. But the soil still moves," Garnock spoke, his voice the sound of a babbling brook. "It moves in two directions, but the rock and caverns of the island are settling intact."

"And?" Leven asked.

"We have followed the trail of the Baadyn. They seek to comfort her, but their kind is of no use to her. She needs freedom, not air. It is a surprise even to us that she lives. Swim where the Baadyn swim and you will find her. But be warned, the remains of Lith are unstable and dangerous. The other Waves and I will swim with you, but we are weak so far below the water."

Garnock lowered back down into the other bubbling faces. Winter looked from the water to Leven.

"Her?" she questioned.

"Dangerous?" Clover asked.

"Didn't I say that?"

"No, you didn't," Winter said.

"I've never been good with details," Leven said. "You and Clover can wait here. Geth and I will go and get back as quickly as possible."

Geth bounced on the balls of his feet, ready to do anything.

"No way," Winter complained. "I'm not waiting on this stupid boat while you two do all the good stuff."

They all looked at Clover.

"Actually, I'll be fine here," Clover said. "I need to talk to the captain about the condition of his boat."

"And I'm not sticking around to listen to that," Winter said. "I'm going with you two."

"We're going to be going under," Leven said dramatically. "And we've got to hurry."

"Good."

"Under the water," Leven clarified.

"Of course," Winter said. "I didn't think we'd be flying under the sky."

Everyone looked up.

"Actually," Geth pointed out, "Winter's been under this water before."

"That's right. So don't worry, Lev," she said. "I'll show you what to do. Are we going right now?"

"No time like the present." Geth smiled.

Geth pulled off the cloak he was wearing and threw it to the deck. He put his right hand on the rail and without saying another thing leapt over the rail and dived down into the blue water, just missing a dead tree floating on the surface. Geth didn't bob back up.

Winter pulled off her cloak. She was wearing a black T-shirt underneath. She slipped off her shoes and with a smile bigger than Geth's, jumped over the rail and into the water. She too didn't pop back up.

Leven looked at Clover.

"Scared?" Clover asked.

"No."

"Because they both took off a lot faster than you."

"I'm just thinking."

"About being scared?"

"About breathing," Leven answered. "I know the Baadyn help people breathe, but I just want to think about it for a second."

"One-banana," Clover counted.

"Cute," Leven said. "It's just that I still don't like water."

"You've been in a lot of it lately." Clover waved off Leven's concerns. "You'd think you would be over that."

Leven pulled off his cloak. He was wearing his inside-out Wonder-Wipe shirt. The two keys were hanging around his neck.

"I'll watch your stuff if you'd like," Clover offered.

"Thanks."

Clover picked up and began to fold Leven's cloak.

"You sure you'll be okay?" Leven asked.

"To be honest, your concern seems a little insincere," Clover said. "It's kind of like you're just trying to stall."

"I'm not."

"I thought you were in a hurry."

Leven climbed up onto the rail, his right hand hanging onto a rope tethered to the mast. The water directly below him was debris free.

"There are millions of Baadyn down under the water," Clover pointed out. "All of them there to help you. You'll be fine."

"Millions?"

"Well, I've actually never really counted."

Leven closed his eyes and dove headfirst into the Veil Sea.

CHAPTER SEVEN

Let the Longing Begin

There are times in a person's life when he or she must make a choice to believe. I choose to believe the sun will rise tomorrow. I also choose to believe that if you go to bed hungry you will wake up ready to eat. I've met a group of men in a faraway country who choose to believe that if you stand on a tree stump for an hour you will gain sympathy for trees. I am already quite sympathetic to trees, so I choose to think they are bonkers. As far as Foo is concerned, I choose to believe that Leven will do what he must to save dreams. And from the message in a bottle I just received, I choose to believe that the gentleman with the short left leg and dry pink eyes will be stopped at the border of Romania before he is able to slip the note to the lady with the big sweaty hands who needs the information to ruin thousands of people's lives.

But that's another story.

I believe in Foo. I have been chased by avalands, threatened by rants, and welcomed by sycophants. I have seen Clover, talked to Leven, and personally thanked Winter and Geth for everything they are doing. I have stood on the shores of Cusp and watched the gloam grow.

I believe in Foo, and though I was whisked away before I personally was able to fight, I choose to believe that Leven was acting in the best interest of everyone and everything when he dove into the Veil Sea to save the longing. I also believe that as the last bit of air in Leven's lungs escaped his mouth, he was very relieved to have the soul of a large, fat, compassionate Baadyn slip over his head.

Leven instantly began to breathe easy and his eyes focused clearly on his surroundings.

The Baadyn are fickle creatures who live on the islands and shores of Foo. They are mischievous creatures who have no trouble causing others grief. But when they begin to feel guilty or dirty, they have the ability to unhinge themselves at the waist and let their souls slide out and into the ocean to swim until clean. The clean souls of the Baadyn have been known for doing all sorts of kind deeds. Most often, however, they would latch onto anyone's head who couldn't breathe underwater.

The view was beautiful beneath the waves. Leven could see schools of oddly shaped fish, so colorful they were blinding. Herds of water deer ran across the depths of the Veil Sea as the soil of what was once Lith snaked in two directions along the trenches of the sea.

Leven spotted Winter farther down, swimming toward a rocky outcrop. She was being pushed down by the Waves. Geth was below her, entering into a dark, jagged hole. Hundreds of brightly glowing Baadyn were moving in and out of the opening.

Leven swam faster through the cold water. Garnock moved in over him, pushing him deeper down into the sea. They watched Winter swim into the dark hole ahead.

A red glowing squid with wriggling tentacles passed in front of Leven and yelped. Leven watched the creature fold into itself as Garnock pushed him farther down and into the dark hole. The softly glowing Baadyn lit the cavern like puffy candles. Leven reached out and touched the rocky walls as he swam deeper.

"It's beautiful," Leven said, his voice amplified by the Baadyn around his head.

Garnock nodded.

The water vibrated as the walls of Lith continued to slowly settle. Garnock washed in over Leven to protect him. The walls stopped moving and Leven swam farther.

The tunnel opened up to show hundreds of Baadyn swirling around the room. The walls were covered with odd patterns and deep markings. Leven swam across and into another tunnel. The tunnel turned sharply and Leven had to move sideways to slip between two smooth walls. Garnock helped push Leven up and through the small crack. The gap opened and another tunnel with an expansive opening expelled Baadyn like bad breath. Leven kicked furiously to move faster.

Once through the wide opening Leven swam up over a

crumbling wall and down into a large, diamond-shaped room. In the center of the room, lying on its side, was a teardrop-shaped cage. In the center of the cage was Phoebe, the very last longing in Foo. She looked excited and scared, her long, sun-colored hair waving in the water in a hypnotic fashion. She was in her short green gown, and her pale skin glowed under the dim light the Baadyn souls provided.

Geth was already at the cage pulling at the bars while the longing reached out to him. Hundreds of Baadyn moved through the space and bars, lighting the scene like a Mexican fiesta.

The water shook and large pieces of rock began to crumble and fall like dry cheese. Geth kicked at the cage as Leven swam closer, groping for the key around his neck.

"Here!" Geth shouted, holding out his hand.

The door was on the bottom of the cage. Geth tried to turn over the entire thing, but it wouldn't budge. Winter and Garnock grabbed hold and pulled along with Leven.

"It's stuck!" Leven yelled needlessly.

One of the smaller Waves moved down beneath the cage, pushing away the dirt below it. The water shook again, causing the soil to move. The iron bars rolled over, giving Geth room to put the key in and open the door six inches.

Phoebe slipped halfway out. Geth, Winter, and the Waves pulled harder and she popped out. The water shook and wide slabs of stone began to shower down, bending the cage inward.

"Let's get out of here!" Leven yelled.

Winter followed Geth and Phoebe up out of the cavern and

back into the tunnel. Stones and walls were dropping everywhere, buckling under the strain of water and dirt.

"Go!" Geth screamed, wrapping Phoebe in his arms and dodging a collapsing ceiling. "Go!"

Baadyn were everywhere, shooting through the water like confused stars. The opening they had just come through was imploding. Leven pushed Winter through the crack and up against the wall.

"The exit's blocked!" Leven hollered.

Geth and Phoebe came into the tunnel and saw there was no way out. They turned and retreated.

"Follow them," Garnock ordered. "You must get out."

Leven and Winter followed Geth back down the crack and out into the once-spacious cavern. Geth was already across the large room, moving into a dark hole.

Leven's arms burned from swimming, and the water was so heavy it made moving a constant struggle. His legs felt like waterlogged tree trunks.

Garnock and the Waves pushed Leven and Winter quickly through the water and into the hole. The narrow passageway scraped Leven's left arm and leg, creating small streams of blood in the water.

"It's getting tighter!" Winter yelled.

"Keep going!" Leven insisted.

"I can see an opening," Geth hollered from up ahead. "Hurry!"

The Waves pushed as the water and walls trembled violently.

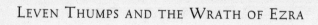

Geth pulled Phoebe up and pushed her through the opening into the deep open sea.

"Come on," he said, reaching for Winter's hand.

Geth pulled Winter to him and pushed her up through the small hole and out to where Phoebe was.

The water and stones trembled again and the tunnel became tighter.

"Out!" Geth shouted at Leven.

"You first!" Leven shouted back.

"Now!" Geth insisted.

Apparently Garnock was taking Geth's side because he pushed Leven, squeezing him up and through the hole. The rocks crumbled further, pinning Leven's legs in at the ankles.

Winter and Phoebe pulled madly on Leven from outside.

"Come on, Lev," Winter pleaded.

"It's not like I want to be stuck," he yelled back. "Pull!"

They tugged harder and Leven popped out of the hole. Garnock followed. Leven turned quickly and could see Geth reaching out of the hole with his right hand. The rocks shook and tightened again, making the hole too small for Geth to get through.

"Geth!" Leven called.

"Go," he insisted. "I'll find another way."

"No way!" Leven yelled, pulling at the rock. "I'm not going up without you."

"Go."

"I will—"

"Geth's right," Garnock interrupted. "We will have to ascend slowly and there's always the possibility that the Baadyn will grow bored and not stick around."

"I'm not leaving Geth."

"Fate holds him now," Garnock said, nodding toward two of his Waves to stick with Geth. "We must get you to safety."

"Go," Geth said again, pulling his arm back into the hole. "I'll be right behind you."

Leven could only see Geth's right eye and a bit of his mouth. But Geth appeared to be wearing the same expression of wonder and amazement that he always did.

"I'll see you up top," Leven said as he started to drift slowly up and away.

"Of course," Geth hollered back.

Leven watched Geth's eye grow smaller and smaller until he could no longer catch sight of it. The only thing he could make out was a gigantic stone mountain quickly collapsing on the bottom of the Veil Sea.

Leven rose slowly. He closed his eyes and tried to see the future. There was nothing.

CHAPTER EIGHT

Leaning Too Far One Way

"Have you ever thought about painting it?" Clover asked. "I mean, you could take a weekend and get a few friends to help."

"She's just fine," Angus insisted. "Why cover up what she is?"

"I'm really good at painting stars."

"Paint a star on my boat and you'll be swimming home," Angus threatened.

"It's called character," Clover argued back. "And if ever someone—"

Clover was interrupted by Winter rising from the water. A large Wave pushed her up, lifting her like a watery goddess from the great depths. The Wave raised Winter up over the rail and set her down on the deck. The Baadyn around her head slipped down and oozed off the boat like a wad of snot. Winter steadied herself and looked at the Wave.

"Thank you."

"My pleasure," the Wave bubbled, slipping back down into the water.

A smaller Wave lifted Phoebe out of the water and up onto the ship. She shook her head and her hair appeared to dry instantly. Her smile seemed almost too big for her face, and her eyes blinked slowly open and closed. Angus took off his felt hat and stared at her.

Clover leapt up onto Winter. "Wow. You guys got her?"

Winter nodded and shivered.

Leven began to rise from the water. Garnock had him on his shoulder, lifting him above the rail and onto the stern. Leven jumped from Garnock and pulled at the Baadyn covering his head. The Baadyn stretched and popped off with a wet snap. Leven shook his dark wet hair and tossed the Baadyn back into the water. He turned to Garnock.

"You have to go after him," Leven ordered. "He's gotta get out."

"He will," Garnock said calmly, his voice the sound of soft running water. "The Waves will stick with him."

"What's going on?" Winter asked.

"Geth's still down there," Leven said. "I'm going back."

"That would be foolish," Garnock said sternly. "You should be in seclusion. You're vulnerable, and your death will help nothing."

"It could help Geth."

"Fate holds him—"

"I know, I know, fate holds him now," Leven said quickly.

"But I'm not standing around waiting to see what fate does."

"The Waves will stay by him."

"I'm not leaving this spot until we have him." Leven held his ground.

As if on cue, the water began to churn and Geth rose out. Two fat Waves were holding Geth by his arms. The Baadyn around Geth's head slipped like runny phlegm back into the water.

Leven and Winter pulled Geth over the rail and onto the deck. Geth flopped down against the floor, coughing and spitting. Leven pushed his wet hair out of his own eyes and smiled. He kneeled down by Geth as the other Waves moved back behind Garnock.

"That was fast," Leven said.

"I said I'd be right behind you." Geth grinned. "The Waves were quick to find another exit. Thank you so much, Garnock."

"We would sooner leave another Wave," Garnock said. "Good-bye, Leven."

Garnock nodded and shrank back into the water. The other Waves did the same, meshing into the foaming mass of gaunt faces and waves. Garnock's face disappeared and the sea boiled as the Waves slowly rolled away in massive, thundering humps.

Everyone turned and looked at Phoebe at once.

"Phoebe," Leven said. "Are you all right?"

"I am now," she said, blinking rapidly. "How kind of you to come for me."

"You're a longing," Geth said.

Phoebe smiled, and the air in Foo suddenly seemed crammed with oxygen.

"There aren't any left," Geth whispered.

"There's one," Phoebe said teasingly.

"A longing on my boat," Angus said in disbelief.

Phoebe touched Angus on the cheek. Angus stumbled backward. He would have fallen right into the sea if it had not been for the rail.

Phoebe turned to Leven. "Thank you."

Leven's face burned red. "Don't mention it."

Phoebe smiled and began to lift off the ground. She rose higher and large translucent wings unfolded behind her, catching the soft wind.

"I should go," she sang.

"Wait," Geth said, sounding like an adolescent teen. "Where are you going?"

"Everywhere," Phoebe answered. She smiled, and the temperature in Foo warmed. She reached out and brushed Geth's arm.

"A lithen," she said, blinking. "How wonderful."

"Geth," Geth said.

"Of course." She laughed. "I'll be back, Geth."

Geth opened his mouth but couldn't say anything.

Phoebe smiled again, then fluttered her wings and drifted away. A few moments later she was out of view.

"Wow," Angus said.

"More like uh-oh," Geth said, finding his voice again. He looked at Angus. "Get us to Cusp as fast as possible. I mean it."

"But . . ."

"Now," Geth insisted.

Angus hurried away.

"A longing?" Geth said urgently, turning to look at Leven.

"What?" Leven answered defensively. "I knew she was in trouble and I had to help. Clover told me to."

"Right." Winter half smiled. "It's Clover's fault."

"I gotta agree with Winter," Clover chimed in. "First of all, I don't remember saying anything, and second, Phoebe's too pretty to be someone you simply save."

"Your grandfather gave you that key to her cage?" Geth asked.

"Right before he died," Leven said, confused. "He said I would need it."

"What a weak soul," Geth cursed. "He's left Foo a mess that only conflict will clean up. And releasing a longing will make things messier. Yes, yes, I realize she's beautiful—I'm not blind. Your grandfather was a coward to leave all of this to you. I think you might be wise to hide the sycophant key someplace besides around your neck and don't tell anyone—or even think about—where. Okay? Not even us. You have to keep it a secret."

"Are you okay?" Winter asked Geth. "You're kind of all over the place."

Geth put his head in his hands, his blue eyes looking confused against the clear sky. Leven sat down on a wooden barrel half filled

with purple apples. He laced his fingers together behind his head and leaned over. Clover patted him on the shoulder.

"It's not easy being the Want," Clover said calmly, making excuses for his burn. "So you let Phoebe out. We all make mistakes."

"It's so confusing," Leven admitted. "I can't see anything but what's in front of me. My eyes are burning, but I can't see the future. I close my eyes and all I can see is darkness. I open my eyes and I see lights creeping into the corner of my view."

"You're settling," Geth said. "The mantle of the Want takes time to assume."

"I didn't want this." Leven wiped his forehead. "I didn't ask to come here and be buried by the seemingly impossible. My hands are bigger, I'm taller, but I feel insignificant."

"You're not," Geth insisted. "Azure and the Dearth will pay, and what you stepped into Foo to accomplish will come to pass."

"You're going to be okay," Winter said reassuringly.

"You don't understand," Leven snapped.

"What don't I understand?" Winter's voice was stern. "Sorry you feel bad, but it's not like you just met a person so beautiful that now you feel completely worthless."

"What?" Leven said. "What are you talking about?"

"I saw the way you all fell over yourselves to stare at her."

"That was Geth."

"Don't argue, you two," Geth said.

"We're not arguing." Leven felt light-headed.

"No," Winter confirmed. "We're just . . ."

Winter looked at Leven. Leven looked right back at her. Winter's cheeks burned red and her green eyes outshone Leven's. The two of them stared at each other and then, as if they were destined to, they began to lean into each other. Leven closed his eyes.

"What are you doing?" Geth asked, concerned.

Winter closed her eyes too and leaned closer. Both of them looked panicked and out of control, but it didn't stop them from moving closer and kissing each other.

Clover's jaw dropped and he pulled something out of his void just so he could let go of it in shock. Even Geth looked caught off guard, as if he'd been given news that he never thought he'd hear in his lifetime.

Leven stumbled back and looked at Winter. His face was almost as red as hers. He looked at Geth and Clover and then back to Winter.

"Well, that was interesting," Clover said happily.

"I don't know what . . ." Leven tried to say.

"No, I . . ." Winter said. "It's not you . . . it's just that my . . . I think I left something down below."

"Hold on," Geth said, stopping Winter. "You don't understand. It's not just you. Her effect—it's already taking hold."

"Whose effect?" Clover asked.

"Phoebe's," Geth answered. "With her release, all of Foo will begin to grow more feeling and . . . well, more passionate."

Winter cleared her throat and continued to blush. Leven looked at his feet.

"Even Azure," Geth added. "If things were heating up before, it's only going to get worse. We've got no time to waste now."

Geth hurried below.

"Wait up!" Clover yelled. "I need . . . well, I don't really need anything, but I just don't want to be alone with these two."

"I really should go below also," Winter said.

"Why?" Leven asked. "Because of what happened? I mean, that's just because of Phoebe. It's not like we really kissed. Well, we kissed, but it wasn't because we wanted to."

Winter smiled awkwardly.

"I mean, I didn't wake up this morning planning to kiss you," Leven explained.

"Don't worry," Winter said, her wet blond hair making her look smaller and more vulnerable than she usually did.

"I feel like a jerk for some reason," Leven admitted. "Or kind of like I'm going to pass out."

"Either way you should probably lie down," Winter said.

Leven squeezed the back of his neck with his right hand and sighed.

"Go lie down," Winter insisted. "Because I'm thinking I might try to kiss you again if you don't. I mean, Phoebe's out."

Leven looked at her. He had never realized how pretty she was.

"You released her." Winter smiled.

Leven stood up very slowly and reluctantly walked below. The *Plud Hag* turned and headed up toward Cusp.

CHAPTER NINE

DON'T FEAR THE REAPER

Ezra paced across the top of the dresser, wringing his hands. His purple plastic toothpick top twisted in the wind of the air conditioner and his green nail-polished body glistened under the pungent glow of the motel's neon sign dripping through the window. Ezra scratched his forehead with his thin wooden tail and clapped his hands angrily. It sounded like a tiny click.

"Something's different," he hissed. "Something's wrong. I feel different all of a sudden."

"Could it be from the fact that the world is falling apart?" Dennis asked. "I saw tanks rolling through the streets today. Everyone's scared of the bugs and clouds and buildings."

"I didn't say something's different about the world," Ezra snapped. "*I* feel different."

Dennis blinked, his eyes tired from staring out the window. He sat up on the edge of the bed and looked at Ezra.

"You don't look different—aside from the fact that you're a toothpick and all."

Dennis had a tendency to speak his own mind these days. With Sabine out of his system he was back to being a simple-minded janitor with wrinkle-free pants and a white shirt. There were traces of black, shadowy lines up and down his arms and body and shaved head, but they were faded, and his mind was mostly clear and open. And the things he had been through gave him a new courage to speak.

Dennis had followed Ezra across the world and back again. They had flown in planes, driven in cars, and crossed the ocean in a large, smelly boat operated by an abusive Russian crew. Dennis had heeded every order Ezra had barked, lifted every object, and done everything the deranged toothpick had ever asked. Now, however, he was tired and wishing that whatever Ezra was experiencing or feeling wouldn't translate to Dennis's having to work any harder or worry any more than he had recently.

After sailing across the ocean they had arrived in North Carolina. From there they had hitchhiked to where they currently were—in Oklahoma waiting for someone neither of them knew, but hopeful that whoever it was would be able to help.

"I feel weird," Ezra snapped. "Sick, even."

"Sick like throwing up?" Dennis asked.

"Sick like throwing up," Ezra mocked. "No, sick like my insides are all girlie."

Ezra looked shocked at his own words.

"Girlie?" Dennis asked, surprised.

"Don't say it!"

"You did."

"I am the one with the girlie insides," Ezra snipped, his one eye blinking rapidly. "I can say what I want."

The motel room was silent except for the sound of the air conditioner. Two doors down a car horn honked and somewhere far away the sound of sirens could be heard.

"Are you sure they're staying here?"

Ezra sighed.

"We've been waiting all day," Dennis continued. "Maybe they weren't really kicked out of their apartment. Maybe they aren't living here now."

Ezra's back tightened as a new knot seemed to grow on his tiny spine.

"You are a swollen pig," Ezra spit. "I would give my left hand, single eye, and all of my pointed toes to have that other idiot back—what's his name, the one who collected garbage?"

"Tim?" Dennis said.

"I'm Ezra, you idiot."

Dennis looked at the ground and wove his fingers together.

"So, Tim was the one who told you about these two?" Dennis asked.

"He told Sabine," Ezra said. "But as usual I was listening in on other people's conversations."

"You must be proud."

"Thank you," Ezra said, confused by his own emotions. "And . . . thanks for being here."

Dennis looked around as if somewhere there was a TV left on and it was playing something offensive.

"What did you say?" Dennis finally asked.

"You've been a good companion," Ezra sighed.

Dennis shook his head and felt his own forehead.

"You're all over the place emotionally," Dennis said. "Why are you saying that?"

"I don't know." Ezra trembled. "Something's wrong with me. I think Geth's doing something. I swear, the moment I meet that selfish fool I'm going to kill him. He takes the good and leaves me with nothing but anger and confusion. Now my insides are turning all rotten and soft and I long to be with friends, chatting. You know, like in that cracker commercial—the one with the cheese and the kittens."

"You have no friends."

Ezra started to wail.

"What now?" Dennis asked.

"What now?" Ezra mimicked. "Can't you see I'm in pain?"

Dennis looked hurt as well.

"Sorry," Ezra said. "I've got to pull myself together. They'll be here soon."

"And you're sure they're from Foo?"

"That garbage man said they were connected," Ezra said. "Plus I can feel it."

"You're feeling a lot of things these days," Dennis said.

"What a pothole you are," Ezra snapped.

"See," Dennis said. "This is why you have no friends."

"I know," Ezra said. "I'm a mess. Call down to the motel desk. See if they know when they'll be back."

"They won't know. You can't just call and have—"

"Call!" Ezra barked.

Dennis stood up and brushed his pants. He looked at himself in the mirror by the TV and ran his hands over his shaved head. It wasn't easy for him to stare at himself, but the last few weeks of his life had made him stronger and more capable. He had even noticed himself standing almost completely straight up instead of slouching when he walked. And on three different occasions he had actually instigated eye contact with people.

"Stop staring at your boring face and call the desk!" Ezra screamed. "It'll be just as washed out and plain after you make the call."

"Thanks," Dennis said sarcastically.

"What a knob."

Dennis picked up the beige phone, pushed the white buttons, and in three rings a gravelly male voice answered.

"What?"

"Um . . . uhh," Dennis tried to think of the right way to ask about somebody else's business. As he was stuttering, headlights pulled into the motel parking lot and brushed across their window.

"What do you need?" the clerk on the phone asked impatiently.

"Well, I was . . . we were wondering if the ice machine was working."

"There's no ice machine." The man laughed. "What do you think this is, a Motel 6?"

Dennis thanked the man for his time and hung up.

"Ice machine?" Ezra seethed. "I'd give anything to work with someone who had at least average intelligence—like a rock, or an empty toilet paper roll."

"I can arrange that," Dennis said firmly. "Knock it off."

"Oh, there's that backbone you were rumored to have."

"I didn't ask him when they would be back because they've just pulled up."

Ezra leapt from the dresser over to the window. He pushed his face up against the glass and stared out. The night was dark but the neon sign lit the parking lot. The car that had just pulled in was parked across the lot.

Its lights shut off and the doors opened.

A large, big-shouldered woman wearing a red sweat suit hefted herself out of the passenger's side. She stood there, catching her breath and looking around. Her expression gave the impression that she currently smelled something foul. On the driver's side a skinny man in a dark robe stepped from the car. He had the hood of his robe over his head and looked like a featherweight boxer getting ready for a quick fight. He wore white sneakers with black socks.

"That's them?" Dennis whispered. "Black socks and white shoes?"

"You're criticizing him? This coming from a man who dresses like you do," Ezra bit back. "Could your pants get any blander?"

"Well, at least I never have to iron my pants."

"Stop talking," Ezra hissed. "It's them, I can feel it. Now, remember our plan?"

"Of course I remember."

"I can't believe I'm putting this in your hands," Ezra growled. "I've never even seen you think well for yourself."

"Don't worry."

Ezra became misty, switching emotions at rapid fire. "You've grown up so fast."

"You really are all over the place," Dennis said, frustrated.

"I know, now let's go."

Dennis picked up a pair of fake glasses resting on the bed. He slipped on a long white lab coat and grabbed a clipboard with a piece of plain yellow paper on it.

"Do I look official?" he asked Ezra.

"Pitiful, maybe."

Dennis picked up Ezra by the head and slipped him behind his ear.

"Don't say anything I haven't whispered to you," Ezra barked. "Understand? I don't want you blowing this by thinking anyone cares about your opinion."

Dennis nodded, picked up his motel key, and walked out the door and across the parking lot.

CHAPTER TEN

THE INVISIBLE VILLAGE

It can be quite difficult to accurately describe something invisible. If you know a person's invisible you might start by saying he or she has arms and legs and a head, but past that point it's not easy to get more specific. I believe the Invisible Village is quaint and lovely, but I'm just going on imagination. I'm certain the buildings have windows and there are doors, but as for the type of flowers growing out of the possible flower boxes, I'm just not too sure. Because of this, this chapter just might take a little more imagination on your part. Thankfully, Foo has not been destroyed and the possibility of dreaming is still there.

Good luck.

Brindle was a fat, happy, red, furry sycophant. He moved through the stone pass and down the twenty moss-covered steps. He had been sent by Rast, the lead sycophant in the Chamber of Stars, to retrieve Lilly. Lilly was Rast's daughter, and the one who had

stolen the sycophant key and given it away. Rast felt certain that Lilly would have answers to help them get the key back and restore their responsibility. Brindle, as usual, was happy to do his part to help.

Brindle leapt four steps at a time trying to keep up with his trail guide. Brindle had met up with an Omitted named Tosia and was now being taken to the Invisible Village. Tosia was tall, with a shaded face and dark hands. He had a long, ratty beard and eyes with white pupils. The dark bags under his eyes were as pronounced as his wide nose. Nothing he wore matched, due to the fact that the Omitted could see everything but themselves and because of this they had to depend on others to tell them how they looked.

"Are we close?" Brindle asked.

"Yes," Tosia answered. "Can't you feel it?"

Brindle stopped walking and let the feelings of the moment wash over him. His heart hurt and his head felt thick.

"Feel heavy?" Tosia asked.

"I do," Brindle answered. "My chest feels tight. It's not a feeling I like."

"The village is a horrible place," Tosia said. "There's no good there."

"I've heard."

"A person with your kind disposition should stay away."

"I must find Lilly."

"The white sycophant?"

"Yes," Brindle said, placing his right hand on his chest to breathe better.

"She's sick," Tosia whispered. "Few have a depression more palpable. She talks often about digging up metal and destroying Foo."

"I know her father," Brindle said.

"Is he a sad creature?"

"Quite the opposite."

"Can you see my shoes?" Tosia asked.

"Yes."

"Do they look okay?"

Brindle stopped to look at Tosia's shoes. "They are on the wrong feet," he said.

"Are you telling the truth?" Tosia asked suspiciously.

Brindle nodded.

"No wonder my feet hurt."

Tosia sat down and untied his shoes.

"Do you know what's happening in Foo?" he asked. "The news we get out here is riddled with holes. The Lore Coils that reach us are pathetic at best. They've bounced around so many times it's hard to understand what they say. Others say that Azure has discovered a way out. And there are multiple mentions of war."

"I fear war is inevitable," Brindle said.

"I've even heard mention of the Dearth rising again. That's impossible, right?" Tosia said as he awkwardly switched his shoes onto the opposite feet.

"Unfortunately, you're wrong," Brindle said. "It's this concern that brings me here to find Lilly. She has a connection to the keys and we are hoping she can help."

"The mythical seven keys," Tosia said. "I don't believe in them."

"I've seen one," Brindle said.

Tosia's eyes ballooned.

"And we fear they might have already been used to open the soil."

"They're real? But if the Dearth rises . . ." Tosia shivered.

"If the Dearth succeeds, all of existence will change," Brindle clarified. "This war will be very different from the last. Most are too concerned with their own comfort this time to worry about fighting. And those who gather to fight are fighting for reasons they don't fully realize."

"Stop," Tosia said. "Our conversation's making me even sadder."

"Sorry," Brindle said. "You asked for news."

"I don't know why I did," Tosia lamented. "I prefer not to know. It's too much for a person to carry around."

Tosia stood.

"Come," he said. "It's not much farther."

Brindle followed Tosia, weaving between thick trees and rocky cliffs. At the edge of a small mountain there was a large wooden gate.

"The village is just beyond that," Tosia said in a hushed tone. "I'm not going a step farther and I advise you to do the same."

"I have to get Lilly."

"The depression will smother you," Tosia said.

"I'll be quick to leave," Brindle said nervously.

"I'd never go," Tosia warned. "In no time you'll be shuffling around wondering what the point is and why you should bother with anything."

"I appreciate your concern," Brindle said. "But I must go on."

Brindle pushed on the gate and it swung up, opening at the bottom for him to walk through. On the other side of the gate was a thin footpath that cut between two tall, skinny mountains. The mountains slouched inward, looking sad.

"Good-bye." Brindle waved, looking through the door. "And thanks."

"Hold on," Tosia said. "Before you go, can I ask, do you think I'm too pale?"

"Not at all."

"Honestly?"

"Honest."

"Describe my eyes," Tosia pleaded.

"There isn't time," Brindle said, uncomfortable.

Tosia looked wounded. "My jealous brother says they're mud colored."

"You have very handsome eyes," Brindle conceded. "Chocolate brown."

Tosia smiled.

Brindle closed the gate before Tosia could say anything else. He moved down the path, flipping the hood of his robe up over his head and turning invisible himself. Brindle's shoulders slouched as the heaviness of the environment began to weigh down upon him.

"I've got to move fast," he said aloud.

He began to run. He ran along the path and came to an opening at the edge of the sloped mountains. Before him was a small green valley. A thin purple river ran through it and the basin was covered with creatures and people walking aimlessly about. Some appeared to be walking in the air.

Brindle reached the cliffside and climbed a large net of ivy down the cliff face and into the valley. Once on the ground he walked straight into something, smacking his face. The impact made his head spin. Brindle reached out and could feel a wall of some sort. He turned and ran into another invisible obstacle. He turned back around and could not find the spot he had just come from.

Brindle's heart beat faster.

He moved onto all fours and crawled in the reverse direction. Running into nothing, he kept moving down what felt like a cobblestone street. Of course all he could see was dirt, but his tiny hands could feel the grooves and textures of each brick.

The stones stopped and Brindle's head knocked into a rough surface. He reached out and wrapped his arms around what seemed like a tree.

He could hear crying and looked up to spot a woman standing there weeping. Brindle moved to comfort her, but there was an invisible wall between the two of them. He tried to climb over the wall but he couldn't find the top.

"Hold on!" Brindle yelled.

The woman didn't move. She just continued to cry.

Brindle loosened his robe and tried to take in big gulps of air. His chest was thumping and his legs became heavy and sore. Not only could he not find a way to get to the woman, he couldn't find a way out of the space he now occupied. He was in the middle of what looked like a wide open field, but he was trapped.

Brindle spun around. Sad, desperate people and creatures trying to find their way out of the Invisible Village dotted the valley.

Brindle breathed in deeply. He closed his eyes and stood still. Stepping forward, he reached out and turned to the right. His ears twitched and his red fur waved lightly. He could sense an opening. Eyes shut, he walked two hundred feet.

Brindle opened his eyes and saw a man sitting on the ground two feet away from him. Brindle was only twelve inches tall but he stepped up to the man and put his small hand on the stranger's right knee. The man was thin, with shoulders narrower than his waist. He had on dirty leather shoes and his pants and shirt were made of black linen. There was crust under his eyes and beneath his nose from dried snot and tears.

The man's crusty eyes blinked slowly and out of sync.

"Who's there?" he asked weakly.

Brindle materialized. The man smiled softly and patted Brindle on the hand with his soiled right hand.

"A sycophant." He sighed. "How nice to think about something besides my plight."

"What is it about this place?" Brindle asked sincerely. "It feels so sad. I've always heard stories, but I didn't understand."

"It's my home," the man said sadly. "I have to live here."

"Why?"

"I can't remember."

"I want to perish," Brindle said honestly. "I want to leave, but I don't know if I can find my way out."

"It's possible," the man said. "Not easy, but possible. Don't worry, though, you'll become accustomed to the hopelessness."

"I don't believe that," Brindle said, loosening his robe around his neck.

The thin man frowned. "Believe what you want. I can say quite honestly that I don't think I have it in me to care."

"I can't even remember what I'm here for," Brindle said, confused. "I think there's a girl."

"Isn't there always?" the man said. "That makes me sad."

"I think it's a sycophant," Brindle said. He was trying hard to think straight. "A white one."

"Lilly?" the thin man asked.

"Yes," Brindle said sadly. "I'm here for Lilly. Do you know her?"

"You learn to know everyone here," he said. "Not many wander in by accident and most stay until they're through with their existence."

"So do you know where she is?"

The thin man lifted his right hand and pointed to the left.

"See that jagged peak?" he asked. "The one with the crooked top?"

Brindle followed the man's finger.

"Yes."

"Last I saw her she was behind there in a two-story cottage."

"Is there a way to get there fast?" Brindle asked. "The village is confusing."

"No," the thin man said. "I'd wish you luck, but in your state you would doubt my sincerity."

"It looks so far away," Brindle complained. "Even if it was a straight shot."

"It is far," the thin man replied. "There's a good chance you might never make it. Of course, you could always wait until it snows. The snow gives our village definition."

"Does it snow here often?"

"Once, maybe twice a year," the man answered.

Brindle didn't know if he wanted to go on living. And if he did want to live, he couldn't remember a reason why he should.

CHAPTER ELEVEN

FAR AND AWAY

The *Plud Hag* traveled all night and reached the docks of Cusp at mid-morning. The boat hadn't even been properly tied off by the crewmen before Leven leapt ashore. Winter was right behind him and Clover was clinging to Geth. All four of them were fighting to control their emotions and trying hard to act as if nothing like an accidental kiss between Leven and Winter had actually happened on the boat.

"Nice detour," Clover complained. "Now everything's even messier."

"I couldn't leave her buried," Leven said loudly.

"I could have," countered Winter.

The docks of Cusp were crowded with people of all types and classes. Hundreds of boats were tied up or taking off. The sky was a clear green with streaks of yellow running along the

bottom, and there were a dozen hot-air balloons hovering in the sky like ornaments.

A dirty, burly fisherman bumped into Leven and continued walking without saying a word.

"Some welcoming committee," Clover said. "One time when my brother came home from his first burn we made signs for him. I still remember mine read, 'Welcome Back.'"

"Clever," Winter said.

Two men carrying a coffin-size box full of bright orange fish pushed past them. The fish were wriggling and complaining while the men were arguing over who loved a certain girl most.

"Phoebe must have flown over," Geth said.

"Great," Winter complained.

"Azure will be at the Far Hall," Geth informed them. "It's the center of Cusp."

"What are we waiting for?" Leven said. "I wish you had cars here."

"Me too." Clover smiled. "One of the best moments of my life was driving a car in Reality."

"You can always travel by balloon," Angus said, stepping off of the boat and butting into their conversation. "Or if you need to go quickly you can move by rope. Personally I'm not comfortable with the rope due to the problems, but I know many use it and think it's safe."

Angus held out his hand and cleared his throat. "If you don't mind."

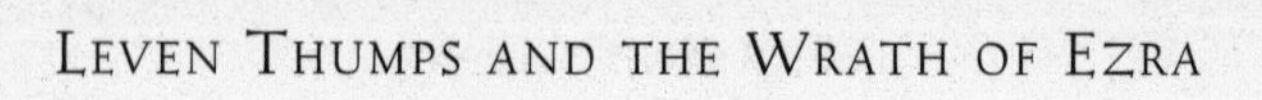

Geth gave Angus a handful of green sticks and a couple of short pieces of rope for his payment.

"Thanks for the ride," Leven said.

"Our pleasure," Angus nodded. "Maybe fate will blow us your way again. Until then, I'll take my leave and wish you well."

Leven, Geth, Winter, and Clover moved down the wooden dock and onto the cobblestone streets of Cusp.

Cusp was the largest city in Foo. Most honest nits and cogs lived within its borders. It stretched from the Sentinel Fields just below the Lime Sea and bordered the Veil Sea all the way up to the Devil's Spiral. The gloam jutted out from below Cusp, but most in the city liked to pretend the gloam and its dirty soil weren't even there.

Cusp was beautiful and diverse. Colorful trees and lush growth flourished along the roads and in the yards of every structure. Birds flew through the balloon-filled sky in magnificent patterns, showing off their colors and skills. The intricate stone streets and tall, aesthetically pleasing homes competed with the trees and rivers for people's attention.

The population of Cusp was close to a million creatures and beings. It was a well laid out city with wide cobblestone streets and neighborhoods reflective of most of the countries in Reality. There were a Russian district, a European sector, and an American avenue. A Polish parish, a French quarter, an African region, a Canadian province, and a Chinese community could also be found. It was all at once quaint, international, and familiar feeling. There were no noisy cars filling the street, only

onicks and other creatures pulling carts or pushing wagons.

For many of the past years Cusp had been a peaceful place where nits manipulated dreams and used their gifts to build the city and better Foo. Cusp was also slow to join sides in the fight to right Foo. Most of the residents were happy to pretend that everything was just fine with Foo and Reality. Recently Azure had spent a lot of energy and time trying to recruit nits in Cusp to join him and the movement to mesh Foo with Reality.

Cusp wasn't dark like Morfit, or remote like Fté. It had architecture and ingenuity. And there was a sense of security and order in Cusp that so much of Foo lacked at the moment.

"It always makes me happy just to be here," Leven said.

"That's just that cage girl making you think that," Clover said.

"Yeah, I don't know how to trust my own feelings anymore," Winter added.

"Phoebe doesn't change your feelings," Geth said. "You'll simply long more for what you always have wanted."

"So when Leven kissed Winter . . ." Clover started to say.

"Hey, there's one of those ropes," Winter said quickly, pointing to one of the many long, taut strands of rope that ran down the street in any number of directions.

The ropes were systematically strung all along the roads and sidewalks. They were held up by dark green poles with what looked like little carved monkeys on top.

"I've never used the ropes before," Geth admitted. "It's a relatively new way to get about. A nit from South America invented it."

"How does it work?" Winter asked.

"Hold onto the rope and say where you would like to go out loud."

"It pulls you there?" Leven asked.

"Kind of," Geth answered.

Winter stepped up to the rope, gripped it with her right hand, and said, "Far Hall."

Nothing happened.

"Wow," Clover said. "I'm glad I didn't blink."

"Is it supposed to . . ."

Winter stopped talking. Her hand was beginning to weave itself into the rope. She tried to pull it back, but she couldn't. The rope pulled Winter into it, stretching her into threads and weaving all of her into the taut line. Two seconds later she was gone, nothing but a shaded bit of rope racing away down the line.

"That's not right," Leven said.

"It's organic or something," Geth said. "You become one with the rope until it hopefully unspools you at your destination. Who's next?"

"I actually don't mind walking," Clover said. "It's kind of a nice day."

"Didn't Angus say there were some problems?" Leven reminded Geth.

"In the beginning a few of the travelers came out mixed with parts of other travelers. I think the kinks have been worked out, though."

"Comforting." Leven smiled.

"Last one there is . . . well, you know." Geth grabbed ahold of the rope, a giant grin on his face. "Far Hall," he announced.

It worked even faster on Geth. His hand wove into the rope and the rope pulled the rest of him into the line as if he were a string unraveling in reverse.

"That's unsettling to watch," Leven said.

"You're not actually going to do it, are you?" Clover asked nervously. "Look, it's just me and you—like old times. We can walk and talk and skip. I'll read something out loud to you as we travel. It'll be nice to stretch your legs. Won't it be nice to stretch your legs?"

"There's no time," Leven said. "Besides, Winter would never let me hear the end of it."

"You might be part of the end of Winter if you try it."

Leven held Clover in his left arm and grabbed onto the line.

"Far Hall."

"Where's my say in this?" Clover argued as Leven's right limb became a long strand of stretched-out twine.

Leven and Clover were pulled into the line.

The feeling was sensational. It felt like being pulled through a tube that was half an inch too narrow. A burning and confusing feeling shot through Leven's body, while long strands of multicolored light spiraled around him as he traveled. He could feel impulses passing through him like freezing cold water in his stomach.

Then, with a sound similar to a full reel of fishing line being let loose, Leven shot out of the rope into a tightly coiled pile of himself. He breathed in and his body gelled together. Winter was standing right next to him with an open mouth.

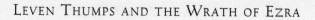

Leven set Clover down and began to pat himself, making sure everything was in place.

"You're all there," Geth said. "Unless there's some strand missing inside of you."

They were standing in a small stone structure that was open on both ends. The rope ran straight through the center.

"That was pretty amazing," Winter said.

A mother and two young children unraveled from the rope directly in front of them. The mother told her kids to keep moving and then walked out of the rope station. A man with a flushed face carrying a large bundle of flowers stepped in and grabbed the rope.

"Thirteen-eighteen Duncan Way."

He was pulled into the thick rope and gone.

"Couldn't someone cut the rope?" Clover asked.

"I suppose," Geth said. "But you'd just be rerouted."

"Let's do it again," Clover said, reaching out.

"Not yet." Leven stopped him. "We have to see if Azure's here."

They stepped out of the rope stop and crossed a large cobblestone street. Onicks shuffled and galloped in both directions, carrying passengers and wares around Cusp. On the other side of the road was Far Hall, a large stone building sitting on a tall granite foundation. Far Hall had a dozen floors and arched windows that looked like webs covering the whole place. It was made of pink

stone that appeared wet under the new morning sunlight. The doors were all wood with round wooden beams that slid across their fronts and locked into place. In each of the rounded windows a yellow-robed nit stood holding a kilve and wearing an expression of focused concentration.

"Azure must be here," Geth said. "They would never have such a heavy presence of security if there weren't someone important or troublesome visiting."

Twenty wide granite steps led to the wide front entrance. Two young boys were walking around shouting about the news in the latest edition of the *Scroll.* Leven climbed the steps quickly with Geth and Winter in tow. Geth addressed the short yellow-robed guard at the entrance.

"Is the Twit in?" Geth asked.

"That's a question only to be asked by those with authority," the guard replied hotly.

"Then will you tell him Geth's here?"

"Geth?" the guard said with surprise.

Geth nodded back.

"Geth the lithen?"

"Yes."

"You can tell him yourself." The guard motioned. "I was raised in a home that still values what you've done."

"Then you were raised well." Geth smiled.

"Come," the guard said. "Follow me."

Inside the front doors, the building opened up like a great cathedral. The ceiling was covered with colored glass that allowed the sunlight to shine down in intricate patterns against the light tiled floor. Thick velvet curtains were draped over hundreds of windows and chairs that would have looked at home in a posh, stuffy castle. Spiral staircases circled up and into large holes leading to other floors and places.

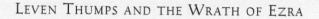

"Is Azure here?" Geth asked the guard.

"He arrived hours ago," the guard answered. "He debates with the Twit in the square chamber."

"It might be best if we were to approach without a lot of notice," Geth said. "Fate would be fortunate to hear what's being discussed without them knowing I'm there."

"Then fate moves me to be on my way," the guard said. "You will find them in the square chamber. There are many others looking on. If it were me, I would approach through the far door and probably not be noticed at all."

"Thank you." Geth nodded.

The guard bowed and backed away.

"There's still good in Cusp," Geth said.

The four of them wound their way up a wide spiral staircase into a light hole. The space was squat, with thick rugs and low ceilings. There were three doors, all tightly closed.

"Around the side," Geth instructed. "There's another door."

Geth turned the corner and slipped into a tiled nook off the tight hallway. The door in the nook was unlocked and opened without noise. The sound of people shifting drifted out and up like tepid wind.

A man inside was speaking.

Geth slid into the back row and scooted down far enough for Leven and Winter to fit in. They were well hidden by the crowd, which began to murmur in agreement with the man speaking.

The room was square with a high, pointed, glass ceiling. Marble pillars lined three walls, holding up a balcony. At the front of the room was a tall seat with a low wooden wall surrounding it and a small strip of fuzzy red flooring in front of it. The remainder of the room was filled with benches for spectators. Almost every seat was occupied and there were some people sitting casually on the floor near the front.

"That's Azure," Winter said with poison in her voice. She pointed toward the man who had been talking. He was now pacing back and forth on the fuzzy flooring.

Azure had on a long blue robe with black markings on the edges. He had broad shoulders and was as tall as Geth. His hair was long and dark and he looked young, like Geth. It seemed apparent by the way he spoke and moved that he was knowledgeable and thought he was smarter than he actually was. His dark eyes looked over the crowd with a manufactured sincerity. His right ear was red and swollen and when he moved he favored his left side so as to keep the ear out of sight.

"We move in bulk, but we seek only peace," Azure said. "We are soldiers in pursuit of peace."

The Twit was sitting in the throne. He wore a high, funny-looking red wig and had a short gray beard and big square glasses. The Twit looked much older than Azure and wore a far less sophisticated brown robe. His hands were small and folded neatly

in his lap right below his round stomach. He unfolded his hands and scratched at his nose, looking both bothered and bored.

A small, thin man with fluffy blond hair and a fancy purple robe was sitting near the throne writing everything down. The back wall of the room was lined with guards all holding kilves.

"You wish to occupy land that rests directly next to Cusp," the Twit said. "If you were the Twit, I wonder if you would be so quick to allow permission."

"If I had the word of someone such as I," Azure said strongly.

"Such as you? There's much sordid talk about one such as you," the Twit said, his red wig jiggling.

"Talk?" Azure smiled.

"Yes, talk," the Twit said. "Of course, people often speak without understanding, but let's see if I understand. You say you wish only to march down the gloam and occupy the stones the lithens have abandoned?"

"Yes," Azure said. "As we continue our search for a pathway out of Foo."

The Twit laughed as others in the square chamber fidgeted in their seats.

"Such a pathway does not exist," the Twit said. "I know because I've read many books addressing the subject."

"You are most learned," Azure said. "But with no offense intended, we believe differently."

"There's also talk of you stealing gifts and digging up metal," the Twit said.

The audience hissed.

"I am not here to debate what those in Morfit do," Azure said. "I . . ."

"I'm not talking of those in Morfit," the Twit said heatedly. "There's talk of gift stealing here on the edges of Cusp, by those who pledge allegiance to you."

"Would you deny those who wish to shed the responsibility of their gifts?" Azure argued. "There are many who tire of what they have been burdened with. Why should they have to hold onto their gifts if they don't wish to? As for metal, I can't be responsible for what a few rogue rants dig up."

"You've brought the rants here. And so many of them," the Twit said. "It's your casual excusing of order that concerns me."

"Rest easy," Azure said. "You will see in time that we seek no malice."

"I should hope so, and Cusp does not seek to regulate all of Foo. The Sentinel Fields are yours to occupy for the time being. However, if your gathering bleeds into the Meadows we will be forced to use our strength to hold you back."

The audience moaned and chattered. An old woman with a wide, floppy hat barked at Azure while others booed her.

"Trust me, we seek no war," Azure assured them all. "We've done nothing to harm you, and when the soil in the gloam settles we will be on our way with all who wish to join us."

"I want no talk of pathways out of Foo," the Twit insisted. "We still believe there is importance in our relationship with the dreams of man. You are an idiot to think as you do, but perhaps the lesson of your failure will be what is required to teach you so."

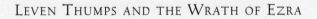

Azure tried to calm his nerves by breathing deeply.

"I will obey your wish," Azure finally said. "But let me say before this crowd and all who have ears, that believing there's no way out is a foolish tradition. We have proof of Geth leaving and returning with others."

Leven looked at Geth.

"That gateway was destroyed," the Twit said.

"We believe there's another," Azure said. "A permanent opening he used many, many years ago."

The Twit shook his head. "That's a myth wrapped up with the origin of the Dearth. Sabine and his shadows searched Foo for years looking for any gateway."

"But there were places they didn't reach," Azure said boldly. "Spots on the Thirteen Stones, and the island of Alder."

"What if your supposed opening went down with the sinking of Lith?" the Twit sniffed impatiently. "What then?"

Azure stood there silently, opening and closing his fists.

"I don't believe it, but what do I care?" The Twit waved his hand. "Waste your time as you wish, but do not bother the harmony of Cusp. We take our calm very seriously."

"I wouldn't dream of it," Azure said with oil in his voice. "We desire nothing but peace."

"That's a lie," Geth said, standing up.

The entire audience turned around as if on hinges. Geth pushed his hood back and looked directly at Azure's blue eyes. The crowd was cheering and clapping, quite happy with the disturbance. They began to mumble and titter with excitement.

Azure's eyes glowed blue and then dimmed.

"Geth," Azure said, shaking, his face pale. "You're the last person I expected to see."

"Sorry to disappoint you." Geth stepped out of his seat and into the aisle. "Azure seeks to overthrow Cusp, your honor. He has awakened the Dearth."

The crowd laughed.

"Geth," the Twit said with enthusiasm. "You live. How interesting."

"No thanks to Azure," Geth said. "He left us for dead."

"Explain," the Twit said.

"I'm afraid Geth's confused," Azure said, trying to regain his composure. "Geth seeks to keep everyone living in the past and captive to the old ways. He tells the story as if he were innocent. It was I who was left for dead."

"That's not true," Winter said passionately. "I was there."

"Hold on, this is not a trial," the Twit barked, his red wig shaking as he did so. "People speak when they are addressed. I paid for this position and you will respect me."

Winter's face burned pink under the reprimand.

"She's telling the truth," Leven said, standing. "Azure's working to ruin Foo."

The Twit's face flushed red. He held up his hands and then took off his glasses and rubbed his swollen eyes. He adjusted his wig and snapped his fingers.

"Drink," the Twit said loudly.

A tall guard entered the room carrying a porcelain pitcher

and stein. The guard poured some liquid into the stein and passed it to the Twit.

Leven closed his eyes as the Twit drank.

"Still coming up blank?" Clover whispered into Leven's ear, recognizing what Leven was trying to do. "Would it help if I hit you on the back of the head?"

Leven pushed back his dark hair and stared at the glass ceiling. The room was warm and the heat he felt in his cheeks was scorching.

"I bet if the Twit were an animal or creature of some sort you could control him," Clover added.

The Twit handed his cup back to the guard and exhaled. He stood and glared at Winter and Leven. He looked at Azure and Azure bowed respectfully.

"Geth," the Twit asked, "are these two interruptions with you?"

Geth nodded.

"You'd be wise to teach them manners," the Twit chastised. "And you say the Dearth is free?"

"Yes," Geth answered.

"Well, I have no concern for the Dearth," the Twit said sternly. "The tales of his existence and desires are stories I was told as a child to keep me from wandering into the Swollen Forest or away from the hills of Morfit. My heart's happy to see you, Geth. You are still spoken of with kindness, but you don't understand what's happening. You were away while much progressed."

Geth looked the Twit directly in the eye. "Progressed?"

"This is a different time," the Twit said calmly. "To hear you speak of the Dearth only confirms my fear that you're lost in a past that has long since slipped away. True, I do not trust Azure completely, but his intentions are clear and if he seeks foolishness then so be it. My concern is with Cusp and our level of society."

"And we seek only for peace and possibility," Azure said.

"You seek to destroy Foo entirely," Geth replied.

"This is not a trial," the Twit said again. "The mood here is attached to my decision. Azure, we will not react to your followers as you wait for the gloam to grow. But if I feel for a moment that the comfort of those in Cusp is being compromised, we will incite our forces and push against you."

"We will be gone the moment the gloam settles." Azure bowed.

"I can't believe this," Geth argued. "He has betrayed Foo. The Thirteen Stones aren't his to possess."

"Enough," the Twit said. "Azure's not on trial and the Thirteen . . . Twelve Stones are not my concern. Our beliefs may differ, but Azure walks our streets freely. And unless you have the money to change my mind, your concerns are not mine."

"Then you're a fool," Geth said.

"Careful," the Twit said. "My affection for you is not without limits. I can process what I see without your help. Now, who's the boy?"

"This is Leven Thumps," Geth pointed.

The courtroom exploded with mumbling and chatter.

"Quiet," the Twit ordered. "I suspected so."

"Everything we lithens have prophesied is coming about," Geth said.

"Don't speak of prophecy," the Twit snapped. "What stability does guessing at the future bring anyone?"

"I'm not guessing," Geth insisted.

"You bring a boy and say he's Leven," the Twit said. "And what if he is? His presence does nothing to guarantee Cusp's quality of life."

"I don't believe it. You choose to relax while Azure gains strength."

"Stop," the Twit insisted, halting Geth. "This conversation is over. Cusp knows how I feel and my thoughts are now public."

The small man with the puffy blond hair was writing frantically, trying hard to keep up.

"You're selling out Foo for the promise of fading comfort!" Winter cried.

"I could have you locked up!" the Twit yelled back. "You should thank fate that I have lunch plans and no time for the paperwork such motions involve."

The Twit glowered menacingly at Winter and turned in a huff. He then walked through a small wood door and out of the back of the room.

Geth looked at Azure, and the two of them locked eyes. Azure's smile made his face look fake and plastic. Geth moved toward him and in an instant Azure was gone.

Leven's stomach lurched, as if in sync with Azure's disappearance.

"Where'd he go?" Winter asked. She looked around the room.

The crowd began stamping their feet in excitement as the guards filed out of the door through which the Twit had exited. Some spectators shouted with enthusiasm for the Twit while others left the square chamber to broadcast the outcome.

"Where's Azure?" Leven called.

"He's never had the ability to disappear before," Geth said. "It's a trick. He must still be in the room somewhere."

Leven moved through the square chamber looking for any sign of Azure. He dropped to his stomach, checking beneath the benches and seats.

"He's not in here," Winter reported.

"Outside," Geth said. "He can't be far."

Leven stood up and held his stomach. His lungs heaved and he coughed until he could breathe freely again.

"Are you okay?" Clover asked.

"I'm fine," he answered.

"What's wrong?" Winter asked frantically, her emotions out of whack. She put her hand on Leven's back.

"My insides are messed up," Leven moaned.

"Can you walk?" Geth questioned.

"Of course," Leven said hotly.

Geth ignored Leven's reaction and ran to the spiral stairs.

"Keep your eyes open!" Geth hollered as they climbed down.

"I wasn't planning to keep them closed," Leven shot back.

The corridors of Far Hall were packed as spectators who had been in the square chamber poured out and mixed with those who were already there. There were all colors of robes covering all shapes of beings, but no sign of blue.

The four of them spilled out onto the main floor.

"Can he shrink?" Winter asked.

"No," Geth replied. "Azure's a lithen. He has no nit gift."

"Maybe he does now," Leven said. "They've been taking gifts in the hopes of being able to bestow them."

"There's no talk of their success," Geth said. "Over there."

Geth pointed to the long corridor that ran down the largest wing. At its end a speck of blue slipped between two marble pillars.

Leven pushed through those mingling in the corridor. Even here the effects of Phoebe could be seen. Dignified nits with tall hats and wigs were all over the place talking and arguing heatedly with one another. Some were expressing their love or reciting awful poetry.

When Leven reached the marble pillars, Azure was gone. All that remained were a tall stained glass window and a wide wooden door.

Leven pushed open the door and ran through it. Outside he found himself in an open courtyard filled with large granite orbs that were arranged in a square pattern. The clouds in the sky streaked across the horizon as if their bellies were smoldering. On

the opposite side of the courtyard Azure was walking quickly toward a rope.

"We've got to get close enough to hear where he's going," Geth instructed. "If he takes off without us hearing, we'll never catch him."

"Go, Clover," Leven commanded.

Clover shivered happily. He leapt from Leven's shoulder and soared through the air. He bounded across the tops of the orbs and ran across the heads of those walking about.

Azure was ten feet away from the rope.

Clover bent his legs and sprang over two old people who were holding hands and confessing their love to each other.

Azure reached the rope and stuck out his hand.

Clover hit the ground and rolled between the legs of a tall, slow-moving man.

Azure grabbed the rope and spoke.

Clover watched Azure become one with the rope and then disappear seconds before Leven, Geth, and Winter made it there.

Clover materialized and jumped onto Leven's right shoulder. He dusted his knees. Leven was breathing so hard from running that he couldn't speak yet.

"You okay?" Clover asked.

"Fine," Leven answered.

"What'd he say?" Geth questioned, not yet breathing easily himself.

"I think he said he's fine," Clover replied. "It's kind of hard to tell exactly, he's breathing so hard."

"Not Leven," Geth scolded. "Azure."

"Oh, he said, 'Fourteen Over Zenith.'"

Geth grabbed the rope and repeated what Clover said.

"All right," Winter said, taking hold and shouting out the address for herself. She was quickly pulled in.

"Ready?" Leven asked Clover.

"Of course," Clover replied.

Leven wrapped his fingers around the rope.

"Fourteen Over Zenith."

Leven was pulled into the rope and shot through the fibers. Lights and warmth twisted around him like fingers being dragged down his legs. He could feel others string through him. Three seconds later he shot out of the rope onto the side of the street, directly in front of a red brick three-story building.

Winter was standing there.

"Azure saw Geth come out," she said quickly. "He took the rope and said, 'Norton Bend.' Geth went after him."

Leven and Winter grabbed the rope. The ride was longer this time. Leven could feel himself rising and lowering as he zipped along.

Leven strung out in front of a large stone outcrop—nobody was there. Winter raveled into place right next to him.

"Where are they?" she asked, panicked.

"Not here," Leven said. "Are you sure he said Norton Bend?"

"I think so," Winter said. "He was sort of yelling. It could have been 'Horton Glen.'"

"There's a Horton Glen, and a Morton Den," Clover said.

"There's a Horton Glen?" Winter asked in disbelief.

"Great—I'll take that one," Leven said, reaching out. "Horton Glen."

Leven zipped into the rope and was on his way.

"Morton Den," Winter said, grabbing the rope.

Two seconds later they were nothing but twine and on their way to two completely different stops.

CHAPTER TWELVE

Completely Strung Out

Leven flew out in front of a round lake filled with green water and yellow fish. The fish popped like hot corn from the surface of the lake. Clouds of blue and gold dipped down into the water, their bottoms turning a wet, drippy purple. There was nobody in the immediate area. A short wooden fence ran through a sandy stretch of land surrounding the lake. In the distance a small shack with a picture of a cooked fish on it sat like a splintery squatter.

"It must have been Morton Den," Clover said needlessly. "I wish we had time to do some fishing."

"We don't," Leven said and grabbed the rope. "Morton Den."

Like skinny tree roots Leven's fingers grew long, twisting into the rope. The sound was similar to the noise of creaking wood. The lights and flashes of warmth rushing though Leven were

dizzying. He could feel himself lift and zip quickly to the right. The sound of thin tinkling bells and long, drawn-out screams could be heard weaving through Leven's mind. Leven spun like a corkscrew and sprayed out of the rope into a recognizable pile of himself.

He and Clover were in front of a large glass building with a stone arched doorway. The cobblestone street was filled with people walking and carts being pulled by onicks.

Once again there was no sign of Azure, Geth, or Winter.

Leven stopped a female cog walking by. "Did you see anyone pop out?"

"Excuse me?" the pretty cog said kindly. She had heather in her hair and wore a dress the color of sunshine.

Leven's cheeks burned.

"A guy in a blue robe and one in a dark green," Leven said slowly. "And there was a girl."

"I didn't see anything," she replied.

The pretty cog walked off.

"I don't think I should have released Phoebe," Leven said to Clover.

"It's sure making you all act goofy," Clover agreed.

Leven looked around frantically. In a patch of clean red dirt on the side of the walkway he saw a large word scratched in the soil.

"That's Winter's writing," Leven said urgently.

"How can you tell?" Clover asked.

"It's messy," Leven answered. "And there's a 'W' beneath it."

Leven clasped the rope again. "Twenty-Seven End of Up."

The rope ride was beginning to feel familiar and comfortable. Leven liked the sensation of others rushing past him. He would have almost enjoyed the journey if it had not been for the urgency in his heart.

Leven was ejected from the rope with a blast. His feet coiled against the stone street as his body wove itself back into shape.

Twenty-Seven End of Up was the end of the line and, by the looks of it, pretty close to the end of the world. The street stopped right up against a large, red, clay cliff. Trees lined the empty street, the low branches holding hands with one another as they stretched across the road, creating a canopy.

Leven looked up. Clover and he were not alone.

"Hello, Leven," Azure said coldly. "How nice of you to come to me. It's been a busy few days and this saves me some time and trouble."

Four rants were standing behind Azure holding Geth and Winter. Geth looked calm as usual, but Winter's cheeks were red and her green eyes stormy.

Leven reached out to hold the rope again, but a rant moved in from behind and seized his wrist. He spun Leven around, holding him tightly in front of him. The rant was huge and Leven could smell his hot, fishy breath on the back of his neck.

"So impetuous," Azure said. "Check him."

A sixth rant stepped in front of Leven and began to roughly search him. Half of the rant searching him was tall and strong. The other half was in the shape of a lumpy avaland.

"Nothing," the rant growled, trying to control his left half.

"Where's the key, Leven?" Azure asked.

"What key?" Leven said innocently.

Azure hit Leven across the face with the back of his left hand.

"Don't be stupid," he said cruelly. "The sycophant key. It once hung around your neck."

"The Want took it," Leven said without missing a beat. "I thought you would know that."

"The Want's dead," Azure said.

"Then I have no idea where the key is," Leven answered. "He took it from me."

"Search him again," Azure barked. "And don't be so gentle."

Leven struggled as the rant threw him to the ground and ripped at the robe he was wearing. Azure helped by pushing Leven's chest down with his own kilve. The rant tore and pulled at Leven. Geth and Winter struggled against their own rants.

"Leave him alone!" Winter shouted.

"Shut up," Azure growled.

The rants finished with Leven.

"Nothing," the largest rant said in shame, pulling Leven back up onto his feet.

"Take them to the cottage," Azure said angrily. "Keep an eye on them. I'll be back once we've covered more ground."

The rants bowed toward Azure and then pulled them all off the stone road and through the forest. A tiny brown cottage covered in moss and weeds stood barely noticeable among the thick trees.

"Inside," the rant holding Leven ordered, pushing him in through the front door.

Leven flew to the ground. The floor had been ripped up, exposing the dirt beneath. Leven lifted his chest to push himself up. Geth came crashing down on him, followed by Winter. The door of the cottage slammed closed behind them all.

"I got your message in the dirt," Leven said, sitting up.

"Sorry," Winter said. "We thought we were chasing after him, not the other way around."

"Is Clover here?" Geth asked.

"Of course," Clover said, appearing.

"See if you can listen to what they're doing," Geth whispered. "Quickly."

"No problem." Clover smiled and then disappeared.

"We shouldn't have followed him," Winter said.

"Why?" Geth asked.

"Honestly," Winter chided. "Don't you see where we are?"

"Exactly where fate would want us to be," Leven answered, looking around.

Geth and Winter stared at Leven—Geth looked proud, like a dad who had just witnessed his son's first home run.

Finally Winter spoke. "That's something Geth would say."

Leven stood and walked around the one-room cottage. The inside was the size of a large living room. There was a wooden trunk sitting in the middle of the torn-up floor and a round stone fire pit in the corner below a leafy funnel for smoke to rise up through. It was dark, but two small windows at the top

corners dimly lit the room. Leven could feel the dirt floor hissing.

"We shouldn't be standing on this ground," Leven said, holding out his hand to help Winter up.

"I'm okay," she said, getting herself up and stepping onto the trunk.

All three of them were barely able to squeeze together and sit with their knees up against their chests on the trunk.

"This might work for a little while," Winter said. "But I can't sit like this forever."

"What's he up to?" Leven asked Geth. "Azure could just get rid of us."

"I think the Dearth would have a problem with that," Geth whispered. "And he wants that key. I'm glad you don't have it."

"I listen occasionally," Leven whispered back.

"I think *rarely* is more accurate," Clover said from on top of Leven's head. "Like I asked him not to talk in his sleep, and he still does."

"Did you hear anything from them?" Geth asked, ignoring Clover's blathering.

Clover materialized. "Azure was talking to a tall rant and he said something about how it's taking longer than expected for someone to gain their strength."

"The Dearth," Geth said quietly.

"He also said he would be able to fix all of that tomorrow at the Meadows when it begins."

"Meadows?" Leven asked, looking at Geth.

"On the edge of Cusp," Geth answered. "The Twit has made it so easy for them. They'll be right next to the shatterball tournament tomorrow."

"Go, Cusp!" Clover cheered. "Anyway, he's going to keep you here until it's over. After that, I think he's planning to kill you."

"What?" Winter exclaimed.

"Why do you say that?" Leven asked.

"Because he said, 'I'm planning to kill them,'" Clover reiterated. "He said he has no use for Geth or Winter and that it wouldn't hurt for Leven to bleed a little."

"Nice," Leven replied. "We've got to get out of here."

"And the guards are still there?" Winter questioned.

Clover nodded. "There's two at the front, two at the back, and two standing out by the road. Why are you all sitting on this trunk?"

"The soil's not safe to stand on," Geth said, pushing his hair back out of his eyes.

"There's good news," Clover continued. "Azure's gone. He went for that thing that's gaining strength."

"And we're about to be killed," Winter said angrily.

"It shouldn't be that hard to break out of here," Leven said.

"Six huge rants," Clover reminded him.

Geth jumped from the trunk to the stone fire pit. He knocked against the hard wood wall.

"Could you get us our kilves?" Winter asked Clover.

"Not without them noticing me shoving them through the window," he answered.

"How about some food?" Winter complained. "I don't want to die starving."

"I can't get you a warm meal, but I've got a few things," Clover said, reaching into his void.

"No way," Leven insisted. "Don't eat anything he pulls out of there."

"I picked up some stuff from the Eggmen."

Clover fished around and pulled out a round blue ball with gold webbing covering it.

"I don't know what this is," Clover said. "But I thought it looked good."

"Don't eat it," Leven warned.

"How about some of that stuff I gave you at sea?" Clover asked. "Filler Crisps. I still have a whole box left."

"That's okay," Winter said. "I'm not doing that again. Don't you have anything chocolate?"

Clover reached deep into his void, his tongue at the corner of his mouth as he stretched. He smiled and pulled his arm slowly back out. In his tiny hand he held a long, thin, foil-wrapped bar of candy. The foil wrapper was dull under the weak light. On the front there was a single word: *Slub.*

"This sounds harmless." Clover shrugged.

He slowly unwrapped the candy and the aroma of chocolate filled the room. There were four small squares hooked together.

"What does it do?" Winter asked.

"I picked it up while we were with the Eggmen," Clover said excitedly. "I think it's new."

"It smells fantastic," Geth said.

"I don't know." Winter hesitated. "*Slub* sounds kind of dubious."

"More for me, then," Clover said happily, breaking off a square and popping it in his mouth. As Clover chewed, his blue eyes grew wide. He licked his small lips and began reaching for a second piece.

"No way." Winter grabbed a square. "I get one."

"I'll take one too," Geth said.

Clover held the last square of chocolate in his hand. He looked at it lustfully and licked his lips.

"I guess if you don't really want it . . ." Clover said to Leven.

"No, wait," Leven said, watching Geth and Winter eat theirs.

"Wow," Winter gasped. "That's the best chocolate I've ever eaten. Give me Leven's."

"I'll take half of it as well," Geth said.

"How about thirds?" Clover offered. "I'll divide it."

"Okay," Winter agreed.

"Hold on," Leven insisted. "If it doesn't do anything, I want my piece."

"It's not doing anything," Winter said.

Leven snatched his piece and put it in his mouth. The rest of them looked at him as if he had just done something incredibly cruel and thoughtless.

Leven chewed and then moaned. "That's the best chocolate I've ever had."

"Do you have more?" Geth asked Clover.

"Yeah," Winter said urgently. "You have to have more."

Clover was already fishing around in his void and complaining, "I know that's it. It was sitting in a pile of other candy when I grabbed it. I wish I had more."

"We should go back," Geth said.

"Yeah," Winter said excitedly. "Let's get out and go back for more."

"I can't remember ever tasting something so . . . what's that?"

Geth pointed toward Clover's nose, where a thick stream of brown was leaking out.

"What?" Clover asked.

"Your nose," Winter said.

Clover wiped his nose and looked at his little hands. His eyes bulged.

"That can't be right," he said with concern.

He lifted his palm up to his nostrils and breathed in. He then licked the back of his hand.

"It's more chocolate," he said. "Fantastic."

"No way," Winter said, standing up on the trunk. "That's disgusting."

Clover let his nose run directly into his mouth. His nostrils began to flow, chocolate running in two streams down to his mouth and onto his neck.

"It's even better than the bar," Clover raved. "Way better."

"Where did you get that candy again?" Leven asked, worried.

"The pile said *flavored*," Clover answered back, his face a chocolaty mess.

"Flavored?" Leven said exasperated. "Are you sure?"

"Yes," Clover argued. "F-l-a-w-e-d—flavored."

Leven put his palms to his eyes and rubbed.

Winter licked her lips—there was chocolate dripping from her nose now. She kept her mouth closed, but the smell of it was so intoxicating she finally breathed some in.

Clover's nose began to flow faster in smooth, thick, chocolate streams. His leafy ears twitched and he was swallowing as fast as he could.

"I told you we shouldn't take anything from him," Leven said, pointing at Clover.

"Too late for that!" Winter yelled, chocolate filling her mouth as she spoke. "You know what, though, it is better!"

Geth had been laughing at Clover and Winter, but now his nose had begun to run.

"It's really tasty," Clover said, trying to make it sound like a good thing was happening.

"It's coming out of our noses," Winter reminded him. The lower half of her face was now completely covered in runny chocolate.

Geth had the stuff all over his hands and arms from attempting to wipe it away.

Leven's own nose began to drip slowly as Clover's started to spurt chocolate out in a large brown arc. Clover spun and sprayed all of them.

"I got some in my mouth!" Leven yelled. "That is completely dis . . . actually, it's really good."

Geth was trying his best to look dignified while eating the chocolate running from his own nose. He was having a hard time pulling it off. Chocolate ran down Winter's front and onto the trunk.

Leven slipped off the trunk, his own nose now blowing out chocolate.

"It's delicious, but there's too much!" Leven hollered.

Geth had it all the way down his cloak and Clover looked like a misshapen and melting chocolate Easter bunny. Winter slid off of the trunk and struggled to get up as chocolate covered the dirt floor like a wave of mud. Geth stepped out of the stone fire pit and lost his footing on the slippery floor. Chocolate was now blasting from Clover's nose like small bombs. The chocolate hit the walls with large wet smacks.

"Turn the other way!" Winter yelled.

Leven held his hand over his nose, trying to stop it from flowing. It was a bad idea. He started to sniff and his head cocked back as a huge sneeze built up inside of him.

"No!" Geth yelled.

Leven blew. Chocolate spray painted the inside of the cottage. Geth and Winter, both covered in chocolate, glared at Leven—chocolate flowing from their own noses like water.

"Wow," Clover said happily, chocolate splashing all over as he spoke. "You'd think it would have stopped by now."

"Thanks a lot!" Winter yelled sloppily.

"I told you not to eat it," Leven sputtered, chocolate filling his mouth.

"I was starving," Winter gurgled.

A large rant opened the front door and stuck his head in. "What's going . . ."

He looked at the huge mess and growled.

"Quick!" he yelled to the other rants outside.

The rant charged into the cottage with two more right behind him. The first one wrapped his arms around Geth and threw him to the floor.

Geth slipped out of the rant's hold like a greased pig and tumbled into Leven. Another rant grabbed Winter's wrist, but the slick chocolate allowed her to pull free without any problem.

Chocolate was shooting everywhere. The room looked like a celebration of mud.

"Get to Angus!" Geth yelled to Leven and Winter in semicode, his mouth full of chocolate. "Get to where we last saw Angus."

Two more rants entered the cottage and knocked Leven to the floor. Leven wriggled in the chocolate, spinning out from under them. He tried to stand but was grabbed at the ankle.

Leven sneezed again, blowing chocolate everywhere and blinding them all.

Geth got to his feet and pulled Winter across the room. He flung her in the direction of the open door. Winter bolted as two more rants raced in. She slipped between them like oil and squirted out into the open.

"Run!" Leven yelled after her.

The chocolate sticking to the heavy robes of the rants was

making it almost impossible for them to fight with any effective style. A big rant with a huge left side of the head lunged at Leven. Clover took a fistful of the chocolate running from his nose and shoved it into the rant's right eye. The rant screamed and missed Leven completely.

Geth picked up the trunk and threw it at two rants while running for the door. He made it out while knocking two more down onto the sloppy, slippery floor.

"After him!" one of the rants yelled. "Stop them!"

Leven grabbed the legs of a rant and quickly pulled himself up. The rant turned, and Leven kicked him as hard as he could in the thigh. The rant filled the room with obscenities.

Leven didn't stick around to apologize; he ran toward the open door. He felt a kilve barely hit him across the back of his right shoulder. Clover jumped onto his neck, holding as tightly as his chocolate-covered hands would allow, his nose still running.

Leven burst into the forest. He could see no sign of other rants or of Winter or Geth. A kilve flew past his head like a spear, thrown by a rant just exiting the cottage. Leven ran up the path toward the cobblestone street. Behind him he could hear the sound of more rants struggling.

"Get him!" one yelled. "Get him!"

"They're pretty mad," Clover observed.

Leven dashed though the trees and out onto the cobblestone road. He slipped and scraped against the street. He could see blood mixing with chocolate on his forearm. He looked up and saw the rant emerging from the forest. Another kilve came flying toward Leven and whizzed past his right ear.

"Get up!" Clover yelled.

Leven begged his legs to lift him. He stood, the rants only a hundred feet away. Leven's head was swimming, but he reached out and snatched the rope with his right hand. Then, as quietly as he could, he said, "Cusp Cove."

Leven's hand wove into the rope just as the rants reached him. He smiled and waved with his left hand.

The rants grabbed for him just as he was being pulled in. Luckily Leven was still covered in chocolate. The rants couldn't get a grip, and Leven slipped away.

CHAPTER THIRTEEN

DEALING WITH DOLTS

It was raining. Water was dripping from the night sky like heaven had gone on vacation and accidentally left the sprinklers running. Traffic was light and the Cozy Hide-a-Way motel was far from filled to capacity. In fact, only four of the twenty-four rooms were currently occupied: one by a lady who was in town to visit her dying friend, one by a man who had lived in the motel for almost a year now, one by Terry and Addy, and one by Dennis and Ezra.

Of course, at the moment, Dennis and Ezra's room was empty while they hung out with Terry and Addy in theirs. It had taken a large heap of lying to get Addy to allow Dennis to come in. But Dennis, with the help of Ezra behind his ear, had told her that he was a doctor interviewing important locals. Addy claimed there was nobody more interesting or important than her Terry and let him enter.

"Nice room," Dennis said.

"It's just the reverse of yours," Terry said, cracking open a beer. "Our microwave doesn't work. Nineteen dollars a night and the microwave doesn't work. We're no better than some fifth-world country."

"Terry loves geography," Addy said.

Ezra whispered something insulting from behind Dennis's ear.

"So you're a doctor," Addy continued. "Terry and I have never had much patience with the M.D. crowd—snooty, snooty people."

"I'm not really that kind of doctor," Dennis said. "I study things."

"A thinker, huh?" Terry scowled. "Where's the money in that? We could use a little money. My wife just lost her job, leaving us high and dry."

"I've had a terrible pain in my back so I'm taking some time off," Addy explained.

"You don't fold napkins with your back," Terry growled. "We needed that job."

"Do you want me to walk out on you?" Addy asked. "Because I will."

"Ah," Terry waved. "Do whatever you want."

"This man's here to interview you and all you can talk about is me losing my job," Addy harped. She turned to Dennis. "Will your article appear in the paper?"

"Of course," Dennis said.

"I'm not surprised you're interested," Addy said. "Terry's getting quite the following. It's the robe."

"Quiet, Addy," Terry said.

"The robe?"

"Found it with a metal detector," Terry bragged. "Look at this."

Terry stood up and closed his robe. He began to hover a couple of inches off of the ground.

Dennis was sincerely surprised.

"Don't know how it works," Terry said. "Addy tried it on and nothing. Can't get it to do anything else. But I tell you what, people respect it. I've been collecting followers at the recreation center. People think I'm prophetish."

"Plus it's slimming," Addy added.

"Quiet, Addy," Terry said. "Always talking."

"And I think it's made him gentler," she said, trying to make her fat face display a smile.

The TV was showing footage of avalands chasing a school bus somewhere in the state of Washington. A woman with tall hair was interviewing one of the children who had been on the bus. Terry turned down the volume.

"Can I ask you two fools a question?" Dennis said, repeating Ezra's words without editing them.

"What?" Addy said, confused.

" . . . Um, I mean, can I ask you a question?" Dennis corrected.

Terry sat back down, eyeing Dennis suspiciously.

"Did you ever know a simple garbage man?"

"Used to have one stop by our old home," Terry said.

"Was he simple with a dumb hat?" Dennis asked, using Ezra's words again.

"Never talked to him," Addy said.

"But did a garbage man ever come and talk to you?" Dennis asked.

"I think that horrible man that was stalking us was a garbage man," Addy said guardedly. "He came to visit us at the apartment we just got kicked out of—knocked right on the door and started asking all sorts of personal questions."

"Like . . . ?"

"No, not at all," Terry chimed in. "I didn't care for him. He was looking for someone."

"Who?"

"Listen," Addy jumped in. "I'm a charitable woman when I need to be. I graciously took in my stepsister's dirty child. The boy ran away and that trash man wanted to know where he went."

"Where'd he go?"

"Who cares, we gave the boy everything and in return he ruined our life." Terry swore. "Look where we live. I can't even make popcorn."

"Wow," Dennis said for both himself and Ezra.

"It really is amazing how underappreciated we are," Terry slurred.

"Was there something wooden by your old house?" Dennis asked.

"Nothing but a tree," Terry said. "A dumb tree that I cut apart. Chopped it right up, then later it picks up our house and destroys it."

Dennis put his hand up to his ear to hold back Ezra from showing himself and attacking Terry.

"What if I could tell you how to get back at the boy?" Dennis said.

"I'm listening," Terry said.

"And possibly use your new robe to do some good," Dennis added.

Terry and Addy stared at Dennis.

"I mean make some money and possibly . . . I can't say that," Dennis said to himself, refusing to repeat what Ezra was telling him to.

"What's wrong?" Addy asked. "Your brain stop working?"

"Something like that," Dennis said nervously.

"Keep talking," Terry ordered. "Make some money and . . ."

"Possibly rule the world." Dennis coughed.

Addy and Terry nodded with interest.

"What's the catch?" Terry asked.

"Do you have a car?"

"You saw us pull up in it."

"How about we take a long ride?"

"If we leave tonight we won't have to pay next week's rent," Addy said.

"You'll pay for the gas?" Terry asked suspiciously.

Dennis nodded.

"Pack up my underwear and socks, woman," Terry said. "I'll get my other pair of pants."

Terry walked into the small closet and Addy stepped into the bathroom, gathering up all her cosmetics.

"Pleasant people," Ezra whispered into Dennis's ear. "They make you look intelligent."

"Thanks," Dennis mumbled.

"I can't help it," Ezra growled. "It's the new me. I can't stop myself from being nice."

Dennis stood up, buttoned his lab coat, and pushed up his useless glasses on his nose. He looked into the mirror that hung on Terry and Addy's wall.

"Even with the glasses you still look boring," Ezra said.

"Thanks."

"Again," Ezra said. "Blame the new me."

CHAPTER FOURTEEN

UNTITLED

Tim Tuttle was a fish out of water, or more specifically a man out of Reality. He had tested fate by swimming into the collapsing gateway that Sabine had built, and fate had snatched him into Foo.

He was now trying to adjust, but his mind was constantly preoccupied with the mistake he might have made by not minding his own business and leaving Winter to fend for herself. He had set out to help her, but clearly now he understood that things were far more complicated and unbelievable than he had anticipated. Tim was now more concerned with getting himself out of Foo than with finding Winter. Unfortunately, neither one of those tasks looked very plausible. If it had not been for his new sycophant, Swig, he would have felt so horrible he might have simply and spontaneously expired.

"Head still hurting?" Swig asked.

"A little," Tim answered.

"It's not far," Swig said kindly. "The Sentinel Fields are just over that third mound. Can I rub your forehead for you?"

"I'm all right," Tim said. "I've never had anyone so quick to take care of me. Don't tell my wife I said that."

"I wouldn't dream of it."

"I'm joking."

Swig laughed. "You have a nice sense of humor, Tim."

Tim rubbed his temples.

"I think I've made an awful mistake," Tim said. "I should be home with my family."

"I'm sorry," Swig said softly. "It's no secret how startling it is for nits to step into Foo. Only a few souls have ever stepped in and been instantly glad to be here."

"I just don't understand why Winter was in Reality."

"According to all those you've talked to, she's quite important," Swig reminded Tim. "There must be a reason—a good reason—she was in Reality."

"I should have just let things be."

"Well," Swig said, "if what we keep hearing is right, there might be a way to get back."

"I hope so," Tim remarked.

"If anyone will know it will be the armies of Azure," Swig said cheerfully. "And we'll be there momentarily."

"So they want to get to Reality, right?" Tim asked.

"That's what that large man with the dirty green hat said."

Swig jumped onto Tim's right shoulder and started whistling.

Tim walked faster, climbing up and over a small hill and down through a shrub-laden valley. At the top of the next hill Tim stopped.

"Do you hear that?" Tim asked. "What is it, a river?"

"There's no river up ahead," Swig answered.

Tim began to walk faster. He ran down a grassy slope and hopped over a dry creek bed that was filled with goats and nervous, whining weeds.

The noise up ahead was growing louder.

"I think it's people," Swig said into Tim's right ear. "Lots of people."

Tim ran faster and then slowed. He came to a complete stop under a large, leafy fantrum tree. He breathed into his hands for three breaths and spoke.

"What if it's people we don't want to meet up with?" Tim huffed. "I've been here long enough to know that not everyone's concerned with my well-being."

"Hold on," Swig said. "Stick here."

Tim sat back against the tree and continued to calm his breathing. A large orange bickerwick skirted around the base of the tree. Having eaten one before, Tim knew how tasty they were. He picked it up, bit it in half, and swallowed. The strange fat bug tasted like toasted marshmallows.

"Good?" Swig asked, appearing on Tim's left knee.

"Not bad." Tim finished up his bite. "So what'd you see?"

"There's a lot of people," Swig reported. "Most of them look nice. I saw a couple of men who looked mean, and a woman with

a really awful scowl. But everyone else seemed to be excited."

"How many are there?"

"A dozen? Maybe more," Swig said. "I'm not good at counting."

"It's not the most detailed scouting report, but it'll have to do."

Tim finished his bickerwick and stood up. Swig patted him on the back and moved onto his right shoulder.

"Feel better?" Swig asked.

Tim smiled. "You really are a remarkable breed."

The noise of those gathered grew louder with each step Tim took. By the time he had crested the last hill he knew full well that there had to be more than a dozen people making so much noise.

Tim took off his ball cap and whistled. The Sentinel Fields were larger than any open space he had seen. The fields stretched on for hundreds of miles in every direction. Light purple stalks of grain with glowing tops blew beautifully all around and the sky here was a different color from the sky over Cusp.

"So, Swig," Tim asked. "How many come in a dozen here?"

"About half a batch?"

"This is way more than half a batch of people."

As far as Tim's eyes could see there were beings and creatures filling Sentinel Fields. They were all organized in large square groups. Each group had a small tent in the center with a flag and everyone was dressed in blue robes.

"I told you I'm not very good at counting," Swig apologized.

"But see, there's that lady with the scowl. Just like I said."

Tim patted Swig on the head and walked down the steep slope and directly into the crowd. Not a single person even turned to acknowledge him. A troop of black skeletons wearing black bandannas and led by two giant avalands pushed through the crowd in front of Tim like some sort of science fiction parade. Tim gawked appropriately.

"I wish my boys could see this," Tim said.

Tim stopped a short man with a friendly face covered in moles.

"Excuse me," Tim asked. "Could you tell me who's in charge here?"

"We all fight for our own freedom," the dotted man answered. "But the rants hold the most passion in their hearts and Azure leads us."

"Is Azure here?"

"It would be a great honor to lead you to him," the mole-covered man said. "A great honor indeed. But Azure is gathering fighters in Cusp. If you wish to join us the rants will assist you."

"Where are they?" Tim asked.

"See all those in the dark blue robes?"

Tim couldn't miss them. There looked to be miles and miles of rants all organized in neat squares.

"All those behind the flags are rants," the man said. "Join us and dream your own dreams."

Tim thanked the man and then moved through groups of women cooking meals and men sharpening sticks. There was a

large gathering of children sewing small pieces of blue cloth. Tim passed beings that looked to be on fire, beasts that he couldn't have imagined if he had been forced to, and long green tents that were emitting sounds of snoring and chaos. Other tents were filled with piles of metal weapons.

"Just so you know, rants are sort of unstable," Swig said.

"Unstable?" Tim asked.

"Sort of. Half of them is always in flux," Swig explained. "They are weak and always halfway entwined with a dream from Reality. And the state of dreams in Reality is making them even less stable."

"I'm just hoping their stable half will be able to help," Tim said. "Maybe they know something that will . . ."

Tim stopped. He turned around, surveying the crowd.

"What?" Swig asked, invisible on Tim's right shoulder. "You look startled."

"Did you hear something?" Tim asked.

"I hear a lot of things," Swig said. "What would you like me to hear?"

The sound rang out again.

"Like a screeching," Tim said. "Someone screaming."

"There's so much talking and festivity," Swig said.

Again Tim heard it and this time he could tell the direction it was coming from.

"Over there." He pointed.

Tim stepped away from the rants and between two long tents.

"It's a woman's voice," Tim said.

"Are you sure?" Swig asked. "It sounds like a goat."

Down past a crowded cook site Tim spotted a large swatch of muted yellow in the middle of fifty or so burning beings. Tim rubbed his eyes.

"I must be wrong."

"I can't imagine that ever happening," Swig cooed, attempting to be a perfect sycophant. "Your opinion is just as valid as any other."

Tim's stride became longer.

"I know that person."

"The one with the goat scream?"

Tim began to push aside anyone in his way. He jumped over a long row of fallen trees and right into the group of burning beings. Without any breath left he stopped just behind the large woman in yellow. He reached out to tap her on the shoulder but his hand went right through her.

"Excuse me." Tim coughed.

She didn't turn around, but one of the burning creatures speaking to her was watching Tim curiously and casually pointed him out to her.

She turned, and right there, at that exact spot, Janet Frore received her fourth life-changing shock since being whisked into Foo.

"You," she gasped.

"And you," Tim gasped back.

Janet collapsed.

Nobody moved to help her, due to the fact that she was a whisp—but many gathered to watch. After all, it's not every day you witness a whisp fainting.

CHAPTER FIFTEEN

TAKE ME THERE

There are so many fantastic things about Foo. The Cinder Depression when the avalands are stampeding at sunset. The Devil's Spiral during the wettest seasons when the water shoots so high the mountains of Morfit can see it. The Green Pond when the blue frogs come out in full force and feed on the bit bugs nesting near the Sun River. But—I can't stress this enough—none of those things compare to the tranquil beauty and awe of any single part of Sycophant Run.

Anyone who doubts the importance of saving true Foo need only spend an hour on Sycophant Run. Some say it has the feeling of how Foo once was and could still be. The kindness of the sycophants and the glorious feeling permeating the air are as powerful and contagious as any fatal disease.

Now, even in a state of concern, and with the possibility of war breaking out, the glad hearts of the sycophants kept

Sycophant Run a place of hope. There was fear in the wind, but their hearts were continually hopeful.

Rast sat alone in the Chamber of Stars. The hollow tree was empty up to the tips of each bare branch. For those who were lucky enough to ever sit at the five-pointed table in the empty tree's belly it was a marvel to behold. Looking up you could see thousands of tiny pinpoints of light. It felt like the middle of the universe and you were just lucky enough to be standing in it. The wind outside of the tree blew lightly, making the points of light dance in a cosmic fashion.

"Lilly," Rast said to himself.

Rast had been unable to sleep for days. He worried about his daughter who had gone so far astray. He worried about the secret of their mortality being out there. And he worried that if Azure continued his quest to mesh Foo with Reality, eventually, no matter how hard they tried, the fight would come to Sycophant Run.

The light in the Chamber of Stars brightened and then dimmed as someone entered through the knothole.

"Rast," the visitor called.

"Reed," Rast said kindly. "I wasn't sure if you'd come."

"I wasn't either." Reed laughed uncomfortably.

"Are you ready?" Rast asked.

"You really think this is necessary?" Reed said. "Perhaps more thought and consideration is needed."

"I have thought for many hours and days," Rast answered softly. "I feel as if we are responsible to make sure."

"Of what?" Reed asked. "We know it's there."

"The loss of our key weighs heavily on me," Rast said. "It was our responsibility and we believed it was safe."

"Lilly has a mind of her own," Reed said kindly. "We cannot forget that the will of others is as precious as our own."

"I feel it is our responsibility to make sure," Rast said again. "We will travel there and back and sleep well because of it. We cannot have our people fight for something that might not be there any longer."

"I won't deny my anxiety," Reed admitted.

"Nor mine," Rast said. "You've told no one?"

"No one," Reed said. "Still, I feel my brain arguing with my heart."

"Opposition in all things," Rast said. "How can we savor what we hold if we know we have no choice but to hold it?"

Rast stood and stretched his small body.

"Come, my friend."

"I am old," Reed said. "But my mind is as worried as a child's."

"Good." Rast smiled. "It will keep us alert."

Rast stepped back from the table and walked out of the tree.

Reed followed.

Outside, the day was near its zenith. Clouds slid through the purple sky like thick cream, leaving intricate patterns of white behind them. As usual the sound of laughter rang out somewhere on Sycophant Run. The lush grass covering the hill stood as tall as it could and a cluster of large flowers opened and closed like hungry baby birds, filling the air with an intoxicating scent.

They walked to a field of yellow boulders and stepped carefully into the center of the rock grouping. Rast bent over and shifted a stone. The rock moved, allowing Rast to extract a short loop of twine. Rast pulled and the ground opened up.

"We'll be to the marsh shortly."

Reed nodded and followed Rast into the tunnel, pulling the stones closed behind him. Rast tugged on a vine and the side of the tunnel pushed back, revealing a hidden cavern and two more tunnels.

"I didn't even know this was here," Reed remarked. "So many secrets in Foo."

"This tunnel has never been a secret," Rast said seriously. "It simply has been waiting to fulfill its purpose."

Reed hefted his satchel up onto his small shoulder and followed eight paces behind Rast as they descended lower into the tunnel.

CHAPTER SIXTEEN

HIDE-AND-EAT

I have always loved secret passageways. What good is a home without a few hidden hallways and a couple of forgotten rooms? Sure, it might provide a roof overhead and a warm place to sleep, but with no mystery or surprise those things are far less enjoyable. I think anyone building a house who doesn't include a hidden pole sliding down into a secret room is just plain crazy. Of course, sometimes hidden rooms take on a far different meaning. Sometimes hidden rooms are necessary to keep people safe and alive. I know the secret tunnels in my current residence have saved my life on a half dozen occasions. There aren't a lot of homes with as many secret passages and rooms as the safe house in Cusp. It was in that house that Leven, Geth, Winter, and Clover had finally found temporary reprieve.

The house sat silhouetted against the large green moon, its high pitched roofline creating a gigantic "A." Deep inside the

house, in one of the many secret rooms, four tired Foo fighters were happy to finally be sitting down.

A shaggy purple rug twisted and wriggled around their feet, carefully massaging their tired soles. Leven could feel the soft strands of fabric brush and polish his toes.

"Nice rug," Leven said.

"Yeah," Clover agreed, lying on his back as the carpet rolled in waves beneath him.

"We were lucky," Winter sighed. "To get out of there."

"Oh," Clover said. "I thought you meant we were lucky that the chocolate finally stopped flowing."

"After two hours," Leven complained. "My nostrils have never been this sore before."

A large fire in a tall stone fireplace burned high and wide. The fire hummed and sang as it danced.

The foursome was safe in a warm house located in the middle of Cusp on the edge of the Canadian-influenced neighborhoods. It was a safe place that housed anyone who still believed and fought for the true Foo. The keeper of the large, three-story stone home was a man named Owen. The home looked relatively plain from outside, but on the inside all the walls and doors could shift and move as quickly and easily as the dreams coming in.

It had taken a couple of hours for the chocolate to stop running and a good twenty minutes after that to wash it all off on the edge of the Veil Sea. From there, stepping carefully, they had made their way by rope to the safe house. They were now resting in soft, high-backed chairs in front of a happy fire, drinking

warm pear cider and awaiting a hot meal. The song the fire was currently humming reminded Leven of his life before Foo.

"Sometimes I really miss Reality," Leven said.

"Is this about that soda stuff?" Clover asked.

"No," Leven said. "I miss Oklahoma. You know, I used to wake up on our back porch and watch the sunrise. I mean, I like Foo's, but there was something about the Oklahoma sun."

"Yeah," Geth said softly. "I remember some of the rainstorms. When I was a tree the rain would hit my higher branches and then bounce off and spatter against the lower ones. I know there was cold rain, but I remember it now as always being warm."

"At night when Janet and Terry had locked me out on the porch, and after they had turned off the TV inside, it was so quiet," Leven said. "I would listen to your branches blow and believe that there was good in the world somewhere."

"I don't know about Oklahoma," Winter chimed in. "But in Iowa I used to love the way the day would settle on the horizon. It was like everything that had happened during the day would fall into the sunsets and disappear."

"I liked the sticks and leaves," Clover said. "Everywhere you went there were sticks and leaves and weeds just sitting there. Here, look at this."

Clover pulled out a dead maple leaf from his void. He held it up and the fire backlit it, showing off every vein and detail. The fire began singing a song about trees. All three of them wanted to reach out and touch the leaf, but the scene was so serene that it felt wrong to do so.

Clover looked at all of them and rolled his eyes. "It's just a leaf."

"I don't remember anything anymore," Winter admitted. "Nothing, only my time in Reality waiting for you. When we first came back to Foo I could see bits and pieces of my other life here, but now, nothing."

"So where would you rather be?" Leven asked.

"Careful," Geth said. "That's a dangerous thought."

"I love Foo," Winter said. "There's a feeling here that's much more intense than Reality. I know that if we were in Reality reminiscing about Foo my feeling would be even stronger."

The fire harmonized.

"How about you, Geth?" Winter asked.

"Lithens aren't big on reminiscing," Geth reminded them. "But I remember wishing that every creature in Foo could feel and experience Reality so that they might better understand how important our task here is. As for where I would rather be, I know this is where fate has placed me. But I'll tell you this: For the first time I believe that we will see Reality again."

Leven and Winter stared at Geth as Owen came in and refilled their mugs with more cider. The top of Leven's mug foamed and crackled.

"Dinner's in ten minutes," Owen said. "And you should know that the layout of the house has shifted since you've been here. The dining hall is now behind you and the hallway out of the door leads up, not down. We had visitors and I thought it best to keep you hidden. They had evil in their eyes."

"Rants?" Geth asked.

Owen nodded. "We are always one of the first places they check."

Owen was a cog. He had the clear markings of blue hands and an orange forehead. He was six feet tall and walked with a slightly hunched back. He had thin red hair and a thick brown beard. His eyes were blue with yellow-flecked centers. He had come from nit parents and had been passionately convinced that Foo needed to exist since as long as he could remember. He had worked for many years in the Cusp government, but now lived a peaceful and secretive life helping those he knew to be true to continuing the fight.

"Thank you again," Geth said.

"To have a true lithen amongst us is an honor. And Leven and Winter—what a thrill," Owen said, stepping back out of the room. "Stay put, they may return."

The door shut softly.

"See Reality again?" Leven and Winter both said quickly, bringing Geth back to the topic he had started.

"The Dearth wants the soil of Reality," Geth said. "If he can move out of the door, then he may be able to accomplish his desires."

"Door?" Leven asked.

"There's a permanent path into Reality," Geth said. "There's opposition in all things, and Foo has always had the potential to bleed out if evil had its way. Your grandfather found this out only after he had become the Want and long after he had created his

own gateway. The gateway you destroyed was so Sabine and Azure and the Dearth couldn't get out. The permanent door is known only by a few and guarded by millions."

"It's on Sycophant Run," Leven whispered.

Geth nodded. "It's also protected by stone surrounding its shore. There's a fifty-mile-wide ring of hard stone that the Dearth cannot move through or make it across."

"Wait a second," Leven said excitedly. "But he's moving the soil two directions."

"What?" Winter asked.

"Remember, the dirt under the water's going in two directions," Leven said, standing up. "He must be moving toward Sycophant Run. They're not going for gifts and the stones. It's a trick while they create a way for the Dearth to get to Sycophant Run."

"Tomorrow we stop Azure," Geth said. "There's no more time. Azure wants that key. The Dearth knows that whoever holds that key has the potential to lock him back up."

"Well, can't they just unlock him again?"

"Yes," Geth said. "But it must take time for him to gain any real strength. He wants out of Foo and into the soil of Reality. That key has to stay out of his hands or none of our lives will be of value."

Owen stepped in again.

"The house is shifting once more," Owen whispered. "They're here in force looking for you and the floor plan must be changed. Stay quiet. If you must escape, the door now leads down into the cellar and beneath the street."

Owen stepped out.

"Does this mean we don't get to eat?" Clover whispered.

"Quiet," Geth said.

The sound of footsteps could be heard running overhead and down the back wall. Pounding echoed off one of the side walls as someone or something banged their fists.

Leven and Winter fell to the ground against the purple carpet—strands of yarn twisted up against them. They kept still, as if lying low might keep them hidden.

They heard rants hollering out orders through the wall. Their voices were muffled but strong.

"What happens if they get in?" Winter asked. "I'm not escaping by eating anything else Clover has."

Clover materialized just so that he could look hurt.

"No offense," Winter added.

Clover shivered and disappeared.

"We don't even have our kilves," Leven said.

Geth crouched down and held his finger to his lips. The wooden doorknob turned and clicked. Geth moved back behind one of the chairs as the fire chanted lowly,

"Closer, closer evil creeps from the soil dark and deep."

Winter gave the fire a withering look.

The building creaked and rumbled while the door opened wider. Owen slipped in.

"Had the house not shifted it would have been a rant coming in," he whispered. "Stay put."

Owen was gone again.

"What kind of place is this?" Clover asked.

"And I thought the Want's home was confusing," Leven said.

"The Want's home shifted due to dreams," Geth said. "This home changes to deceive."

The thundering sound of multiple feet running across the ceiling and descending down the wall could be heard. Everyone held their breath and pushed themselves closer to the floor. The thundering sound diminished until there was nothing but the pesky fire chanting,

"Light above and dark below—back to the dust we all must go."

"What's up with Owen's fire?" Leven whispered. "I've never heard flame be so specific."

The doorknob rattled once more. It turned and the door slowly swung open.

"It's just me," Owen alerted them. "They've gone, and they're not happy."

"Any sign of Azure?" Geth asked.

"No, only his rants."

Everyone stood up and Clover materialized.

"Don't dwell on the worrisome any longer." Owen smiled. "You will eat and rest tonight and your minds should be occupied with thoughts that comfort you."

Owen pulled the door open and two pretty cogs carrying large trays entered the room. They placed them on the round wooden table as two more, far less pretty, cogs came in with even larger trays of food. All four cogs arranged the food on the table as smells stronger than light swirled around the room and under everyone's nose.

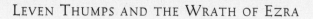

"That smells . . ." Winter's mind failed to produce a word strong enough to explain how amazing it was.

"Our means are not endless," Owen said. "But we wish to match the caliber of our guests."

"Thank you, Owen," Geth said nobly.

"Yes," Leven added.

"Sit," Owen insisted. "Sit and enjoy. I'll have news for you as you digest."

Winter almost trampled Geth as she made her way to the table. They all sat and began piling their porcelain plates with food as beautiful as it was aromatic. Leven loaded up on cream steaks and buttered carrots, while Winter went after the smoky breaded sheep and stacks of thick, fluffy wheat cakes dripping in creamy syrup.

"Save some for me," Clover said needlessly, seeing how as each serving plate was depleted a cog would bring in another, piled high, to replace it.

Clover took handfuls of popped pastries and half a meat pie. He passed the other half to Geth, who was already downing a quarter of a loaf of bread covered in rich dark gravy and slices of peppered sheep.

"I never want to stop," Leven said with a half-full mouth.

"Me neither," Winter added, wiping syrup from her chin.

"Who says we have to?" Clover mumbled, shoving muffins and cookies into his void.

The fire had changed its tune and was now singing about the importance of friendship. None of them were listening; they

were far too interested in what they were gobbling down.

Thirty minutes later Owen came back into the room. Everyone was reclining and moaning except Winter, who was still eating.

"I hope it was all to your liking?" Owen bowed.

"It was perfect," Leven said, a crumb of bread sticking to his cheek.

Owen smiled, his orange forehead wrinkling.

"We have the information you requested," Owen said.

Geth nodded.

"Azure will be attending the match tomorrow. He will be sitting in the Twit's seats. He's making an effort to be seen as a friend of Cusp in front of the crowd. Everyone within five hundred miles will be there. I should add that most of Cusp is only mildly bothered by Azure. A number of citizens find him and his ambition interesting, quirky even."

"Interesting?" Winter said, disgusted. "It sure was interesting the way Azure tried to destroy us all."

"Azure has also been spotted all over," Owen said. "He has been busy. There are reports of him traveling the road between here and Fté. Also he has been seen in Morfit and all around Cusp."

"How?"

"I'm not sure," Owen said. "Those reports are not verified."

"And the Dearth?" Geth asked.

"He has risen, but has not been spotted."

Winter swallowed her last bite of scorched caramel pie.

Owen smiled again but then quickly looked sad. "Sleep—the door now leads to a top room with plenty of beds. The home will shift a number of times during the night. If trouble occurs, the window will always take you out. It's probably best, however, to stay put until I retrieve you in the morning. There's a washroom next to the room, but should that change, you'll find a pot in your chambers. Sleep—a clear mind can be a terrific advantage."

They all stood and followed the curiously self-assured cog out of the room and up the stairs.

CHAPTER SEVENTEEN

Evil Is Always Dark at the Core

Standing tall is a very admirable thing. There are very few stories in history of heroes who slouched to the rescue. Likewise, most individuals don't look up to people who are drooped over. I once heard a song that said something about standing for something or else falling for something else—the song made sense, I'm sure; I've just never been great with lyrics. The important thing is good posture. Since the dawn of time adults have been telling children to stand up straight, only to get old themselves and begin to walk with a stoop. We are born curled up, straighten out, and then end up with a hunch.

Fate is funny that way.

Of course, it could be argued that nobody slouched lower and yet had more power than the Dearth as he stood waiting inside the small tent in the open field miles outside of Cusp.

His strength had grown and he was now able to stand on his feet and lift his head up when he spoke.

Azure entered the tent.

"You stand," Azure flattered the Dearth.

"Of course, my strength's coming quicker now. The key?"

The Dearth stretched out his long, dark right arm and opened his tar pit of a palm. Hundreds of black strings ran from his arm to the soil.

"I am close to finding it," Azure said. "Dwell on the good: You are free and the war will soon be in full gear."

The Dearth closed his open palm and lifted his head higher.

"You speak as if your words will comfort me," he oozed. "I find no comfort in your mistake."

"Nor do I," Azure said sharply.

"Leven?"

"Waiting for your arrival."

"I can't feel him standing," the Dearth hissed.

"He knows you are in the soil," Azure said. "They step carefully, hoping to avoid you."

The Dearth turned his dark, sticky head and smiled. His face looked like an oil slick on a dirty road.

"How amusing," he spoke. "How can one hope to avoid the soil forever? Eventually all creatures must rest on the earth."

Azure remained quiet.

"Where is he?" the Dearth asked.

"We have him," Azure lied.

The Dearth turned to Azure and flicked out his long, scaly

tongue. His tongue lashed Azure on the cheek near his bleeding ear. Azure winced, struggling to hold his temper against one as powerful as the Dearth.

"Do you think I cannot feel?" the Dearth cried.

"I . . ."

"You lie," the Dearth spit, black juice running from his sticky mouth. "They are free, slipped through your fingers."

"We will find them," Azure insisted. "I have hundreds searching even now. It was a blessing that we had them momentarily."

"Blessing?" the Dearth asked. "What a foolish word. Next you will speak of fate."

"We will find him."

"Of course you will," the Dearth said. "Time cooperates?"

Azure nodded.

"Your ear still bleeds," the Dearth tisked. "How can I trust you completely when you still battle your own self?"

"Don't doubt my desire!" Azure shouted.

"So much passion," the Dearth mocked. "Point that energy toward finding the key. After Cusp, it will be our only loose end. The troops are ready?"

"They move closer even now."

The Dearth reached up and picked at his own face. He pulled a noodlelike strand of puss from his chin. The lengthy blemish fell to his dark shoulder and oozed into his skin.

"There's word of a longing," Azure said bravely.

"I've felt it," the Dearth said. "So many hot tempers and emotions. Let's see you use this to our advantage."

"I will," Azure committed.

"The battle for Cusp may be more heated than planned."

"We will succeed with you beneath us," Azure flattered.

The Dearth moaned and soaked up more soil into his being. "I am still too weak to walk."

"We will drag you with honor," Azure said calmly.

"You speak so kindly now, but I know you are as dark and selfish as I."

"I'm here only to serve."

The Dearth coughed and choked, sending small wads of dirt and phlegm out over the room. Azure stared into the distance, trying to control his thoughts.

"The time's finally coming," the Dearth said happily as he fell back to the soil. "Fate's time is up."

"It's a great day for Foo," Azure said.

"It's a final day for Foo," the Dearth hissed.

Azure moved to pick up the Dearth.

"No," the Dearth insisted. "I must speak with Leven first."

"We'll find him," Azure argued, bothered by the subject.

"That won't be necessary," the Dearth bubbled. "Keep the fire burning out front. I want our visitor to be able to find us."

"How is . . ."

"Leave me to correct what you have left dangling," the Dearth scolded.

Azure nodded and stepped from the tent, fighting hard to control his own thoughts. He walked through the few rants surrounding the fire and past the wagon as it sat there drenched in

moonlight. Azure climbed up a small dirt ridge and onto a fist-shaped stone outcrop that jutted out over a wide stream. Azure walked to the edge of the stone, stared up at the moons, and hissed like a hoarse wolf.

His mind began to race freely.

It was so exhausting to constantly keep his thoughts away from the Dearth. How satisfying it was to be able to think as he pleased. Azure thought of Sabine. He knew that for many years Sabine had operated under the influence of the Dearth. Azure marveled at Sabine's strength to have endured it.

Azure thought of Reality. He thought of the power he would have and of the legions of followers he would control. He thought of the single key that Leven held and how he would gladly lock the Dearth back up himself once he had used his power to destroy the sycophants and find the way out. Then Azure would control everyone and everything he pleased.

Azure turned and lifted his head again to the moonlight.

CHAPTER EIGHTEEN

Pulling Back the Curtain

The black asphalt highway stretched forward forever, looking as if it ran directly into the future. The landscape on both sides of the road was brown, with lighter shades of tan accenting the occasional patch of sagebrush and tumbleweeds. The sun was just beginning to tilt downward, creating short, stubby shadows that in time would be stretched out properly.

Addy was asleep in the backseat, her large bulk spread out over both seats. Her relaxed body jiggled slightly as the speeding car vibrated. Terry was at the wheel driving, his right cheek filled with sunflower seeds. He lifted a Styrofoam cup to spit out one of the shells. He set down the cup and fiddled with the radio. There were no clear stations. And all static-filled stations were going on and on about the world falling apart and clouds and bugs attacking everywhere.

"Do you think you could turn it down?" Dennis asked.

Dennis sat in the passenger's seat looking out the side window. He still wore the white lab coat and fake glasses. Ezra was tucked behind his right ear snoring softly.

Terry turned up the static.

"Seriously," Dennis said. "It's just noise."

"Well, maybe I like noise!" Terry shouted.

Dennis rolled down his window, letting the wind blow forcefully through the car. Ezra flew into the backseat, landing in Addy's bag of half-eaten Cheetos. He opened his eye and then went back to sleep.

"Close your window!" Terry ordered.

"No radio," Dennis said, enjoying the feeling of speaking his mind.

Terry flipped off the radio and Dennis rolled up the window.

"This is just about the ugliest piece of earth I've ever seen," Terry whined. "I'm glad it's not a part of my country."

"New Mexico is part of your country," Dennis pointed out.

"Right," Terry said sarcastically.

"So tell me about that robe," Dennis asked. "What's with it?"

"It's mine," Terry said defensively.

"I'm not looking to take it," Dennis said calmly.

"Where are we going, anyway?" Terry bellyached. "I'm sick of driving. Look at this place, nothing but dirt and more dirt."

"I don't think it's too much farther."

"So there's going to be money, right?"

Dennis nodded. "And what about this boy, Leven?"

"What about him?" Terry asked. "My sister's half-sister dies while giving birth to him and we take him in. I don't remember much about him growing up. I remember I never really liked his name. I always thought he should be called Dirk. But people never listen to me. He was a quiet kid—didn't eat much. Then he ruined our lives."

"How?"

"Look at me!" Terry yelled. "I'm in a car with a stranger driving someplace I don't think I'll be happy to arrive at."

"Did he ever talk about a place called Foo?"

"I don't know what he talked about," Terry said. "Addy did all the child rearing."

"But your house was frozen?"

"The trailer wasn't even paid off."

"How could he have done that?" Dennis asked. "Don't you wonder why you can float and how all that happened?"

"I was never good with biology."

"What about all the things happening in the world?"

"Things?" Terry questioned. "Like the Super Bowl?"

"No, things like on the radio and TV. Things like those dirt creatures and bugs that pick people up. Or what about those tornadoes and clouds that attack people?"

"I don't pay much attention to politics," Terry confessed.

"You haven't seen the news?" Dennis asked. "You haven't seen pictures of buildings moving and airplanes being turned upside down?"

"I've seen some stuff," Terry admitted.

"What if I told you I know what's happening," Dennis said. "And that Leven's involved."

"I'd tell you I'm listening," Terry answered. "At least until we get decent radio reception again."

"Well," Dennis said. "Here's what I know and why I believe you might be the right person to tell the world about it."

Terry spit the rest of his sunflower seeds into the cup and placed it between his legs.

"Go on," he signaled.

Dennis began to spill it all, and for the first time in Terry's life he really listened. Dennis told him why buildings were moving and planes were being turned upside down. He told him about bugs that can carry people and things called avalands. He told him about Foo and how he had spent weeks in Germany trying to build a gateway. He told him about Sabine and how meshing Foo with Reality would bring great powers—powers much like those woven into the robe Terry was now wearing. He told him what he knew about Leven and Winter.

"Is that why my house froze?" Terry snapped.

"Most likely," Dennis said.

"Children have no sense of responsibility."

Dennis told Terry everything except for the part about Ezra. Terry just sat there digesting the information and staring into the distance while driving.

"It's a lot to think about," Dennis admitted.

Terry was still silent.

"There's more," Dennis finally said. "I didn't find this all out on my own. I had help."

"Who?"

"He's actually here with us now. His name is Ezra."

"Is he like the Force or something?" Terry whispered nervously.

"No—he's right here in the car."

Terry looked around suspiciously. "Is this one of those hidden camera shows?"

"No."

"Then you must be out of your mind," Terry complained angrily. "No, I take that back, *I* must be out of my mind. Believing you and falling for this Foo junk."

Terry slammed on the brakes and the car skidded off the road, coming to a stop in a tremendous cloud of dust on the dirt shoulder. Addy was thrown forward onto the floor behind the front seats. Her impact into the seat backs knocked Terry and Dennis into the dashboard and sent the bag of Cheetos flying into Dennis's lap.

"Get out," Terry said. "No, give me your money and then get out, Mr. Make-Believe."

"What's going on?" Addy screamed, trying to pull herself out of the floor space she was wedged into.

"This loon is trying to take us for a ride," Terry yelled. "And I just now came to my senses."

"No," Dennis said. "I'm not—"

"Ahhhhhhhhhh!" Addy screamed directly into Dennis's

ear as she leaned over the front seat. "What's that?"

Addy pointed to the dashboard where Ezra was now poised. He was standing as tall as he could, his plastic purple hair wriggling and his green nail-polished body shining under the light of the sun. Ezra was tiny, but he would have looked almost impressive if it had not been for the Cheeto he had stuck around his torso.

Terry reached out as if to flick Ezra away.

"No," Dennis said, hitting Terry's arm. "That's Ezra."

Terry pulled his arm back and grimaced.

"I don't know if I should feel better or worse," Terry whispered.

"What's going on?" Addy snapped. "One minute I'm sleeping peacefully and the next moment I'm thrown around and looking at a toothpick."

"Way to sum things up," Ezra sniffed while trying to push the Cheeto down from his middle.

"Here," Dennis said, picking up Ezra. "I'll get that off."

"No," Ezra complained. "I can . . ."

"Just let me pull it . . . there."

"Would you get your . . ."

Dennis set Ezra back on the dashboard. Ezra cleared his throat and repositioned his feet to steady himself.

"I seen a lot of things," Terry said quietly. "A lady next door to us had a dog with two tails. But I never seen a thing like that. Is it real?"

"Is it real?" Ezra said, disgusted. "Have you bathed recently?"

"Can I touch it?" Addy asked Dennis.

"If you'd like your eye pierced," Ezra growled. "And don't think for a moment that Mr. Boring here's the one you should ask permission from."

"Terry and Addy," Dennis said graciously, "I'd like to introduce you to Ezra. He was once a part of your tree."

"The same tree that messed with my house?" Terry asked, making fists with his hands.

"That was Geth then," Ezra spit. "If it had been just me I would have burned the place down."

"How rude," Addy said.

"With you in it," Ezra added.

Terry smiled and then tried to look mad.

"So this Foo place is real?" Terry asked.

"Six words strung together clearly. That's probably close to a record for you," Ezra sniffed. "Yes, Foo is real, and if you listen to what we say you'll be the one to inform the world and profit from it."

"We're not taking orders from a toothpick," Addy barked.

"Hush," Terry said. "Hear the man out."

"Man?" Addy ground her teeth. "It's a sliver of wood."

"I know it's a lot to take in," Dennis tried. "But it's true."

"Thank you, white bread," Ezra said. "Now could we get moving?"

Terry put the car into drive and slowly eased back onto the road.

"And if the large one in the back can stay quiet for a bit, I've got some things to say," Ezra declared.

Addy started to talk but Terry signaled her to stop.

"She'll be quiet," he said.

"I most certainly will not," Addy snipped.

"Do you want to be rich?" Terry asked.

Terry, Addy, and Dennis were quiet as Ezra paced back and forth across the dashboard telling them all they would need to know to help bring Foo to Reality. He explained his vision for Terry and the part he thought he should play. And he talked quite passionately about how excited he was going to be to finally pay back Geth for what he had done to him. Ezra then cackled and laughed until everyone in the car was either uncomfortable or deeply concerned.

CHAPTER NINETEEN

THERE IS NO "I" IN ABDUCT

Nobody enjoys lifting heavy things. If you meet people who claim they do, they are either not telling the truth, or they are part of a confused group of people whom someone should keep a close eye on. Who in his right mind lines up for the chance to heft a piano or a safe filled with gold bricks?

Not me.

Of course, I would rather lift a car above my head than carry the heavy feeling Brindle was holding while working his way through the Invisible Village.

Halfway across the valley Brindle could hardly remember his name, much less the reason he had come. He kept running up against obstacles he couldn't see and people who were even more depressed and confused than he was.

After getting trapped for over an hour in what must have been a courtyard, Brindle finally found a wide road that went

straight for more than three hundred feet. He almost felt a bit of hope—almost. But then he hit another wall and simply didn't have the will to find a way around it.

Brindle fell to the ground and crossed his small legs. More than anything he wanted to be back on Sycophant Run laughing and feeling good, but he couldn't shake the heavy feeling holding him in place.

A sad-looking, skinny nit stuck in a second-story room paced back and forth right above Brindle. The nit had long, dirty hair and an unshaven face. He was wearing wide striped pants and a green, ratty vest. Brindle looked up and called out to him.

"Hello?"

The nit looked down and sighed.

"Hello," he called back, his voice muffled by the invisible walls and floor he was having to talk down through.

"Are you okay?" Brindle asked.

"Is anyone here okay?" he answered.

"Are you stuck?"

"I can't find the door out," the skinny nit said. "There's a window but I'm scared to jump."

"You should just—"

"Don't talk to him," a new voice interrupted. "He's a stupid nit who was foolish enough to step up into an unknown room."

Brindle turned to face the direction the voice had come from.

"Who said that?" Brindle asked.

"Excuse me?" the voice asked back. "Just who are you?"

"The name's Brindle. I'm a sycophant."

"I can see that," the voice snipped. "I hate sycophants."

"I'm sorry to hear that. I'm looking for . . ." Brindle couldn't clear his head to remember his mission.

"I've heard what you're looking for," the voice said. "Why?"

"If you tell me what I'm looking for, I'll see if I can remember why," Brindle said.

"You're looking for a white sycophant."

"That's right . . . Lilly," Brindle said in a fog.

"Why?"

"Her father," Brindle said. "He needs her."

There was silence for a few moments. Brindle looked above him and could see right up the skinny nit's nose. The nit was kneeling on the second floor trying to hear what was being said.

"He needs her to come home," Brindle clarified.

"When has my father ever needed me?" Lilly said, materializing, her voice angry. "He's a foolish sycophant who lives by the rules of a backward tradition."

"Lilly!" Brindle gasped.

"Of course," she answered. "How stupid he is to think you can come fetch me. I am not at his beck and call. I'd sooner burn the whole of Sycophant Run than return."

Lilly was no more than twelve inches tall, but her leafy ears gave her a couple more inches of height. She was completely white and wore a pale yellow robe with blue on the edges. Her green eyes were wide and wet around the rim. She looked like a friendly stuffed animal, not a threat to anyone.

"If you won't return, then what of the key?" Brindle asked.

"Oh." Lilly sniffed. "That makes much more sense. He wants the key. I knew he didn't want me."

"He wants you, but if you refuse to come, at least give us the key."

"What a thick breed," Lilly said. "I don't have it."

"You took it."

"Brilliant deduction," Lilly said. "But I . . ."

Lilly couldn't finish her own words, her emotion slipping up into her throat.

"Gave it to Winter," Brindle finished for her.

"Don't say her name!" Lilly screamed, scratching at her own ears. "Don't ever say that name around me."

"She has returned," Brindle said.

"I know that," Lilly said impatiently. "The whole of Foo felt the Lore Coil she set off."

"She'll want to see you," Brindle said.

"How dare you," Lilly spit. "How dare you lie to me? How could you know that?"

"She was your burn."

"She abandoned me," Lilly snapped. "Set me down and walked away."

"I don't know her reasons," Brindle said. "But I know she fights for . . ."

"You know nothing!" Lilly yelled.

"Come with me," Brindle said, his strength building as he argued. "You can find her. Besides, what have you here but misery?"

"You have no idea what I have," Lilly snapped. "And you are as big a fool as my father if you think I would ever come with you. She left me, and every sycophant I have ever met answers in the same way: It's fate."

Brindle looked around and sighed.

"Isn't that what you believe?" Lilly challenged hatefully.

"I believe your father loves you," Brindle replied.

"Then you're a half-wit with far more heart than brain," Lilly seethed. "I will never return. Not even to die. My bones will rest here."

"I am sorry for your hurt," Brindle said sadly.

"You know nothing about me," Lilly snapped.

Brindle looked around at the Invisible Village.

"Perhaps you're right." Brindle gave in. "Can you lead me out?"

"I'm inclined to let you rot," she said. "But I would loathe running into you ever again. If I lead you out, will you leave for good?"

"Get me out of this valley and I promise I'll never come back," Brindle said.

"Come," Lilly growled.

"Can I follow?" the skinny nit above shouted.

Lilly turned and started to walk away. Brindle looked up at the man and shrugged.

"If you can get out," Brindle yelled, "you can follow!"

The man frantically raced around the upstairs room looking for the door. Unable to find it, he jumped out of the upstairs window and fell down to the ground a few feet away from Brindle. His shoulder snapped but he jumped up, too afraid of being left behind to complain.

Lilly wound through the Invisible Village as if she could see every wall and road. Brindle and the nit followed her, trying hard to make sure they were always only a few steps behind.

"How do you know the way?" Brindle asked.

"I've had years to map it out," Lilly called back. "I've seen it covered in snow many times. Now stop talking."

"Why's it invisible?"

"Stop talking," she growled.

It took over an hour to walk back across the valley and up to the ivy-covered cliff side Brindle had first come down. Lilly stopped just below the cliffs.

"There," she pointed. "Go straight up and over and you will be out of the village. Don't come back."

The skinny nit pushed past both of them laughing with glee. He ran up the path and into the cliffs toward freedom.

"Thanks," Brindle said. "Can I tell your father anything?"

"You can do what you please," Lilly sneered. "I personally

prefer he think me dead. I want no part of any of it or any of you."

Brindle stuck out his hand to shake Lilly's good-bye. Lilly put out her hand without thinking and as quick as a snake Brindle grabbed her wrist and bit down.

Lilly had no time to react. She looked at Brindle with surprise and then collapsed into a small heap on the ground.

"Sorry," Brindle whispered sincerely. "But he said I could bite you."

Brindle picked up Lilly and slung her over his shoulder. He then slowly hiked up into the cliffs and over the path, happiness returning to his heart with each step he took.

CHAPTER TWENTY

Not Everyone's Attractive

My favorite number is thirteen—I don't know why, it just always has been. I can't remember ever preferring another number more. Sure, seven's okay, but I'm most happy with thirteen. If I have to pick a number between one and twenty, I'm going to pick thirteen. If I were a race-car driver, I'd have the number thirteen painted on my car. And if I were a world-famous football player, my jersey would have thirteen on the back of it. True, I'll most likely never be a race-car driver or a famous football player, but it's still a great number. Of course, some people think there's something wrong with the number thirteen. Most hotels don't have a thirteenth floor simply because people are superstitious about it. I know a man who won't go out on the thirteenth of each month and a lady who will never buy any groceries that expire on the thirteenth.

People are different.

For example, I learned while wearing a costume and playing cards that Leven's favorite number is eleven, and the Dearth likes thirty-two. Of course, at the moment neither one of them were thinking about their favorite numbers. The Dearth was thinking about Leven while Leven was wondering how in the world anyone could have designed a bed as comfortable as the one he was lying on.

The beds in the safe house were made from the feathers of Tea birds and air-filled shavings of gunt. The mattresses were covered in material that the Children of the Sewn had made from the remnants of the softest and lightest dreams. To Leven it felt like sleeping on a cloud that was lying in a hammock that was propped up by marshmallows.

There were twelve (one less than thirteen) of the soft beds lining the edges of the room. The walls were covered in thick, green, velvet wallpaper, and small wooden shelves hung every three feet. On each shelf a fat orange candle with a yellow flame burned upward. The ceiling was a web of small twigs strung together with black twine and ivy, and the single large window was propped open to let the soft breeze drift in.

Leven, Geth, and Clover picked beds near the window, while Winter took the largest one on the opposite side of the room.

"What's the deal with these beds?" Leven slurred, his face resting against a giant pillow.

"I don't know, I'm already asleep," Clover mumbled back.

"It's like heaven," Winter called from across the room. "Except softer."

Geth was snoring lightly.

"He never snored as a toothpick," Clover complained, switching beds to be one farther away from Geth.

"He's probably dreaming about Phoebe," Leven said groggily.

"She was pretty," Clover whispered.

"I guess she . . ."

Leven fell asleep mid-sentence. His mind relaxed as thick waves of light rolled through his brain. He could see spots of blue blending with triangles of orange and pink. Leven could see Terry and Addy yelling at him. Addy was wearing her sweats and had a green night masque spread on her face. Leven could see Oklahoma and feel the wind blowing across the prairie and over his arms and face.

As Leven's body sunk further into the bed, his dreams became stronger and more vivid. He could see his grandfather the Want and his wrinkled, shriveled-up eyes. He could see Clover clinging to the bottom of his bed, and Winter freezing Brick and Glen, the bullies from his old school. Leven could also see Geth as a tall tree, his branches long and twisting in the blue sky.

"What do you see?" his old neighbor asked him in his dream. She was an elderly woman wearing a ratty bathrobe and plastic curlers in her hair. In Reality she had never even spoken to Leven. Now, her voice was soothing and full of concern. She touched Leven's arm.

"What do you see, Leven?"

Leven wanted to speak, but he couldn't move his mouth.

"Stand up, Leven," she said. "Come with me."

Leven felt himself standing in his sleep, his mind cloudy and

confused. He moved across the room, opened the window, and, without stopping, crawled out. He dropped ten feet and crashed to the soft ground, still asleep.

"Get up," his neighbor prodded kindly.

Leven stood, his eyes closed and his mind not his own. The sky was windy and the night was cold and black.

"Leeeeven," the wind howled.

Clover dropped from out of the window and onto Leven's shoulder.

"What are you doing out here?" Clover asked. "There could be rants."

The streets were completely dark and empty. Leven opened his eyes, but he was still fast asleep.

"Well, maybe there's none now, but they could come back," Clover insisted. "Wait a second, are you still sleeping?"

Leven didn't answer. Clover waved his hand in front of Leven's eyes. The glow from Leven's gold eyes shone against Clover's tiny hands.

"Leeeeven," the soil whispered.

Leven mechanically patted Clover on the head.

"You're sleeping," Clover deduced.

The soil whispered again. Leven looked up at Clover.

"I need to go somewhere," Leven said foggily.

"Where?"

"Far," Leven slurred. "Fast."

"I know how you can get there fast," Clover said excitedly.

Leven looked at Clover, his eyes glowing but glazed. Clover

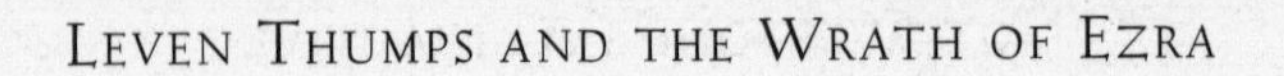

took out a long tube with an orange wrapper. The wrapper read Lofty Toffee, and it had a gold star on it that exclaimed, "You'll feel lighter than air!" On the back of the tube a slogan was printed: "One bite and you'll take flight."

The soil whispered again and in his dream Leven saw his neighbor stick out her hand and wave him closer.

Leven reached for the candy.

Clover handed it to him. "You probably should bc awake before you eat that stuff. Candy can be tricky enough if you are alert. But of course if you were awake you'd probably say no."

Leven was too busy listening to the soil to hear Clover. He opened the tube without looking at it.

"Stay here," he told Clover listlessly.

"No way," Clover said. "Last time I shirked my job you took a ride in the Devil's Spiral without me. Besides, you're sleeping and won't remember telling me to stay."

Leven took a huge handful of the buttery-smelling candy and handed it back to Clover. Clover took a few pieces for himself and then wrapped it back up and put it away. Leven flipped his handful of Lofty Toffee into his mouth and chewed.

Leven stood there asleep, seeing images in his head and trying to wake up his mind enough to talk to Clover. He could feel his body fizzing and then, like an elevator dropping, he plummeted downward. Before he hit the ground the wind picked up his pieces and blew him up over the homes. He was a million pieces of fluffy toffee being swept up over Foo.

The sensation was dreamlike and thrilling. Leven couldn't tell

if he was awake or asleep. His arms and legs were snapping and cracking like Pop-Rocks in a wet mouth. He could feel his breath being stolen and then pumped quickly back into his lungs. His vision was similar to that of a fly; he could see hundreds of images in multiple directions. Leven tried to speak, but his mouth was as hollow and silent as a vacuum.

His body spun farther up and raced through dark clouds, moisture clinging to the tiny bits of him. His body felt empty but his heart felt like a ball being lobbed through the air.

"Leven."

His body followed the voice. He descended, rose up again, and then drifted down above a field of full-grown tavel. He twisted in and out of the tavel stalks and then blew through the opening of a tent and down onto a floor of clean dirt.

Leven felt his body gel as he fell into a sleeping heap on the cold ground. He lay there silently for a few moments and then began to moan.

"Leeven," a voice whispered, interrupting his moaning.

Leven slowly opened his eyes. He closed them again and slept.

"Leven."

"What?" Leven mumbled, his eyes still closed.

"Leven."

The chilling voice pierced Leven's soul. He opened his eyes in a panic. His heart suddenly raced and he could feel that something was terribly wrong.

The smell of buttery toffee filled his nostrils.

He sat up and looked around. It was pitch-black, but as Leven turned his head, his eyes shone dimly. The room looked empty, and he could feel the cold dirt underneath him.

"Clover?" he called out.

There was no answer.

"Geth? Winter?"

"They're not here," a voice in the dark whispered slowly.

Every hair on Leven's neck stood at attention. Leven sat up and scooted backward.

"It's just you and I," the voice said dryly.

"Who are you?" Leven asked.

There was a soft, disturbing laugh. "I believe you know exactly who I am."

Leven looked as hard as he could toward the voice. His gold eyes burned brighter and gave the room a faint definition.

"Who are you?"

"Don't insult me," the voice said.

"The Dearth?"

"See, you do know me."

"Am I still in the house?" Leven asked.

"No," the Dearth replied.

The soil sizzled and hissed. A short rant entered the tent carrying a small lamp. He placed the lamp down in front of the Dearth and left.

The Dearth had his back turned and was slumped over. Leven could see the Dearth's spine and his spindly shoulders. His tarlike skin bubbled in spots. Small bits of hair were growing out

of the back of his dark head and there was a long swath of brown fabric wrapped around the Dearth's waist.

Leven scanned the room but could see nothing else.

"Would you like to go back?" the Dearth asked, still facing the opposite direction.

"I'm not sure what you mean," Leven said honestly.

"Yes," the Dearth said. "You could go back to Reality, or back to Geth."

"Either of those would be fine," Leven said, his heart pounding in his throat.

"I should thank you—you've helped our cause by letting the longing loose," the Dearth hissed.

"It wasn't meant to help you," Leven insisted.

"Don't be angry," the Dearth said. "Someday you'll come to understand how what we seek is truly the greater good. Had you met up with Sabine before Geth, you might very well be fighting for us."

"I would never fight with Sabine."

"Never's a long time," the Dearth said. "You say Sabine is bad, but at the instruction of a soul such as Geth you have killed Sabine, and Jamoon, and now you seek to do me harm."

"I fight for Foo," Leven said, trying to keep his thoughts to himself. "I am a part of this now."

"How nice," the Dearth said.

"Why am I here?"

"You give some beings hope," the Dearth said. "And that just won't do."

"What?"

"Hope is a poison and I wish to put an end to every bit of it."

"How can you say that?"

The Dearth turned around slowly. The features of his face were prominent. His eyes bubbled and his mouth was a black hole. His forehead looked like a sticky wad of rot with a couple dozen bristly hairs growing out of it. He stuck out his tongue.

Leven gagged.

The Dearth's tongue was a thin, decaying rope of black. He whipped his tongue around and then retracted it slowly, flecks of it dusting off as he did so. He looked closely at Leven.

"Such strong eyes," the Dearth gurgled. "Such strong, bright eyes. And sadly I can see the confidence of Geth in the way you sit. Such a useless breed, the lithens are. Poor Azure has to redeem an entire race."

"I would do anything Geth asked," Leven said boldly. "And your words mean nothing to me."

The Dearth's tongue extended and withdrew. Scaly pieces of tongue drifted down through the air.

"Why am I here?" Leven demanded again.

"Well, Leven, I plan to kill you," the Dearth said calmly.

"Is that supposed to scare me?"

"You asked," the Dearth hissed. "I told you."

"How did I get here?"

"You blew in," the Dearth answered. "Do you know what I am?"

"I already answered that."

"No," the Dearth said, breathing strong. "Not my name. Do you know *what* I am?"

"I don't care."

"I think you should," the Dearth said acridly. "You see, I am the life force beneath the soil. I have been around since the creation of Foo, and each dirty soul buried at death becomes a part of me. How quickly they realized my true desires and locked me away. The keys kept me trapped—a prisoner beneath the soil. But truth be shared, I would still not have been able to rise had not so many hearts turned dark."

Leven was silent.

"Now I want Reality. I want the power to be whole in Reality. I want to take what's here and create something better there. I want what's mine, Leven."

The Dearth paused as if for dramatic effect.

"Am I supposed to clap?" Leven asked. "You won't succeed."

"You know, I worried about that as well," the Dearth said icily. "It seems that as long as the sycophants live freely, as long as they can perch on someone's shoulder and tell them what they can be, hope will always linger. And as long as they keep me from their shores, I am trapped. But I am happy to say that the sycophants are no longer a problem."

Leven opened his mouth to speak, but the Dearth had other ideas. Strands of darkness snaked across the ground toward Leven. The darkness slipped up his legs and wrapped around him like a boa constrictor. Leven tried to scream, but the blackness was pushing up against the bottom of his chin and choking the

air out of him. Leven tore at the strands with his hands as more of the Dearth's strings shot over and wrapped around his arms.

The Dearth pulled Leven up onto his feet and dragged him closer. Leven struggled for breath as the Dearth smiled at him. The tip of his decaying tongue whipped up against Leven's right cheek.

"The time for hope and dreams is dying," the Dearth moaned mockingly, his dark eyes boring deep into Leven. "And there is no fate strong enough to save you."

The strands of black tore at Leven, pulling his skin and stretching him. He could feel his ribs being pulled apart. The Dearth's tongue lashed out at Leven's face again, and his rank breath made Leven's sight go black.

"Your time is . . ." the Dearth stopped talking. His eyes became as wide as prunes and he held Leven back to stare at him. "It's not possible."

Leven gasped desperately for air, his body being squeezed to death.

"The Want?"

The Dearth held Leven back even farther. He released his grip on Leven's neck and began to tremble, his body jiggling like mud.

"How?"

"I can't breathe," Leven gasped.

The Dearth loosened his grip around Leven's chest.

"That's impossible," the Dearth said. "How can you be the Want?"

Leven's eyes burned and he could see right through the Dearth. He could see the hundreds of dark veins and pitch-black organs. He saw the Dearth's raisin-size heart beating weakly. The Dearth's body began to shake and rumble. He set Leven down and retracted the black strands.

Leven stood up straight, breathing in deep and rubbing his neck and arms.

"For someone who's been in Foo for so long," Leven said, "you should know that *impossible* is not a word we have to submit to."

The Dearth was shaking uncontrollably. "You killed the Want?"

"By accident," Leven said.

"He was your relative?"

"My grandfather."

The Dearth began to moan and scream. He tilted back his sticky head and howled. His body dripped and ran, pooling up black puddles all over the tent.

"Now might be a good time to get out of here," Clover whispered into Leven's ear.

"You're here?" Leven said, surprised.

"Of course," Clover said. "Now get out."

Leven dashed toward the door of the tent, pushed it open, and burst out. A handful of rants were standing around a fire in the distance. They spotted Leven and instantly gave chase.

"Run!" Clover yelled.

"Thanks for the suggestion!" Leven yelled back.

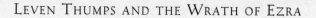

Leven ran into the field of tavel as fast as he could. He pushed the stalks of purple and green aside, taking steps twice as long as his normal gait.

"They're coming fast!" Clover screamed. "And there's a ton of them."

"Where were you?" Leven yelled back.

"I was there the whole time," Clover answered. "I just thought it might be smart to stay hidden. I was just about to save you when he let go."

"Right," Leven called back.

"You can thank me later."

Leven tore through the tavel, the sound of angry rants close behind him and swatches of growth snapping under his step. A large moon was sliding down the far side of the dark sky and Leven could see nothing but the high stalks of tavel for miles and miles.

"I don't know where I'm going," Leven admitted. "I don't know where I am."

"Who cares?" Clover screamed. "Just go!"

"He didn't seem too happy about me being the Want!" Leven hollered.

"People like that are always miserable."

Leven turned and ran between two tight lines of tavel. He slipped down behind one of the rows and rolled to the ground.

"What are you doing?" Clover whispered.

"Shhhh," Leven said quickly.

The rants were systematically pushing through the tavel

searching for Leven. They swore and hollered, slicing at the tall stalks with their kilves. Two ran past them, their feet kicking dust up into Leven's face.

Leven could feel the dirt beneath him moaning in confusion.

"We've got to get moving," Leven said. "Find some stone."

"That way," Clover pointed.

Leven stood and ran in the direction Clover had pointed. The growing tavel was so thick he could barely push through it. Leven's movement attracted the attention of the rants and they shouted to follow after him. The moon held its height in the sky, curious as to what was happening.

"Where's the stone?" Leven yelled as Clover held tightly to his neck.

"I don't know," Clover answered.

"But you said this way."

"I thought one of us should make a decision."

The rants were all behind them, running in a line. Leven turned and headed toward the direction of the moon.

"How did we get here anyway?" Leven asked.

"Candy."

"You're joking."

"No."

"Do you have more?"

"Yes, but the wind will just blow us back to that ugly guy!" Clover yelled. "What's the deal with his hair? It's gross."

"You're obsessed with people's hair!" Leven yelled back. "Find some stone. I can still hear him hissing beneath us."

"What are you going to do?" Clover screamed. "Stand on a rock while they tackle you?"

Leven zipped down another row of tavel, looking for any sign of some way out. The rows went on for miles with no hint of a break. Leven could see a rant pushing through the tavel and coming at him from the side. The stalks of grain rolled up and down as he got closer, reminding Leven of the avalands that had chased Winter and him on the Oklahoma prairie.

Another rant was closing in from the left. Leven's legs popped and burned like hot oil, his lungs exhausted.

"Please," Leven pleaded, begging his gift to kick in. "Please."

"I'm not sure good manners are going to help us right now!" Clover yelled. "In fact, you might try swearing."

Leven could hear rants right behind him, swinging their kilves. He could feel the wind from their movement, and they had apparently taken Clover's advice about swearing.

Leven couldn't breathe. His side was cramped and each step felt like a blow to the kidney.

"Please," Leven whispered.

His gift didn't kick in, but the ground beneath him began to rise. Leven stumbled, but caught his stride as the ground lifted.

"What's happening?" Clover yelled. "You're wobbly."

"The ground's lifting."

"Avalands!" Clover yelled.

The avaland beneath Leven was huge. Its back was covered with tavel stalks and its body was stony. The avaland rose above the ground running, its huge dirt legs thundering across the field.

Leven could feel the avaland's simple thoughts. He knelt down on the back of the charging beast and grabbed onto two of the stalks of growing tavel.

"Faster," Leven commanded.

The avaland moved even quicker. A kilve shot past Leven and pierced the avaland's back. The avaland bucked and thundered

faster, leaving the rants chasing after them and buried in dust.

"Which way is Cusp?" Leven yelled.

"Head toward the smallest moon," Clover answered.

Leven shifted his grip and the avaland turned slightly, heading directly toward the smallest moon in the sky.

"How can you control this thing?" Clover shouted.

"I don't know!" Leven shouted back. "I can feel what it's thinking."

"You're like a black skeleton," Clover said. "Cool. Captain Black."

"It's Leven." Leven smiled.

"Dirt Jockey?" Clover tried.

"Leven."

"All right," Clover said. "I'll keep trying."

The avaland's huge feet pounded the ground, streaking across the field. Leven felt free and powerful, a sensation he had not had much experience with. The evil of the Dearth was fresh in his mind, but he had seen through the evil and now knew that victory for Foo was just as close as the possible defeat.

The avaland brought Leven and Clover all the way to the edge of Cusp. From there they rode the ropes back to the safe house. Owen was more than a little surprised to have them knocking on his door so late.

"But I thought you were sleeping," Owen said.

"Apparently I sleepwalk," Leven explained.

"Would you like a room with no window?" Owen asked.

"No," Leven answered. "I don't think it will happen again."

Owen led Leven and Clover back to the room. They had to take three different flights of stairs and cross through more than two dozen rooms.

"I don't know how you ever find your way around," Leven said.

"It takes some time to learn." Owen smiled.

Once Leven reached his room he woke up Geth and sat on the edge of his bed to fill him in. Geth's blond hair was a tangled mess, and his speech was tired, but his eyes still looked excited.

"He let you get away?" Geth said, surprised.

"I think he was confused by me being the Want," Leven explained, drinking a glass of warm milk that Owen had set out.

"He'll seek you even more now."

"I could see right through him at one point," Leven said. "It was as if his whole inside was known to me."

"How far was he?"

"Pretty far," Leven said. "We traveled a long distance on the avaland."

"And Azure?"

"I didn't see him at all," Leven answered. "But I have no memory of traveling there. He could have met me and led me into the tent, for all I know."

"He's supposed to be at the Meadows tomorrow," Geth said. "Let's hope he's still there."

"I don't like the Dearth, Geth," Leven said solemnly. "It's even worse than Sabine or Azure. He looks like the kind of thing you'd find in a haunted cellar. I'd love to not have to meet up with him again."

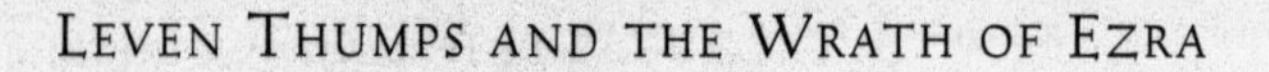

"I wish that were possible," Geth said.

"Me too," Clover said, materializing. "He was really unattractive."

"Well, you should sleep now," Geth said.

"I'd love to," Leven said tiredly.

"I'll lock the window," Clover volunteered.

"We'll head to the Meadows as soon as we awake," Geth said. "Tomorrow could be a big day for Foo."

Geth said a few other things, but Leven only heard a couple of them. The warm milk began to take effect and he quickly fell fast asleep.

CHAPTER TWENTY-ONE

SHATTERBALL

The rope ride to the Meadows, where the shatterball tournament was taking place, was quick and crowded. Leven could feel hundreds of other passengers weaving through him as he spun along. He was ejected at the back side of the Meadows near a row of quaint brownstones. Winter shot out right after Leven, and seconds later Geth was standing there patting himself down to see if all of him had made it.

"So many people traveling," Geth said. "I was certain I'd come out with extra pieces."

Clover held up a string. "Do you think this is something important?"

"Let's hope it's just string," Leven said.

People were popping out of the rope at a rapid rate. The four of them moved out of the way and across the wide cobblestone

street. They walked between two tall brownstones and out to the Meadows.

"Wow," Winter said in awe.

On the other side of a wide dirt road stood a lush green field larger than most cities. The field was covered with hundreds of thousands of people and small booths selling food and assorted shatterball paraphernalia. There were trees and shrubs and numerous stone walls that sectioned off smaller areas within the Meadows. In the sky hundreds of hot-air balloons drifted, and in the center of the Meadows four monstrous trees towered above everything. The four trees were spaced out like the corners of a large square and each was at least two hundred feet high.

"Keep your heads low," Geth warned. "Walk on stone. The longer we stay unnoticed the better. Avoid all rants. Azure wants that key, but if things turn bad he might decide it's best to just kill us on the spot."

"Nice." Leven smiled.

"What if he disappears again?" Winter asked. "We should probably split up so we can spot him from more places."

"Okay," Geth said. "Winter and I will approach him from behind; Leven, you move at him from the other side. I know your gift's not working, but if it kicks in we could use the help."

"Let's hope it does," Leven said.

Winter and Geth stood up and, walking on a short stone wall, moved toward a large rock archway that spanned the entrance to the Meadows. The archway was covered with beautiful small flowers that opened and closed like blinking Christmas lights.

Leven followed them at a safe distance. He saw them reach the archway. A sign above the gate read:

Use of all gifts prohibited on the Meadows unless instructed.

A large cog with a wrinkled orange forehead held out his blue palm to stop Geth and Winter as they tried to enter.

"Waiver?" he questioned.

"We have none," Geth replied. "But we have this."

Geth pulled out a small sack of money and handed it to the cog.

"I figure it's enough to take care of us and the nit coming in behind us," Geth said kindly.

The cog looked back in Leven's direction. He hefted the money and surveyed the scene for anyone watching him.

"What do I care?" the cog finally said. "Put your kilves in the bins and move in."

Geth and Winter retrieved their kilves from behind their backs and placed them into one of the wooden barrels next to the archway. They slipped through the stone gate and into the crowd. A few moments later Leven moved to the archway. He put his kilve in one of the barrels and waved at the cog. He was motioned through without a single word exchanged.

"Tight security," Clover whispered.

Leven pulled the hood of his cloak up over his head and moved to the edge of the massive crowd.

The Meadows were like heaven, but with noise and bugs. The venue and the location were as perfect as any outdoor creation could be. The hundreds of hot-air balloons were hovering at

different levels, their flames sounding out as they moved sideways across the sky. Above the balloons was a fat layer of gray hazen. The clouds rumbled and shook as small lines of light sizzled through them. The ground was covered with hordes of carts selling almost anything you could imagine and thousands of couples walking hand in hand or professing their love.

"Head to the tall trees," Clover whispered in Leven's ear.

Leven pushed through the lovesick crowd. His eyes were focused straight ahead, searching for any sign of Azure. The trees got closer and larger. Leven walked through a second gate sectioning off some stone bleachers. He looked up and stopped.

"What's that?" Leven asked in awe.

"That's the arena."

Hanging in the center of the trees, filling most of the space between them, was a gigantic glass sphere. It looked as large as a small moon and glowed slightly purple. The glass sphere was suspended by four huge branches, one from each of the four trees. The branches wrapped around the bottom of the sphere and kept the entire glass structure floating almost twenty feet off of the ground. The field beneath the hanging sphere was barren aside from a few hundred pieces of litter that spectators had thrown down from the seating. The rest of the four trees' branches were filled with assorted spectators waiting to watch the match.

"Impressive," Leven said, momentarily forgetting that he was there for anything besides gawking. "It's huge."

"Over six stories high and wide," Clover said. "It's made out

of gunt. They heat it and stretch it to form. It takes months and many craftsmen to create each one. They're a work of art."

"Can they break?"

"If the game's a good one."

The glass sphere appeared to be completely sealed except for one large hole in the bottom and a tiny one up top. Inside the glass eight robed nits stood around the hole. Four of the nits were in blue robes and four were in orange. The whole thing looked like a giant glass planet with people standing in it.

"What do they do?" Leven asked. "The people inside?"

"The blues are called Pidgins and the orange players are called Pawns. The Pidgins are from Morfit. The Pawns are from Cusp," Clover whispered. "You'll see them move when it starts up."

"Is one color better than the other?"

"Always go with orange," Clover lectured. "Blue obviously has something to hide."

"Really?"

"I don't know," Clover admitted. "But if it were true it'd be interesting. I'm just never going to root for Morfit. Not after being there. Besides, that Johnny Chapman is so smug and he's their team captain."

"And you don't like him?"

"I just think that long hair and a bad attitude don't necessarily make you cool."

Leven patted Clover on the head.

A large musical band made up of nits and cogs sat around the bases of two of the humongous trees. The band members

were holding a wide assortment of unusual wooden instruments and drums. A whistle blew and the band began to play. The pounding of the drums was so loud that the glass sphere above began to vibrate.

The music was intoxicating and made Leven miss Winter.

Leven could see a section of tent-covered seats over at the far end of the littered field. Sitting in the middle seat was a tall man in a blue robe. Leven was too far away to see him clearly, but he knew it was Azure. Leven watched Azure whisper to someone short who was next to him.

"Do you see Geth and Winter?" Leven asked Clover.

Another loud whistle sounded and the men inside the glass steadied themselves. Everyone looked up.

"Here it comes," Clover said, not answering Leven's question.

The crowd began to chant and scream, drowning out the music. Some threw small white balls at the glass court. The tiny hollow balls bounced off, falling to the littered field beneath.

"We should get closer to Azure," Leven said.

"Wait," Clover insisted. "It's starting."

Three men in white robes walked into the center of the littered field below.

The crowd cheered.

"Those are the officials," Clover said. "They're also nits with the gift of flight."

One of the officials blew a whistle and all three flew up from the ground. One flew to the top of the glass sphere. The other

two flew slowly around, circling the huge ball, their eyes focused on the players inside.

The official on top pulled a black ball the size of an orange out of his robe. Leven could barely see it from where he stood.

"That's the pit," Clover explained.

The official held the pit above the small hole at the very top of the sphere. The hole was just a few inches wider than the ball. The crowd began to count down from ten. The Pidgins and Pawns inside slowly began to fly around in circles.

The official dropped the black pit and it fell through the small hole down into the sphere. It bounced with a piercing twang against the bottom near the large hole. The pit ricocheted wildly inside of the glass court. The players flew around, knocking into one another and maneuvering for the pit. They were incredibly fluid and zipped around each other in mesmerizing and skilled motions.

Leven couldn't take his eyes off of them.

"I wish I could fly," Leven said.

"Me too," Clover replied. "I'm tired of you just walking."

"So what are they trying to do?" Leven asked.

"They grab the pit and push it back up into the top hole while trying to shove their opponents down through the bottom hole. They can't touch the glass unless they are shoved into it. If they touch it themselves the other team gets a point."

"How does it end?"

"When the sphere is shattered or there's only one player left inside. If the sphere breaks when a team slams an opponent

against it, that team wins. It can get pretty intense. Sometimes the spheres are so strong the game lasts for hours. No one is allowed out unless they are thrown out or they're the last player."

Leven watched a Pidgin slam a Pawn and send him hurling across the court. The orange Pawn hit the wall and slid down the side. He fell limply through the hole and out of the sphere, flailing wildly as he dropped the twenty feet down to the littered field below.

"When they fall out they're not allowed to fly to stop their fall."

"Brutal," Leven said.

"Yeah, I usually watch that part with my hands over my eyes. Sometimes they break arms and legs as they hit the ground."

The crowd threw white balls at the poor player who had just dropped out.

Inside the sphere a Pawn flew into a Pidgin and pushed him violently into the glass.

The spectators cheered riotously.

"Everyone's pretty pumped up," Clover noted.

Two blue Pidgins spun up around a Pawn. The orange Pawn grabbed the black pit as it bounced off the wall. He shot up and shoved it through the small hole in the top. The small pit hovered above the sphere until the official grabbed it and inspected it.

The official looked at the pit and then raised a finger on his right hand.

The crowd roared.

The official dropped the black pit back down into the court and blew his whistle.

Leven watched the pit bounce around. One player grabbed it and his opponent hit up against him, smacking it out of his hands. A Pawn then threw a Pidgin into the wall and the Pidgin slid down and dropped out of the hole. The movement was jarring and felt spliced together.

"Did you see that?" Leven asked.

"See what?"

"There was . . . something happened."

"Yeah, the Pawns are winning," Clover said. "Did you see how dumb that guy looked falling out?"

"No," Leven said. "Something happened."

"That's what keeps people's attention," Clover said slowly. "It's called a game."

Another Pidgin flew into a Pawn and grabbed him by one arm and one leg. He spun him around and threw him against the glass, where he hit headfirst and slid down out of the hole. He fell to the ground with a great thud, grass and litter exploding as he landed.

"There it was again," Leven said. "Did you see that?"

"I told you I put my hands over my eyes when people fall."

Leven looked in Azure's direction. Azure sat calmly watching the game.

"I think we need to find Geth," Leven said urgently. "Something's happening."

The Pawns scored and the crowd was whipped up into a

messy frenzy. Spectators threw hundreds of little white balls up against the glass court. The clicking of the balls combined with the screaming was deafening.

Leven moved along the back of the stone bleachers and pushed through the crowd, looking for Geth and Winter.

"What's wrong with you?" Clover asked.

"I think I'm going mad," Leven said.

"I had an uncle who did that," Clover said. "Now he makes rugs."

"Great."

The Pawns scored again as they sent another Pidgin down the hole and onto the littered field. Leven felt it again.

"Can't you feel that?"

"I don't know what you are talking about," Clover said. "Does the game make you nervous? I mean, it's a contest, there has to be a winner and loser."

"Find Geth," Leven said. "Find him and get me to him."

Leven's forehead was wet with perspiration. He stopped and watched the glass sphere. A large Pidgin thrust the smallest Pawn into the wall. The entire glass ball swayed. Leven could see the beginning of a crack where the hit had occurred. It slowly began to lengthen. The crack paused and then continued sideways, sounding like dry bones shattering.

Leven closed his eyes. There was nothing but darkness. He pulled the hood of his cloak tighter over his head and breathed deeply.

Nothing but darkness.

He threw his hood back down and sucked in some air. The chanting of the crowd felt like a fist repeatedly pounding Leven's chest. The spectators' emotions were out of control.

Leven opened his eyes and the entire scene went quiet. He could see everyone still shouting, but he couldn't hear any of them. He blinked and the noise was back.

A hand grabbed Leven on the neck and spun him around. Leven threw his hands up as if to push back.

"Lev," Winter said, "what's wrong with you? You're sweating like mad."

"I don't know what's wrong! Where's Geth?" Leven said frantically.

"He's . . ."

"Just take me."

Winter pulled Leven by the hand and wove through the thick throngs of enthusiastic fans.

"Did Clover find you?" Leven yelled.

"Of course," Clover said, from on top of Leven's head. "Do you still feel like my uncle?"

"Something's going on!" Leven shouted to Winter as she led the way. "Time's not acting right."

Leven slammed into a tall cog carrying three glasses of pink ale. The liquid seemed to freeze in time and then in an instant it blew out all over the crowd.

"Sorry," Winter said as they continued to rush through.

"I don't understand what's happening," Clover said.

"Time's messed up," Leven said.

Geth was standing behind a short stone wall that was blocking the tents from the field. Leven stumbled into him.

"What is it?" Geth asked, holding him up. "You're as white as gunt."

"Something's happening," Leven whispered fiercely. "I'm not sure, but I feel like someone's picking away bits of my time."

"I don't understand," Geth replied.

The Pidgins scored and the place erupted in cheers. Thousands of white balls were thrown up against the sphere.

"Watch," Leven said, pointing to the glass ball.

Two players slammed up against the inside of the court and the beginning of a new crack was born.

"I don't see what you're saying." Geth looked concerned.

"Time's stopping and starting or something," Leven insisted. "I don't know how, but I can feel it."

For the first time ever Leven saw a wave of fear cross Geth's face. Geth turned to look in Azure's direction.

"What is it?" Winter asked.

The Pidgins scored as the Pawns lost another player.

"There," Geth pointed. "The man with his cloak pulled up, sitting behind Azure."

A short robed being leaned into Azure and whispered something. Geth could see a smear of blue beneath the man's nose.

"Azure is stopping Time," Geth said.

"He can do that?" Leven asked, scared.

"He's done it before."

"I felt this way at Far Hall," Leven said.

"That's how he disappeared," Geth said.

"But why is he stopping it now?" Winter asked frantically.

"I'm not sure."

"It just stopped again," Leven said.

"For how long?" Geth asked.

"I have no idea," Leven admitted. "But it's not for brief moments. It feels long."

"How long?" Winter repeated.

"I don't know," Leven insisted.

"Maybe that's why I feel so hungry," Clover said, trying really hard to sound concerned.

"It doesn't work that way," Geth said. "He's doing something with that time. While we all sit here he's setting up our demise. It must be the Dearth. He's buying the Dearth time."

"I figure he's stopped it at least six times so far," Leven said. "For how long I'm not sure."

They moved along the back of the stone wall.

Two players slammed into the inside wall of the sphere and a loud, cracking noise began to chirp like an alarm.

The fans were whipped up and frothy.

"He's stopped it again," Leven whispered fiercely.

"We could lose days just trying to get to him," Winter pointed out.

"Just keep moving," Geth insisted. "It's all we can do."

Leven knew that what seemed like a short walk could take weeks to complete.

"Want me to mess with him?" Clover whispered into Leven's ear. "I can get there faster than you."

Leven nodded.

"But be careful."

"Of course." Clover smiled, having no idea what he was really stepping into.

CHAPTER TWENTY-TWO

Coming to an Uncomfortable Understanding

Tim bent down and tried to help Janet up. Unfortunately, she was a whisp and there was nothing to hold onto to help up. He tried again, but achieved the same results.

"She's not there," Tim said, amazed. "I can't pick her up."

The echoes surrounding Tim laughed.

"What happened?" Swig asked.

"I think she fainted," Tim said.

A tall, fiery being knelt by Tim and gazed compassionately at Janet. Tim looked at him and contemplated screaming and running away.

"She'll be fine," the being said. "She's very resilient."

Tim was speechless. His brilliant mind was still trying to comprehend the environment and creatures he was now a part of.

"I am Osck," the tall being said.

"I'm Tim." Tim extended his hand.

"I have no use for that," Osck said. "I've my own."

Osck showed Tim both his hands.

"You have something on your head," Osck observed.

Tim touched his ball cap, staring curiously.

"Look," Osck said. "She's beautiful even when silent."

Tim looked around, wondering who he was talking about.

"Oh, her?" he said, pointing to Janet.

"Yes," Osck said. "You know each other?"

"She was the mother of a girl I'm looking for," Tim said.

"Yes, she has spoken about a girl," Osck said. "Her eyes get smeared and interesting when she does."

Janet began to stir. She was wearing an old yellow housedress with faded red flowers on the front. It looked like the same outfit she had been wearing when Tim had last seen her. Her hair was loose, and her face looked far more relaxed than Tim remembered. Her heavy body seemed less bulky as a whisp.

Janet blinked and smiled at Osck. She sat up and made eye contact with Tim. Once again she gasped.

"How can you be here?" Janet screeched.

Osck looked at her like she had just done something beautiful.

"I'm not sure how I got here myself," Tim replied.

"Are you whole?" Janet reached out. Her hand passed right through Tim's arm.

Osck touched Tim on the shoulder.

"He's a nit," Osck said. "Are you here to fight the battle with us?"

"I'm here to find Winter," Tim said, looking at Janet.

Janet put her hand to her mouth. "How's that possible? Winter's here?"

"I think so," Tim said softly.

Janet began to cry.

"I like how she looks when she does that," Osck pointed.

Swig was invisible and sitting on Tim's shoulder. He laughed at Osck's words.

"You were asking about Winter when I last saw you in Reality," Janet said. "When I sent you away."

"And I've been searching for her ever since."

Janet looked like she had been punched in the face.

"And I did nothing," she mourned.

"Yet," Osck said comfortingly, "that's the thing about possibilities. They are always around."

"Apparently Winter's well-known here," Tim said to Janet. "A lot of people in Cusp have heard of her. They say she's fighting the war. I was hoping she might be here."

"I don't understand," Janet said. "How could they know her?"

"She's from Foo."

Janet closed her brown eyes and then opened them slowly.

"She's a nit, isn't she?" Janet asked. "She froze my hair once."

"She has frozen a number of things," Tim said. "My hope was to find her and make sure she was safe. Now, however, I'm not certain I can even save myself."

"You must march with us, then," Osck said passionately.

"Azure's army has room for all who want their freedom."

"March?"

"Today we begin the hard march into Cusp," Osck said. "Once Cusp is taken we will be one step closer to finding a way out of Foo."

"Is that possible?"

"Azure promises it is," Osck said. "Then Janet and I will be together. She will be whole and I will reflect her. So will you march?"

"I'm not sure," Tim said.

"And I'm not leaving without Winter," Janet insisted. "I turned my back on her once, but not again."

"What's in the other direction?" Tim pointed to the far horizon.

"The Swollen Forest," Osck said. "And Morfit is back a bit where the sky is black."

"Could Winter be there?" Tim asked.

Osck shrugged. Fiery streaks of light raced through his veins, and Tim could see his own reflection in Osck's shoulder.

"I don't know where Winter is," Osck pointed out naively. "But your chance for reunion is best if Azure succeeds."

"I've heard both good and bad about Azure," Tim said. "A lot of people in Cusp fear him and think he's misguided."

"Most in Cusp fear the possibilities Azure promises," Osck said firmly, his ears burning like red-hot flames. "Azure promises multiple gifts and freedom for all. The day's coming when we will dream our own dreams. March with us."

"I will until I discover that Winter's somewhere else," Tim said. "I've got to finish this."

"Same here," Janet said passionately.

"What of us?" Osck said sadly.

"Osck," Janet said tenderly, "I will never be truly whole until I have found her and told her I'm sorry."

"Then we will find her," Osck said. "And we will be one of those groups."

"Groups?" Tim asked.

"Where there's people who live in a house."

"A family?" Tim smiled.

"Yes," Osck said. "What about you, Tim? Do you live in a house with people?"

Tim nodded.

"Do they all wear things on their heads?"

"Just me," Tim said.

"Would it be possible for you to stand so that I can reflect the top of you?" Osck asked. "The top of your head is fascinating."

Tim took off his ball cap. He looked at it in his hands. He had tucked it into his pocket before he had been snatched into Foo. He had gotten it years ago from his wife, Wendy. She insisted it wasn't because he was going bald, but because the sun can be harmful to people with large foreheads. The front of the cap had a picture of a bulldog on it.

Tim stared at the hat for a few seconds. He handed it to Osck.

Osck squinted and stepped back.

"No," Tim said. "I want you to have it."

"But I don't have one to give you," Osck pointed out.

"Will you help me . . . us . . . find Winter?"

"Of course."

Tim held the hat out farther.

Osck took it carefully. He looked at the bulldog and turned the hat around in his hands. He placed it on his head and smiled. His smile turned his ears red, causing them to spark up. The hat caught fire and in two seconds it was nothing but ashes.

"Thank you," Osck said as ashes drifted off of him. "Your head looked better when you were wearing it. That's quite a sacrifice."

"I've got to be dreaming," Tim murmured to himself.

"You're not," Swig whispered from the back of Tim's neck. "Are you sure you want to join up with all these people?"

"I'm not sure of anything anymore," Tim said quietly.

"Are you hungry?" Osck asked.

Osck walked Tim over to one of the cooking circles and loaded him up with a plate full of gravy-covered sheep, stick-beaten potatoes, and a large mug of rich, cold milk. With a full stomach things seemed much less worrisome but just as unbelievable.

CHAPTER TWENTY-THREE

Blue Hole Lake

In most of America fall was getting long in the tooth and large bits of winter could be felt in the early mornings and late at night. But in Santa Rosa, New Mexico, the weather was still warm enough for the inhabitants to wear shorts and sandals.

It was early morning, and the mild chill of a new day was beginning to slide off of visitors and settle only in the cold ground beneath their feet.

Santa Rosa was waking up. Of course, the small town would never really get all the way up. The best it could hope for was a slouch. It was a lazy spot with brown homes and buildings that sat on the edge of dirt roads like boxy spotted frogs. There were a few paved roads and only a couple of restaurants that looked as if they wouldn't pass a board of health inspection. Interstate 40 cut through the middle of the town and most cars traveling the freeway were content to just keep on going.

Dusty, faded signs and billboards touted Santa Rosa as the diving capital of the Southwest. The claim seemed absurd, since the town was landlocked and barren, but thanks to some extraordinary sinkholes filled with water, numerous divers would come and practice their skills in Santa Rosa.

The most famous sinkhole was called Blue Hole Lake. It wasn't much larger than a community pool, but it was over eighty feet deep. It was an artesian spring that pumped more than three thousand gallons a minute of water up and then downstream. On a day when few scuba divers were practicing in it, the water was so clear it was said you could spot a nickel on the bottom of the lake from up top.

The small lake was surrounded by a short brick wall on two sides and a high stone cliff at the back. There were some stairs at the front for people who preferred to walk carefully into the lake and a cement platform off the north wall that allowed the less cautious to dive in. A couple of worn picnic tables sat near a dive shop that, on its best days, didn't look like much more than an abandoned building.

"Not much of a town," Dennis said, taking in his surroundings. "There doesn't look to be a single building that couldn't use some repair."

"Thanks for the commentary," Ezra said.

"It's just so brown," Dennis added. "Remember Germany?"

"No," Ezra mocked. "I've completely forgotten what happened to me just a short while ago. I'm so stupid that I have no memory of an entire country or that we were just there."

Dennis shook his shaved head and mumbled something under his breath.

"Smart retort, baldy," Ezra snickered.

"You realize I could just flick you out into the water and never have to bother with you again?" Dennis asked.

"You realize that even though you've become more assertive, your IQ hasn't risen a bit?"

Dennis held Ezra with two fingers and positioned his other hand to flick him.

"Frightening," Ezra yawned. "Where's that round woman, Addy?"

"Buying food."

"There's a shocker."

Ezra and Dennis had gotten to town the night before and rented a room at a motel called the Tower, with maroon doors and weekly rates.

Terry and Addy had their own room next door. The confused couple were still trying to digest all the new information that Ezra had given them. The idea of Foo is not always easy to take in. Especially for people with small, unimaginative, selfish brains like Terry and Addy.

"So you're sure this is it?" Dennis said, pointing at Blue Hole Lake.

"I hate answering pointless questions the first time," Ezra scolded. "And here you are asking for the tenth time. Yes, I'm sure it's it."

"And there's a hole down there beneath that grate?"

"That's what that website said," Ezra answered, defeated. "There are two grates, actually."

"The water's so clear."

Dennis was correct in his description. The water in Blue Hole Lake was crystal clear and the temperature stayed at a consistent sixty-three degrees. There was a large grate at the bottom of the lake covering the natural spring. The sides of the lake were rocky and sloped inward like an upside-down bell. The website also talked about the hidden caves and openings beneath the lake under the grates.

Two divers were currently in the water practicing their diving skills. Every few moments a fistful of bubbles would percolate to the surface. The parking lot next to the lake was almost empty. A couple of tourists walked around taking pictures and commenting on how beautiful the water was.

"There's no way we could swim down through that grate without being seen," Dennis whispered. "Besides, it's gotta be sealed closed."

"You have no vision," Ezra said. "By the time we are done using . . . I mean, helping Terry and Addy, people are going to be begging us to drain this lake and open the gateway."

Ezra stopped talking and began to tremble. Dennis looked down at the angry toothpick sitting quietly in his shirt pocket. Ezra burned hot, turning red as he did so.

"Are you okay?" Dennis asked.

"Quiet," Ezra sobbed.

"Your emotions are a disaster."

Ezra leaned his head against Dennis and sobbed. "What has Geth done to me? I'm nothing but pain and confusion."

"And nail polish," Dennis said.

Ezra poked Dennis through his shirt pocket. They walked around the lake one more time and then out into the parking lot.

"We'll set the tent up just over there." Ezra pointed to an empty field across the street. The ground was covered with nothing but dirt and small scrub and rocks.

"It's beautiful," Dennis said sarcastically.

"I know," Ezra smiled.

"And you think Terry can pull it off?"

"It's debatable. You humans have such a difficult time doing anything right," Ezra said. "But if Terry fails we'll steal his robe and you can do it."

"I hope he doesn't fail, then," Dennis said.

"You have so little gumption," Ezra snapped. "If there's one thing I have discovered about you people in Reality it's that so many of you are just waiting around to believe in something. We'll give the masses what they want."

"And you're sure this gateway works?"

"I went through it once a long time ago, while I was still a part of Geth."

"Why?"

"I can't remember," Ezra said. "I can't remember anything, only what I can feel."

A large, white van with dusty windows and a red stripe running along its side pulled into the parking lot. The doors flew open and six kids spilled out. The two parents opened their doors and started immediately yelling at their kids to stay away from the water.

"Look, don't touch!" the mother screamed. "And watch out for clouds and dirt and bugs and any shifting buildings."

Dennis and Ezra watched the kids fight with one another all the way over to the Blue Hole.

"You'd make a horrible dad," Ezra said cruelly.

"Where'd that come from?" Dennis asked.

"I just think, based on your personality and looks."

"Thanks," Dennis said, laughing.

"I was being serious," Ezra demanded.

"Someday you might actually be glad I was around." Dennis smiled.

"I don't see that ever happening," Ezra ranted. "Now, let's get back to the motel. Tomorrow's coming."

"I'm aware of that," Dennis said.

"Maybe your IQ is changing."

Dennis walked down the road heading back toward their cheap motel. It was a mild day and the traffic and town seemed slow.

The motel was right off of the main road, and when they finally got there, Terry and Addy were inside Dennis's room waiting for him and the person they called "toothpick." But unlike the hundreds of times Clover had affectionately called Geth *toothpick,* Terry and Addy had no affection for Ezra whatsoever.

"It's about time," Terry whined. "We've been sitting here for over half an hour."

"Sorry," Dennis said. "We didn't know you were waiting."

Ezra rolled his eye at Dennis.

"No regard for our time," Addy snapped. "No regard whatsoever."

"We were—" Dennis started to say.

"We were?" Terry complained. "Hear that, Addy? Suddenly it's we this and we that."

"Well, *we* are sick of it," Addy pouted.

"I'm not sure what you're talking about?" Dennis said.

"We've been thinking," Terry said.

"There's the problem," Ezra growled.

"You better keep quiet, toothpick," Terry said ominously.

"What's going on?" Dennis asked.

"We aren't sure we want any part of this," Addy said. "We're professionals; I had a job back in Oklahoma."

"And I was looking," Terry added.

"Sure, sure, your future was rosy." Ezra laughed.

"I'll snap you in three," Terry threatened.

"I'd like to see you count that high," Ezra spit.

Terry looked at Ezra with rage. Addy looked both disgusted and disgusting.

"You going to let a toothpick talk to you like that?" she barked.

"Hold on," Dennis insisted. "Let's talk about this."

"I ain't talking to a toothpick," Terry said. "We've made up our minds and we are going to take what we know and sell our story. Addy thinks she can get twenty thousand dollars from the *National Enquirer*—twenty thousand dollars."

"Money!" Ezra screamed. "Your vision's as puny as your brains."

"Twenty thousand dollars!" Addy yelled.

"You promised to help," Dennis tried.

"Terry never keeps his promises," Addy said proudly.

Terry nodded toward her. "That's true."

"What about Leven?" Dennis asked.

"Who?" Terry asked.

"Leven," Dennis said sadly. "The lake here could bring him back."

"I ain't sharing my money with that kid," Terry complained to Addy. "It's not his. He didn't do a thing to earn it."

"Oh no, no way," Addy insisted. "No."

"No?" Dennis said, suddenly reminded of his own horrible childhood. "Don't you want to find him?"

"That's the dumbest question I've ever heard," Addy said. "If we have the money, what do we need him for?"

Dennis's bald head was swimming. His insides felt sick and out of line. He could see himself as a janitor sitting in his small closet. He could see his parents, who had done so little to help him be more than he had turned out to be. He could see Terry and Addy writing off their responsibility for a few thousand dollars.

"He's your responsibility," Dennis said angrily.

"Who?" Terry asked again.

"All this talking's stupid," Addy barked. "We had the professional courtesy to tell you what we were doing and this is how you treat us?"

"There's nothing professional about you two," Ezra snipped. "Unless you're talking about the strength of your breath."

Terry reached out and snatched Ezra from the top of the dresser. Dennis tried to stop him, but he was too slow. Terry held Ezra up to his face and breathed his professional-strength breath on him.

"I ain't listening to a toothpick no longer," Terry seethed.

He pinched Ezra's head with his right thumb and index finger, and with his left hand he quickly and cruelly pulled off Ezra's tail.

Ezra screamed. Dennis jumped toward Terry to stop him, but Addy moved her big body between the two.

"What you gonna do, baldy?" she sneered.

"Put him down," Dennis demanded.

Terry held Ezra up and, as if the toothpick were a wishbone, he pulled both Ezra's legs and snapped his right leg off.

"No!" Dennis shouted as Ezra screamed.

Terry flicked the cursing toothpick to the ground and smiled. "We're out of here."

Addy moved to leave and Dennis lunged at Terry, hitting him in the face. Terry fell back onto one of the beds and bounced to the floor. Dennis found Ezra under the desk and picked him up carefully.

Addy helped Terry up much less compassionately.

Terry and Addy stood at the door looking back in at Dennis.

"You're lucky I'm a man of restraint," Terry said, holding his chin. "I'll tell you this, I don't want any part of you or Leven. I could go the rest of my life without ever caring a single second about your well-being."

Addy nodded in agreement.

"We did more than the average person would have done for that boy," Addy sniffed. "We can't save the world."

Addy opened the door and she and Terry self-righteously walked out of Dennis's and Ezra's life forever.

Unfortunately for them, fate was about to offer up a very short forever.

CHAPTER TWENTY-FOUR

THE JOURNEY OF A HUNDRED FEET

The shatterball game was down to three players—two Pidgins and one Pawn. The glass sphere was swaying like a pendulum and there were three large cracks in three separate spots. Everyone in the Meadows was stamping and screaming and throwing small white balls at the sphere.

"Stay low," Geth said. "And tell me when you feel time shift again."

Leven could see Azure more clearly now. His right ear was red, swollen, and bleeding slightly, the blood mixing with his long, dark hair. On his face he wore an expression of complete smugness. Azure lifted a clay stein and took a long, deep drink.

Leven pulled his own hood closer around his face and held Winter's hand tightly as they moved through the wave of spectators.

"This is bad," Winter said. "We have no idea how much is happening when time stops."

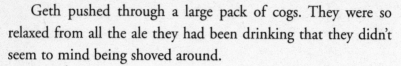

Geth pushed through a large pack of cogs. They were so relaxed from all the ale they had been drinking that they didn't seem to mind being shoved around.

Leven looked to the game and watched a Pidgin hit up against the wall. The sphere was pelted with thousands of white balls.

"He did it again," Leven said. "Time shifted."

They stopped behind a wagon where a cog was selling roasted pieces of warm meat smothered in dark cheese and folded into thick, soft pieces of splotch bread. The delicious smell was distracting to both the nose and the stomach.

"How come I can feel time stop?" Leven asked Geth.

"You're becoming the Want," Geth whispered. "Azure can pause time, but he can't stop what's changing in you. Your body must feel that gap in time he's creating."

The three of them moved to just below the stone bleachers leading up to Azure's seats. A woman selling sticky apples was standing between them and a clear view of Azure.

"He stopped time again," Leven whispered.

The two Pidgins zipped around the Pawn and slammed him into the wall. The glass cracked further, but the gigantic sphere was still holding together. The Pawn pulled away and grabbed the black pit as it bounced up at him. He shoved it into the small hole at the top and the score scrolled across the side of the glass sphere.

As the pit dropped back into the court the Pawn spun and flew backward into an opponent. Caught off guard, one of the

Pidgins was blown into the side and fell helplessly from the sphere.

The crowd was now clapping in rhythm and throwing anything they could find at the glass arena.

"They have no idea what's happening," Geth said sadly.

The two remaining players shot toward the far side of the sphere. The Pawn twisted and clamped his legs around the Pidgin's. He rotated and slammed the Pidgin up against the glass.

A crack began to split from the impact and rip down and under the bottom of the glass sphere. Small shards of glass rained down like glitter on the field but the ball continued to hold together.

The spectators all over the Meadows were out of control.

The Pidgin hooked the Pawn with his arms as he flew over him. He flipped the player around and then with full force of flight slammed him backward into the glass wall.

"We have to keep moving," Geth said.

Leven felt time stop. The feeling made his knees buckle.

He closed his eyes and the world was silent.

He opened his eyes and found himself standing in a completely different place. It was quiet and the sound of a small fire popping could be heard. Azure was sitting in front of him in a large chair covered in white roven hide. The room was dark and a tiny fire was burning in a round stone oven off to the side.

The shock of being in one place one moment and somewhere completely different the next was jarring, but it was

Azure's current actions that caused Leven much greater concern.

In his left hand Azure held Clover by the neck. Clover hung there limply as Leven tried to register what had just happened and what to do next.

CHAPTER TWENTY-FIVE

How Sycophants Die

The word *thing* is an interesting word. At first glance it looks like the front half of one word combined with the last half of another. It's a versatile word. It can be good, as in, "what a nice thing," or, "she has a thing for you." Or it can be bad, like, "the thing under the bed," or "here's the thing, you're fired and you smell bad." Add an "s" to the back end of it and it becomes something that most people in the world can't get enough of.

Things.

People love things. They collect things. They store things. They cherish things and then move on and cherish other things. People also buy things. Some buy a lot of things simply because their neighbors have those same things—which is a weird thing if you really think about it.

It's remarkable what we'll do for the sake of things when in reality things couldn't care less about us.

Leven possessed very few things, but he cared for a number of them. One of the things he cared most for was Clover, and at the moment things did not look good for his friend.

The small fire in the stone oven lit only the center of the square room. It was cold and there was no sign of natural light anywhere. The floor was dirt and the ceiling was higher than the firelight reached. Azure was sitting in a chair with his legs crossed. He uncrossed his legs and stood up, holding Clover by the neck.

Clover shivered pathetically, keeping his eyes closed.

"Put him down," Leven insisted calmly.

Azure scratched his ear with his free hand.

"Release him," Leven reiterated.

"Giving orders, are we?" Azure smiled darkly. "I think you're in the wrong position to do that. You see, the person from the position of strength calls the shots."

"Put him down," Leven said again.

Azure looked at Leven and laughed.

"You know," Azure said, "I am surprised by one thing. I mean, you're obviously inexperienced, but I was under the impression that Leven Thumps was a small boy. You're taller than I was expecting, which means you've probably had more than your fill of turmoil and experience here—growing so rapidly. "

"Put Clover down," Leven said, stepping forward.

"Ah yes, Clover." Azure sighed slowly. "I had forgotten the name of Antsel's beloved sycophant—Clover. You know, Leven, I must admit I always found it disgusting that Antsel cared for this

thing. But Antsel's dead. And now this dirty wad of hair is yours."

Clover blinked.

"Where are we?" Leven demanded. "Where are Geth and Winter?"

"They're fine for the moment," Azure said coldly, his voice the sound of freezing water. "They're still right where they were, blissfully unaware that time's standing still. I must say, I was surprised. One moment I'm enjoying myself, watching the game, and the next I have someone's pesky sycophant attempting to bite me."

Azure lifted up Clover and looked him in the closed eyes. He petted Clover on the head.

Leven shivered.

"Did you send him to harm me?" Azure asked innocently. "And here I was hoping we could be friends. Do you even understand what's happening?"

"You're showing your strength by picking on a small sycophant?" Leven said sharply.

Azure scratched at his infected ear, trying not to look bothered by what Leven had said.

"Are you aware of how powerful distraction can be?"

Leven stared Azure down.

"We are closer now than ever before to bringing about the meshing of Reality and Foo. So close."

"That ought to make your master happy," Leven said.

Azure flinched.

"It's no secret that you're just a tool for the Dearth," Leven said.

Azure closed his eyes and inhaled. He picked at his ear.

"The Dearth is an ally in this battle to free Foo," Azure sniffed. "I am a tool for nobody."

"If that makes you feel better," Leven said. "You have turned your back on fate and are the worst example of a lithen there could be."

"Geth has gotten to you." Azure laughed. "You sound like his parrot."

"Geth fights for the dreams of everyone," Leven said. "Not just the selfish desires of a few."

"Stop talking," Azure insisted. "You have no idea what the Dearth is capable of and how close we are to achieving it."

"You won't succeed."

"I take it back. You are a child," Azure mocked. "I'm disappointed, Leven. In fact, I'm so bothered by all of this that I'm tempted to kill both Clover and you and be done with it. But the Dearth wants you alive for some reason, and he will be here soon to deal with you personally."

Leven was silent.

"So," Azure sighed quietly. "I guess Clover's death will have to do for now."

Leven laughed.

"You find that funny?" Azure asked.

"You can't kill Clover," Leven said strongly.

"Oh," Azure smiled wickedly. "That's where you're so wrong."

Leven closed his eyes and breathed in and out slowly.

"You know," Azure went on, "there has been one thing that has kept us from reaching Sycophant Run—that silly secret. We've spent years trying to find it and here you stumble into Foo and find it for us."

Azure held Clover up and shook him.

"The Dearth knows many things. And there's no way to mesh Foo with Reality while the sycophants selfishly keep us from reaching their shores."

Leven tried to look calm, but his heart beat wildly in his chest.

"It's quite simple, really," Azure said.

"I don't know what you're talking about."

"Shhh, shhh, shhh," Azure said, holding his finger up to his lips. "Quiet now, Leven. I can't stand to have the air filled with needless child blather. Why should Clover's last moments be occupied by fruitless talking? You doubt what I know. How's this? There are three steps to killing a sycophant."

Leven stared straight ahead.

"Let's see, first you distract his mind from Foo and his burn. I've found metal to be the most effective distraction."

Azure pulled out a silver rod from his cloak. It was twelve inches long and polished, with small round ends. Azure held it up to the firelight and its glint was almost blinding. Azure stood the rod on the edge of the stove. It shone like a fluorescent lightbulb.

Clover's eyes focused on the rod.

"Second, hold the sycophant by the nape of his neck. It relaxes the poor creature. I guess fate's concerned about them being comfortable if they do happen to get killed."

Azure held Clover up by the nape. Clover hung there silently, smiling and staring at the metal rod. He looked like a cat being lifted by his mother.

"Look how content he is," Azure hissed, petting Clover cruelly.

"Put him down," Leven commanded.

"Third, and this is where it gets painful," Azure said. "You know the first two steps are so calm—almost pleasant. Distract them, relax them, and then . . ."

Azure slowly pulled something small from his cloak. He held whatever it was tightly in his free hand.

"Do you know why sycophants always return to Sycophant Run to die?" he asked.

Leven was silent.

"Perhaps you don't know," Azure said. "After all, you are relatively new to Foo. Let me explain. Sycophants do all that they can to make it back and pass away on Sycophant Run. Do you want to guess why?"

"This isn't what you want to do," Leven pleaded.

"Wrong, that's not why." Azure smiled. "And for the record, this is exactly what I want to do. All those lovely histories and stories about how dedicated sycophants are to the land in which they were born. You know, when I hear too many sweet stories I get suspicious. They return home to die because it's comforting,

but most important, because it leaves all of their bones safely on Sycophant Run."

"What do you want from me?" Leven asked. "Why even worry about Clover? Set him down and we'll talk."

"We're already talking," Azure pointed out. "I'd hate to think of what would happen if someone were to get ahold of some sycophant bones and create thousands of tiny shards capable of piercing the center of a sycophant's heart. How does the secret go?"

Azure opened his hand to reveal a sharp sliver of bone. He stepped closer, repeating the complete secret. The fire grew as he spoke.

"Distract their minds from Foo and fear, hold fast the nape alone, with accuracy the heart you pierce, found dead by the bone of their own."

Azure held the bone shard in front of Clover.

Clover disappeared.

"You don't know anything," Leven said calmly. "You're forgetting the fact that sycophants can go invisible. What good is distracting them if you can't see them?"

Azure laughed. "Of course. Many have suspected and guessed at just how Clover's kind can die. Some have gotten close, but always lacking was the way to overcome their invisibility."

Azure waved his hand in front of Clover's invisible face.

"Two words," Azure whispered. "Alderam Degarus."

Clover materialized and Leven gasped.

"And there he is," Azure said soothingly. "Just like magic. The

Sochemists say the words translate to 'Only the trees live on.' Of course, how would they know, seeing how it's a language that none of us are aware of? Supposedly it belongs to the trees."

Leven's knees buckled. He caught himself and put his hands to his stomach. "How?"

"Your very brain leaked the secret as you stood stock-still below the Devil's Spiral. Whoops. So much for their immunity," Azure smiled. "Now as we distract thousands, the Dearth steps closer to controlling all of Foo and all of Reality. The sycophants will be wiped out like a disease. And to think we couldn't have done it without you. Thanks for standing still long enough to ruin your friend. Now, I'd finish you off here if it weren't for the Dearth's wishes. So I suppose I'll let you suffer from a distance."

Azure dangled Clover out in front of him, facing Leven.

"Say good-bye, Clover."

Leven's eyes flashed brilliantly, lighting the room and blinding Azure. Enraged, Leven leapt forward and grabbed Azure's wrist while reaching for Clover.

There was a second flash, and instantly Leven was back at the Meadows standing on the far edge and feeling as if there was no hope left anywhere in the world.

CHAPTER TWENTY-SIX

Killing Me Softly with Blinders On

Tim was hopeful. For the first time since falling into Foo he believed that getting back to Reality and seeing his family again might actually be possible. The armies of Azure were large and so determined that it seemed as if they could tackle and overcome almost anything.

His heart felt lighter than it had at any other point in Foo. Tim also understood that so much of what he felt came as a result of Swig's kindness. Not only did the little sycophant speak and behave in a way that made Tim comfortable, but the mere act of having a sycophant helped his mind and soul blend into Foo. It was a remarkable thing.

In the short time Tim had known Swig, he had come to count on him. In fact, there was a small part of Tim that was beginning to

worry about what might happen to Swig if Tim did make it back to Reality.

"Are you okay?" Swig asked from Tim's right shoulder.

"I really am," Tim replied.

"I'm so happy to hear that."

Tim reached up and patted Swig on the back.

"You might want to walk faster," Swig said. "Osck is getting away."

Tim smiled and quickened his pace. The armies of Azure were moving. They had been granted permission to travel closer to Cusp to wait for the soil in the gloam to settle. But the whispers and speculation in camp indicated they were moving closer to capture Cusp and squelch the last stronghold of unbelievers.

Tim looked out over the vast group of undulating soldiers. The sight was awesome and a bit frightening. He quickly caught up to Osck.

"How many people are there?" Tim asked Osck.

"People?"

"Fighters?"

"Thousands and thousands," Osck said proudly. "Rants have even come down from behind the pillars. Now walk faster. We must make good time."

"For what?" Tim questioned.

"For war," Osck said, marching even faster.

"You're certain there'll be war?"

"I am counting on it," Osck replied. "I wish to be whole. I

wish for Janet to be whole. We have no future while we are kept locked up here in Foo."

Osck looked back at Janet, who was walking twenty feet behind.

"But what if Reality doesn't change you?"

"I don't even think such things," Osck said. "We must walk faster."

Tim shook his head as Osck moved away.

"I hope I'm doing the right thing," he mumbled to himself.

"Don't worry," Swig comforted.

"Yeah, don't worry, you are," Janet replied. "Sorry to listen in to you talking to yourself, but we're doing the right thing."

"How can you know?"

"I trust Osck," she answered.

"But you love Osck."

Janet looked at Tim as she walked quickly.

"I do," she admitted, more to herself than to Tim. "So you can't love the people you trust?"

"No, I'm just saying that maybe your judgment is skewed."

"Maybe it is," Janet smiled, realizing that her old self would have flown off the handle after such a remark.

Tim looked at Janet as she lifted her large legs to march.

"Can't you just drift?" he asked. "I mean, do you have to actually walk?"

"Yes," Janet said with a trace amount of bitterness. "You'd think I could fly, seeing how there's nothing to me."

"Strange place," Tim said needlessly.

"Reality will smooth out its edges," Janet said sincerely.

"I just don't want it to ruin it," Tim said. "It must be important."

"How could it ruin it?" Janet asked. "We will just make both better."

"And do you think we'll really fight Cusp?"

"I do," Janet answered. "Osck said so."

"What's with these?" Tim asked, taking a small blue band out of his pocket. "They've given them to almost everyone but I don't understand why. Aren't they blindfolds?"

"There's no direct killing in Foo," Swig said, clinging to Tim's left shoulder. "In order for someone to die, it must be an accident. The blindfold allows you to swing your sword and accidentally kill."

"That's horrible," Tim gasped. "And absurd."

"It's the way of Foo," Swig replied, sliding down Tim's back and settling on the front of his right shoe. "The largest wars fought many years ago over metal were all fought blindfolded."

"Going into battle with your eyes closed?" Tim said, disgusted. "It's foolish. What if I hit someone on our side?"

"It happens," Swig said. "But the sight chiefs call out and keep most of the fighters in check."

"I can't kill someone," Tim said. "Especially not while being blindfolded. It's one thing to stand up and confront evil, but I don't even know if this is the right cause."

"Do you want to see your family again?" Janet asked.

"More than anything."

"And I want to see Winter," Janet said. "I want to hold her. I want to beg her to forgive me. But we'll never be able to do those things unless we stop those who are keeping us locked up."

Janet pumped her fat legs faster in an attempt to catch up to Osck. Tim marched silently until Swig spoke up.

"Do you need me to say something?"

"What?" Tim asked.

"Is there something you would like me to say?"

"About what?"

"You're worried," Swig said. "I want to speak the words you need to hear."

"I don't just want to hear what I want," Tim said. "Sometimes the words you need to hear are the hardest to listen to."

"I don't understand," Swig said, confused. "How bad must life be to not feel better when told you look handsome or beautiful? Or that you're the most wonderful person alive?"

A line of black skeletons ran quickly past Tim and Swig, their dark bones clicking as they jogged.

"Sometimes it's okay to worry, Swig," Tim finally said.

"Not if I'm doing my job right."

"You're doing it perfectly," Tim said kindly. "I just don't want to do anything that isn't right. It's one thing to make mistakes that hurt only me, but it's a whole other thing to embark on something that might change or destroy another person's existence. I don't know what to do."

"You look handsome," Swig tried.

"I'm lucky to have you," Tim said, laughing.

"It's not luck," Swig said seriously. "It's fate."

Tim looked around him. The sky was yellow with red streaks running through the bulk of it. White hazen filled the air, making all kinds of interesting and complicated shapes and patterns. Behind Tim thousands and thousands of beings marched forward bravely—all of them hoping that by overtaking Cusp and finding a way out they might be more than they were now. In front of Tim were thousands more with the same wish and ambition.

"Come!" Osck yelled from up ahead. "Come, Tim. Walk with Janet and me."

"They're yelling for you," Swig pointed out.

Tim jogged to catch up.

CHAPTER TWENTY-SEVEN

THE GLASS BREAKS

Leven looked around anxiously, wondering where Azure had just moved him from. One moment he was looking at a doomed Clover and the next he was here. He didn't recognize the part of the Meadows he was now standing in—it was flat and there were no visible structures. The crowd was thinner and less aggressive this far out. Leven could see the four gigantic trees holding up the glass court in the far distance.

"Azure!" he screamed, knowing it would do no good.

Leven took off running through the crowd. It had been some time since he had felt so helpless. Clover's life was being threatened and he didn't even know where he was. Sweat was running into his eyes as his dark hair clung to his forehead. Leven was sick of running, sick of cruelties, and sick to death with worry that Clover might be hurt.

Leven pushed people aside, tearing through tents and

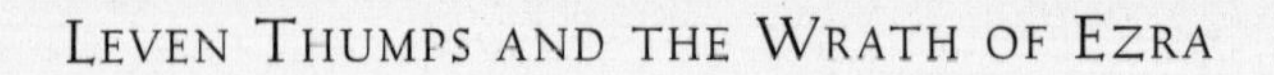

gatherings on his straight path to Geth and Winter. A fat cog with huge arms and legs saw Leven coming and stood his ground. Leven plowed him over, never missing a beat.

"Out of my way!" Leven yelled. "Move!"

Leven reached the tightly packed area of spectators circling the huge trees. The glass sphere glowed in the light of the shifting sun. Leven looked toward the seat Azure had occupied earlier and was surprised to see Azure sitting there. Leven ran faster, looking directly at him.

Azure's eyes caught the motion of Leven tearing through the crowd. He looked over the spectators and directly at him.

Leven stopped.

Azure nodded and then smiled the greasiest, most sinister and uncaring smile Leven had ever seen—and Leven had seen Terry, Addy, and Sabine all smile before. Leven's heart became a knot of cold stone and hot fear.

He pushed through the throngs of people and up behind Geth and Winter. They were both looking at Azure, and Geth was speaking. They seemed completely unaware that Leven had even been gone.

"If we move to the other side of the seats we can approach him from behind," Geth said.

"No!" Leven yelled. "He knows we're here and he has Clover!"

"What?" Winter asked. "What are you talking about?

"He knows we're here and he has Clover," Leven repeated frantically. "I was here and then I wasn't. He stopped time and now he has Clover."

"Can't Clover just . . ." Winter started to say.

"He knows the secret," Leven said urgently. "He was going to kill Clover seconds before he moved me back."

Geth didn't need to hear more—he sprang onto the stone seating.

It's conceivable that Geth might have gotten to Azure before he could instruct time to pause again. It is also conceivable that Geth might have even been able to restrain Azure and put an end to it all. Sadly, no one will ever know, because at that same moment the last Pawn slammed the last Pidgin into the wall and the entire ball shattered like a bomb, blowing glass all over the Meadows like stinging snow.

The crowd was worked up into a state of near insanity.

In the emotion of the moment almost nobody noticed the thousands of blue-robed soldiers spilling into the far side of the Meadows. Organized in squared-off sections, they poured endlessly onto the scene. The rants in front wore blue blindfolds and were swinging metal swords. They marched forward thrusting their weapons at an even level.

Hundreds of nits and cogs were struck down before the crowd even realized what was going on. Countless spectators lost their lives in the first wave of attacks. The back of the Meadows began to rise as avalands barreled beneath them.

Azure stood up from his seat and smiled. Six rants quickly escorted him away.

"Azure's leaving!" Geth yelled. "And his troops are coming."

The ground beneath Leven vibrated. He grabbed Winter and

pulled her toward him. Winter's legs clipped Geth's and he tumbled into them.

"There are avalands below us!" Geth yelled.

The three of them slid backward, slamming into a food wagon and sending hot meat and cheese everywhere. Leven's head hit a collapsing section of stone seats.

A tall black skeleton swinging a metal double-edged sword jumped from the back of an avaland and landed in front of Leven and Geth. He clicked his teeth and screamed. Leven looked around for a weapon of his own. Before he could react, Winter kicked the skeleton's legs out from under him, causing him to fall forward onto his own sword. The weapon slashed the sinew holding the top half of the skeleton together. Bones scattered.

Leven and Geth looked at Winter in awe.

"Thanks," Leven said.

"Don't mention it." She smiled.

Winter pulled the sword from the half-skeleton. The skull yelled obscenities at her as she stripped him of his weapon.

"Nice mouth," Winter said.

The ground beneath them continued to crack and split. All over, innocent nits and cogs were falling down into the craters the avalands were creating. Those who weren't being dragged under were just standing there motionless.

"Can you hear that?" Leven asked.

"What?" Geth yelled.

"The ground," Leven said. "It's speaking, yelling almost."

Geth looked around at everyone as they stood there doing nothing.

"It's the Dearth," Leven said. "He's holding them still."

"Keep moving," Geth ordered. "Don't stand still."

Winter was standing like a statue.

"Pick her up," Geth said. "Find stone to stand on."

Waves of blue soldiers continued to crest over the far edge of the Meadows and spill onto the crowd—a thick stream of fiery echoes following behind them. Avalands popped up from the dirt like small mountains. The fear and surprise were setting off hundreds of emotion-filled Lore Coils. Leven's head was crammed with screams and shouting as the coils rippled through him.

"We've got to get off the field!" Leven hollered.

He pushed through a wall of motionless nits and broke into a run, carrying Winter over his shoulder. Geth was right behind him.

"What are you doing?" Winter yelled as her head cleared.

"Saving you again."

"Put me down," she demanded. "I'll save myself."

Leven set Winter down.

The whole area was teeming with rants. Creatures and beings Leven had never seen before marched in dutiful lines, looking to accidentally take the lives of anyone in their way. Behind each group of blindfolded fighters there were two beings chanting and guiding them into areas where they should attack.

A lifeless cog was lying on the ground.

Leven looked at the cog and breathed deep. His neck and face burned. Leven turned and ran, barreling down a rant and knocking him into another, causing an entire row of assailants to fall like dominos.

Legions of roven flew overhead in patterns. Screaming, they dropped buckets of burning liquid on organized spots as hot-air balloons tried to drift away, or caught fire.

Those who weren't held fast by the voices beneath the dirt began to recognize what kind of danger they faced. Some picked up kilves and rocks and waged a counterattack. Those who had gifts used them to fight, freezing assailants and pulling lightning down from the sky.

A large group of half-frozen rants squirmed and screamed on the ground as those nits who could burrow dove beneath the soil. Any nit who could levitate objects tried to toss around stones and kilves, but the forces of Azure's army were so vast and swift.

A troop of black skeletons were struck with lightning, their dark bones glowing with electricity. A few nits had used their gift of shrinking to shrink down. It was a foolish idea, as they were easily trampled.

An avaland with two black skeletons on its back rushed past Leven and burrowed under the ground. Dirt sprayed up and over them in large, heavy waves.

The weather was no longer making any sense. The suns were bouncing around in the sky as clouds drifted in and began to spray rain over everything. The thunder and lightning joined in and the temperature was rocketing up and dropping rapidly.

"What's up with the sky?" Leven yelled.

"Azure's messing so heavily with time he's thrown everything off!" Geth yelled back.

A small moon pushed its top up and ducked back down below the horizon. The light of the sky flickered like film running through a projector as the suns surged.

Leven moved to run but was stopped by Geth's hand on his arm.

"We've got to find Clover!" Leven hollered.

"Of course," Geth said. "But running into the troops might not be the best course of action. Fate might need *him* to save *us* if we did that."

"What do we do?" Leven yelled.

"Stand still," Geth said.

"Nice plan," Leven criticized. "No wonder Azure doesn't want to be a lithen."

"No," Geth explained. "Try to feel where Clover is."

"I'm no sycophant," Leven reminded Geth. "I don't have that skill."

"But you *have* been connecting with creatures," Geth said.

"Try it," Winter ordered.

The scene was so horrific and chaotic. Noise and weather were shooting around like fireworks. Those few nits who had previously been playing shatterball were now flying through the air fighting for one side or the other.

"I can't think straight," Leven argued. "My gift's not working."

"Where's Clover?" Geth asked calmly.

"You're not listening."

"Where's Clover?" Geth asked again.

Leven closed his eyes, more out of disgust than agreement. The noise around him softened. He could hear voices that belonged to dreams he couldn't yet see. He could feel the cries and fear of some animals caught in the battle. He could see a thin beam of light shoot into the sky. Leven's thoughts shifted and he could see images of himself and Winter woven into that light. The light began to descend and the beam angled so as to blind Leven.

Leven held his hands up to block the light. His eyes flashed

open and noise rushed back into his head like angry traffic. Leven could still see the faint line of light. It shot out across the field and into the distance.

"That way," Leven pointed.

"Nice," Geth said excitedly.

"Follow me!" Leven yelled.

Leven jumped over two short stone walls and dove against the back of a rant who was pummeling a cog. The rant flew to the ground, his body skidding across the grass. Leven put his

right foot down on the rant's right wrist and yanked the kilve from his hand. In one swift move that seemed to surprise even him, Leven swung the kilve backward and came down with the thick end on top of the rant's head.

The rant just lay there moaning on the ground.

"Did you see that?" Leven said, impressed with himself.

"See what?" Winter asked, holding two kilves.

Leven turned to see two rants lying on the ground.

"Don't worry," Winter insisted. "You'll get better."

Winter tossed one of the kilves to Geth, who was smiling.

"Her attackers were smaller," Geth tried to help.

Leven shook his head and grinned. "Come on."

The three of them pushed through the field swinging their kilves and moving quickly across the ground. After a few hundred feet it was obvious how much more skilled Geth was. He swung and moved his kilve as if it were a part of him. He thrust it forward, catching rants under their chins and lifting them off the ground. Then with a flick he sent them flying.

Leven and Winter gladly let Geth take the lead.

Geth was like a kilve master. He twirled the kilve, clipping six enemies, and then thrust it down and sideways, knocking two more out cold. Leven tried to imitate the moves but he never had quite the same result.

Geth's ability attracted some attention. A huge avaland moved in from the right side, carrying two black skeletons on its back. The skeletons held tall, thin staffs in their hands. Their staffs were longer than kilves, and so thin they looked fragile.

One of the skeletons thrust his staff downward. The weapon took on the characteristics of a whip and wrapped around Winter, binding her. Leven grabbed hold of Winter and pulled, yanking the black skeleton off the avaland. The second rider jumped off toward Leven and Winter. Leven twisted his kilve and pulled it backward, catching the skeleton in his bony stomach as he descended. The kilve sliced through and bones scattered everywhere. The skeleton's head tumbled, still cursing at Leven.

Winter was trying to free herself as the other skeleton got to his feet. Geth's kilve came down on top of him from behind. The bones clattering against each other sounded like a dull wind chime.

The skeleton's head rolled to the side and it tried to bite Leven on the ankle. Leven kicked it away, sending it flying into the back of a fighting rant.

The avaland the skeletons had been riding, turned to face Leven. It opened its huge mouth and dirt billowed out. Winter backed up, but Leven stood still. The dirt beast lowered its head.

"Get on it," Geth said. "The creature trusts you."

Leven jumped up and grabbed ahold of the growth protruding from the avaland's forehead. He scaled the face of the beast and sat where he had seen the skeletons perched. Geth and Winter followed him up and sat behind him, gripping the vines and roots that covered the avaland's back.

Leven looked up and could still faintly see the beam of light pointing him toward Clover.

"Ride," Leven commanded.

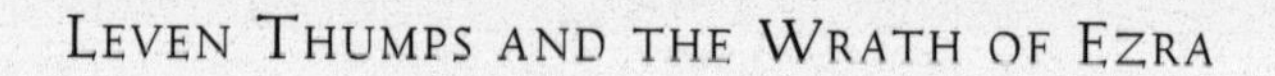

The avaland roared across the meadow, bowling down anyone or anything in its way.

"This is much better!" Winter yelled.

The balloons overhead were dipping and lifting in an effort to avoid the lightning and weather. Leven could see wave after wave of rants spilling over the hill and into the Meadows. Leven's heart sank as he looked out over all those who now lay silently on the ground.

All around, innocent nits and cogs were beginning to surrender. It was obvious they were no match for the endless armies of Azure.

"They're giving up!" Winter cried. "I can't believe it."

Leven shifted, and the avaland seemed to connect with the faint beam of light Leven could see. Up ahead were thousands of rants all packed together tightly and swinging metal weapons.

The avaland parted the mass of assailants who tried to jump on its back and pull off its passengers. Winter kicked a rant in the face and sent him hurling back down into the crowd. Geth held his kilve like a lance and took out a handful of enemies with one forceful jab. Leven threw his kilve like a spear and managed to tag two.

Up ahead the edge of the field met a high stone wall, creating a dead end. The faint beam of light Leven saw seemed to pierce the stone. The avaland continued toward the cliff at full gallop.

"They can't go through stone!" Winter yelled, holding onto Leven. "Make it stop!"

"I can't!" Leven called back.

"Make it turn," Geth suggested.

"I can't make it do anything," Leven cried. "Either we jump, or we're . . ."

Before Leven could finish his sentence the avaland bucked and then dove headfirst down into the soil. They held on tightly as the great beast wormed its way under the ground. Dirt rumbled overhead and pushed the three of them tightly against the avaland.

It was dark, but light broke through as another avaland crossed their path from a different direction. The air was filled with dirt and hard to breathe. Leven could feel his lungs struggling to find enough oxygen.

The avaland moved into a large underground cave. Like a saving gift, air rushed around the three of them and they all gladly breathed deeply.

Torches lined the cave walls and Leven could see dozens of large tunnels with avalands moving in and out of them. The beast they were riding on ran up a steep, stony slope and into a massive cavern.

All three of them gasped in awe and amazement.

The cavern's ceiling was covered with bright flecks of gold, and stone archways circled its edges. A great fire burned in a blue clay pit in the center of the room and smoke filled the air in patterns of stars and sunbeams. Around the fire were massive piles of metal weapons guarded by black skeletons.

Leven, Winter, and Geth rode through the room undisturbed. So many avalands were moving in and out that no one noticed the three of them. They hugged their ride as tightly as possible, hoping to blend into the back of the beast.

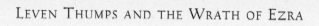

A rant with a massive left side stood at the far edge barking out orders. All around the cave stood small cottages. Some looked to be growing out of the sides of the cave and others were stacked on top of rocks or tucked down in tunnels. Most of the small cottages had fires burning in them that lit the windows like oval stars.

"I didn't know this place was here," Geth said excitedly.

"You sound happy that it's here," Winter whispered.

"I am," Geth replied.

"Clover should be here," Leven said. "I can feel it."

"Is he alive?" Winter asked.

"I hope so," Leven said, wanting more than anything to believe it.

The avaland stopped at the opening of another cave. Leven slid off its back and Geth and Winter followed. The avaland was blocking anyone from seeing them. They were trapped between two small cottages—one was lit, the other was pitch-black.

"Stay," Leven said, not exactly sure how to talk to the beast.

The avaland grumbled and collapsed on the ground, blocking the doorway and keeping them hidden.

Light flashed on in the dark cottage and Leven could see a streak of blue move through the front of the house.

"Azure," Geth said needlessly.

Through the front window they watched Azure drag a little man across the floor. The man, Time, collapsed on the ground, and Azure stood over him speaking.

"What's he saying?" Winter asked.

"If I could hear through walls, I'd tell you," Leven answered.

Geth was already moving to the front of the cottage. He tried the door and then signaled to Leven and Winter that it was locked. He motioned that he was going around the other side. Leven and Winter then moved around their side, meeting up with Geth at the back.

The back of the cottage was dark and ripe with mold and rot from the cave's dampness. Luminescent ivy grew thick and dense across the rear wall. The back door was locked, but thanks to the rotted door frame Leven was able to easily and quietly push it open.

They carefully stepped inside. The back door led to a small hall and the hall opened into a dark kitchen. The kitchen was filled with old fruit and vegetables. A dead duck hung from a hook near a broken window.

The three of them crouched down and moved through the kitchen. They could hear Azure talking.

"You still have work to do!" he yelled. "You're not done."

"I'm done," a weak male voice replied. "I can't do more."

"You were rewarded greatly," Azure said. "You can't be done. You are required only to sit still."

"I *am* sitting still, and yet time continues to move," the weak voice said. "My time has passed."

"No!" Azure shouted. "One more stop. The Dearth's disappointment isn't a pleasant thing. I must finish them off, and we have no influence over your successor. He keeps time even now and avoids the soil."

The sound of someone falling against the floor could be heard. The three moved around a short wall to get a better look. Azure was standing over the small, nearly lifeless man. Azure kicked him and the little man let out a final moan.

Azure sniffed and tugged at his mangled ear.

"It's over," Geth said, stepping forward and showing himself to Azure.

"How—" Azure sneered.

"Where is he?" Leven interrupted, not caring about anything but Clover.

"Where is who?" Azure barked.

"Where is he?" Winter said, ignoring him.

"I'm not sure what you're speaking of," Azure said, stepping back.

"Clover," Geth clarified. "What have you done with him?"

"Clover? What a fool you are, Geth," Azure seethed. "A lithen with no vision. Reality has made you dispassionate and pointless. Foo and Reality are about to combine, we'll have endless power, and yet you're worried about a single sycophant?"

Geth delivered a perfect hit to Azure's face. Azure stumbled backward, catching himself by bracing his hands against the wall.

"Where is he?" Geth said.

Azure rubbed his chin. His face was already swelling.

"He has to be close by," Leven said angrily. "You couldn't have taken me far."

"I think it's probably too late." Azure smiled, spitting blood. "Poor Clover."

"I don't believe it," Leven raged.

Azure stood tall and pushed his hair back. His infected ear was bulbous and bleeding and his blue eyes were as hard as granite.

"Do you know where you are?" Azure asked.

"I don't . . ." Leven started to say.

"Of course you don't," Azure said. "Do you know what's about to happen?"

Geth pushed his blond hair out of his face. The two lithens locked eyes.

"Do you realize what would happen if I called out?" Azure asked. "Thousands would descend upon us and simply wipe you out. You have tricked fate by stealing in and out of Foo. You are not invincible. I, on the other hand, might have to endure a few more of your weak right jabs, but I will live to see you die."

"We only want Clover," Leven tried to reason. "What good is he to you?"

"Alive?" Azure questioned. "Not much. Dead? Well, his bones would provide hundreds of shards to silence hundreds of other sycophants, and thus make our journey onto Sycophant Run and through the caves that much easier."

"Is there no reason left in you?" Geth asked. "Have you forsaken all thought and decency?"

"Nice words," Azure said. "But I simply saw the way things were going and hitched a ride with the greater power. The Dearth will rule both Foo and Reality and I'll know power like no other lithen has ever experienced."

Winter looked bored. She shook her head and scoffed.

"You have something to say about that?" Azure asked, bothered.

"What a couple of idiot men," she said. "You and the Dearth make quite a pair. You realize that if he were to take over Reality, you would eventually wither away and die?"

"That's lithen lore," Azure sniffed. "Man will continue."

"Are you sure?" Winter asked. "Are you confident that when the Dearth gets his way there will be any life for you?"

"Shut up," Azure said, scratching violently at his ear. "Shut up. You understand nothing."

"I'm thinking it's you who is confused," Geth said. "Come on, Azure. It's not too late. Zale held you in the highest regard. You can still save Foo."

"Your brother Zale is dead," Azure barked. "A lot of good it did him to fight for Foo."

"He died with honor."

"I'd rather live with reward."

Azure rocked back and forth on his feet and then lunged forward, head butting Leven without warning. Leven dropped to the ground and Geth jumped over him, giving Azure chase.

Azure ran out of the front of the cottage and into the cave. Winter leaped at him and Geth ran directly into her. They went down in a heap of blond hair and limbs. Leven stumbled over both of them as he dashed to the front door. They all exploded out of the cottage and stopped short.

Azure stood smiling at them, fifty rants behind him. They all

held kilves and all had blood in their right eyes. Geth and Winter held up their own kilves in defense. Winter blew her hair out of her eyes and sighed.

"I wish I could say I was surprised," Leven said.

"Think we can take them?" Geth asked.

"I'm usually up for a fight," Winter replied. "But maybe they'll take us to Clover."

Leven was the first to put up his hands in surrender. Geth and Winter dropped their kilves and followed suit. Three rants moved in quickly behind them and bound their arms. Then, in a not-so-gentle fashion, Leven, Winter, and Geth were escorted away.

CHAPTER TWENTY-EIGHT

PALMS UP

Trouble is a tricky thing. At its most intense it can be incredibly dangerous, and at its least it can be bothersome. Being in trouble is bad. Getting out of trouble is good and is often the subject of some touching after-school TV special starring a boy who wears sweaters and a girl with a barrette in her hair. Some people are trouble. Perhaps you know someone with a scar on his cheek and a leather vest who doesn't wipe his feet on the mat before coming inside. That's trouble. Some people seek trouble—they are called trouble junkies or peculiar. For these people their lives just don't seem to work unless something is going wrong or they have something troublesome to complain about.

People like that are the exact opposite of sycophants.

Sycophants seek nothing but happiness. They believe the very oxygen they breathe has the potential to make them happier. Even as Rast and Reed walked across Sycophant Run on their

way to a troublesome task they had interest and wonder in their worried hearts.

"This really is exciting," Rast said reflectively. "I mean, if you think about it, we're making history."

"I suppose that's true," Reed answered. "But making history isn't always a great thing."

"We've nothing to fear," Rast reminded Reed. "It's not as if it will kill us."

"That's true," Reed said again. "I wonder why I'm nervous?"

"You're always nervous," Rast joked.

The dirt path they were walking along descended into a field of lush green turf and white glassy flowers that shone like marbles under the sun.

The field ran into a thick stretch of fantrum trees. Once through the trees, Rast and Reed arrived at the edge of a great chasm. Hundreds of feet down, at the bottom of the chasm, the orange water of the Glint River was running strongly.

The Glint River divided most of Sycophant Run from a small portion near the Hard Border. The chasm between the two sides was about a third as large as Fissure Gorge and was rumored to have once been a part of that gorge during the creation of Foo. The walls rising up from the river were covered with ivy and squirming, shifting moss. The moss moved up and down the walls in waves.

Glint Chasm was a beautiful, spectacular, dangerous place that most sycophants never traveled to—and if they did, they rarely, if ever, made it past the point where Reed and Rast now stood.

"I haven't been out here for years," Rast said.

"It feels like the edge of Foo," Reed replied seriously. "Except for the fact that we can see the other side. So what now? There's no complete bridge."

"This way," Rast waved, walking on a thin trail that ran along the edge of the chasm.

After about two hundred feet the trail stopped. Rast looked to his left, then to his right.

"Lost?" Reed asked.

"I don't think so." Rast listened to the wind streaming out of the chasm. "There are no birds out."

"Should there be?"

Rast shrugged and stepped off of the trail and into the long grass at the edge of the forest.

"There it is," Rast said, relieved.

"There what is?"

Rast pointed beyond the grass to a thick tree stump. The stump rose above the soil no more than an inch. The top of the stump was covered with moss. Rast stepped up to it.

"Shoo," he waved, motioning the moss to leave.

The moss hissed and crackled but eventually slid off of the stump and into the grass.

"I was worried I had brought us to the wrong spot," Rast said.

"I was just worried," Reed halfway joked.

The rings of the tree could be clearly seen on top of the old stump. Rast counted five rings in and pressed down. The sixth

ring sank into the stump about an inch. Rast counted in three rings from that and rubbed the wood.

The center of the stump popped open and a dank, dirty smell escaped.

"You first," Reed insisted.

Rast smiled and stepped up on the wide tree stump and then down through the open center of it. The opening led to a vertical tunnel with small wooden pegs sticking out of the wall. Rast climbed slowly down the pegs. Reed followed right behind him, closing the stump as he entered.

It was dark, but a small amount of light came from below them.

"Is that an opening?" Reed asked.

Before Rast could answer they had reached the light and dropped down from the wood pegs. They were now in a huge, open cave that looked out into the chasm. The cave was bigger than a large warehouse and its floor was covered with straw and leaves.

"Who lives here?" Reed asked. "I feel so small."

"Birds," Rast replied. "Really big birds. Here they come."

Rast turned to see a gigantic red bird swoop down into the chasm and dive straight for the cave. Reed moved back against the wall. Rast stood up straight, trying not to appear frightened. In comparison to the bird, the two sycophants looked no larger than a couple of worms.

The bird screamed, and its call echoed forcefully off the stone walls as it drew closer to the cave.

"Should we be scared?" Reed yelled.

"I'm trying not to be!" Rast yelled back.

A second bird with bright yellow feathers trailed the red one. The lead bird landed in the cave, scratching its large talons in the straw as it came to a stop. It turned its big head toward Rast and Reed and looked down its beak.

It blinked.

"Well, well, it's been many years," the bird said, its voice as big as its size. "We have seen no sycophants near our chasm since Geth and his brother Zale were here with their visitors."

The second giant bird fluttered to a stop in the cave. He looked at Rast and Reed and then, as well as a creature with a beak can, he smiled.

"How fantastic!" the yellow bird exclaimed. "Who knew this day would offer up something as interesting as visitors?"

"Things have been kept in check," Rast said. "But now we have need to visit the marsh."

"Two sycophants," the red bird said. "No lithen to guide you."

"There aren't many lithens left," Rast said sadly. "Can you lift us across?"

"How sad," the red bird remarked. "We would be happy to take you across, but we do not tote just any sycophant."

Rast lifted his small left hand and showed the birds his palm. There, clearly for the birds to see, was a dark star. Rast moved his hand from high to low, imitating a shooting star. Rast then looked at Reed, and he did the same.

"Two points of the star," the yellow bird said. "Very impressive."

"Can you take us to the marsh?"

Both birds nodded respectfully. The red one lifted his right talon and waved Rast over. Rast climbed onto the talon. The red bird closed it, securing Rast inside. Rast looked as if he were in a round cage as the red bird balanced on one foot. Reed stepped up to the yellow bird and climbed into his left talon.

"Ready?" the red bird asked.

"Very," Rast replied.

"What a bright day," the yellow bird chirped. "It makes all the difference to have something to do."

Both birds screamed and then shot from the cave out over the chasm. Unlike Fissure Gorge, the air in the Glint Chasm was open and clear. The birds dove straight down and spun upward, darting across the chasm.

The wind howled as the sound of birds screeching and two sycophants laughing it up filled the air.

Rast would have been happy to ride in the talon of the great red bird forever. The sky was cool and the bird was having some fun with his task—diving up and down and blasting through hazen. Unfortunately, there was no time to spare.

Rast spotted the short trees on the edge of the marsh. He sighed and then felt his stomach drop as the bird descended. He could see Reed and his bird to the right. The ride had placed a wide smile across Reed's normally worried lips.

The two birds skimmed across the top of the short trees and

out over the marsh. Hundreds of rivers and inlets ran like spider veins through the vast orange marsh. Rast spotted the circular river and knew the red bird was headed right toward it.

"I can't land," the bird warned loudly. "My talons stick to the mud."

"I understand!" Rast yelled back.

The red bird got as low to the ground as possible, and as soon as he was over the circular section of water he opened his right talon and let Rast fly all by himself.

Rast splashed into the water with a tremendous "thwap." He could feel water going up his nose, and his legs and arms burned from rubbing up against the marsh grass. He hit a muddy bank and stuck to the side like a 3-D carving. He opened his eyes and witnessed Reed making his landing.

"Thwap."

Reed bounced on the surface of the water and back up into the air. He screamed and flailed and then splashed down only a few feet from Rast. He struggled in the water trying to find his footing. He crawled up onto a wide, flat rock and shook water from his head and body.

"Reed," Rast called.

Reed looked around, confused. "Where are you?"

"Right here," Rast said. "Pasted to this mud bank."

Reed kept searching but still couldn't see him.

"Talk some more," Reed suggested.

"What do you want me to say?" Rast complained. "I'm right here in front of you."

"Ahhh," Reed said, swimming across the few feet of water and up to Rast. "Are you stuck?"

"Very."

Reed clawed at the mud and pulled Rast's right arm free. He pushed his feet up against the muddy wall and yanked. Rast popped off and into Reed's arms.

"Thanks," Rast said awkwardly.

"I didn't know they were going to just drop us," Reed complained.

"I wanted that to be a surprise."

Rast jumped into the water and washed himself off. He climbed out into the thick marsh and tried his best to shake himself dry.

"Where now?" Reed questioned.

"That way," Rast pointed.

Reed followed closely behind as Rast worked his way to the center of the circular growth.

"I'm no longer sure this is the best idea," Reed admitted.

"No longer sure?" Rast laughed. "You've been against it from the start."

"Well, I've always had well-thought-out opinions," Reed said seriously. "So what if it's not there? So what if it is there? What difference does it make?"

Rast stopped. "I guess I'm hoping it's been destroyed. The land has shifted, and time has been long. I'm not sure how something so fragile could last."

"Good," Reed said. "It must be ruined. Now let's go back."

"I need to know how it is," Rast said. "We let the key get away; I won't be caught off guard by this."

"So it's to protect *you* from possible embarrassment?" Reed asked incredulously. "We're treading out here so you won't have egg on your face?"

"So *we,*" Rast said, spreading his arms, "*all* of us, won't have egg on our face."

"I don't care if I do," Reed argued. "In fact, I like eggs."

"What have we been taught since our births?" Rast asked.

"Many things," Reed replied, frustrated.

"Since the first sycophant opened its eyes we have been taught that without us Foo will fail. Those are not just words."

"Of course not," Reed agreed.

"The secret was compromised, and now the Dearth seeks to get out of Foo. I can't let that happen."

"You're going to break it?" Reed said frantically. "You're going to break the map?"

Rast was silent.

"But that's . . . I don't believe it," Reed said.

"I said nothing," Rast whispered.

"Exactly," Reed replied. "That's what scares me the most."

Rast began walking again and Reed reluctantly followed. They reached the center of the circular marsh. The grass was so thick it was hard to see anything but orange. Rast moved the grass around until a single stalk that was lighter than the others stood out. Rast grabbed ahold of the stalk. It was coarser and much denser than the other orange grass.

"That's it?" Reed asked.

Rast nodded.

"Pull it," Reed suggested.

Rast gripped the stalk of grass with two fingers and tugged it three times to the right. The grass slipped out like a loose string. The spot where it had been began to unravel in a circular pattern. The marsh twisted and dropped like a large spiral staircase—steps of green growth and solid stone plummeted hundreds of feet.

The two small sycophants stepped back from the growing opening. The entrance began to expand rapidly, the stairs and steps becoming wide slabs of stone that an army could easily march down. Rast and Reed continued to move away. By the time the opening stopped growing it was the size of a football field, with hundreds of mammoth steps that spiraled downward into darkness.

Rast and Reed peered over the edge.

"You first," Reed insisted.

Rast smiled and jumped onto the first wide step. He ran across it and jumped down to the next.

"Are you sure about this?" Reed called out.

"Positive," Rast called back, already four more steps down. "Come."

Reed moved onto the first stair and, much more gingerly than Rast, jumped down to the second.

"I'm coming!" Reed yelled.

Rast was too far down to hear. Reed picked up his pace.

CHAPTER TWENTY-NINE

Nothing Justifies the End

Tim Tuttle felt like he was trapped on a deadly roller coaster. The armies of Azure were flowing onto the Meadows and wiping out anything that stood in their way. Hot-air balloons were dropping from the sky as they burned, and lightning and rain exploded everywhere.

Tim had on a blue robe and held a rusted sword that had been buried in soil for hundreds of years. Osck was up ahead swinging his sword, willing to take out anyone who tried to stop him. Tim, on the other hand, was looking for some way to get out of the operation. Each moment caused him to feel more and more uncertain about his decision to join this side of the fight.

The blindfolded rant in front of him screamed.

At first Tim had refused to wear a blindfold. But those around him had gently insisted. He did so, but only after making two small holes in his so that he could see out.

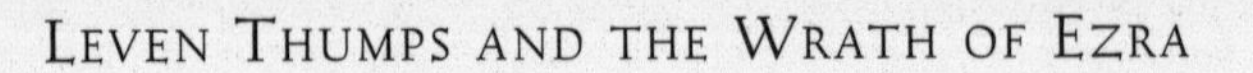

Janet was running with Tim. She had been unable to keep up with Osck and her face was red and sweaty, but her gaze was solid and determined.

"This can't be right!" Tim yelled to her.

"It has to be!" she shouted back.

"Why?"

"Because Osck is an honest man."

"Osck isn't even a man," Swig pointed out.

Janet winced. "You don't know what you're saying."

"He's right!" Tim yelled. "I think you know it, too. This isn't our fight."

"It will be when they break through to Reality," she hollered. "We would be forced to fight then."

"Maybe so," Tim shouted. "But this is wrong!"

"Even if it is, it's too late now."

"It's never too late," Tim insisted.

"I can't betray Osck," Janet said.

"You won't betray anyone by being just," Tim said. "Look around—this is wrong. I'm here to help Winter, not to kill people."

The basket of a hot-air balloon crashed down directly in front of Tim. Tim flew over it, falling to the ground on his face. He pulled himself up and looked back. Inside the basket was a small man wearing a green robe. The man lay there moaning as hundreds of rants swirled around him. Tim fought the stream of rants and worked himself back to the basket. He knelt down and put his face up to the man's to listen for life.

The man breathed weakly.

"Hold on," Tim said.

Tim pulled the man out of the basket and wrapped him around his neck like a gangly shawl. He then ran crosswise against the crowd. Rants batted them around as Tim just tried to get out of the way. A metal spear flew past him and he watched it pierce the ground.

Tim moved into the space between a large boulder and a fallen tree. He laid the balloonist down and checked for signs of life. Tim slapped him lightly on the face.

"Come on," Tim pleaded.

"You might want to hit him harder," Swig suggested.

"Is he alive?" Janet asked.

Tim turned to find Janet looking down over his shoulder.

"What are you doing here?" Tim asked.

"I can't do this," Janet admitted. "I must have changed. There are so many dying. What if one of those being cut down is Winter? This isn't making me whole, it makes me feel even emptier."

Tim was silent.

"Is he alive?" she asked again.

"He's still breathing," Tim said.

The balloonist groaned and his eyes fluttered open. He screamed as if the moment called for it.

"It's all right," Tim said. "You're okay."

"Who are you?"

"I work for the Iowa Sanitation Department," Tim said out of habit.

"Oh," the man blinked.

"Stay with him," Tim told Janet. "Make sure he's okay."

"No way," she said. "He'll be fine. I'm going with you and Swig. I didn't leave Osck to sit by this man . . . no offense."

"None taken," the man grunted.

"When you find Winter I want to be there," Janet insisted.

"Okay," Tim agreed. "We'll run with the armies, staying to the edge and keeping our eyes open. It's not much of a plan, but I suppose we'll test this fate that Foo is always speaking of. It's probably best that we not admit our lack of allegiance."

Tim helped the man get comfortable and then turned to Janet.

"Ready?"

"No."

"Good, neither am I."

Janet actually smiled.

The two of them and Swig charged out of the hiding spot and back into the river of rants and soldiers surging across the Meadows.

Tim held his sword in front of him and peered out of the holes in his blindfold. The surge began to slow as all over nits and cogs were giving up. Many of them fell to the ground and were being bound up by soldiers.

The armies of Azure continued to shoot burning arrows up into the hot-air balloons. Lightning hit one of the four tall trees and split it in half. The tree cracking made the thunder seem like a whisper. All around, Lore Coils exploded as beings suffered and

experienced moments of intense fear and tragedy. Tim could hear voices and cries floating across the Meadows in a horrible cacophony.

"Stay to the side," Swig kept yelling. "Stay to the side, Tim!"

Rovens were now landing on the field, herding the surrendering nits and cogs into groups. There were also many wounded and lifeless rants littered about.

"You've got to look like you're fighting," Swig said.

Tim swung his sword around, looking very much like a garbage man pretending to be a pirate.

Three avalands roared across the path, circling around other nits. Horns began to blast, signaling the fall of Cusp. The armies of Azure were spilling into the streets of Cusp as those in their homes locked their doors and hoped it would all just go away.

The conquerors destroyed homes, cut the ropes for travel, and ruined anything that might bring the citizens of Cusp comfort. Other soldiers shifted position and began to march toward the gloam.

"I can't believe they did it!" Swig yelled. "Cusp has given up without a fight."

"I hope Osck is okay," Janet cried.

"Keep running," was Tim's only reply.

There were still troops marching around the Meadows and securing their prisoners. Tim and Janet reached the side of the Meadows near the stone cliffs. Hundreds of soldiers were marching down through tunnels created by avalands.

"Where are they going?" Janet yelled.

Before Tim could answer, the rants they were marching with turned and headed into a tunnel, dragging them along.

"I guess we'll find out."

Tim pulled off his blindfold and kept in rhythm with those marching. After about two hundred feet the tunnel sloped upward and into a massive cavern. Piles of weapons were scattered about and small fires burned in more than a dozen different fire pits. Little cottages dotted the rocky cavern walls and soldiers were drinking from small springs and gathering weapons.

Tim peeled away from the group and ducked behind a weathered cottage with a moldy thatched roof.

"What is this place?" Tim asked.

"I have no idea," Swig answered. "It's not on maps."

Across the way a tall black skeleton addressed a cluster of rants.

"Go see what he's saying," Tim said to Janet.

"Me?"

"They can't hurt you," Tim reassured. "I need you to listen in."

Janet moved across the cavern toward the group. She stepped up to the skeleton's side. He looked bothered that she was there, but he kept talking.

"Some spy," Swig said from Tim's shoulder.

Tim watched Janet's face light up as she listened. She leaned in closer and the skeleton brushed her away. More soldiers began to move in as groups of other soldiers moved out. Janet ran back to Tim.

"Leven's here," she said breathlessly.

"And Winter?" Tim asked.

"He didn't say," she answered. "But Leven has to know where she is, right?"

"You would think so," Tim said thoughtfully. "Where is he?"

"He didn't say. He just said that Leven was locked up and that Azure was dealing with him. He also said that most of the army was now going to head to the gloam and march to Sycophant Run."

Swig gasped.

"What?"

"They're marching to Sycophant Run," she repeated. "And he also said some words I couldn't understand."

"Do you need to go?" Tim asked Swig.

"Where would I go?" he answered.

"Are your people in trouble?"

"You're my people," Swig said.

"Amazing creatures," Tim said kindly.

Swig looked proud.

More soldiers marched out.

"Let's find Leven," Tim said, concerned. "We'll worry about the rest of the world falling apart when we get to that point."

Swig disappeared and Janet drifted behind.

CHAPTER THIRTY

THE BIONIC TOOTHPICK

A large, square magnifying glass was propped up on the motel desk. A tall gold lamp shone down and lit up the desktop. Dennis was sitting in a chair leaning over the magnifying glass and breathing slowly. Beneath the magnifying glass, a weak, deformed Ezra lay in pain.

"Hold on," Dennis said. "I've just got to remove this."

Dennis pulled off the small, bent sliver where Ezra's tail used to be.

"Owwwwww!" Ezra screamed. "I thought you were helping me."

"Hold on," Dennis insisted.

Dennis cleaned off the flaky green nail polish where Ezra's right leg had once been.

Ezra winced.

"Sorry," Dennis said.

"I could have taken him," Ezra said angrily.

"Right."

"Don't patronize me," Ezra growled. "He took me by surprise, and you did nothing."

"He took me by just as much surprise."

"Well, way to have my back."

"Do you want me to fix you or not?"

Ezra answered by panting shallowly and blinking his single eye under the bright light.

"Good," Dennis said.

Dennis took a silver paper clip out of the desk drawer and straightened it out. He clipped it in half and then bent one of the ends with a small pair of tweezers. He twisted the bent end around Ezra's waist and pinched it closed, creating a new metal leg. Dennis bent the leg slightly at the knee.

"Are you done?"

"Done," Dennis answered.

Ezra rolled over and pushed himself up with his thin, nail-polished arms. His new leg was stiff and made it hard to stand. He spun in a circle until he caught hold of the edge of the lamp and could pull himself up.

He balanced on his new metal leg. He couldn't bend it, but he could lift it with his hip and step forward. His new appendage made a soft clicking sound.

"Not bad," Ezra said happily. "It makes me look interesting."

"You actually didn't need help in that department," Dennis said. "You're a living toothpick with purple hair and a green body. That's interesting enough."

"Still," Ezra said. "Maybe I should break off my other leg and arms and replace them with metal. I'd be a more imposing world ruler if I were all metal."

"I wouldn't suggest that," Dennis said.

"That only makes me think I should do it more."

Ezra stomped across the table and jumped onto Dennis's arm. The bottom tip of his new leg snagged Dennis's shirt and he had to tug at it to get it free.

"You'll get used to it," Dennis said.

Ezra leapt from Dennis's arm to the floor and began to run around in small circles to break in his new leg.

"Thanks," Dennis said sarcastically.

"You're not welcome," Ezra replied, picking up his pace. "*Thanks* is what someone says when they have a limited vocabulary. This leg makes me even more certain that I will be triumphant. How could I fail when I'm half machine?"

"More like one-fourth," Dennis corrected.

"Leave it to you to ruin a perfectly good conversation by applying math to it."

Ezra's new leg got stuck in the carpet. Dennis bent down and picked him up.

"Would it kill you to file down the end a bit?" Ezra asked.

Dennis held Ezra back under the magnifying glass and opened the file on his Swiss Army Knife. With short, methodical

strokes he filed down the sharp edge of Ezra's metal leg.

"There," Dennis said, pulling Ezra out from under the magnifying glass. "It shouldn't snag on anything now."

"I wish your word came with a guarantee," Ezra scoffed. "I'm certain that right when something crucial is happening I will get snagged again."

"Thanks for your faith in me." Dennis laughed.

"I have no faith in you," Ezra said seriously.

"Thanks."

"Limited vocabulary," Ezra sniffed.

Dennis set Ezra down on the bed. Ezra jumped up and down a few times and then reclined against the edge of the pillow.

"Can I be honest with you?" Dennis asked.

"I wish you wouldn't," Ezra answered.

"I know you have nothing but acid and insults for me, but I am so much happier to be here than where I once was."

Ezra put his hands to his ears to block out Dennis's talking. "La, la, la, la."

"I don't know what to believe in all the time," Dennis went on. "But I remember working in that law firm and feeling as if there was nothing for me. I would wander those halls like a ghost that nobody could see. I thought I was one of those people who would walk the earth and die without purpose. I remember thinking that if I choked to death in my apartment nobody would even notice until the rent came due and my landlord came looking for it."

Ezra rubbed his eye and moaned. "Why won't you stop talking?"

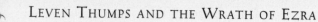

"Say what you want," Dennis said, waving it off. "But there's something between you and me. There's a reason why I ordered that sandwich and you were sticking up in it. I think I believe in fate. I never would have thought I could accomplish something great, but now I know that before I die I will play a part in something big."

"You've been watching too much daytime television."

"Say what you want."

"You're a fool."

Dennis stared at Ezra.

"What? That's what I wanted to say."

"I'm not doing this to make you happy," Dennis said. "I'm doing this because I know that in the end I will have had a part in something larger than I could have ever dreamed. And, I've grown attached to you."

Ezra started to weep.

Dennis smiled. "There, that's the emotionally unstable toothpick I know."

Ezra turned over and cried into the pillow.

"Listen," Dennis said, "I'm sorry. If we're going to do this we have to have a plan."

"I have a plan," Ezra sniffed.

"Let's hear it."

Ezra sat up and ran his hand through his purple hair.

"People like things that are interesting," Ezra said. "So we'll put up a large tent to meet in, and we'll call you Today's Wizard."

"Today's Wizard?" Dennis said. "That's your plan?"

"It's a work in progress," Ezra scoffed. "I have more."

Dennis pulled out a pad of paper from the motel desk and grabbed the cheap pen next to it.

"Shoot," he said.

Ezra began to explain.

ii

The dark of night dripped down like melting plastic. It stuck to the roads and buildings and made walking and driving seem like more of a trial than usual. The neon signs and headlights in view shone no more than a couple of inches from their source.

The interstate was fairly empty, with more vehicles heading east than west. Terry sped quickly westward in the far right lane.

"Is it supposed to be so dark?" Addy asked. "What sort of people live in a place like this?"

"Dark is dark," Terry reasoned. "We got bigger problems. Why won't they pay?"

"They don't believe us," Addy grimaced. "They sit there in their big offices with nice haircuts and tell me things they think I don't understand."

"That makes no sense," Terry sniffed.

"They won't give us any money unless they see you float," Addy snipped. "We gotta drive to them and let them inspect us. Nobody trusts nobody these days."

"Then they'll give us money?" Terry asked. "Once they see me float?"

"They'd better," Addy said. "We should take care of that robe."

"I ain't going to hurt it," Terry said. "I like wearing it."

"You should take it off," Addy insisted. "Keep it in a box or something for safekeeping."

"I'll think about it," Terry said, bothered. "They'd better give us enough money. Otherwise we could have stayed with that bald guy."

"And share our money with Leven?" Addy asked. "No way. It would be just our luck to have him come back and start whining about us taking care of him. He's still too young to just leave on his own. And the courts are always siding with the children."

"We'll get our own lawyer," Terry said. "That boy already cost us thousands of dollars to raise. He should pay us."

"You might have something there," Addy said excitedly. "All right, if he asks for money we'll threaten to collect what we've already spent on him."

"Even if he doesn't ask," Terry suggested, "let's see if we can collect. You didn't ask to take care of him. He was thrust upon us."

"I shouldn't have to pay for having a big heart," Addy said indignantly.

"I'll say you shouldn't," Terry spit. "This isn't Russia."

"We might have a real case," Addy said greedily. "And when we win we'll have more money than we've ever had. Now take that robe off so it doesn't get ruined."

"I'll take it off next stop."

"Just take it off now," Addy demanded, pulling on the right sleeve. "We'll get no money unless you float."

"It's fine," Terry complained. "I'll take it off later."

"Just pull it off now." Addy tugged.

"I'm going seventy miles an hour."

"Just slide it off behind you."

Addy grabbed at the robe, pulling Terry's arms back and yanking the robe. Terry's hands slipped from the wheel and the car swerved. Terry lunged for the wheel, but Addy was still pulling and he fell toward her.

"We should have stopped first!" Terry yelled.

It's difficult to believe, but for once in his life Terry might have been right. The car swerved the opposite direction as Terry slammed his foot on the gas pedal by accident, barely missing a stray dog that was foolishly crossing the interstate. Unfortunately, Terry couldn't avoid hitting something far more substantive.

CHAPTER THIRTY-ONE

THE CANDOR BOX

The caves and caverns beneath the cliffs were vast and confusing. All around, troops of soldiers and black skeletons were marching and moving avalands and prisoners out of the caves. Leven and Geth and Winter were taken to a large metal cage in a small cavern. They were thrown in, locked up, and left alone.

"I can't think of anything but Clover." Leven stood up.

"Me neither," Winter admitted.

"He's exactly where he should be," Geth said, trying to comfort them.

"What's that supposed to mean?" Leven argued.

"Careful, Lev," Winter said. "He didn't mean anything."

Leven looked at Winter with frustration. He couldn't tell if he wanted to yell at her or kiss her. He knew also that his feelings toward Geth were largely due to Phoebe's presence.

"You have to trust that Clover's life will lead to good," Geth

said. "There's nothing I would like more than to make sure Clover is safe, but I would be a scoundrel if I promised you that fate might not have other plans for him. He has already helped change the world, something quite spectacular for a sycophant. Who knows what his life—or death—might still accomplish."

The words were harsh, but coming from Geth they sounded so sincere that Leven couldn't help but mellow.

"I know," Leven said, sitting down on the floor with his legs crossed. "I know you're right. But it's Clover."

"Well then, breathe deep and put some pressure on fate to come through."

Leven took a deep breath as a tall, normal-shaped rant stepped up to the cage. Two other rants were behind him. Leven stood again.

"The girl," the lead rant grunted.

"No way," Leven snapped. "Winter stays here with us."

The rants laughed.

"I didn't realize that you were the one giving orders," the lead rant said. "The girl, now."

"I said—"

One of the rants hit Leven in the chest with the thick end of his kilve. He flew back against the far bars and fell to the ground. Geth tried to move forward, but one of the other rants had reached in and pulled him up against the bars.

The lead rant opened the cage, grabbed Winter by the arm, and yanked her out. He slammed the cage and locked it.

"We'll be back for one of you later," he threatened.

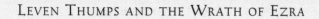

"You can't just take her!" Leven yelled.

"Really?" he growled. "Because that looks to be exactly what we're doing."

The rants walked off with Winter, leaving Leven and Geth alone.

"We have to do something," Leven said.

Geth began checking the bars for any that were loose or designed to open. The floor of the cage was cement and the ceiling was stone. Leven shook the door but it didn't budge in the least, thanks to the lock on its front.

"Can lithens do anything besides think optimistically?" Leven asked, frustrated. "Don't you have a secret power or something that can help?"

"What about you?" Geth asked less harshly. "Can't you get the avalands to bust us out?"

Leven closed his eyes and tried, but nothing happened. He slumped dejectedly to the ground on his rear.

"It doesn't work," Leven said. "They won't hurt her, right?"

"I hope not," Geth answered. "Winter's strong."

"And pretty," Leven said without thinking.

"What?" Geth smiled.

Leven looked shocked. "I didn't mean it. I was just thinking . . . it's that stupid longing. I'm saying things I don't mean."

"Don't call Phoebe stupid," Geth said seriously. "She's a longing."

"Oh yeah, I forgot you've got a thing for her."

"I don't have a thing for her," Geth insisted. "Longings and

lithens have a long history and I just think that she and I would have a lot in common."

"And Winter and I wouldn't?"

"I'm not saying that."

"Just so you know, Winter and I have been through a lot," Leven said. "I knew her for days before you ever met her in Reality."

"Well, Phoebe would understand me," Geth argued, his eyes showing that he was as confused by what he was saying as Leven was. "Hold on, she's . . ."

Geth put his hands up and took a deep breath.

"What?" Leven asked.

"I just think that Phoebe and I have much more of a chance than you and Winter."

"Why?" Leven asked. "Because you're both so old?"

"Just because we're ageless is no—"

Leven stood up and charged into Geth. The two of them rolled across the floor and banged up against the metal bars. Leven's head hit the bars hard, causing him to see stars for a few moments.

Geth stood up, reached his hands down to help Leven up, and started to laugh.

"It's not funny," Leven insisted.

"I know," Geth said. "I'm sorry."

Leven sat up and rubbed the back of his head. "Your girlfriend is making things messy."

"I like the sound of that," Geth said.

"You're not acting very lithen."

"Weird," Geth said in a daze.

"Listen," Leven sighed. "We've got to find a way out of here. Or neither of us will ever have a girlfriend again."

"The cage is solid," Geth said. "We might . . ."

They could hear the sound of footsteps approaching. The rants stepped out of the shadows, pushing Winter forward.

"Winter," Leven said with way too much enthusiasm.

"Step back," the large rant said. "Or we'll knock you back."

Leven and Geth stepped to the rear of the cage. The rant opened the door and threw Winter in.

"You." The rant pointed at Geth.

Geth looked at Leven and Winter and then stepped up to the open door. The rants pulled him out and slammed the door closed on Leven and Winter. They marched off into the darkness with Geth.

Leven knelt down by Winter.

"Are you okay?" he asked.

"Fine," she said. "They didn't do anything but ask me questions."

"Who asked them?"

"Azure," Winter answered. "There was this booth and it makes you tell the truth. I apparently know nothing that they care about. They want to know about the key."

"Oh," Leven said, looking into Winter's green eyes. "The key."

Leven and Winter simultaneously backed up and away from each other.

"Listen," Leven insisted. "It's probably best that we talk about things that are nonemotional. Phoebe's got everything all messed up. I actually attacked Geth."

Winter laughed. "You attacked Geth? Why?"

"Well . . . that doesn't matter."

"Who won?"

"I don't know; it was confusing."

Winter brushed her hair back behind her ears and Leven felt light-headed. He held onto his side of the cage as if his life depended on it.

"So, a truth box," Leven said casually. "I was worried about you."

"That's nice of you," Winter replied. "Actually, I think the candor box has a lingering effect. I feel like I want to tell you things."

Leven fought himself for a moment and then blurted out, "What things?"

"I know that Foo is falling apart, that your father's alive, that Clover's in danger, and that people are dying all around us, but I can't stop thinking about that kiss—the accidental one."

"Me neither," Leven admitted.

"But we should forget it," Winter said sadly. "I mean, who would want to start out a relationship on false emotions?"

"Yeah, that's crazy," Leven agreed. "Who'd want that?"

"I mean, it's just Phoebe making us nuts, right?"

"Right," Leven said, letting go of the bars and stepping closer to Winter. "We're not children anymore. We should be able to act responsibly despite Phoebe."

"Right. I mean, you're Leven and I'm Winter, and we're responsible friends," Winter mumbled, moving across the cage.

"Good friends," Leven replied.

"Maybe even best friends," Winter said, closing her green eyes and leaning in.

"Best friends who once accidentally kissed and now are going to kiss on purpose."

"You're tall," Winter said happily.

"You're beautiful," Leven replied.

Leven leaned in and closed his eyes.

"Ahem," Geth cleared his throat on the other side of the bars.

Leven and Winter turned toward him with red faces. The rants had brought Geth back at a rather awkward moment. Some of the rants laughed.

"Back against the bars," the large one ordered.

The door was opened and Geth was tossed in.

"Come on, Romeo," the large rant joked.

Leven stepped out and the door was shut again. He was too embarrassed to turn back and look at Winter. He walked with the rants out of the cavern and into a high-ceilinged room next to it. The room, like the rest of the massive caves and caverns, was cold and dreary. Organ pipes lined two walls and a large, ornate organ sat in the middle of the far one. A cog with long gray hair and a tattered robe sat in front of the organ. His feet were chained to the base of the instrument. In the center of the room Leven noticed a wooden box about the size of a phone booth. Azure was standing in front of the box scratching his infected ear.

The rants pushed Leven into the room and Azure motioned for him to step into the candor box. Leven put up no fight. Azure closed the door and slid the bolt shut. At about neck level hundreds of holes created a screenlike opening to look out of. The organist began to play low notes—notes so deep and low Leven could feel them pushing at his soul.

"Why are you here in Foo?" Azure asked.

Leven was surprised to find himself replying, "Because Geth brought me."

The organist moved his fingers and a new set of low notes pushed up through Leven's body.

"Do you trust Geth?"

" . . . Yes."

"There's some hesitance in your answer," Azure said. "Why?"

The organ drew it out of him. "Sometimes I'm not sure he knows what we're doing."

Azure smiled. "Go on."

"As a lithen he's so happy with the present and the thrill of the future that I'm not sure he understands how scared I am."

Leven couldn't believe what he was hearing come out of his own mouth.

"You're much more forthcoming than the others," Azure said. "You killed the Want?"

"Yes."

"He was your grandfather?"

"Yes."

"Did you know this?"

"No."

The music coming from the organ was so low it was almost inaudible. But Leven could feel it working and massaging the truth from his soul.

"Where's the key, the one your grandfather gave you?"

Leven shook. "I'm not sure."

Azure laughed. "You can't fool the truth. What did you do with it?"

"I left it in the remains of Lith."

Azure looked shocked by the answer. "What?"

"It's buried with Lith."

"Impossible."

The music played even lower.

"The key your grandfather gave you. Where is it?" Azure yelled.

"Buried with Lith."

Azure's face burned a bright red, contrasting against his blue robe and eyes, but coordinating quite nicely with the blood dripping from his infected ear.

"You can't . . ." he started. But his tantrum was interrupted by the sound of gongs ringing through the caves.

Azure looked around, startled. Fear flashed across his eyes.

"The Dearth is whole," he whispered.

Gongs rang out in deafening choruses.

Azure looked at Leven in disgust. "What a stupid child you are."

Azure motioned for the large rant.

"Take him back to the cage and then gather everyone in the Sanatorium," Azure said with excitement. "The Dearth is whole."

Azure pulled Leven out of the candor box and pushed him into the arms of the large rant.

"Get him out of here," Azure ordered.

The rants marched Leven back to the cage and locked him up with Geth and Winter. Then without so much as a *good-bye* or a *see you later* they ran off.

"What's happening?" Winter asked. "Where are they running to?"

"And what's with the gongs?" Geth questioned, helping Leven to his feet.

"Azure said the Dearth is whole and apparently everyone wants to see him," Leven said, still feeling light-headed from the candor box.

"How heartwarming," Winter said.

"I don't want to see him." Leven shivered. "I've seen the Dearth at half strength. I can only imagine what he's like now."

The sound of trumpets and gongs and glad hollering rang throughout the caverns—shouts of Cusp being conquered and the Dearth being whole bounced off the walls like thousands of tiny Superballs.

"How do you think the Twit feels now?" Leven asked.

"If he's uncomfortable, then he probably feels bad," Winter said.

"He's most likely dead," Geth said seriously. "Azure has planned this thing out well, and if I were him I would have had the Twit taken out so that all of Cusp would be confused and weak."

"What did he ask you?" Geth questioned Leven. "In the box?"

"He asked about the key."

"And you told him," Winter said sadly.

"Kind of," Leven said quietly.

"Kind of?" Geth questioned. "I was in that box. There's really

no 'kind of' answer. I was glad I didn't know where you put it."

"Well, he asked me about the key my grandfather gave me," Leven whispered. "But my grandfather gave me two keys. So I told him about the one that we used to get Phoebe out with. He thinks it's buried in Lith."

"Brilliant," Geth said with awe.

"You know, if we hadn't gone to get Phoebe, that key would be with the sycophant key and I would have had to give it up."

"Wow," Winter said sarcastically. "And if you hadn't gone to get her none of us would be so emotionally messed up and crazy and wondering if we are ever going to feel normal again."

"So it's a trade-off." Leven smirked.

"It'll level out," Geth assured them. "It's just that there has been no longing for so long. The emotions of it will settle eventually."

The shouting and gong ringing began to soften and soon the cave they were in was as quiet as any respectable library.

"How long do you think they will keep us here?" Winter asked.

"Until they're done with us," Geth answered.

Winter hit Geth in the arm—hard.

"I'm just saying that's what I would do."

They heard footsteps approaching and were silent as Azure stepped into the cavern and up to the cage. He looked taller and even more sinister than before. His ear bled profusely and he wore a smug expression.

"There's someone who wishes to speak with you," Azure said.

There was no sound of footsteps, but in the faint light a shadow cast itself against the tunnel wall. The shadow grew taller as the visitor came closer. Winter moved toward Leven and they stepped back in concern.

The shadow grew taller still.

"It is my honor," Azure spoke, "to present the Dearth."

All three of them went pale.

CHAPTER THIRTY-TWO

SMALL, FEAR-FILLED HEARTS

Sycophants are a wonderful breed. Their kind support of those who are snatched into Foo gives so many hope and does volumes to keep the balance in Foo. But like anyone else, they can grow tired of their task and need a vacation or break from the burns they serve.

Fortunately for the sycophants, they have the ability to bite. All one has to do is to sink his teeth into his burn, and the poor nit will fall to the ground, knocked out until the sycophant chooses to bring him to. Considerate sycophants always make sure to bite their burns only when absolutely necessary, and always in the privacy of their burns' homes. That way the poor nits can lie there blissfully dreaming about how great sycophants are without anyone noticing. It's not uncommon, however, for a sycophant to simply get fed up while out in public and bite his or her burn there and then, leaving the poor person to lie on the

side of the road or on a bench for days until the sychophant comes back.

If you look around Foo carefully it's not hard to spot a number of nits just slumped over in a field or under a tree waiting to be awakened.

A lot of sycophants use their "me time" to travel back to Sycophant Run, or to just catch up on sleep. But a number of sycophants spend their time at one of the few hidden hostels scattered around Foo—secret spots where sycophants can hang out and relax without a single nit, cog, rant, or being taller than they are. There is a popular hostel up above Fté and a nice one near the green pond. But one of the most frequented hostels is hidden in the trees near the edge of the Swollen Forest and the Veil Sea. There are hundreds of small tree binds to stay in and a gigantic sycophant-size tavern and park. Normally the hostel was a happy place where sycophants gathered to be themselves and rest up. But as Brindle entered it now, it seemed anything but happy and relaxed.

Sycophants were running in all directions, collecting their things and fussing over what to do. Groups of them were gathered around tables, and the tavern door was open, allowing moans and groans from unhappy sycophants to escape.

Brindle had walked through the park carrying Lilly over his shoulder. He was tired and thirsty and in need of rest. He entered the noisy tavern and sat down at a table with dirty mugs on it. He propped Lilly up in the chair next to him.

A frantic sycophant in an apron ran past.

"Excuse me," Brindle said. "Can I get a drink?"

"Not from me, you can't," he said. "I'm leaving."

Brindle stood up and walked to the bar. A harried sycophant was trying to fill drink orders as fast as he could.

"Peach malt," Brindle said.

The sycophant nodded and kept filling drink orders.

"Hey, I know you," a skinny yellow sycophant said. "You sit in the Chamber of Stars, don't you?"

Brindle nodded.

A few other sycophants stopped talking and looked over.

"What can you tell us?" the yellow one begged. "What are we going to do?"

"About what?" Brindle asked, wishing his drink would hurry.

"About what?" a red sycophant cried. "The secret's out."

"Well then, there's nothing we can do about that."

"But we could die."

Brindle's malt was delivered. He took a long, deep drink and set down the half-empty mug. His cheeks warmed and his ears perked up. Most of the tavern was now waiting for him to say something.

"Listen," Brindle finally said. "Night always gives way to day. This is a dark moment in our history, but it is not something we won't survive."

"But they know how to kill us," a short green sycophant wailed. "The words are floating around on numerous Lore Coils. Morfit has printed the secret and has placed it in the library, claiming it is a document of importance—our death sentence, a

document of importance. Lobs are reporting those who are looking for bones and the locusts are whispering about the soil having reached our land."

Brindle took another drink and then closed his eyes.

"Please," he urged. "Keep your hearts light—this is a peak of fear, but potentially a period of great growth. I believe that we will not only be okay, but we will be better because of it."

Most in the tavern began to cheer and whisper happily.

"Be wise," Brindle added. "Stay far away from those who would do you harm."

"The gloam has connected to our home," a sycophant with an eye patch said. "The armies of Azure are beginning the trek, with the Dearth leading the way."

"I didn't say I'm not frightened," Brindle added. "But my heart is light because of hope. We must remember that without us Foo will fail."

"It's hard to believe that in a time like this," the yellow one mourned.

"And yet it is more true than ever," Brindle said.

"If we can't fight for fear of being put in a trance by metal—or worse yet, killed," a gray sycophant said, "then how do we stop them?"

"I believe it's up to Leven," Brindle said.

Brindle answered with such sincere conviction that he created a tremendous Lore Coil. Leven's name floated out of the tavern, through the hostel, and out over Foo.

"Let's be ready to help where we can," Brindle added.

He took a drink from his refilled mug. He wiped his mouth with the back of his hand, stepped over to Lilly, and threw her back over his shoulder.

"Who's that?" an orange sycophant asked.

"Nobody you need worry about," Brindle answered.

Then he smiled, wished them all well, and headed out.

CHAPTER THIRTY-THREE

THE END OF TERRY AND ADDY

Nobody likes bad news. It's never nice to be handed a piece of information that will ruin your day. Sadly, we all are told things we'd rather not hear at some point in our lives. You can try to hide from bad news, but it always finds you. Like a starving monkey who knows you possess the last banana on Earth, bad news can cling to you and scream incessantly. Even if the bad news involves someone you don't care about, there's still that little bit in the pit of your stomach that wishes you hadn't heard it.

That's exactly where Ezra and Dennis found themselves Sunday morning when they were awakened by a knock on their motel door.

The sun was just coming up and the ugly orange curtains covering the windows were beginning to leak light into the room. Ezra had been sleeping on the chair. He sat up and wiped a little

morning drool from the corner of his mouth. Dennis jumped out of bed and peeked out between the curtains.

Two police officers were standing there, one male, the other female. The male officer had a thick mustache and the female had a thin one. There was a squad car parked in the spot next to the room.

"Cops," he whispered fiercely to Ezra. "Be quiet and don't say anything."

Dennis threw on his white shirt and wrinkle-free pants.

"What am I going to say?" Ezra growled. "We're pinched. I bet that fat woman gave us up."

"Just don't say anything," Dennis repeated.

Dennis's hands began to tremble. He skipped putting on his shoes and opened the door. Dennis clasped his hands behind his back and stood up straight. His bald head glinted brightly in the morning sun. Luckily both officers were wearing sunglasses. Ezra climbed up onto the latch for the door chain and pushed himself close to the wall to listen. He was only a few inches from Dennis's left ear.

"Is there a problem?" Dennis asked.

"I'm afraid so," the female cop said. She had a badge that read *Elma,* and her partner's name tag said *Keane*.

Officer Keane cleared his voice. "We're sorry to bother you, but do you know a Terrell Hillary Graph?"

"I don't know anyone . . . you mean Terry?" Dennis asked.

"Perhaps," Officer Elma answered. "He was staying in the room next door."

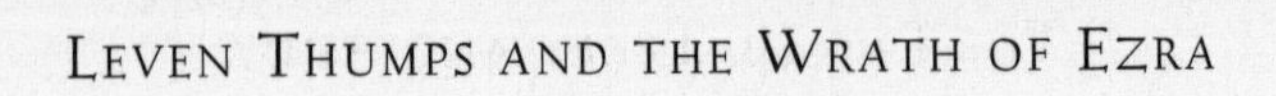

"Yes," Dennis said cautiously. "That's Terry."

"And Adelia Wilbury Graph?" Officer Keane asked.

"Addy," Dennis answered, an awful feeling coming up in his throat like a sour meal.

"There's been an accident," Officer Keane said. "Very late last night."

"An accident?" Dennis asked, wishing he could sit down.

"From what we can put together," Officer Keane explained, "and we're still going over eyewitness reports, but it was real dark, and according to one source Terrell and Adelia were driving down the interstate, swerved to . . . um, *hit* a stray dog, and ran head-first into a semi truck delivering adult undergarments."

"Diapers," Officer Elma added.

"I hate to be the bearer of bad news, but they didn't make it," Officer Keane clarified. "I'm sorry for your loss."

Dennis couldn't believe it. He stood there with his mouth hanging open.

"Say something," Ezra hissed.

"I can't believe it," Dennis finally said. "How did you find me?"

"There were a few things that survived," Officer Elma answered, nodding toward their patrol car.

Dennis looked at the cop car.

"We traced Terrell and Adelia to this motel," Officer Elma continued. "The clerk told us you were an acquaintance of theirs."

"Ask them about the robe," Ezra whispered.

Dennis waved Ezra away as if he were scratching his own left cheek.

"Are you okay?" Officer Keane asked, concerned.

"Just itchy," Dennis answered.

Ezra put his right hand over his single eye and sighed.

"It has been dry," Officer Elma said. "How well did you know them?"

"We . . . I didn't know them well," Dennis said sadly. "They gave me a ride."

"Do you know if they had family?" Officer Elma asked.

Dennis was about to mention Leven, but Ezra's persistent hissing stopped him.

"No," Dennis answered. "I don't think they did."

"The license plate on their car was from Oklahoma," Officer Keane said. "Is that home?"

"I think so," Dennis said, rubbing his bald head. "I think it was home for them."

"Ask him about the robe," Ezra demanded in a whisper.

Dennis ignored Ezra. "It's just so sad."

"Again," Officer Keane said, "sorry to be the bearer of bad news. If you have any other information that might help us track down family or friends of theirs, please let us know."

Officer Keane turned to his partner and she pulled a business card from her front shirt pocket and handed it to Dennis.

"And if you remember anything immediately, we'll be right next door getting a cup of coffee at Denny's."

"Thanks," Dennis said, closing the door.

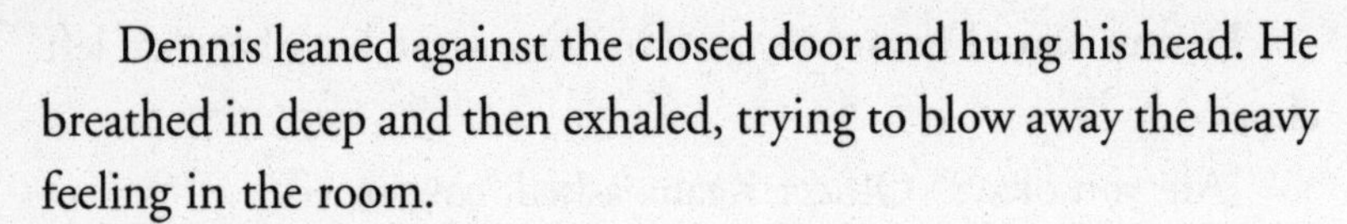

Dennis leaned against the closed door and hung his head. He breathed in deep and then exhaled, trying to blow away the heavy feeling in the room.

Ezra looked at him.

"I can't believe it," Dennis said sadly.

"I know," Ezra agreed. "Terry's middle name was Hillary?"

Dennis stared at Ezra in disbelief. "You are the worst person I know."

"Then why do you stick around?" Ezra asked.

Dennis looked around the room and then back at Ezra.

"Because I'm probably the second worst," Dennis answered. "This is horrible—one minute they're alive and the next they're gone. It's so sad."

"I know," Ezra said. "We needed that robe."

"You're the worst person," Dennis scolded.

"Well, you're the second worst," Ezra mocked. "And if you were capable of any real malice you would've asked where the robe was."

"I didn't need to," Dennis said sadly.

"What do you mean?" Ezra barked. "We needed that robe."

"No," Dennis explained. "I didn't need to ask because I could see it in the back of their squad car."

"Fantastic." Ezra laughed. "Those goobers left the car while they're getting coffee."

"I'm not breaking into a police car," Dennis argued.

"I can't do it!" Ezra screamed. "I've only got one leg."

"You've got two," Dennis growled. "One's just metal."

"What a nob!" Ezra yelled. "I'd kill you if I were taller. We have to get that robe."

"I'll check if their car door's unlocked," Dennis said. "But we can't just break into a police car."

"So that's the extent of what you'll do?" Ezra sniffed. "Bold—no wonder you ended up where you did."

Dennis blew off Ezra's response and opened the motel door. He looked out carefully. There were only four other vehicles in the parking lot aside from the police car.

Dennis could see the Denny's next door. He could also see through the windows. The two cops were currently sitting at the bar with their backs toward the glass.

Dennis slipped out of the room and walked up to the police car. He could see the robe sitting in a box next to the back window.

"Try the door!" Ezra yelled.

Dennis bent down as if tying shoelaces on his bare feet. As he stood back up he grabbed the car door handle and pulled.

It was locked.

Dennis stood up straight and looked back toward the motel door.

"Try the other doors!" Ezra ordered.

Dennis reached for the other door and yanked the handle quickly. It too was locked, and so were the two doors on the other side of the car. Dennis turned and headed back into the motel room.

"Get back out there," Ezra commanded. "If you can't do this, what good are you?"

"The doors are locked."

"Thank goodness you aren't in charge of anything really important," Ezra sneered. "I want to get to Foo, and we might not be able to do that without that robe."

"It's a police car," Dennis argued.

"It's a police car," Ezra mimicked. "What's that thing at the top of your neck, anyway?"

Ezra jumped out of the motel room and hobbled with remarkable speed up to the rear right tire of the squad car. He climbed up the tire tread and onto the top of the wheel. From there he swung out and grabbed ahold of the gas tank door and then inched up onto the bottom edge of the back window.

Ezra tapped rapidly against the glass with the top of his head.

It did nothing.

Ezra began to scratch at the glass with his metal leg.

"Someone's going to see you," Dennis warned, stepping up to the car and leaning down to whisper to Ezra.

"Someone's going to see you and wonder if you could possibly be any paler," Ezra insulted him. "This isn't working. Break the window."

"No," Dennis said.

"When are you getting a spine implant?" Ezra said, disgusted. "I'm going in."

"What?"

"I'm going in."

Ezra jabbed his head into the seal beneath the back door

window. He burrowed into the seal, wriggling and working his way down into the door's insides.

"What are you doing?" Dennis whispered with concern.

Ezra didn't answer—he was far too busy crawling through the door's innards.

"This is so stupid," Dennis complained. "There's no way you can get in there."

Ezra appeared in the backseat of the squad car. He looked out of the window toward Dennis. He smiled, but it wasn't a friendly, next-door-neighbor type of smile. It was more like a deranged, I-can't-wait-to-berate-you type of smile.

Ezra climbed up into the back window and pulled the dark purple robe out of a shallow open box. The robe was charred and wrinkled, but it looked to be mostly intact.

Ezra slowly dragged the robe across the backseat and up to the door. He looked around for a latch to open the door. Dennis could see him scream something, but he couldn't hear him clearly through the glass.

"There's no way to unlock it from inside!" Dennis shouted through the glass. "It's a police car. Just get out. They'll be coming back."

Ezra gestured wildly.

"I can't hear you!" Dennis screamed back. "Get out!"

Ezra continued to mouth the same thing over and over: "Break the glass."

"I'm not breaking the glass," Dennis insisted. "Get out."

Dennis could see inside the coffee shop. The cops were getting up from their bar stools and moving toward the front of the restaurant.

"Get out!" Dennis yelled. "They're coming."

Ezra just kept mouthing, "Break the glass," over and over.

The cops were almost out of the restaurant. Dennis looked around angrily. He spotted a good-size rock sitting in the sad-looking motel landscaping. He picked up the rock and knocked it against the window. A large crack spread across the glass.

"Harder," Ezra mouthed.

Dennis pulled back and slammed the rock into the window again. The glass pushed inward and shattered over the backseat and on top of Ezra. Dennis reached in and grabbed the robe. He pulled it out, extracting both the robe and Ezra, who was clinging to its edge.

"They're coming!" Ezra screamed.

Dennis tossed the robe under the police car.

"Hey!" Officer Keane yelled. "Hold up there."

Dennis stood up straight.

Both officers ran across the parking lot and up to the squad car. Officer Elma looked at the shattered window and pulled out her gun.

"What happened?" Officer Keane asked frantically.

Dennis shook slightly.

"Did you see anyone?" Officer Elma asked.

"There was a guy," Dennis said.

"A guy?" Officer Elma said, putting her gun back into her

holster and pulling out a pen and pad. "Anything else?"

"He was tall," Dennis offered.

"This neighborhood's going to the dogs," she growled.

"I know, and it used to be so nice. Of course, the whole world is falling apart," Officer Keane tisked. "Did you see his face?"

Dennis shook his head.

"What was he wearing?" Officer Elma asked.

Dennis looked down at himself. "A white shirt and tan pants."

"No-good punk," Officer Keane cursed.

Officer Elma's radio sounded. She pushed a button and responded by shouting out some numbers.

"We gotta go," Officer Keane translated. "More trouble on the interstate. You have our card."

The two cops hopped into their damaged squad car and pulled out of the parking lot with their lights blazing, not noticing the robe they had been parked over.

Dennis just stood there.

After thirty seconds Ezra crawled out from under the robe.

"Wow." Ezra laughed. "You're quite the criminal. You had no problem giving your own self up. What a useless wad."

"I was just being honest. Besides, I got you out of the car," Dennis reminded him.

"I got me out," Ezra replied. "You just wielded a rock when I told you to."

Dennis picked up the robe and looked at the material. The deep purple color was as rich and textured as a Magic Eye puzzle.

Dennis felt that if he stared at the fabric long enough he'd be able to see patterns and pictures that were not visible to the naked eye.

"Terry and Addy are gone," Dennis said seriously.

"Then you've got some practicing to do," Ezra said coldly. "Put the robe on."

"What?"

"Put the robe on."

"It belongs to Terry." Dennis's voice was melancholy.

"He won't be wearing it ever again," Ezra sneered. "Now put it on."

"A little respect," Dennis said.

"Why?" Ezra asked. "You've never done anything to deserve it."

"I think I like you better when you're all girlie inside."

Ezra poked Dennis on his right bare foot.

"Owww."

"Put it on."

Dennis slid on the robe. It felt warm and comfortable and it complemented his white shirt and wrinkle-free pants perfectly.

"I never noticed you were so tall," Ezra said with amazement.

"It's the robe."

"Wow!" Ezra exclaimed. "It really improves your image."

Dennis bent down and reached out his right arm. Ezra jumped into his hand. Dennis looked over at the room where Terry and Addy had once stayed.

"It's just so weird," he said softly.

"I know," Ezra said, amazed. "I never thought there was any way to improve your image."

"No, that they're gone." Dennis shook his head and carried the mean and angry toothpick into the motel room and shut the door.

It is easy to say that Addy and Terry had it coming to them—that their mistakes and wrongdoings ultimately did them in. But those words don't change the fact that two lives were now gone. Gone was the chance for Terry and Addy to realize what they had done and the opportunity to make peace with it. Gone was the option to make the world a better place instead of leaving it worse off. Gone was the possibility that someday Leven might be able to show his rotten guardians what he had become.

Ultimately, however, Terry and Addy were just plain gone.

CHAPTER THIRTY-FOUR

EVIL IN A VEST

Leven had to blink several times to make sure his eyes were working properly. He focused on the man and tried to make sense of it.

"That's the Dearth?" Winter whispered.

"It can't be," Leven whispered back.

Geth moved to the front of the cage and stared intently at the being Azure had just introduced. He was a short, older man who wore a soft smile and a quaint English cap. The hair showing above his ears was neat and gray, and even in the low light his deep blue eyes could be seen. He had on corduroy pants and a plaid vest over a button-down shirt with rolled-up sleeves. He looked like the kind of person you might find sitting in a pub working on a crossword puzzle on a warm afternoon.

"Good day," the Dearth said with a British accent.

All three just stared at him.

"Who are you?" Leven finally asked. "Because you're not the Dearth."

"Smart lad," the Dearth spoke. "But you see, I most certainly am. Leave us for a moment, would you please, Azure?"

Azure walked away and the Dearth stepped closer to the cage.

"You can't be," Leven argued. "You were all black and oozy, and there was that pus."

"Please," the Dearth spoke. "Do you think I would present myself to Reality looking like that? And forgive me for losing myself the last time we spoke. It's not often that I'm taken by surprise. I was weaker then. Things are much different now. Just look at me."

"I can't believe it," Leven said.

"We've done our research," the Dearth said, smiling.

"Research?" Geth said, disgusted.

"It seems that older men wearing vests and speaking with accents are among the most universally trusted beings. When I walk out into Reality, they will see a harmless old man who is simply happy to be free from Foo. I will smile and thank them and they will freely allow all those behind me to flow into Reality. Only after we've moved enough beings out will I show my true self and enslave any who choose to fight against me."

The Dearth's bare feet wriggled and oozed into the dirt. A small mound of dirt rose up behind him and created a place for him to sit.

The Dearth sat.

"I don't understand," Leven said.

"Of course you don't," the Dearth said mildly. "Let me explain."

"I don't care," Leven said, throwing up his hands. "You can take the shape of a basket full of kittens and talk about dirt all day, but just tell me where Clover is."

"Ah . . . I'm very sorry 'bout that," the Dearth spoke. "But you must put the sycophant from your mind, please—'tis the folly of man to care more for their pets than their own blood."

"Clover's not my pet."

"No, no, not anymore," the Dearth said sadly.

"Where is he?" Winter demanded, tears coming to her eyes. "If he's dead, we want to see him."

"Ah, Winter," the Dearth said softly. "You have become quite lovely. I thought you to be a child, and yet you stand there like a woman."

Winter's green eyes dimmed as she blushed.

"And Geth," the Dearth continued. "How I wish I had someone with your pluck on my side. You have been put through the hoops and still you stand there proud and determined to do your duty. Admirable—stupid, but admirable."

"You know it won't work," Geth said. "Foo won't fail."

The Dearth stared at Geth and spoke in a measured tone. "Even now I can see it in your eyes, Geth. For the first time you realize that just maybe you are wrong and that Foo, alas, is doomed."

The words were most damaging to Leven and Winter.

"Look," the Dearth said. "Look at these two. My, how they

put stock in what you say. Don't falter, Geth—your sure footing gives them hope."

"This is crazy," Leven said. "You can't just march into Reality."

"I can and will," the Dearth said cheerily.

"They'll stop you," Geth said.

"That's the most interesting part," the Dearth said. "There's very little about you, Geth, that I don't know. For example, your body has been in a state of flux. Growing and shrinking back and forth. You're aware that part of you is missing, and well, that part is in Reality helping me to ultimately destroy Foo. Even now, what's left of Sabine is trying to get the attention of your missing piece. And they'll soon convince thousands of what they should do when I come through."

"I don't believe it," Geth said.

"Yes, you do," the Dearth countered. "The longing's release has made our armies passionate and Cusp has been taken even more quickly than I had anticipated. The soil that once belonged to Lith is now connecting to Sycophant Run, and the troops have already begun to march toward the opening that your missing piece has pointed out so clearly. I thought I would have to wriggle around in the soil of Sycophant Run for a while before finding the opening, but thanks to you that isn't necessary."

"Where's Clover?" Leven asked again.

"My goodness," the Dearth said. "Like a broken record. *I* should ask *you* some questions. Like, where's the key? But you've already exposed yourself and we now know the key rests in the

remains of Lith. We'll find it. But it's a pity, really, it was the only reason we were keeping you alive. You mean nothing to me now."

Footsteps sounded. Azure was back.

"It's time," Azure said respectfully.

The Dearth sighed. "So soon?"

"The soil has settled and the message has been sent," Azure said.

"Don't do this, Azure," Geth said calmly. "You'll be destroyed just like everyone else."

"Oh yes," the Dearth said. "The lithen party line: 'all hope will die and so will any living being.' Rubbish. Azure knows that when the dust settles he will stand by my side with unlimited power."

"Then he's a dolt," Geth said. "Mankind cannot survive without hopes and dreams. It is our responsibility as lithens to protect that."

"It's not true," Azure said. "We were brought up on lies, Geth."

The Dearth gave the three prisoners the once-over.

"Well, I've enjoyed our conversation," he said. "Azure, you may kill Leven and Winter when you please—the last thing we need is for a new Want to mess things up. So extinguish him while he's still vulnerable. But keep Geth alive, will you? I'm not certain what would happen to his missing part if he were to die now."

The Dearth tipped his cap to them.

"Cheerio."

He then walked out, dragging his soiled feet with him.

"Don't go anywhere." Azure smirked, following the Dearth from the cavern and into the dark.

"This is bad," Leven said.

Geth stood silent and still.

"Geth," Winter said, touching his arm.

Geth didn't move. His eyes, however, bounced back and forth as if he were a machine trying to process some stubborn information.

"Are you okay?" Leven asked.

Geth's blue eyes looked like they had been pulled out, stomped on, and then shoved back in.

"I used to believe that the whole of Foo would gladly stand up and defend our home to the very last dream," Geth whispered. "Now it seems as if everyone is willing to walk into Reality and let it all slip away."

"I'm not," Leven insisted.

"Me neither," Winter said.

Geth smiled faintly. "That makes three of us against the world."

"I like the odds," Leven said.

Geth looked at Leven intently. "You're so much more than you once were. Where's that boy I used to have to pull along?"

"I don't know," Leven replied. "He's probably somewhere in the past with that toothpick I used to have to drag around."

Geth breathed in deeply. Color pushed back into his cheeks as if nature was redrawing him. He looked

20 percent more lithen than he had just moments before.

"It's going to feel great to win this thing," Geth said seriously.

"You're telling me." Winter beamed.

"And listen," Leven added. "For the record, I'm not going to stop believing that Clover's still alive and okay."

"We'll find him," Geth declared.

"Then we've got to get out of this cage," Winter noted.

"Can you do anything yet as the Want?" Geth asked Leven. "Anything?"

"No," Leven answered.

"Then our only chance is to overpower them when they come to kill you two."

"Real nice," Winter said.

"I can't see another way out," Geth said, pulling on the door again.

"Maybe this will help," a low voice said from the shadows on the side of the cavern.

Everyone was silent.

"Who said that?" Leven asked.

A thin man in a blue robe holding a heavy rusted sword stepped carefully into the light. Next to him was the same whisp Clover had once lost track of up near the turrets.

Winter rubbed her eyes and choked on her own breath.

"Janet?" Leven said in disbelief.

"You know her?" Winter said in shock.

Janet was already running toward Winter. Janet slipped through the bars and tried desperately to hug Winter—she was

crying and wailing and a complete mess. Leven thought she was attacking Winter and tried to shoo her away.

Winter struggled to dry heave her vocal cords back into operation. Tim stepped up to the cage and lifted his sword. Leven and Geth backed away and Tim slammed the sword down against the lock, shattering both the weapon and the latch. Tim shook his arms, pain from the hit causing him to quiver.

"Who are you?" Geth asked.

"We're here for Winter," Tim answered. "Come on."

Tim pulled open the door and Leven and Geth ran out. Winter, however, was still standing there in disbelief. It's one thing to run into your banker at the bank—they look so normal there and in their proper place. But it is something altogether different to run into your banker at, say, a convention for the preservation of collectable thimbles. And it is something entirely different to run into your neighbor and your nasty guardian in the dark caves of a hidden realm right before you are about to be killed.

Winter's brain tried to digest what she was seeing but she couldn't get her voice to work or her legs to move. Tim ran into the cage and, with Swig's and Leven's help, pulled Winter out. Tim hugged her and looked into her startled eyes.

"I can't believe it," he said. "Are you okay? You're older."

Winter still wasn't able to speak, and poor Janet couldn't touch or hold Winter because of her whispy condition. All Janet could do was hover around weeping with joy and regret and talking about how grown-up Winter looked.

"You're here for Winter?" Geth asked happily.

"All the way from Reality." Tim nodded. "But we'll gladly help out anyone she's locked up with."

"Brilliant," Geth said. "Let's stick to the shadows, and step only on the stone."

They all edged to the far side of the cavern and ran through the shadows. Outside the cavern, the tunnels were bigger and wound in all directions, including up and down.

"Over there," Tim pointed.

They darted down a dark tunnel and into an alcove stacked with clay jugs. They ducked down behind the containers.

Winter gasped as if breath had finally been breathed into her. Tim put his arm around her.

"How?" Winter asked in amazement. "How did you find me?"

"It wasn't easy." Tim laughed.

"And your children," Winter asked. "Darcy and Rochester, and your wife, are they okay?"

"Last I heard."

"And you're with her?" Winter said, disgusted, nodding toward Janet, who was sitting next to her wringing her hands and shaking nervously.

"And me," Swig pointed out.

"Not that I'm not thankful for you letting us out," Leven interrupted, "but who are you?"

"It's a long story," Tim replied.

"Talk fast," Geth suggested.

Tim launched into what he had been through, as Winter stared at him and Janet in amazement. Tim told them all about Ezra and Dennis and how Sabine had finally perished. He talked about the condition of Reality and how everyone was crazy and nervous about the state of the world. He told them how they had tried to build a gateway but it had only worked once—on him.

"The missing part of me is named Ezra?" Geth asked.

"Yes," Tim answered. "And his wrath is something to be concerned about."

Geth looked at all of them. "I used to have issues," he said.

"Men and their anger," Winter complained.

"We've got to get out of here before our absence is noticed," Geth said.

"It's not going to be easy sneaking you three out," Tim said.

"I'm not getting out yet anyway," Leven insisted. "I'm not leaving without Clover."

Winter put her arm around Leven. "I know how you feel, but if we don't escape, all that Clover has done will be for nothing."

"You can go," Leven said steadfastly. "But I'm not. I'm finding Clover."

"We'll stay together, then," Geth said. "Tim, you and Janet would be best to keep acting as if you are with the armies. If they catch you with us, it won't do anyone any good."

"I won't leave Winter," Janet said.

"You left me plenty of times in Reality," Winter reminded her, still not believing in Janet's change of heart or feeling comfortable around her.

Janet began to cry harder.

"I know it's a lot to take in," Tim said to Winter. "But she really has changed."

"And I know I should just accept it, but seeing you and her is still almost impossible to believe," Winter said.

"Maybe time will help," Tim said. "We'll split from you three, to help find your sycophant. We can cover more ground in two groups, and if we're stopped we can just look confused."

Janet already did.

"Good, and if you find Clover first, release him and he'll be able to track us down," Geth said. "Otherwise we'll meet you at the gloam."

"I have no idea what that is," Tim replied.

"I do," Swig said.

"It's where all of Azure's troops are now heading," Leven said. "Follow them."

"Above the gloam there's a forested cliff on the over side. We'll meet you at the top of that," Geth said.

Tim hugged Winter and Winter tried to smile at Janet.

"I'm so sorry," Janet cried.

Winter didn't know what to do. Tim, Swig, and Janet moved out from behind the jugs and ran quickly.

"Any idea where we should start looking for Clover?" Geth asked Leven.

"I've got no feeling whatsoever," Leven answered. "I wish—"

Winter held up her hand. "Someone's coming."

The sound of dozens of soldiers marching nearer swirled around their ears.

"There are some coming from the other direction as well," Geth said.

The noise increased until both groups of soldiers were right in front of the alcove.

"You," they heard Azure say. "Take your regiment and join those marching to Sycophant Run. Make sure all of you carry weapons. The Dearth will travel with you."

"As you desire," a deep-voiced rant replied. "Do we wear our blindfolds?"

"That won't be necessary. Cusp has folded."

"What about the rants who are wounded?"

"Everyone is being moved out," Azure said. "You are some of the last. We're marching on. I'll join you as soon as I take care of a couple of . . . loose ends."

"What about the—"

"No more questions," Azure interrupted. "Go."

All the soldiers marched up while Azure headed down.

"Let's wait a second before . . ." Geth started to say.

Leven wasn't in the mood to wait. He grabbed one of the empty clay jugs. Moving as quickly and silently as he could, he charged down the tunnel in Azure's direction.

Azure looked back, thinking Leven was just another rant. "What now? I said . . ."

Leven had not been brought up by nice people. He had never really been taught to be kind to others. In fact, on a

number of occasions Terry had told him that kindness was only for rich people who needed tax write-offs. Despite the bad upbringing, Leven was well aware of right and wrong. And despite how wrong it might sound, Leven had never felt quite as right as when he slammed that clay jug into Azure's head, knocking him out cold.

Azure fell to the ground as shards of the broken container clanked and chirped against the stone floor.

Winter came running up behind Leven. She looked down at Azure and then back at Leven. Geth joined them. Leven grinned at them both.

"Sorry, I couldn't wait," Leven said.

"I can see that," Geth said.

"I have a plan," Leven admitted. "Quick, grab his feet."

Geth grabbed Azure's feet and Leven took his arms while Winter picked up his kilve. They ran down the tunnel and past the cavern they had been held in.

"Aren't you going to lock him up?" Winter said.

"No."

Leven and Geth carried Azure into the organ room. The poor nit was still chained to the organ. He shook when he saw Leven and Geth carrying Azure in such a way.

"Don't say a word," Winter said to the nit, catching on to what Leven was thinking and waving Azure's kilve.

Winter opened the door on the candor box and Leven and Geth crammed Azure into it. Leven shut the door and slid the thick bolt to lock it.

"Play something," Leven ordered the nit.

"But I can't just . . ."

"Play something and we will cut you free before we go."

The nit began to play the organ. The sound was mellow and deep. Leven could feel the notes in his own chest.

Through the holes they could see Azure begin to stir. His head swayed and then his eyes popped open. The shock of his predicament caused him to shake and curse violently. He beat against the inside of the box.

"How dare you?" Azure said, his anger mellowing in the soothing music. "How . . ."

Leven stepped up to the holes and smiled.

"Do you know what I'm going to ask you?" Leven questioned.

Azure relaxed even further.

"Lower," Leven told the organist.

The music became even deeper and softer. It felt to Leven as if he were standing on an air-hockey table, hovering slightly.

"Do you know what I'm going to ask you?" he repeated.

"Yes," Azure said reluctantly.

"What?" Leven questioned.

"About your sycophant," Azure answered unwillingly.

"Is he okay?"

Azure was trying to stop himself, but he couldn't; the candor box was working perfectly. "Clover's . . . Clover's . . ."

Leven pounded on the box. "Is he okay?"

Azure relaxed completely and gave in.

"Clover is . . ."

CHAPTER THIRTY-FIVE

CONNECTING WITH THE DEARTH

It's not easy to know or predict exactly what's coming. Tomorrow's full of hope, but certainty? Who knows? What's up ahead could potentially be anything. I suppose that's part of what makes life so interesting. If I knew that next Thursday at three fourteen I would be receiving an award for good posture, that would be great. But I'd probably get so nervous I would start slouching and the award would then be given to someone with a straighter back. I don't like to think about such horrific things—and good posture is nothing to joke about.

Neither, of course, is predicting the future.

Some people on TV claim they can see your future. I've seen a man who throws down silverware and reads the patterns it makes on the ground to get an idea of tomorrow's weather. And once, a woman with long hair and a deck of playing cards told me she could see my future. She went on and on about how

someday someone would be holding this exact book and reading this very line at this very moment.

Eerie, isn't it?

I should thank you for being a part of my future, but first I must warn you about a piece of the past. You see, it seems that when Sabine was killed, the faint marks left on Dennis's skin began to take on a life of their own. They had been shifting silently across Dennis's body, but now they wanted to say something. And what they wanted to say had everything to do with the future. And whereas predicting the future isn't always exact, the images and words forming on Dennis's bald head were dead-on. Unfortunately, Dennis was too tall for Ezra to see the top of his head and because of that, the information printed on his scalp had so far gone undetected.

Until now.

Dennis scratched his shaved head. His brain was buzzing with anticipation and unease. He was not taking the death of Terry and Addy well. Despite how rotten they were, they were still humans and their deaths were sad to Dennis. But almost as unsettling was the fact that now Dennis would have to step up and play Terry's role.

Dennis was not one to seek the spotlight, but the robe helped. He looked over at Ezra. The skinny toothpick was polishing his paper-clip leg. Ezra liked his new appendage. It wasn't as responsive as his other leg, but it was sharp at the end and, as Ezra had cackled many times, "Indestructible!"

"It's still a paper clip," Dennis said in an effort to humble Ezra.

"You're still just a fleshy bag of disappointment."

"This is going to be hard to pull off," Dennis said.

"Why do you even speak?" Ezra replied.

The motel room was cold, and the smell of bleach permeated the air. Ezra and Dennis had been trying to work on their plan, but it kept turning into a shouting match, with Ezra demanding that Dennis be tested for actual brain function and Dennis threatening to break Ezra in half.

"It's not much of a plan," Dennis said for the tenth time. "It seems like a spotty way to build an army."

"Have you ever felt good about yourself?" Ezra said, disgusted. "You more than anyone should know that people need to believe in something. We'll just give them something new to believe in."

"You yourself said you don't know that much about Foo."

"I know enough!" Ezra yelled. "I know Geth's there, living an emotionally balanced life while I suffer. I know he came here for Leven, and I know that I will never rest until Geth is made to pay for what he did. I was part of a perfectly good tree; now look at me."

Ezra hobbled in a sad little circle on the top of the dresser. He coughed twice, trying to really sell the fact that he was pathetic. Dennis just stared at him.

"I get it. You've been terribly wronged."

"Terribly," Ezra sniffed.

"That's still not going to make people want to join up with you. In fact, it will probably make them want to do just the opposite," Dennis argued. "So we tell them about Foo, we preach about the opening in the Blue Hole Lake, and then what?"

"I'm being completely honest when I say that I wish I was working with a stuffed cactus instead of you."

"You would be refuse on the street if it wasn't for me," Dennis said.

"Refuse?" Ezra yelled. "Who are you, the queen of England? Well, I'd rather be refuse than trash."

"What's that supposed to mean?"

"Once again I have to explain the obvious to you," Ezra spat. "It means you are a wet spine of an individual and even your hair was smarter than you, seeing how it got out while it could."

"My hair has nothing to do with this," Dennis said hotly. "How about I pick you up and flush you down the toilet?"

"You wouldn't—"

Dennis silenced Ezra by pinching his mouth closed. He picked up Ezra and held him out in front of him as if he were a dirty sock. Dennis headed for the bathroom. Ezra thrashed and kicked, trying to scratch at Dennis's hand as he carried him. The purple plastic topper on his head wiggled wildly. Ezra reached down with his arms and grabbed hold of his metal leg. He strained to bend it slightly. With a bend in the leg Ezra was able to kick up and jab the paper clip into Dennis's fingers.

His second kick drew blood.

"Owwwww!" Dennis yelled, dropping Ezra to the ground. "That really hurt."

Ezra dashed as quickly as he could under the dresser, looking much less feeble than before.

Dennis reached down for him, but Ezra was too quick. He ran to Dennis's foot, opened his tiny mouth, and bit down on the back of his ankle.

"Ahhhhh!" Dennis screamed.

Ezra dashed under the bed, hollering like a warrior.

"Come out!" Dennis yelled.

Ezra was suddenly quiet.

"Come on," Dennis insisted. "Where are you?"

Dennis dropped to his knees and looked under the bed. A soft noise sounded from behind him.

"Whissssh."

Dennis scuttled around on his hands and knees and checked under the dresser.

"This is ridiculous," Dennis fumed. "Where are you?"

"Whissssh."

Dennis quickly flipped around and lifted the end of the comforter up and looked back under the bed. Ezra had jumped up and stuck himself in the comforter, hiding himself in the ugly pattern printed on it. He was now perched inches away from Dennis's bald head.

"Come on," Dennis said, peering beneath the bed. "You're being a baby."

Ezra leaned forward and opened his mouth to take a bite of

Dennis's scalp. The faint bits of darkness moved across Dennis's head like flickering ticker tape.

Ezra held his bite mid-chomp.

"What's that?" Ezra asked.

Dennis lifted his head and stared Ezra directly in his single eye.

"What's what?" Dennis asked, amazed at how well Ezra blended into the comforter.

"Your typically washed-out head is spelling stuff," Ezra said.

"What?"

"Your bald head," Ezra exclaimed. "It's finally saying something worthwhile."

"What are you talking about?" Dennis jumped up and ran to the mirror hanging on the wall. He tried to look at the top of his head but he couldn't see it clearly.

Ezra climbed up on top of the bed and jumped over to Dennis. He caught hold of the back of Dennis's pants and pulled himself up the back of Dennis's shirt as if it were a cargo net. He reached Dennis's neck and moved to glance into the mirror too.

"I can't see anything," Dennis said.

"Don't you have a makeup compact?"

"What?"

"One of those makeup mirrors," Ezra explained.

"Why would I have a makeup mirror?" Dennis asked, confused.

"'Cause you're a girl," Ezra said.

"You're the one who's always crying."

"I'll bite your neck."

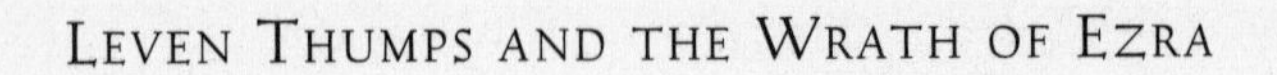

"I'll shove you down the sink," Dennis said angrily.

They both growled at each other for a few minutes until Dennis had had enough.

"This is stupid."

"It's pronounced *I'm,* not *this.*"

"Come on," Dennis said, trying to keep his cool. "Knock it off. Now, what does my head say?"

Ezra climbed up the side of Dennis's head.

"Do you mind sitting down?" Ezra asked. "It's windy up here."

Dennis sat down on the floor, crossing his legs and leaning up against the side of the bed.

"Does it really say . . ."

"Shhhhh," Ezra insisted.

Ezra was standing on the top of Dennis's head. He pivoted on his metal leg, looking over the complete scalp. Ezra moved his arms and hands as if he were a fortune-teller looking into a crystal ball.

"What do you see?" Dennis whispered.

"Lots of things," Ezra replied. "Can you feel the images?"

"No," Dennis answered. "I used to feel them more when Sabine was still alive. They were darker then."

"Sabine still lives in you," Ezra said with a hushed awe. "It's faint, but I can see what he knew."

"Sabine can't live in me."

"Whoooaa," Ezra said. "When you said that, the markings on your scalp went wild."

"Can you make it stop?" Dennis sounded concerned.

"Are you kidding?" Ezra snapped. "This is just what we were looking for."

"What?"

"All of Foo and everything we need to know is right here," Ezra said, thrilled.

"I don't want that on my head."

"You have no choice," Ezra demanded. "This is what we need. Now, stop talking and let me read it."

"I'm still not happy," Dennis insisted.

"How could you be?" Ezra sniffed. "Look at you."

Dennis shook his head with disgust and Ezra wobbled.

"Will you let me read?" Ezra asked indignantly.

Dennis sat still and closed his eyes. He could see his old life. He could see the many days and years he had put into being a janitor at the law firm of Snooker and Woe. He could see all the many people passing him in the hall and trying as hard as they could to not make eye contact. He could see his parents' disappointment in him as he grew up.

"I've always hated the way I looked," Dennis said honestly, letting some real feelings slip out.

"Why are you telling me?" Ezra asked. "I'm not Oprah."

Dennis had never been the big man on campus or even the slightly significant guy at any school. He couldn't remember anything in his childhood being warm or thrilling or good for his self-esteem. And nothing in his adulthood had been much better. He had settled at almost every point and turn in his life. Even

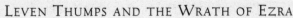

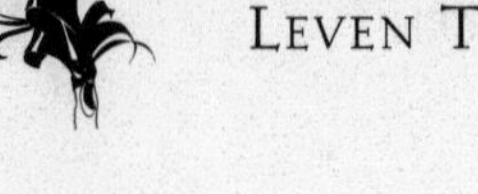

what he wore was a clear sign that he had no personal opinion or taste with any flavor to it.

"What do you see?" he finally asked.

"Apparently Foo is much more than I have felt or could remember," Ezra said excitedly. "Wow. Do you know somebody called the Dearth?"

"How would I know anyone from Foo?" Dennis asked.

"Sabine was looking for the gateway to bring the Dearth here."

"Is that good or bad?"

"Whatever the Dearth is," Ezra said, "it's incredibly powerful."

"So what should we do?"

"Shhhhh," Ezra snapped, his purple hair twisting lightly as he read Dennis's head. "Amazing. I think I like this Dearth guy. This is going to be perfect."

"What's going to be perfect?"

"Our plan," Ezra cackled. "We will prepare the masses to welcome the Dearth. Then when he comes through I'll explain to him how I answer to no one and that he now answers to me."

Ezra pumped his tiny fist.

"A toothpick will rule the world," Ezra growled. "And Geth will die knowing that the anger he shed ended up with everything."

"You got all that from my forehead?" Dennis asked, amazed.

"Don't wait around for a *thanks,*" Ezra said. "We've got work to do."

Ezra jumped from Dennis's head onto the bed. He leaned down and straightened his metal leg.

"And what's in it for me?" Dennis asked boldly.

"You'll be co-ruler of the world. Duh," Ezra said.

Dennis imagined a future where he had confidence in himself. He could see something coming into view, and no one was more surprised by the possibility than Dennis himself.

ii

The sun coming up over the flat, barren desert was beautiful. The starkness of the scene was awe inspiring in a steal-your-breath type of way. Tumbleweeds smacked up against the interstate guardrails. The wind would tease them and then pick them up and send them onto the freeway, where unsuspecting cars and trucks would obliterate them head-on.

Dennis watched a jackrabbit jump from its hole, run across the blowing dirt, and descend into another hole. The wind made Dennis's soul feel even more unsettled.

"I have no idea what I'm doing," he said to himself.

Ezra was sleeping in the pocket of Dennis's dark robe. Ezra had taken to the pocket, calling it the perfect place for a toothpick of his stature to rest. Dennis had taken to the robe as a whole. He felt good wearing it. Unlike the dark shawl that Sabine had once been, Terry's robe was comforting and made Dennis feel strong in a different type of way.

A large commercial tent had been delivered and set up on a small piece of land across the street from Blue Hole Lake. The tent was white with thick blue stripes running up and down all over it. Inside Dennis had set up fifty folding chairs and placed a wobbly podium at the front. The dirt field outside of the tent could easily accommodate hundreds of cars if the need arose. Dennis was standing in the parking lot looking out toward Blue Hole Lake. The lot felt incredibly empty.

"Hey," Dennis said, smacking the pocket Ezra was sleeping in. "Get up. How are we planning to get people here?"

"I'm tired," Ezra growled.

"You're a toothpick," Dennis snapped back. "Toothpicks don't get tired. They get used and then discarded."

"Thank you for the fascinating explanation of toothpicks," Ezra mocked, climbing out of the robe pocket and looking around. His purple tassel was smashed on one side, giving him bed head.

"Your hair's a mess," Dennis said.

"Your smell's offensive," Ezra replied.

"Come on," Dennis insisted. "Can't we get past the childish insults?"

Ezra shrugged. "Stop making it so easy."

"How are we getting people here?" Dennis asked again.

"Remember those flyers we made?" Ezra said slowly.

"People aren't going to see a flyer on their car windshield and say, 'Hey, this looks interesting. Let's go.'"

"Really?" Ezra said. "Then who's that?"

A beat-up red truck was pulling into the dirt parking lot. It stopped near the side of the tent and a woman wearing shorts and a tank top got out. She had short legs and spiky hair.

"Who are you?" she asked Dennis.

"I'm Denn . . . Professor Wizard," Dennis said uncomfortably, using the name they had put on the flyer.

Dennis and Ezra had argued for hours over what stage name he should use. Dennis thought he should be Professor Shock; Ezra thought that the name Today's Wizard would bring many more curious people to the tent. In the end they compromised, and Professor Wizard had been created. Ezra had also wanted Dennis to carry a wand, but Dennis had put his foot down, altering his image only by always wearing the robe.

"Is it true what the paper said?" the woman asked.

Dennis nodded.

"You know why everything's happening?" she said. "Them bugs and dirt and all that windy cloud stuff?"

"Say something comforting," Ezra whispered from behind Dennis's left ear.

"I do," Dennis answered.

"That's probably the only time in your life you'll get a chance to say that," Ezra quipped.

"What's happening, Professor?" she asked earnestly.

Dennis looked around before remembering he was the professor.

"What's happening?" she asked again. "My sister was picked up by bugs two weeks ago. Normally I would have thought she

was just making stuff up, like the time when she claimed she saw Gandhi in soap scum around her tub, but she was telling the truth. Even the news talked to her."

Ezra started to whisper and Dennis talked.

"It's okay," Dennis said. "I'm going to introduce you to a new word—Foo."

"Foo?"

Two more cars pulled into the parking lot.

"Come inside," Dennis said. "I think you'll want to hear this."

The woman followed Dennis into the tent and took a seat in the front row. Dennis stepped behind the podium and gripped the edges. The other people had made their way in. There was a man and a woman, both with long hair and vests, and there were also two women holding onto each other for support. They stepped timidly into the tent, both of them clutching their purses as if Dennis was going to pounce on them and wrestle the purses away.

"Come in," Dennis said, waving. "Have a seat."

Everyone sat down.

"Tell us what you think it is!" the spiky-haired woman shouted.

Dennis's hands trembled and then, as if a strong sedative were kicking in, his body began to warm up and settle down. He looked at the people's faces. Everyone appeared eager to hear what he was going to say next. He loved the feeling. Coupled with the sensation of the robe, it was almost enough to lift him from the ground.

"What are you doing?" the long-haired man pointed.

"I'm . . ."

"Floating," one of the timid women said. "He's floating."

"Is it a trick?" the spiky-haired woman asked.

Dennis looked down, surprised to see his feet dangling in the air. He was only a few inches off the ground, but he was most definitely floating.

"Say something," Ezra insisted in a whisper. "Follow my words."

"No," Dennis said aloud.

The small crowd looked at him in awe.

"No?" the vest-wearing woman asked.

"No, I mean I can find my own words," Dennis said, directing his comment to Ezra, but allowing the crowd to hear it.

"I believe you," the spiky-haired woman uttered. "Say your own words."

"There's a place," Dennis said. "A fantastic place, a place where all the oddities that now plague us have come from."

"What place?" the second timid woman asked.

"Foo."

The few spectators began to mumble and whisper amongst themselves.

Dennis raised his hands and smiled. His body lowered to the ground and he had never felt so surefooted. He recalled all the things Ezra had explained to him from the markings on his head.

"The bugs are called sarus."

"The bugs that picked up my sister?"

Dennis nodded. He went on, "And the clouds that are messing with planes are called hazen."

"What about those windy monsters we keep dreaming about?" the timid women asked in unison. "We can't stop dreaming about them."

"Telts," Dennis said. "They are telts, and the creatures that rise from the dirt are called avalands."

"How can you know that?" the vested man asked. "You're just making it up."

"I know about it because I know about Foo."

"So you're, like, prophetic?" the spiky-haired woman asked in a hushed tone.

Dennis didn't react to the question.

"What else do you think you know?" the man asked skeptically.

"I know that in a short while the inhabitants of Foo will begin to spill into our world, bringing things far more odd and dangerous than bugs and clouds," Dennis said solemnly. "I know that unless we are ready, we will be in grave danger."

Everyone shivered.

"When you say *spill,* how do you mean?" the vested woman asked.

"There is a small lake right across the field," Dennis said.

"Blue Hole?" the man asked.

"Yes," Dennis answered. "Shortly the water will drain and thousands will shoot up from the caves below."

"And they hate us?" one of the timid women asked.

Dennis began to float again. He hovered in the air like a weak balloon caught in a small draft.

"How do you do that?" the man asked.

All of the women "Ahhhed."

"Is there a wire?" the man questioned further.

Not patient enough to wait for an answer, the man got up and walked around Dennis. He waved his hand beneath Dennis's feet and looked closely for wires above him.

"I gotta tell someone!" he shouted. "What's this place called, the one that's going to spill?"

"Foo," Dennis said with authority.

"Foo," the two timid women whispered reverently.

Dennis lifted his arms up and, moved by the moment, clapped his hands. The small gathering instantly reacted, running for the tent exit. In less than ten seconds Dennis and Ezra were alone again.

"Wow," Ezra said. "That was even easier than I anticipated. But I still think you should have listened to me."

"This is all real," Dennis said softly. "Foo, Geth, Leven, and us having power? It's all real."

"I've been telling you," Ezra said.

"I know," Dennis replied. "But now I can feel it. It was like I was speaking about something I knew personally."

"Don't get all hopped up on your new ability to feel," Ezra insisted. "Now, sit down and let me read your head. If I'm right,

people will be coming back and you'll need more information. I want a huge gathering to snuff out this Dearth character and make me king."

"The USA doesn't have a king," Dennis pointed out.

"Foo S of A does," Ezra said loudly.

"Foo S of A? That's horrible," Dennis scoffed. "Have you been thinking of that for long?"

"It came to me a couple of nights ago," Ezra said, bothered. "It's not bad."

"It's awful."

Dennis sat down on a folding chair and let Ezra hop on top of his head.

"Let's see what we've got," Ezra said excitedly.

Dennis listened to Ezra as he read the top of his mind.

CHAPTER THIRTY-SIX

ONE-WORD ANSWERS

The power of a single word can be amazing. I suppose it's not often thought about, seeing as how the world is filled with words and often their value can seem insignificant. Words are everywhere. They litter the sides of buildings, occupy armies of signs, and decorate millions of pithy T-shirts. Computers and magazines spit out more pointless words these days than at any other time in history. Sure, there are some good words in there somewhere, but it's not always pleasant to dig around looking for them.

That, to me, is the reason why a single word properly placed is so powerful. If you are down on a knee waiting for your soul mate to respond to your proposal of marriage, *yes* is a pretty fantastic three-letter word, whereas *no* with its two tiny letters could ruin your mood for months, if not years. The word *fire* is comforting if you've just come in from a long day of snow skiing. But it is far less enjoyable to hear if you are standing in front of a firing squad after being interrogated for hours about where you were on the night of October 13 and why there is blood on your shirt.

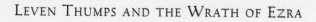

For the last time, I was at the library and it was jam.

Single words can be very powerful, and there was certainly great impact in the single word that Azure finally uttered from the candor box:

". . . alive."

Leven felt his entire body drop two inches before catching itself. Winter smiled like it was Christmas and she was opening the cutest pony on the block. And Geth, well, he clapped his hands, which for a lithen is pretty out of control.

"Clover's alive?" Leven asked, wanting to make sure he had heard right.

"Yes," Azure said defeatedly, his ear bleeding badly.

"He's alive?"

"Yes."

"You're sure?"

"Yes."

Leven jumped. "Where is he?"

"Down below us," Azure answered, his face scrunched and confused.

"Who has him?" Leven asked.

"He's locked up."

"Where?"

"In the infirmary storage cabinet."

"Why?"

"We were going to run tests on him."

Leven wanted to dash around the room screaming with joy, but Geth cut him off.

"We should go quickly. Leave Azure—with any luck, no one will ever free him."

"The nit," Leven said, pointing toward the organist.

Geth broke the nit's shackles with Azure's kilve, and the four of them left the room. Not surprising to any of them, the organist split from the pack and ran to find his own way out. The caves and caverns were much quieter now and had a deserted feeling to them.

"How do we get down?" Leven asked.

"There." Winter pointed.

A thin tunnel between two fatter ones sloped down steeply. They waited behind a stone archway as four rants approached.

"If I took down the two biggest, could you and Winter get the others?" Geth whispered to Leven.

"Is that a challenge?" Leven asked. "Because . . ."

Winter was already charging into the largest rant. The element of surprise worked well. She knocked him over, slamming the back of his head up against the stone wall. He went down hard. One of the other rants grabbed Winter by her hair and yanked her head backward. He let go the moment Geth connected the kilve to his gut and then spun it around to knock him out cold with the other end. Leven was wrestling a third one to the ground, and Geth finished him off by cracking the kilve over his skull. The last rant had Winter by the wrist and was flinging her sideways. Leven charged the rant and grabbed him around the neck. Winter twisted free and applied an amazingly solid kick to the rant's right side while Geth hit his legs out from beneath him.

They dragged all four of the rants to a trash hole near the archway. They stripped them out of their robes and shoved them into the trash hole. Leven had never seen a rant without its robe on. The sight was amazing and concerning. Two of the rants were half windy telt; one was half monkey, half man; and the other was half man, half female president. The seams between the rants' two sides looked like stretched-out scars.

"If they get to Reality will they be made whole?" Leven asked.

"They'll die," Geth said, slipping on a blue robe. "But the Dearth has promised them they'll be fixed."

"This robe's way too big," Winter said, drowning in the robe she had put on.

"It looks great," Leven said, putting on his own.

They flipped their hoods up and, dressed as part of Azure's army, ran across the juncture and down the skinny tunnel Winter had previously pointed to. The path curved and descended even further, opening into a long cavern filled with empty beds.

"This place is amazing," Leven said. "Why would they leave it?"

"Too much stone," Geth replied. "The Dearth needs soil to sustain himself and control others. The cavern worked for Azure, but not for the Dearth."

"I have no idea where the infirmary is," Leven admitted.

"Just keep going down," Geth said.

They reached a hallway with tiled walls and a smooth, glassy floor and quickly followed it.

"What are you doing?" Leven said suddenly. "We've got to get Clover."

Geth and Winter turned to look at Leven. He was standing still and talking to himself.

"What?" Geth asked.

Leven looked up. "Winter was hugging me."

"I was not," she said, baffled.

"Yes you were," Leven insisted.

"Actually," Geth said, "she wasn't."

"Why would I say she was if she wasn't?" Leven argued.

"Wishful thinking," Winter said, shaking her head. "Come on."

The hallway turned and they were now in a stone tunnel again.

"Phoebe," Leven said. "Where did you come from?"

Geth and Winter stopped and turned to look at Leven again.

"I guess you're pretty happy, aren't you, Geth?" Leven said. "Phoebe, how did you find us?"

"What are you talking about?" Winter looked dumbfounded.

"I'm talking about Phoebe," Leven said. "She's right . . . well, she was right next to Geth."

Geth turned around. There was nothing but empty tunnel in both directions.

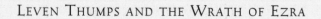

"Are you okay?" Geth asked.

"I'm fine," Leven insisted. "Phoebe was there."

"Maybe it's some sort of tunnel mirage," Winter joked. "Come on."

"I saw Phoebe."

"Was she hugging you?" Winter mocked.

"I . . ."

"Come on," Geth said nicely.

At the end of the tunnel they hid behind a small fountain while a few lone rants and cogs marched past carrying weapons and supplies.

"Is that a picture of a Band-Aid?" Leven asked, pointing to a marking on the wall.

"A Band-Aid or toilet paper," Winter said.

"Either way, couldn't that be pointing to the infirmary?"

The picture pointed to a row of wooden doors. Some were open and some were shut, but all led into the same large room. Metal tables with sharp instruments strewn across their tops encompassed the room. The walls were lined with glass canisters. All of the containers appeared to have something worrisome floating in them. The floor was one big mosaic of different-sized stains and splotches. Lamps hung from the ceiling on chains.

"I don't like this room," Winter said quietly.

"Don't leave, Winter," Leven pleaded. "We've got to get Clover."

"What are you taking about? I'm not going to leave."

"You were."

"No I wasn't," she insisted.

"I saw you go back out the doors," Leven said, trying to keep his voice down.

"I'm worried about you," Winter said. "You seem . . ."

The sound of something shaking made them all jump.

"What was that?" Geth said excitedly.

They heard a noise—it sounded like a cat stuck in a closet, or a sycophant trapped in a cabinet.

"Clover!" Leven exclaimed.

They ran across the room. Leven knocked over a table, flinging devious-looking tools everywhere. Some of the instruments stuck into the wall and ceiling.

There were six small cabinets against the wall, but only one was rattling. Leven grabbed for the handle and pulled. It was locked tight.

"Clover, is that you?"

There was a muffled reply.

"That's Clover's muffle!" Winter cried.

Leven grabbed one of the tools that had stuck in the wall and pulled it out. He jammed it into the edge of the cabinet door. Geth and Winter gripped it with him. With all the strength they had, they popped the door open and peered inside.

Two glowing blue eyes slowly materialized.

"It's about time," Clover said. "I'm starving. Hey, what are you guys wearing?"

Winter grabbed him and he threw his small arms around her neck. "We thought you were dead."

"No," Clover said, dismissing her comment with a wave. "I think they were testing things, but I was pretty bored, and that cabinet stinks."

Leven pushed his hood down. Clover leapt to Leven and held onto his right ear as he leaned out to pat Geth on the shoulder.

"I'm so glad you're okay," Leven said, trying not to sound too emotional.

"Me too," Clover replied. "Now, let's get out of here—if you heard some of the things that went on in this room . . ."

Clover shivered.

"Stick to the shadows and the stone," Geth reminded them.

They all followed him with quick steps and considerably lighter hearts than just moments before.

CHAPTER THIRTY-SEVEN

A Very Fragile Pattern

Rast and Reed scurried through the dark tunnel trying to calm their small hearts while still making good time.

"We're almost there," Rast said. "I remember."

"Shouldn't we see some light soon?"

"Yes," Rast answered.

"So, what are you going to do?" Reed asked.

"I'm not sure," Rast replied.

"You know you're going to have to make a decision," Reed said. "Because I'm not staying down here any longer than I have to."

"Oh, I see," Rast said. "So the future of everyone is dependent on your comfort."

"I didn't say that," Reed insisted. "Usually I like underground tunnels, but this one just feels too serious."

"I know what you mean," Rast whispered. "This is not an ordinary cave."

"Okay," Reed said. "We'll make sure it's there, you'll contemplate destroying it, and then we'll get out."

"You're a good soul," Rast said kindly.

"I see some light," Reed said. "Quick."

The two small sycophants ran speedily down the dark path toward the faint light. The tunnel turned and the light became greater.

"Hurry!" Rast said with excitement.

"My legs are only four inches long," Reed argued. "I'm moving as fast as I can."

"Leap more," Rast suggested.

"I don't mind leaping," Reed said. "It's the landing that hurts my old knees."

"I'll meet you at the light, then," Rast said. "I don't mind sore knees."

Rast leapt from wall to wall, bouncing back and forth in a quick pattern that propelled him forward. The tunnel grew wider as the light grew brighter. The sound of an underwater river running strong filled his ears.

"Do you hear that?" Rast stopped and yelled. "Water."

Reed caught up to him, breathing hard. "Yes, yes, I can hear the water and see the light."

"It's just around the next bend," Rast said.

Reed put his hand out and held onto Rast's arm.

"You're not nervous, are you?" Rast joked.

"A bit," Reed admitted. "What if it's not there?"

"Then my hard decision is made for me," Rast said. "Come."

They walked together down the trail. The light up ahead looked like a bright ghost rapidly gaining weight.

"There it is," Reed whispered.

"It's still whole," Rast said, half happy, half sad.

They climbed three wide steps and walked onto a flat open path.

"The map of glass," Reed said reverently.

Light from a single hole that tunneled hundreds of feet up to the top of the cavern dropped through and rested squarely on the back of the large piece of glass. It was ten feet tall and thirteen feet wide. It was framed in stone, and the images on it were brightly colored. The entire plate had a gold sheen to it, and some of the markings looked permanent, while other marks shifted as the light shone through. The trail to Reality was clearly marked on the glass. A heavy dotted line wound through intricate tunnels and up through watery rooms.

"It looks so fragile and thin," Reed said.

"And yet it still stands."

"The trail winds through rooms of water," Reed pointed. "How is that possible?"

"That's why the map is so crucial," Rast explained. "Follow the guide and you will walk through the water without getting wet and with air to breathe. Go it on your own and you will surely drown. The path through the water also changes as the light through the map sees fit."

"How do you get back?"

"Once you get through the maze, the water drains and the path remains open for three days," Rast said.

"Plenty of time for Azure to move thousands into Reality," Reed said sadly.

"If we break the map, then the way is lost," Rast said.

"But our role is not to destroy," Reed whispered. "And would eliminating the map really guarantee our success?"

"It stops the Dearth."

"For a time."

"What would you do?" Rast asked sincerely. "You heard the Lore Coils, even down here. If the secret has reached us here, who in Foo doesn't know how to destroy us?"

"Maybe our kind should move through the caves."

"Reality's not fit for sycophants. Our role has changed," Rast said sadly. "With the secret out, we are vulnerable. Our people will be forced to hide and keep away."

"Some will stand up for us," Reed said. "Many nits would die for their sycophants."

"It doesn't matter," Rast said. "If the Dearth gets through because we can no longer stop his armies at our shores, then we have failed all of Foo and all mankind. One rock though the map will at least stop them."

They were quiet, listening to the water run through the caves.

"What a dark day," Reed finally said soberly.

Rast walked across the trail and over to the side of the underground river. He picked up the biggest rock he could lift.

He carried it over and stood by Reed.

"The Dearth will want our heads," Reed said. "Taking his exit will not sit well with him."

Rast lifted the rock above his head.

"All this risk for the sake of dreams?" Reed asked. "We're offering up our people so that those we don't even know can continue to dream."

"We are simply doing what's right," Rast said. "There's no other measurement to live by."

Rast swung his arms back and threw the rock directly at the bottom of the map. The rock arched slightly and then spun toward the glass. Before it got closer than six inches, it was batted back.

It landed on the ground between Rast and Reed. They both just stared at the rock.

"Try it again," Reed said.

Rast picked the rock up, spun around, and let it fly. The rock went higher this time, but before it hit, something darted in and batted it away. The rock landed behind Rast and Reed.

"What was that?" Rast asked. "Something stopped it."

"Throw it again."

Rast picked the rock back up and threw it with all of his might. This time the rock shot straight toward the glass. A flicker of dark intercepted it and knocked it back.

Reed picked up a small pebble and threw. Rast grabbed his rock and did the same. Both stones were swatted back.

"Knock it off," a small voice demanded. "What are you thinking?"

"Who said that?" Rast asked.

"I said that."

Rast blinked, and there flying above his nose was a small winged being. It was dark green with clear, fluttering wings, and no more than an inch tall. It had little horns on its green forehead and a fuzzy green body.

It smirked at Rast.

"Who are you?" it asked.

"I'm Rast. I am . . ."

"Throwing stones at the map?" it scolded. "What are you thinking?"

"Not much," a second, brown thing said.

"Sorry," Rast said. "Are you thorns? I haven't seen your kind in ages."

"Well, maybe we haven't seen your kind in ages either," a third, black thorn said.

"Yeah," the green thorn said. "It's your fault."

"I'm not blaming anyone," Rast said.

"Of course you aren't," the brown thorn mocked. "You're too busy throwing stones at my map."

"Your map?" the green thorn argued. "I thought we agreed this month it's mine."

"Well, it will be my map next month."

"No it won't," the black thorn bickered. "It will be mine because you forfeited your turn, remember?"

"I didn't forfeit. I was resting."

"Resting your turn? How do you rest a turn? This is me," the

black thorn mocked. "Look at me, everyone! I'm resting my turn. You forfeited."

As the three thorns quarreled, Reed leaned in closer to Rast. "What should we do?" he whispered.

"I'm not sure," Rast answered. "I know thorns are incredibly possessive of things. They must be attracted to the map."

"Well, the rocks are right there," Reed pointed out. "Maybe if we throw them while they're distracted. . . ."

Rast and Reed slowly picked up the rocks.

"The map winked at me," the green thorn declared. "That means I'm number seven."

"So now the map's winking?" the brown thorn argued. "Last week it blushed and now it's winking? You need to get out more."

Rast and Read threw their stones.

Without missing a beat the three thorns zipped in and batted them back.

"What, you think we're stupid?" the green thorn asked.

"Yeah," the brown thorn agreed. "Think we can't argue and keep an eye on you at the same time? Look at these two. Sad."

"Go home," the green thorn fluttered.

"Listen," Rast said. "Some bad things will happen if that map isn't destroyed."

"Ooohhh," the black thorn shivered. "I'm scared. You guys shaking like I'm shaking?"

The green and brown thorns laughed as they fluttered about.

"The only bad thing that's going to happen is if you hurt my map," the black thorn said.

"Again with the 'my map,'" the brown thorn squabbled. "Your time is two months away."

"And I'm two seconds away from hurting you."

"That's even less frightening than these fur balls," the brown thorn said.

As brown and black argued, green began polishing the map and singing to it.

"Glass and light feels so right, you and me together."

"I think we should go," Reed said.

"But the map," Rast said sadly.

"It's in the hands of fate," Reed said softly. "As it should be. They're not going to let us destroy it."

"Okay," the black thorn gave in. "You get to say the map is yours on odd days, and I get to say it's mine every other even day until spring."

"Where does that leave me?" the green one yelled. "And if you bring up that time-share idea again, so help me I'll go mad."

"Keep your voice down," the brown thorn said. "You know loud noises bother her."

"Let's get out of here," Rast said.

"Yeah," Reed agreed. "This is getting weird."

Rast and Reed walked quickly and quietly back through the caves—both of them knowing that for the first time in the history of Foo, their people were about to face real danger.

It was not a good feeling.

CHAPTER THIRTY-EIGHT

A MOMENT TO BREATHE

The meadow was littered with wounded beings and debris. Blue soldiers marched in straight lines restoring order in the chaos and gathering prisoners. In the far distance buildings burned in Cusp. The dark smoke from the fires rose up into the dusk and the hazen fed on it greedily. The sky was balloon free, but rovens in small clusters patrolled the air, screaming to make sure their presence was known.

The weather was still undecided, warmth hovering in some spots and the cold refusing to leave others. Weak lightning struck occasionally, and the sky continued to shift colors like an out-of-sync movie.

Azure's army had moved in and conquered with little regard for what things would look like after. Hundreds of Lore Coils of different strengths still drifted around, most of them concerning the battle or the sycophant secret. The words *Alderam Degarus*

hung in the air. And anytime they were whispered, sycophants in the immediate area would turn visible and scream in fear.

The brick path Leven and everyone walked had been torn up in hundreds of spots by the avalands that had stampeded through. The bricks ended at the far edge of the meadow right above the field leading to the gloam.

As they stepped onto the new path, it began to rain.

Leven, Geth, Winter, and Clover marched through the mud. Winter cursed the heavy, wet robe she had to drag through the muck.

"This robe is so huge," Winter complained.

"Sorry," Geth said supportively. "The mud's hard to move through, but it should also make it difficult for the Dearth to listen and communicate."

"You know what I think?" Clover said. "I think we need a name."

"We've got names," Winter said.

"No, a group name," Clover pointed out. "Like 'The Marchers.'"

"That's horrible," Leven said. "We're not always marching."

"I was thinking about the month of March," Clover said defensively.

"That makes even less sense." Leven laughed. "It's not March."

"True," Clover replied, jumping onto Geth's wet-cloaked head. "Well, then, what do you suggest, toothpick?"

"I suggest we hurry."

"No, that has no appeal." Clover waved. "How about, 'Four Friends'?"

"Descriptive," Winter said. "The hem of this robe weighs about two hundred pounds."

The rain pounded harder. Clover disappeared, and two seconds later he was back.

"The Brotherhood of Foo."

"I'm a girl," Winter pointed out.

"The Sisterhood?"

"Let's just think on it a while," Leven said.

"I've really been the only one to suggest anything," Clover said. "Besides Geth."

"Geth wasn't suggesting," Winter argued.

Clover disappeared.

A cart pulled by two onicks moved through the mud and past them. The wheels of the cart created long, thin lines of water that slowly spread out, like thick fingers.

"Not much farther," Geth said. "We'll move off the trail and approach the knoll from Sentinel Fields."

"Do you think Tim and Janet are far?" Winter shouted through the rain.

"It would be a guess any way I answered," Geth replied. "But let's hope we meet up."

"I don't want to see her," Winter said. "She was horrible to me."

"Sorry!" Geth shouted. "But she's here. Fate must have some reason for it."

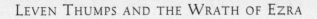

"She seems remorseful," Leven said, rain filling his eyes.

"She was awful," Winter argued.

"Hey, where'd you get those clothes?" Leven asked Winter.

"Funny."

"Seriously, how did you . . . am I seeing things again?"

"Apparently," Winter snipped. "Because I'm still wearing this awful robe."

"What's up with my vision?" Leven yelled to Geth. "I can't figure it out."

"It appears that you see the things people want or need."

"Winter wanted to hug me?" Leven asked, smiling, water dripping down his face and pasting his long, dark bangs to his forehead.

"I think he sees what *he* wants," Winter complained.

"Do you see those soldiers way off to the right?" Leven asked.

"Yes!" both Geth and Winter said.

"Are they holding trophies?"

"No," Clover answered.

Leven looked around quickly.

"What about that woman in the cart behind us?" Leven asked. "Is she holding a baby?"

"What woman?" Winter asked. "There's just a tiny old man wrapped in a blanket."

"This isn't good!" Leven shouted into the rain. "I can't even trust what I see."

"Yes you can," Geth said calmly. "You know what's real."

"No I don't," Leven argued.

"I could help," Clover said. "Like one of those helper dogs in Reality."

"This way," Geth ordered. "Hurry."

The four of them veered off the path and around a small cluster of thick trees. On the other side of the trees was a row of orange bushes being pelted by rain. The bushes bled into more trees that ran up a steep hill.

"We're going up," Geth said, "between the white trees."

"Wait!" someone yelled. "Hold up!"

Leven turned back to see Tim and Janet running toward them.

"They found us," Leven said. "Hey, what's Winter doing with Janet?"

"I'm not with Janet," Winter said.

Leven looked to his right, where Winter was standing. "Sorry, you were running by her. I guess that's what she wants, not you."

Tim and Janet caught up to them. Tim hugged Winter and Janet tried to.

"Hey, there's that whisp . . . Pam," Clover whispered to Leven. "And the balding guy?"

"It's Janet, and the guy is Winter's neighbor from Reality or something."

"And they're here?"

"You found your sycophant!" Tim cheered, looking at Clover. "We were worried when we found no trace of you. The caves are barren; the last troops were moving out as we left."

"Any sign of Azure?" Geth asked. "Did he get loose?"

"I guess," Tim answered. "We saw him yelling at some soldiers."

Swig appeared and Clover looked bothered.

"Come on," Geth said kindly. "We should move."

They hiked through the trees up to a small, flat knoll shaped like an upside-down cauldron. It provided a panoramic view of the gloam reaching out into the Veil Sea. Geth crawled to the edge and looked out from under the dense growth.

"Fantastic," he cried.

Leven dropped down and moved over to Geth. From the very edge he could not only see the gloam stretching out, he could also see the thousands and thousands and thousands of soldiers dressed in blue gathered at the shore waiting to cross the gloam.

"There are so many," Leven said, depressed. "I didn't realize there were that many in all of Foo."

"Some must have come from beyond the Pillars of Rant," Geth said. "They have prepared well. I like a worthy opponent."

Winter crouched down next to Leven. "Listen to them down there," she said. "They sound like the sea itself."

The troops in front carried tall, weblike staffs that were covered in shimmering, plate-size pieces of metal. When shifted, the metal pieces sparkled like sequins.

"To distract the sycophants," Geth said solemnly.

"They *are* really neat to look at," Clover said naively.

Leven moaned.

"When the rain stops, the avalands will rise and carry most of them swiftly across the gloam to Sycophant Run. If they know where the opening is—like the Dearth said—they could be

moving troops into Reality in less than a full day. Any suggestions?" Geth asked.

"We give up," Leven joked.

"What's wrong with moving into Reality?" Tim asked honestly, crouching down near them. "I need to get back. I have a wife and kids."

"So do most nits that wander in," Geth said. "But that's fate. And because of that, you have been able to think and to hope and to dream. Once the Dearth moves so many into Reality, you along with everyone else will perish with hopelessness."

"But I have to get back," Tim persisted.

Geth rolled over and sat up. "It would be best for all mankind if you never did."

"I don't understand."

"Your world floats in a sea of space that reaches farther than man could ever comprehend. It spins so that you can stand. It turns so that you can experience, and what you experience is possible only because mankind is balanced. That balance will begin to erode the moment the Dearth moves through. It's what we lithens have always feared."

Tim rubbed his eyes and face.

"Every one of those soldiers down there believes that Reality will make them whole, mend their souls, give them substance, or cure what ails them," Geth continued. "Unfortunately, it will do just the opposite and drag humankind down with it. It's not lithen rhetoric, or a child's fairy tale—it's simply the truth."

It began to snow.

Tim retreated into his own head, lost in thought.

"You don't paint a pretty picture," Leven said.

"I didn't say it was hopeless," Geth replied.

Winter laughed. "You may as well have."

Clover appeared and whispered, "If I come up with a name for our group, does it have to involve those three?"

Leven shook his head.

"Good," Clover said. "Then how about, 'The Four Who Don't Need Those Other Three'?"

"Actually, that name sort of involves them," Geth pointed out.

"In a clever way. Not everyone will get it," Clover defended quietly. "I just think it's weird having them around. It's like that aunt who comes to your birthday and gives you ribbons for your hair and makes you wear them in front of the other boys in your class."

"What are you talking about?" Winter laughed.

"Fine," Clover sighed. "I'll keep thinking."

Leven patted Clover on the head. The small sycophant smiled and then disappeared.

"We should get some sleep," Geth said. "Morning will clear our thoughts. The stone might not be the most comfortable, but it should keep us undetected."

"I wouldn't mind some food," Winter said.

Leven and Geth got up to forage for bickerwicks while Tim and Winter built a small fire.

"It needs more wood," Tim said. "I'll be right back."

"But it's burning . . ." Winter tried to stop him, but he was gone, leaving her alone with Janet.

Winter pushed the new fire around with a long stick and kept her green eyes down.

"This must be so hard for you," Janet finally said.

"No," Winter said. "It's fine. I mean, the last time I saw you, you were sitting on the couch drinking from a hose and telling me how little I mattered."

Janet wiped her non-eyes. "What a fool I was. The sad thing is, I'm probably still sitting there on that couch."

Winter looked up.

"I hadn't thought about that," she said. "But I suppose if you're a whisp here, then most of you is still just like you always were in Reality."

"I don't want to go back," Janet said honestly. "I hate being nothing here, but I dread even more returning to what I was."

"I don't blame you for that," Winter said. "You were awful."

The small fire began to grow and warmed the dry area beneath the trees quite well.

"I was so scared when I stepped into this place," Janet said. "I wasn't whole, I had no idea where I was, and I was seeing things I never could have imagined. I've never had a good imagination. I was so frightened. But it didn't take me long to realize that what I was most unhappy about was how I had treated you."

Winter looked at her.

"I want to say it was no big deal," Winter said softly. "But it was."

"I know that," Janet sniffed. "I'll try my hardest to convince

you I'm sorry. My form can't change in this condition, but I know my insides have."

Leven and Geth returned with a bushel full of bickerwicks and two purple plants that looked like puffy rolls of paper towels. They tore off pieces of the plant and rolled up toasted bickerwicks inside them. The roasted bickerwicks tasted sweet and flavorful.

The seven of them sat around the small fire as snow built up on the boughs above them. The sound of the Veil Sea and of the armies below rose in the air like steam off a warm lake. Leven looked around at his companions.

"It's unbelievable," Leven said.

"I agree," Winter replied, biting into her rolled-up bickerwick. "Absolutely delicious."

"Yeah, the food." Leven nodded. "But I mean, it's unbelievable that we are all here."

Everyone looked around, slowly understanding what Leven was getting at.

Leven flipped his hood down. His face was sober and his chin well-defined. Long, dark strands of hair hung down over his gold eyes, and the white streak in his hair reflected the firelight.

"I thought Clover was dead, but here he is."

Clover materialized and then disappeared back and forth a few times for effect.

"And Winter, your neighbor and his sycophant are here. And your . . . and Janet is here too."

Winter looked at Janet and Tim and Swig and smiled. Tim

finished what he was chewing and smiled back while Janet glowed.

"And us," Leven said, looking at Geth and Winter. "I'd be nothing without you two."

Winter looked beautiful lit by the fire. Her long blond hair fell across her face like a veil and her green eyes shone out like stones that most men would fight over. She curled her pink lips into a smile.

"You'd be remarkable regardless," she said warmly.

The small fire hummed.

Leven realized that they were all exactly where they wanted to be at the moment.

"When I looked over that edge earlier and saw those armies, I felt as if I had a new understanding of *impossible,*" Leven said softly. "But I look at us here, still living and having made it this far, and I can't help but think that it's they who have their work cut out for them."

Geth's eyes danced, reminding Leven of the toothpick he had once been.

"To dreams," Geth said, raising his rolled bickerwick in a toast. "And to the restoration of Foo."

"To Foo," everyone replied.

The fire sang "amen" as the snow continued to fall. It was easily one of the top five meals Leven had ever eaten.

"I wish Phoebe were here," Geth said.

Everyone was too busy munching to give him a hard time about it.

CHAPTER THIRTY-NINE

SUSPICIOUS MINDS

Ezra was right. It didn't take very long for the word to spread about Dennis's ability to float and his explanation for what was plaguing the entire world. People began to flock to the Tent of Answers and Possibilities. By the end of the day there were more people than chairs, and two news crews had come to film Dennis hovering. By the following morning the national press had picked up the story, and hundreds of people began to flood into the sleepy town of Santa Rosa looking for both answers and possibilities.

Dennis was taking to his new role beautifully. It was as if his personality had been born the moment he had put on the robe. He loved the feeling of others listening to him. And he had no problem with Ezra reading what was on his mind so he could repeat those facts and figures about Foo to all who came.

A woman had come from Texas and brought her electric

keyboard. She was so convinced Dennis was the real deal that she had agreed to play music for free until the day Blue Hole opened up and Foo came to Reality. She was now playing music softly as the people spilled into the tent in anticipation of hearing Dennis speak. They had to open the sides of the tent so that more people could hear.

Dennis came in from the side wearing his robe with the hood up. He stood at the front and flung his hood back, exposing his shaved head.

The crowd clapped. As usual, Ezra was tucked behind Dennis's right ear, ready and willing to feed Dennis suggestions and information.

"Tuesday," Dennis began. "Today is Tuesday."

The crowd seemed to like where this was going.

"Once," Dennis continued, "when I was like you, I used to go to work on Tuesday."

The crowd hollered in agreement and the music grew louder.

"And on Wednesday, and on Thursday and on Friday and on Monday—and even sometimes on Saturday."

The crowd shivered.

"But no more."

There was a nice round of clapping and some happy music.

"What if I told you that all your dreams could come true? What if I told you that the events happening today are simply the signs of what's to come?"

One lady giggled excitedly as Dennis began to hover.

"Well, we can be scared—or we can be prepared."

Dennis wiped his large forehead, feeling quite happy with how things were going.

"In a short while, thousands of beings will rise from the caverns below Blue Hole Lake. But what they don't realize is that we know about them. We are aware and—if you are committed—ready to claim the wonders and miracles of Foo for ourselves."

The crowd cheered and the keyboardist played "Roll Out the Barrel."

"Then every dream you've ever dreamt will be fulfilled. Impossible tasks will be commonplace and possibility will be beyond endless. You see me floating?"

Everyone nodded in awe.

"That's nothing," Dennis said kindly. "Soon the possibility of so much more will be yours to take. All we need is to gather ourselves here on the edge of the gateway and prepare to stop what's coming. Will you prepare?"

Dozens of audience members replied, "Yes."

"Will you prepare?" Dennis asked again.

"Yes!"

"Now let me tell you about a problem called the Dearth," Dennis said. "He will step from that lake and wish to take your existence. Will we let him?"

"No!"

Dennis smiled as he looked out over the crowd. His heart felt too big for his chest and his arms and legs tingled with the excitement of a captive audience. He bowed slightly.

Dennis went into great detail about Foo and the worrisome

things happening in Reality. He closed by saying, "More at eleven."

Dennis flipped his hood back up and walked out.

The crowd continued to chant. Many dialed friends and family on their cell phones, begging them to come to Santa Rosa and be part of Dennis's clan.

"They're more gullible than I thought," Ezra whispered as Dennis walked away through the cars.

"This is going to work," Dennis said.

"I've been telling you that for days," Ezra complained.

"They're listening to me."

"Well, in all honesty, they're listening to you say what I want."

"Still," Dennis said thoughtfully.

At eleven the crowd was twice the size. Thanks to the Internet and the Associated Press, people were coming in droves. Dennis was the first person to offer some sort of explanation for what was happening. A few other wackos around the world had tried to act like they knew what was up, but they had no real explanation. Dennis not only seemed to understand telts and avalands but he could hover when he talked. Dennis also had a plan. He was asking the world to gather around Blue Hole Lake and prepare to overtake the trouble that would pour out someday soon. His plan also promised those who helped great riches and possibilities in Foo.

Gullible people liked that.

"Across the street is a small lake," Dennis said loudly.

"Blue Hole," the crowd murmured.

"For hundreds of years people have speculated just where the caverns beneath it lead," Dennis said. "Well, there's no longer need for speculation. In a short time the lake will drain. Soon afterward, hundreds of thousands of creatures, much like those who have been plaguing us now, will spill up into our world. Their desire is to control Reality and their leader is called the Dearth. They might have succeeded, if it were not for the fact that we know they are coming. And because we know, dreams and imagination will be your only limitation, and your boring and monotonous lives will be filled with adventure and fulfillment."

The audience screamed and shouted with joy.

"Call all who want to be a part of it. Fill this barren land with those who want more," Dennis exhorted. "Foo awaits all of us. More tomorrow at nine."

The crowd clapped and hooted. Dennis stepped out from behind his podium and walked though the crowd high-fiving and shaking hands. Halfway through the masses he turned and made an escape through the side of the tent. He broke out into the open and took long strides across the parking lot.

"Don't look now," Ezra said, "but some people are following you."

Dennis turned and looked. Two thin men in brown suits stood about a hundred feet behind them.

"I told you not to look," Ezra said.

"How do you know they're coming toward me?" Dennis said. "There are people everywhere."

"You've got a point," Ezra replied. "Most people are repelled by you. Still, they look determined."

Dennis walked faster. He was tired. His feet hurt and his head was still swimming from the attention he had just received. His heart beat loudly and suddenly he wanted nothing but to be back in his motel room lying on the bed.

The two men turned and went a different direction.

"I guess they didn't want you," Ezra said.

"Good," Dennis said. "I'm exhausted."

Dennis crossed the wide road in a diagonal line heading toward the motel. A large black car pulled onto the road and sped toward Dennis. Dennis stepped into the vacant dirt lot next to the motel. The car followed and slammed on its brakes just before hitting Dennis and Ezra. A huge cloud of dust washed over them.

The two thin men with brown suits climbed out of the car and walked up to Dennis with purposeful strides. One of the men had a large mole on his chin and the other had a mustache under his nose. Neither one looked very kind, thanks to the hard expressions they were sporting.

"Can I help you?" Dennis asked.

Mole looked Dennis up and down.

"Are you the one with the tent?" Mustache asked.

"Yes," Dennis said.

"Professor Wizard?"

Dennis nodded.

The men reached into their suit coats and pulled out wallets. They flashed gold badges at Dennis.

"Neat," Dennis said, not knowing how else to respond.

"You bet it is," Mustache said. "This badge gives us the right to take a little bit of your time."

Mole grabbed Dennis's arm. "You're coming with us."

A number of spectators had gathered around, curiously watching.

"What's this about?" Dennis asked.

"You'll find out soon enough."

"I've done nothing wrong," Dennis said boldly.

"We'll see about that," Mustache barked. "Into the car."

"You can't take him," one of the crowd argued. "He didn't do anything."

"We'll let the government decide that," Mole said, pushing Dennis into the large black sedan.

Ezra whispered to Dennis and Dennis yelled out to the spectators, "Keep gathering. The Dearth is coming!"

"Quiet," Mole ordered, "or we'll charge you with inciting a riot."

The door slammed and Mustache climbed into the driver's seat. He started the car and revved the engine loudly. He threw the car into drive, and dust and rocks blanketed all of those standing around as the vehicle raced off.

"Perfect," Ezra whispered. "Just perfect. There's nothing like a little action to get things noticed."

Neither Mustache nor Mole said a single word during the two-hour drive west toward Albuquerque. Ezra, on the other hand, quietly whispered things to Dennis during the whole ride.

At the edge of Albuquerque the vehicle exited the highway and drove south. They stopped at a checkpoint, flashed some identification, and then sped farther south. The area was barren and deserted. There were no homes or structures, just desolate dirt roads that stretched out along the east side of the Monzano Mountains.

The car turned left on one of those deserted roads and drove right up to the side of the mountain. A large bunker built into the side sat there like the opening to Earth's stomach.

The car stopped and Mole helped Dennis out of the car.

"Find out where we are," Ezra whispered.

"Where are we?" Dennis asked nervously.

"That's a question," Mole replied.

"Am I not allowed to ask questions?"

"Did you not give him the 'no questions asked' speech yet?" Mole complained to Mustache.

"I didn't have time."

"No questions," Mole insisted.

"I don't understand what we're doing," Dennis said, confused.

"I'm sure they're aware of that," Ezra whispered.

"Inside," Mustache ordered, opening a large white door and waving Dennis into the bunker.

The bunker was empty. There were a few boxes in the far corner and a couple of mousetraps along the edge. Four chairs circled a metal table in the middle of the room, and a suspended light shone down like a brash flashbulb that was determined to shine. The entire place wasn't much bigger than a large warehouse and reeked of sulfur.

Ezra swore.

"What was that?" Mole asked.

"I said it stinks," Dennis said innocently.

"Sit down," Mole said, pointing to the chairs.

Dennis walked over and sat in one of the middle chairs.

"Actually, could you slide over?" Mustache asked. "It's probably best if you're not in the middle."

Dennis moved into a different chair.

Mole and Mustache sat down. They looked at their watches and brushed the knees of their trousers. Mustache pulled out a small comb and ran it though his namesake. Mole whistled a bit, stood up, paced around the chairs and table, and then sat back down.

"Are we waiting for something?" Dennis finally asked.

"No questions," Mole replied.

After a few more minutes Dennis heard the sound of another vehicle pulling up outside. The door of the bunker opened and an impressive-looking person in an army uniform walked into the bunker. He had short brown hair and dark eyes. He also had two deep dimples in his chin.

Mole and Mustache saluted him as he took a seat across the table from Dennis. He pulled out a folder and clicked his pen. He then sniffed twice and looked directly at Dennis.

"Professor Wizard," he said with contempt. "Or should I say, Dennis O Wood."

"Either one's fine," Dennis said nervously.

"Oh, so you admit to being both?"

Dennis nodded and Dimples scribbled something on the folder.

"I don't want to get into sources, or who I heard it from," Dimples said. "But there've been some reports about you giving explanations to what's happening around the world."

"It was probably me you heard it from," Dennis said helpfully, "because that's what I've been doing."

"I see," Dimples said, making more notes. "How is it that a janitor from back east has become a know-it-all out west?"

"Well, we drove most of the way," Dennis answered.

"Not how did you get here," Dimples raged. "How do you know what you think you know, but you can't possibly know?"

"About Foo?"

All three military men grimaced uncomfortably. After regaining some composure, Dimples spoke. "Yes, about Foo."

"Tell them to shove it," Ezra whispered.

Instead Dennis went with, "You wouldn't believe me if I told you."

"Try us," Dimples dared.

"Why do you even care?" Dennis asked.

Dimples looked at Mole and Mustache. He stood up and turned to face the door. He folded his hands behind his back.

"The world is in turmoil," Dimples said. "You are aware of that?"

Dennis nodded his shaved head.

"I mean, countries are preparing for war over all these things that nobody can explain."

"I can," Dennis said.

"So you say," Dimples snapped. "Did you know there are accounts going back thousands of years of the existence of a place called Foo? Egyptians referenced it as *Pfu,* the Russians *Foo,* with their own style of *o*'s, and in Asia *Fu* . . ."

"Like in 'everybody was kung fu fighting,'" Mole chimed in.

"Yes," Dimples agreed. "Like that song. Well, it seemed the talk always surrounded dreams and images that were bleeding into Reality. The chatter was always dismissed because there's no proof in dreams. A few select beings, however, have kept their eyes and ears open for any further insight. One of those interested parties is your government. We weren't originally concerned, but about fifty years ago a man by the name of Hector Thumps reported to his local government about a place he had been to and how he had gotten back. He was dismissed as crazy, but we kept an eye on him just in case. The government lost track of him for a bit, but then he showed up again, this time with a child. He gave the child to a nice family and was never seen again. Guess what we did then?"

"You watched the child?"

"Well, yes," Dimples said awkwardly. "I didn't think you'd guess it right off. Anyhow, the child was unspectacular and, to be honest with you, he did nothing flashy or Foo-like. Nope, Elton Thumps grew up rather normal and married a nice woman. Unfortunately for him, it was about this time that the country

got very suspicious about things they didn't understand. A couple of high-ups began to wonder if there wasn't some power or advantage in knowing about Foo, and the only sort of real connection they had was Elton. They tried to talk him into helping, but he knew nothing of Foo. He told them he was a child when he was brought here and had no knowledge of it. For some reason the government didn't believe him. So they had to make a few adjustments."

"Adjustments?" Dennis asked.

"They might have accidentally faked his death and taken him far away. And when his wife died giving birth to his child a few days later, they might have told him that the child had died as well."

"I like their style," Ezra whispered.

Dennis just looked baffled.

"You have to understand, the government was suspicious. We kept some tabs on the child who was born, but a short while ago he disappeared. It was at that same time that odd things began happening in the world. And now you claim to know things and are connecting it to Foo."

"Why are you telling me all of this?" Dennis asked.

"Because we've got nothing," Dimples said, his hands shaking and eyes bulging. "I'm getting all kinds of pressure from my commanders to produce something and I have nothing—nothing. The world is falling apart. Countries are preparing for war and they're putting it on my shoulders. Me. I'm up for retirement in six weeks, and if I can just give them something to focus on until—"

Mole slapped Dimples. "Get ahold of yourself."

Dimples put his hand to his face and stood up. He breathed deeply and tried to regain his composure.

"How is it you know about Foo?" he finally asked Dennis.

"I'm not sure I want to answer that," Dennis said. "It seems to me that you went to great lengths to hurt Elton Thumps. How do I know you're not planning the same for me?"

"Don't worry about Elton, he's completely forgiven us," Dimples said lamely.

Dennis laughed nervously. "I'm not sure I believe that."

"You're a smart man," a new voice spoke.

A tall man in a long coat and stiff hat stood in the doorway of the bunker. He took off his hat and walked with purpose up to the table. He was somewhere between forty and forty-five, with thick dark hair and brown eyes. His chin was as well-defined as his smile. He was tan and wore glasses that fit his scholarly face.

Mole stood up and offered the man his chair. The man sat down and smiled at Dennis. He removed his gloves and extended his right hand to shake.

"Dennis, is it?" he said.

Dennis nodded, looking at the man's slightly blue hands.

"It's nice to meet you, Dennis. I'm Elton, Elton Thumps."

Ezra swore and Dennis repeated it.

"Now," Elton said, smiling, "what can you tell me about my son?"

CHAPTER FORTY

SPLIT DECISIONS

Before everyone had even finished eating, Winter had drifted off to sleep and Clover was snoring. The trees and bushes kept the area dry and cozy and it didn't take more than a few more minutes before they were all out.

Leven slept fitfully. He tossed and turned, his head full of images of rants and war. He was on the outside of the group, lying on the edge of the stone ground next to the bushes. He flipped over and tried to get comfortable on his back. His brown eyes flashed open and then burned gold. He closed his eyelids and tried to think of his father and mother, or of anyplace warm and safe.

Leven felt old, although only a short time ago he had been a child.

The stone was hard and difficult to get comfortable on. He settled his back just a bit onto the dirt beneath the bushes. The

dirt was so soft compared to the rock. Leven pulled back, knowing he shouldn't. After a few more restless minutes he leaned against the dirt once more.

Something scratched at his ankle and as he moved to itch it, thick, rubbery strands of black whipped around his mouth and body. He tried to scream but his face was covered. Instantly the strands coiled tight, trapping Leven. The black strings slipped him silently from the others and into the cold, wet forest.

Leven was drawn in like a retracting measuring tape. He slapped up and down against the ground—pulled down the hill and across miles of land. He plowed through the dirt like a cartoon dog burrowing through a field. He weaved in between stones and soldiers and flew across the Sentinel Fields and out onto the gloam.

Once on the gloam Leven was picked up and slammed down on the soil with a tremendous smack. He moaned.

"Get up," a kind voice said.

Leven pushed himself up onto his knees, his back to the voice. His whole body felt like one giant bruise.

"You don't have to put on the act for me," Leven said. "I'm very aware of your true being."

Leven stood up and turned around. He was standing on the gloam a couple of miles out from the shore. The night was dark and Leven could hear the Veil Sea on both sides of him. The gloam itself was about a mile thick and nothing but hard soil. The dark sky above was clear, and stars fizzled like sparklers around the two fat moons.

"You are aware of very little," the Dearth replied.

Leven studied the short man in his vest and cap, his feet meshing with the ground. There was nobody else around. All the troops were still on the shore, asleep or preparing to march in the morning. Leven listened to the sea and hoped that Garnock was aware of what was happening.

"Do you think I don't know what you're thinking?" the Dearth said. "The Waves will not protect you. Cry all you want; they are tending to something much more important to them."

"Garnock!" Leven yelled.

"Here, I'll help," the Dearth said. "Garnock! Garnock, old boy!"

The wind whistled down and around the two of them.

"You don't seem to understand," the Dearth said sympathetically. "This is but a moment. You have stepped in at the end, but this second has been planned and organized to take place just as it is for thousands of years. And now you are approaching the end of your sad life."

Leven's lungs struggled for air as he tried to stand still.

"It's true, I may have underestimated you," the Dearth said. "Or, more precisely, I may have not ever factored you in—which was a mistake. Had I known you were of the same blood as the Want, I might have acted differently. He was successful at very little, but he did well keeping that thought from me. So many secrets, no wonder he went mad."

Leven's hair blew and he could see the moons drawing near

to observe. The scene was vast and cosmic, but it felt more intimate than Leven was comfortable with.

"Why your allegiance to Geth?" the Dearth asked sincerely.

"I believe him."

"But you can step with me and have real reward."

"Why do you even care?" Leven argued.

"You know, you're right," the Dearth said. "I don't. When Azure said you had escaped, I yawned. I can't fight ignorance, and you're a fool to side with anyone but me. I offer possibilities in the face of death."

Leven's head buzzed. He looked up to the stars and then down to the Dearth. The scene was different now. The Dearth stood there alone and the world behind him was nothing but soil—no sky, no water, no life. The view was as miserable and heavy as anything Leven had ever seen. Leven's heart shrank like a tomato left far too long on the vine.

The Dearth's eyes widened. "What do you see?" he asked suspiciously.

"What you truly want," Leven replied, disgusted. "Lithen party line? You lied. Geth's right: You know exactly what will happen when you move into Reality. It will destroy everything."

The Dearth frowned. "I'm afraid so," he said. "Everything will return to dust and I will be plagued by mankind no longer."

"You can't," Leven said angrily. "I'll tell Azure the truth."

"Oh," the Dearth said sadly. "About that, it might be a tad

late. You see, Azure suffered an accident earlier this evening and isn't feeling all that well."

"What?"

"He's been left for dead," the Dearth said bluntly.

"I don't believe it."

The Dearth wriggled his feet and the dirt near Leven began to tumble and bubble up. Azure's motionless body rose to the surface. Azure was covered in soil, his body twisted and bent. There was a large wet stain across the front of his right shoulder. Leven could see Azure's chest rise and drop slowly. Azure coughed, and dirt fell from his mouth as he settled on the soil.

"What have you done?" Leven asked, kneeling by Azure. He took Azure's wrist and felt for a pulse.

Azure's eyes opened and he coughed again.

"He never completely fit in," the Dearth said sadly. "A little bit of good infected him until the end. He stood on too much stone. And when he lost the key and killed Time, that was just inexcusable. We'd be done with all of you and even closer to Reality had he not messed up. Besides, as only you now know, he won't live much longer anyway. No one will. There's still a bit of life left in him, but the accident has left him in ill repair."

Leven looked into Azure's eyes. They were clear and so different from what they had once been. Azure coughed again and blinked. Leven shifted him to make him more comfortable.

"Leave him be," the Dearth bit. "He's a piece of the past."

The Dearth's body seemed to split open and drop to the ground. A black head and black limbs whipped out; the image of

the kindly old man was replaced by a dark beast. The Dearth grabbed Leven and lifted him.

Leven tore at the black, digging his nails and fingers into the goo. The Dearth hissed and dropped Leven down directly on top of Azure.

Leven screamed and scuttled off of Azure. The Dearth wrapped one of his many limbs around Leven's ankle and slapped him like a fish against the ground. Leven twisted and grabbed hold of the black limb. He pulled himself toward the Dearth and bit down on his shoulder.

The Dearth screeched. Then, like a wave of dirty water, he washed over Leven and coiled tightly around his two legs. Leven tried to kick but the hold was too great. The Dearth drew into the ground, sliding beneath the soil like a sinkhole and dragging Leven with him.

Leven clawed at the soil, fighting violently to stay above ground. The Dearth inhaled wickedly, gathering strength, and pulled Leven down. Azure was dragged along with them, moaning in pain. The soil collapsed over Leven as he sank. The Dearth let go of his legs and contracted the soil, cocooning Leven.

"Such a pity," the soil whispered in stereo. "Both of you have come so close to seeing me in my glory, and now to perish only moments before."

Leven could see nothing, but he could feel Azure's foot right above his head. Leven pulled on Azure and dragged himself up through the soil. He grabbed Azure's shoulders and climbed even farther, pulling Azure up with him. Leven's head pushed out of the dirt and he opened his eyes to find himself staring directly at Azure.

Azure was whispering something as Leven grabbed at the ground. Leven scrambled up out of the dirt and onto level soil. He turned and pulled Azure up behind him. Leven stood and took two steps before the Dearth snatched him from behind and reeled him back like a reluctant yo-yo.

The Dearth rose up above the soil and pinned Leven down with three of his sick, twisting limbs. Leven was lying five feet from Azure. The Dearth smiled and black drippings spilled from his mouth.

"What an unwilling victim you are," the Dearth hissed.

He shot one of his limbs out over the ground. It raced past Leven like a snake and off into the distance.

"Why are you doing this?" Leven asked. "You'll destroy everything."

"I like the sound of that." The Dearth laughed, soil raining down on Leven as he did so. "Everything comes from the soil—everything. I'm just putting everything back in its place."

The limb he had sent out retracted. The Dearth had retrieved a long, curved sword from some soldier miles away on shore. Leven was still pinned down and unable to move.

The Dearth lifted the sword and held it two feet above Leven.

"Ready to die?" the Dearth asked.

Leven struggled to get out.

"Sorry you don't get a choice in the matter," the Dearth said.

Leven closed his eyes as the Dearth swung the sword down

with force. Leven felt a heavy thud fall across his body. He opened his eyes to see Azure lying on top of him with the sword in his back.

Azure looked at Leven. "Sorry," he moaned.

The Dearth pulled the sword from Azure's back and rose up higher.

"How beautiful," he cackled, the wind and the sea screaming behind him. "A last attempt to do some good. Fool."

The Dearth threw the sword back down at Azure as he lay over Leven. Leven twisted and rolled Azure out of the way and onto his back. The sword struck the soil and the Dearth screamed. Leven moved away from Azure and tried to climb onto his feet.

He was too slow. The Dearth clipped him at the ankles and pulled him down against the ground with a sharp clap. Leven's lungs exploded as he struggled for breath. The Dearth covered Leven with cords of black and held him tightly against the soil on his back. He lifted the sword up again.

"There's no one left to save you," he crowed proudly.

"You won't win!" Leven yelled, dirt and wind filling his mouth.

"I beg to differ."

The Dearth thrust the sword toward Leven's neck. Leven closed his eyes as the sword landed directly across his neck with a thud. The sword flew back, shaking violently.

Leven's eyes flashed.

The Dearth tried again, this time plunging the sword

toward Leven's stomach. The sword hit and slid to the side.

He tried again.

Nothing.

Again.

Nothing.

"No," the Dearth moaned, drawing back.

The Dearth wrapped five of his black strands around Leven's neck and squeezed. Leven could still breathe perfectly.

"No," the Dearth thundered, releasing him.

Leven sat up, feeling his neck. "Did you plan for this?" he asked.

"No!" the Dearth yelled. "It's too soon for you to be whole."

"I don't make the rules," Leven said. "I just . . ."

Leven moved quickly to take advantage of the Dearth's shock. He grabbed the sword from his limb and in a single smooth stroke sliced the Dearth in two. The top half of the Dearth fell to the ground while the bottom half wriggled and drew into itself. Leven watched the Dearth's face and shoulders ooze into the ground.

Leven dropped the sword and ran to Azure. He lifted him up under his arms and wrapped Azure's right arm around his shoulder.

Azure stared at him.

"Hold on!" Leven yelled.

Leven dragged Azure as the dark night and the tumultuous sea played out around them. Leven's legs felt no burn as he moved down the gloam. He looked up at the dark sky and could see the

light that all the moving stars and moons desired to glow. It lit up the night like a fluorescent bulb.

Black shoots sprang up from below Leven and grabbed hold of his legs. The Dearth had regrouped.

Leven fell to the ground with his back against the soil, Azure rolling to the side. The Dearth moved up over Leven. He was coughing and holding himself together where Leven had sliced through.

"How dare you?" he growled.

Leven lay still on his back, a strange calm filling his heart.

Hundreds of thick black sprouts burst up from the ground and wrapped tightly around Leven. The Dearth tried to pull him back under the soil, but Leven didn't move.

"You're whole!" The Dearth cursed.

Leven smiled, looking up at the night sky. He moved his arms as he lay there and the strands of black flew off him.

"You won't stop me," the Dearth said. "Feel that?"

The ground rumbled beneath Leven's back. It shook as if keeping time.

"You can't dam an entire army," the Dearth smiled viciously.

Leven lay there with his eyes closed, feeling the ground shake as thousands of soldiers began to march down the gloam toward Sycophant Run.

Leven could see light in his mind. He could see the mess the immediate future would be and the beauty a restored Foo could bring about. The possibility felt almost impossible.

"I'll kill you!" the Dearth screamed.

"You can't," Leven said, sitting up.

"Then I'll find the one who can!" the Dearth screamed.

The Dearth slithered down into the soil and disappeared—leaving Leven alone with nothing but the rumbling of the ground and the thought of the one person who could actually follow through with the Dearth's threat.

"Impossible," Leven said to himself.

The wind howled and the ground shook as Leven picked up Azure and moved down the gloam.

CHAPTER FORTY-ONE

THE SON WILL COME OUT TOMORROW

Elton Thumps stared at Dennis. Dennis scratched his nose self-consciously.

"What do you know about Leven?" Elton said. "You claim to know so much about Foo."

"I know he's alive," Dennis said weakly.

"That's a fifty-fifty guess," Elton said, the kindness in his voice slipping just a bit. "Listen, Dennis, I think you are getting into something you don't have the fortitude to complete. This isn't for you."

Ezra whispered something from behind Dennis's ear.

"Don't tell us what we can or can't do," Dennis insisted.

"Us?"

"Me," Dennis clarified.

Elton looked at Dennis carefully.

"Why are you even involved in this?" Elton asked. "Terry and Addy I could see, but you—you have no connection."

"I have what I know," Dennis said forcefully.

Ezra whispered an insult about Elton. Dennis smiled.

"What was that?" Elton asked.

"What was what?" Dennis said.

"I heard a noise, and then you smiled."

"I'm a happy person," Dennis explained.

"No," Elton said. "No, you're not. I've read your file many times."

Ezra whispered something else.

"There it is again."

"Quiet," Dennis said, more to Ezra than to Elton.

Ezra did not like being told what to do. He whispered again. Elton jumped up from where he was sitting and walked around the table and up to Dennis.

"I think he's wired," Elton told Dimples, Mole, and Mustache.

"We patted him down," Mole said.

Dennis stared straight ahead and tried not to look nervous. Ezra pushed back as far behind Dennis's left ear as possible.

Elton circled slowly around Dennis. He looked at the back of his head and then stopped moving. Elton's jaw dropped.

"What?" Ezra said. "Your small brain can't process someone as powerful as me?"

"What *is* that?" Elton asked in awe.

Dennis jumped up, but not before Elton had reached in and pinched Ezra. Ezra was screaming and kicking as Elton held him up in front of his face.

"Unbelievable," Mustache said.

"Get me a jar," Elton said.

Dimples scuffled away.

"I wouldn't do that," Dennis said. "You should let go of him now."

"I knew you weren't important by yourself," Elton said cruelly to Dennis. "This is the missing piece."

"And you're the missing link!" Ezra screamed.

Dennis moved to get Ezra, but Mole and Mustache held him back.

"Easy now," Elton said. "You wouldn't want to end up on our bad side."

Dimples returned and handed Elton a glass jar. Elton dropped Ezra in and then twisted the lid closed.

Ezra was furious, bouncing around the inside of the jar like an over-caffeinated evil toothpick.

Elton set the jar on the desk.

"At least put some airholes in it," Dennis said.

Elton pulled out a small pocketknife, opened it, and violently jabbed two slits into the lid.

"There," Elton said smugly.

Dennis pulled free from Mole and Mustache and slammed his right fist into Elton's left cheek. Elton fell backward onto the

table, his glasses flying off. Mole and Mustache grabbed Dennis again. Elton stood up straight, trying to act calm.

"You shouldn't have done that," Elton said, wiping blood from beneath his nose.

"Don't tell me what I shouldn't do," Dennis said. "Now let him loose."

Elton picked up the jar and looked at Ezra. The angry toothpick was pounding at the glass with his paper-clip leg. Elton smiled and tightened the lid.

"You shouldn't have done that," Dennis said.

"Really," Elton replied. "And why is that?"

"Because eventually you're going to have to let him out," Dennis answered. "And when you do, I would hate to be you."

"Well, that makes us even," Elton Thumps said, "because I would hate to be you. Now sit down. I've got a few more questions."

Mole and Mustache pushed Dennis down into his chair while Ezra continued to scream and run around the jar making unpleasant gestures.

"Let him out," Dennis demanded.

"The issue is not up for debate," Elton said. "I—"

Dennis sprang forward again, ramming his head into Elton's chest. Elton fell backward as Mole threw a strong blow to the back of Dennis's neck. Dennis dropped to the ground, his head hitting the concrete floor. The room flashed and then went dark.

ii

Dennis came to, moaning and tied to a metal chair. The rope was wrapped around his ankles and arms and chest. He tried to move, but the chair just chirped against the ground. He looked around slowly, his head feeling like a huge wad of wet clay bobbing from side to side as he tried to hold it up.

He was in a different bunker. It was large, like the previous one, but this bunker was filled with barrels and boxes all around the edges. There was a small window above the closed front door. A thick, concentrated beam of light shot through the window and down to the floor twenty feet in front of Dennis. At the exact spot where the light touched the ground sat the glass jar holding Ezra. Ezra was pushed up against the side of the jar staring at Dennis. The back of Ezra was beginning to smoke from the intense sunlight being focused on him. Ezra gasped, his arms stretched wide and his mouth open as he started to smolder. He was exhausted from running around the jar, and the heat had stolen every last bit of his energy. The purple tassel on Ezra's head began to smoke.

"No!" Dennis shouted. "No!"

Dennis rocked violently back and forth in his metal chair, trying to break loose. Ezra was mouthing something, but Dennis couldn't hear him through the jar.

"Hold on!" Dennis yelled.

He pulled at the ropes around his wrists until blood began to

drip. Dennis tried to jump up in his seat and hop toward the jar. The chair moved an inch closer. Dennis jumped again, the binding of the rope making it hard for him to breathe. He moved two inches closer.

Ezra's right arm sparked into flame. Ezra weakly patted it out.

"Come on," Dennis cursed himself. "Move."

Dennis hopped forward half an inch.

Ezra's left arm began to burn. Ezra dropped to the floor of the jar and tried to roll the flame out.

"I'm coming!" Dennis yelled.

Ezra looked up and mouthed something as his back burst into flame. Dennis jumped and jumped in his chair. He could see Ezra's whole little body starting to burn. Dennis flipped his shoulders forward and yanked the chair onto its front legs. The chair pivoted and began to drop forward. Dennis twisted one final time and the chair flew sideways against the floor. One of the legs barely reached Ezra, clipping the jar and sending it up into the air. The chair settled on its back with Dennis staring up. He watched the jar bounce off a metal drum and then drop onto a red rusted barrel. The barrel lid popped open and the jar slid down into the barrel. There was a small splash followed by a hissing rush of air. The barrel lid settled on the side and then tipped and slid to the floor in a loud crash.

Dennis lay there on his back, tied to the chair, trying to catch his breath. His body couldn't make up its mind whether to start crying or throw up. Dennis turned his head and looked at the barrel. It was about five feet tall and two feet wide and obviously contained some sort of liquid.

"Airholes," Dennis moaned, knowing that Ezra's jar would be filling up with whatever was in the barrel and sinking to the bottom.

Dennis rocked back and forth like a tipped-over turtle, frantically trying to roll over or move. It was no good; he was useless. Dennis closed his eyes. The barrel gurgled and a final pop of air escaped the top.

Dennis lay there in silence. It was so quiet that he could hear a couple of mice scurrying around behind him. He half hoped someone would remember he was there and he half hoped he would be left alone to die.

Dennis heard a soft metallic scratching. He turned his head, listening for it. Again the noise sounded, and Dennis could tell it was coming from the barrel Ezra had dropped into. Dennis held his breath and listened carefully.

After a minute of silence the sound could be heard again. This time it was louder and had a slight echo.

"Ezra?" Dennis said hopefully. "Is that you?"

There was a short tap followed by a long scratch. Dennis fought his ropes to get free, but it was no use.

"I'm trapped," Dennis said.

There was another tap and then, like a wicked purple sun rising over a rusted metal rim, Ezra emerged.

Dennis smiled.

Ezra flung his arms over the rim of the barrel and pulled himself up onto it. His purple tassel was wriggling menacingly and his green nail-polished body was glowing. His metallic leg shone as if it had been polished repeatedly for years.

"Ezra," Dennis said happily.

The glowing toothpick looked down at Dennis and smiled. His single eye blinked and he looked almost proud. Ezra hopped from the top of the barrel and zipped up to Dennis. Dennis could feel warmth radiating from him.

"I'm sorry," Dennis said.

"You saved me," Ezra replied. "And look at me, I'm more powerful than ever. I have no further insult for you."

Dennis looked dumbfounded.

"Of course, I might change my mind if you continue to make it so easy," Ezra said.

Dennis smiled. "If I could get untied, we could . . ."

Ezra touched the rope around Dennis's chest and it disintegrated. Ezra zipped around the chair and in less than two seconds Dennis was free and dusting bits of rope off of him.

"That's a new trick," Dennis said.

"I'm a new toothpick," Ezra growled. "And I've a new nemesis."

"Elton?"

"Nobody puts me in a jar. I will use him if I need to, but I will not rest until he and Geth are destroyed." Ezra's purple tassel smoldered. "You and I will rule both the realm of Foo and the sad Reality we are now fighting in."

"Let's get out of here, then," Dennis said.

Ezra jumped up onto Dennis's shoulder in a single bound. His body glowed and he clenched his fists. Dennis walked toward the doors. Before he could even comment on the fact that they were probably locked, Ezra reached out his right hand and the two metal doors blew outward and off of their hinges. They flew fifty feet and slammed into the black vehicle that was parked out in front.

Dennis looked at Ezra on his shoulder. "I like that," he said in awe.

"Not as much as me," Ezra cackled.

Through the open door they could see Elton and Mole and Mustache climb out of the smashed vehicle. The three men were yelling and running toward the doorway. Ezra stretched out his other arm and the entire front of the bunker began to pull away from the mountain. Elton and his cronies stared at the tilting wall in horror.

Ezra growled and the wall came tumbling down on top of Mole and Mustache. Elton had been in the path of the missing doors and now stood surrounded by piles of stone and board. Mole and Mustache moaned from under the wreckage.

"What's happening?" Elton asked, trying to remain calm.

"Things have changed," Dennis said.

Ezra spoke into Dennis's ear, quite comfortable with him doing his speaking.

"We'll need at least fifty tanks," Dennis said. "Some helicopters and planes might help as well."

"I can't . . ." Elton started to say, but Ezra flashed his tiny hands open and Elton fell to the ground.

Dennis walked through the rubble and stood over Elton.

"Do you want to occupy Foo?" Ezra seethed.

Elton nodded.

"Then we'll need everyone you can get," Ezra barked.

"I'll have to make some calls," Elton said, standing back up. "I'll need to contact my leaders."

"Do it," Dennis commanded.

iii

Ten hours later a massive convoy of tanks and military vehicles was making its way out of Albuquerque and moving toward Blue Hole Lake. The sides of the vehicles had banners that read: *Military Relief Effort.*

Dennis was in the backseat of the lead vehicle with Ezra on his knee. Elton was there as well, and a general with more medals than hair was questioning the toothpick in disbelief.

"A whole realm?" the general asked. "Untapped land?"

"A whole realm," Ezra answered, bothered. "Can't these things go faster?"

"The convoy's moving as fast as it can," the general said.

"What's the deal with the Military Relief Effort signs?" Dennis asked.

"We feel there's no need to get people too concerned."

"Were you elected to your position?" Ezra asked cruelly.

"No," the general said, clearing his throat.

"I didn't think so," Ezra sniffed.

"You know, we're putting a lot of trust in you two," the general huffed.

"Would you like me to turn your body inside out from your mouth?" Ezra asked seriously.

The general laughed uncomfortably while Elton shook his head.

"Trust what you want," Ezra said. "But in a short while Foo will spill from the opening, and if we don't strike first, then we will be destroyed."

The general shrugged. He looked down at Ezra and tapped his own nose with his right index finger. "I suppose we've gone to war over far less."

"See," Ezra said. "That's the spirit. This will all work so much better if you just listen to me."

"I've always been an out-of-the-box thinker," the general bragged.

Ezra and Dennis stared at the general.

"Wow." Ezra laughed. "This is going to be easier than I thought." Ezra's vicious cackle filled the large vehicle and added to the overall feeling of uneasiness about what was unfolding—none of them realizing that what they were driving into was the beginning of the very end.

GLOSSARY

Who's Who in Foo

Leven Thumps

Leven is fourteen years old and is the grandson of Hector Thumps, the builder of the gateway. Lev originally knew nothing of Foo or of his heritage. He eventually discovered his true identity: He is an offing who can see and manipulate the future. Lev's brown eyes burn gold whenever his gift kicks in.

Winter Frore

Winter is thirteen, with white-blond hair and deep evergreen eyes. Her pale skin and willowy clothes give her the appearance of a shy spirit. Like Sabine, she is a nit and has the ability to freeze whatever she wishes. She was born in Foo, but her thoughts and memories of her previous life are gone. Winter struggles just to figure out what her purpose is.

GETH

Geth has existed for hundreds of years. In Foo he was one of the strongest and most respected beings, a powerful lithen. Geth is the head token of the Council of Wonder and the heir to the throne of Foo. Eternally optimistic, Geth is also the most outspoken against the wishes of Sabine. To silence Geth, Sabine trapped Geth's soul in the seed of a fantrum tree and left him for the birds. Fate rescued Geth, and in the dying hands of his loyal friend Antsel he was taken through the gateway, out of Foo, and planted in Reality. He was brought back to Foo by Leven and Winter.

SABINE (SUH-BINE)

Sabine is the darkest and most selfish being in Foo. Snatched from reality at the age of nine, he is now a nit with the ability to freeze whatever he wishes. Sabine thirsts to rebuild the gateway because he believes if he can move freely between Foo and Reality he can rule them both. So evil and selfish are his desires that the very shadows he casts seek to flee him, giving him the ability to send his dark castoffs down through the dreams of men so he can view and mess with Reality.

ANTSEL

Antsel was a member of the Council of Wonder. He was aged and fiercely devoted to the philosophy of Foo and to preserving the dreams of men. He was Geth's greatest supporter and a nit. Snatched from Reality many years ago, he was deeply loyal to the

council and had the ability to see perfectly underground. He was a true Foo-fighter who perished for the cause.

CLOVER ERNEST

Clover is a sycophant from Foo assigned to look after Leven. He is about twelve inches tall and furry all over except for his face, knees, and elbows. He wears a shimmering robe that renders him completely invisible if the hood is up. He is incredibly curious and mischievous to a fault. His previous burn was Antsel.

TIM TUTTLE

Tim is a garbage man and a kindly neighbor of Winter. In Reality, Tim and his wife, Wendy, looked after Winter after being instructed to do so by Amelia. When Winter goes missing, Tim sets out to find her.

DENNIS O WOOD

Dennis is a janitor whom fate has picked to carry out a great task. He leads a lonely life and has never dreamed.

JANET FRORE

Janet is a woman who believes she is Winter's mother but has no concern that Winter is missing. She has spent her life caring only for herself.

TERRY AND ADDY GRAPH

Terry and Addy were Leven's horrible-care givers in Reality.

OSCK

Osck is the unofficial leader of a small band of echoes. He is deeply committed to the meshing of Foo with Reality. He has also taken a very strong liking to Janet Frore.

AZURE

Azure is a lithen and a contemporary of Geth. He sat on the Council of Wonder and was a great friend of Geth's brother Zale. He turned to evil when he decided to stand still too long and let the influence of the Dearth overtake his mind and heart. A small bit of good still infects him, and it manifests itself by swelling and bleeding from his right ear. He is no longer his own man.

THE ORDER OF THINGS

BAADYN

The Baadyn are fickle creatures who live on the islands or shores of Foo. They seek mischief to a point, but when they begin to feel guilty or dirty, they can unhinge themselves at the waist and let their souls slide out and into the ocean to swim until clean. The clean souls of the Baadyn have been known to do numerous good deeds.

BLACK SKELETONS

These great warriors rose from the Cinder Depression many years ago. They occupy the land nearest Fté, and are known for their ability to tame and ride avalands.

COGS

Cogs are the ungifted offspring of nits. They possess no great single talent, yet they can manipulate and enhance dreams.

THE DEARTH

It is said that there is none more evil than the Dearth. His only desire is for the soil to have the last say as all mankind is annihilated. He has long been trapped beneath the soil of Foo, but has used his influence to poison Sabine and Azure and any who would stand still long enough to be fooled. In his present state, the Dearth works with the dark souls who have been buried to move the gloam and gain greater power on his quest to mesh Foo with Reality.

ECHOES

Echoes are gloriously bright beings that are born as the suns reflect light through the mist in the Fissure Gorge. They love to stand and reflect the feelings and thoughts of others. They are useful in war because they can often reflect what the opponent is really thinking.

EGGMEN

The Eggmen live beneath the Devil's Spiral and are master candy makers. They are egg-shaped and fragile, but dedicated believers in Foo.

FISSURE GORGE

Fissure Gorge is a terrific gorge that runs from the top of Foo to the Veil Sea. At its base is a burning, iridescent glow that creates a great mist when it meets with the sea. The heat also shifts and changes the hard, mazelike air that fills the gorge.

GIFTS

There are twelve gifts in Foo. Every nit can take on a single gift to help him or her enhance dreams. The gifts are:

See through soil

Run like the wind

Freeze things

Breathe fire

Levitate objects

Burrow

See through stone

Shrink

Throw lightning

Fade in and out

Push and bind dreams

Fly

GLOAM

The gloam is the long arm of dirt stretching from below the Sentinel Fields out into the Veil Sea. It is said that the Dearth uses the black souls of selfish beings buried in Foo to push the gloam closer to the Thirteen Stones in an effort to gain control of the gifts.

GUNT

The gunt are sticky creatures that seal up and guard any hole too deep, thus preserving the landscape of Foo and preventing disaffected beings from digging their way out. Once gunt hardens in the holes, it can be harvested to eat.

LITH

Lith is the largest island of the Thirteen Stones. It has long been the home of the Want and a breeding ground for high concentrations of incoming dreams. Lith was originally attached to the main body of Foo but shifted to the Veil Sea along with the other stones many years ago.

LITHENS

Lithens were the original dwellers of Foo. Placed in the realm by fate, they have always been there. They are committed to the sacred task of preserving the true Foo. Lithens live and travel by fate, and they fear almost nothing. They are honest and are believed to be incorruptible. Geth is a lithen.

LONGINGS

A near-extinct and beautiful breed, longings were placed in Foo to give the inhabitants a longing for good and a desire to fulfill dreams. They have the ability to make a person forget everything but them.

LORE COIL

Lore Coils are created when something of great passion or energy happens in Foo. The energy drifts out in a growing circle across Foo, giving information or showing staticlike images to those it passes over. When the Lore Coil reaches the borders of Foo, it bounces back to where it came from. It can bounce back and forth for many years. Most do not hear it after the first pass.

NITS

Niteons—or nits, as they are referred to—are humans who were once on earth and were brought to Foo by fate. Nits are the working class of Foo. They are the most stable and the best dream enhancers. Each is given a powerful gift soon after he or she arrives in Foo. A number of nits can control fire or water or ice. Some can see in the pitch-dark or walk through walls and rock. Some can levitate and change shape. Nits are usually loyal and honest. Both Winter Frore and Sabine are nits.

OFFINGS

Offings are rare and powerful. Unlike others who might be given only one gift, offings can see and manipulate the future as well as learn other gifts. Offings are the most trusted confidants of the Want. Leven Thumps is an offing.

OMITTED

The Omitted are very insecure and untrusting beings. They can see everything in Foo except for themselves and their reflections. They are dependent on others to tell them how they look. They reside in caves and trees in the mountains outside the Invisible Village.

ONICKS

Raised near the Lime Sea, these winged beasts travel mostly by foot. An onick is loyal only to the rider on its back, and only as long as that rider is aboard.

RANTS

Rants are nit offspring that are born with too little character to successfully manipulate dreams. They are constantly in a state of instability and chaos. As dreams catch them, half of their bodies become the image of what someone in Reality is dreaming at the moment. Rants are usually dressed in long robes to hide their odd, unstable forms. Jamoon is a rant.

ROVENS

Rovens are large, colorful, winged creatures that are raised in large farms in the dark caves beneath Morfit. They are used for transportation and sought after because of their unbreakable talons. Unlike most in Foo, rovens can be killed. They are fierce diggers and can create rips in the very soil of Foo. When they shed their hair, it can live for a short while. They often shed their hair and let it do their dirty work.

SARUS

The sarus are thick, fuzzy bugs who can fly. They swarm their victims and carry them off by biting down and lifting as a group. They can communicate only through the vibration of water. They are in control of the gaze and in charge of creating gigantic trees.

SHATTERBALL

Shatterball is a popular sport played in a suspended giant orb of glass created by special engineers in Foo. The players are nits who have the gift of flight. It is a violent and exciting game that

ends either when the orb is shattered or when only a single player remains inside. It is played with a small black ball called a pit.

SOCHEMISTS

The Sochemists of Morfit are a group of twenty-four aged beings who listen for Lore Coils and explain what they hear. They are constantly fighting over what they believe they have heard. They communicate what they know to the rest of Foo by using locusts.

SYCOPHANTS (SICK-O-FUNTS)

Sycophants are assigned to serve those who are snatched into Foo. Their job is to help those new residents of Foo understand and adjust to a whole different existence. They spent their entire lives serving the people to whom they are assigned, called their "burns." There is only one way for sycophants to die, but nobody aside from the sycophants knows what that is.

THORNS

Thorns are possessive and whimsical beings. They are as small as bees, but they have great strength. They often live and hover around things they have grown attracted to, spending their days protecting and taking care of what they admire.

THIRTEEN STONES

The Thirteen Stones were once the homes of the members of the Council of Wonder, with the thirteenth and largest, Lith, occupied by the Want. Each of the smaller stones represented a different one of the twelve gifts. With Foo in disarray, many of the stones are empty or are being used by others for selfish reasons.

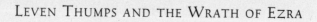

TURRETS

The turrets of Foo are a large circle of stone turrets that surround a mile-high pillar of restoring flame. The turrets sit on a large area of Niteon and are surrounded by a high fence. The main way to the flame is through the gatehouse that sits miles away.

THE WANT

The Want is the virtually unseen but constantly felt sage of Foo. He lives on the island of Lith and can see every dream that comes in. He is prophetic and a bit mad from all the visions he has had.

WAVES OF THE LIME SEA

The Waves of the Lime Sea are a mysterious and misunderstood group of beings who guard the island of Alder. Their loyalty is to the oldest tree that grows on the island.

WHISPS

Whisps are the sad images of beings who were only partially snatched from Reality into Foo. They have no physical bodies, but they can think and reason. They are sought after for their ideas, but miserable because they can't feel and touch anything.

THE ADVENTURE CONTINUES
IN BOOK FIVE,
LEVEN THUMPS AND THE RUINS OF ALDER

CHAPTER ONE

When Peace is Shattered

Two small sycophants stood on a tall gray rock and gazed out over the Veil Sea. The dark waters were choppy, and the largest moon was pulling and pushing huge waves up upon the shores only to call them back again. The shores were covered with sycophants all poised and waiting for battle.

"They're coming," Rast whispered, his voice sounding old and tired.

"I know," Reed replied. "I'm worried that each breath might be my last."

The night felt poised to fall and shatter, as if someone had stacked it precariously on a high shelf and now the smallest motion might send the whole thing tumbling down. Orange flares shot across the sky, drawing lines from one end of Foo to the other.

"Keep your heart light," Rast pleaded. "Please."

"It's not in my nature," Reed admitted. "But I'll try."

Rast smiled at his friend. Rast was one of the most important sycophants and the brightest point in the Chamber of Stars. He had been entrusted with the well-being of Foo, and now the entire realm teetered on the brink of collapse. Rast stared at the thousands of sycophants who were all poised and waiting along the shore for battle. In the past, the only way to see the sycophants would have been to look through the special glasses he had. Now, with the secret of the sycophants floating around everywhere, and so many lore coils exposing the words that stole the sycophants' invisibility, there was no need for the glasses. Rast, along with anyone who had vision, could easily see every sycophant.

"Everything's changed," Reed complained. "How can we ask our children to fight when they are visible?"

"They must," Rast said. "And they still have their claws."

The claws Rast was speaking about were temporary and usually came on during the few years all sycophants spent committed to guard the shores of their homeland. The claws were tremendous and razor sharp and shot out from their knuckles and could slice through just about anything. Their claws were extremely effective weapons, especially when sycophants were invisible. Now, however, they would be fighting against larger foes without the ability to disappear.

"I wish Brindle were here," Rast said. "His heart is always light."

"He'll be back," Reed said, too worried about himself to think of others. "We'll win this, right?"

Rast looked at his friend and sighed. He put his small hand

on Reed's shoulder. Reed was a kind but anxious sycophant. He was one of the lower points in the Chamber of Stars.

"I can only hope," Rast answered.

"Foo can't fail," Reed argued.

"Can you hear that?" Rast asked in a hushed whisper.

Reed jumped and then steadied himself. "Hear what?"

"Look," Rast said, pointing. His voice was filled with sorrow. "The gloam now connects to our home."

Reed looked, but there was nothing but darkness and thousands of sycophants standing motionless and on guard. "I can't see anything but our troops."

"See how the black of night moves right above the gloam?"

Reed slowly shook his head.

"We should have shattered that map," Rast said.

"We tried," Reed shivered.

"Well, it's too late now," Rast said sadly. "Can you feel that in your feet?"

Reed fell to his knees and pressed his palms down against the stone. "What am I supposed to . . . the ground's shaking."

"Ready the captains," Rast ordered. "Claws out and eyes wide. Look over there now."

Reed looked toward the gloam and could faintly see thousands of twinkling bits of sliver reflecting under the moonlight. The lead rants were carrying huge silver poles, and the staffs were strung with thousands of coin-sized pieces of silver.

"Reed," Rast ordered, "I was wrong. Claws out and eyes like slits—don't look at the metal."

Reed leapt from the stone as the largest moon increased in intensity, doubling the light of the night. Rast could see the armies clearly now. The shimmering metal looked like a net of sparkling lights. All over, sycophants who should have been fighting for their home began to stare at the silver and fall into a trance. Their small bodies splashed into the water or onto the shore, lying there motionless, looking like rag dolls.

"Keep your eyes closed and fight!" Rast demanded, screaming out to those in front of him. "Remember: Without us, Foo fails."

Thousands of rants spilled onto the shores of Sycophant Run. They were swinging metal swords and wooden kilves. Rast jumped from the pointed stone and sprang up over a dozen considerably younger sycophants. He struggled up onto another flat stone and looked out over the scene.

Rast's small heart slid down into his right foot. He watched as thousands and thousands of sycophants were thrown aside or trampled over. Stunned or wounded, the valiant beings fell. Everything in him told him to turn and run, but Rast knew that this was the sycophants' last chance to stop what was happening. His eyes became wet and he could no longer see clearly.

Reed climbed up next to him. "There's too many, Rast. And the metal is putting so many of us in a trance."

"I see cogs and echoes fighting as well," Rast said sadly. "Why would they fight against us?"

"It's the whole of Foo spilling onto our shores," Reed cried. "They want out and we've failed to keep them away."

Rants circled in and around the numerous troops of sycophants. Some sycophants were slashing away with their claws out and eyes closed, but most were dropping like stones as their minds became transfixed on the shimmering metal.

"We should retreat," Reed yelled. "We should hide until these fools have gone away."

"And let them just walk out of Foo?" Rast asked.

"What choice do we have?"

Rast looked at all the thousands of sycophants. He watched as wave after wave of attackers rolled off the gloam and joined the battle. Two sycophants were hurled over their heads, flying back into the trees and crashing to the ground.

"We must retreat," Reed said.

Rast looked at Reed. "Let me at least get my hands dirty first."

"But . . ."

Rast screamed and then plunged down from the flat stone directly onto a huge rant. Reed shrugged, screamed even louder, and took on an enemy of his own.

CHAPTER TWO

I'M NOT SLEEPING ANYMORE

Leven tossed and rocked, trying desperately to find some more sleep, but the dream he had just experienced kept his mind racing. So, despite the exhaustion that had been brought on by lack of rest and even more by Leven's battle with the Dearth, sleep was not coming easily. As he lay on the floor, his mind whirled and whined like a rusty hamster wheel. He could hear Geth breathing lightly across the room.

"Are you awake?" he asked softly.

There was no answer. Geth had found sleep, and only the sound of wind pushing through the leaves above answered Leven.

"*Worry,*" the wind seemed to whisper.

Leven turned onto his side.

"*Worry.*"

Leven opened his eyes. His pupils warmed slowly, sending a ray of gold up into the roof of the tent. He could see the stitches in the fabric.

Leven lifted his right hand and held it up to his view. His fingers looked the same, but he knew that something had changed. The Dearth had been unable to kill him. He had seen the blade crash down against his own neck and nothing had happened. His mind played the image over and over in his head. Leven caught his breath and sat up.

"*Worry,*" the wind moaned. "*Worry.*"

Leven could hear the sound of splashing water in the distance. He turned his head and closed his eyes. When he opened them back up a moment later, they dimmed until they were as dark and brown as they used to be.

Leven stood up and shifted his right ear away from the wind. It was faint, but the sound of splashing water still trickled through his brain.

"Clover," Leven whispered, "is that you?"

The thought disappeared like a bubble as he looked down and saw Clover curled up in a ball, sleeping by Geth's feet. Geth mumbled something and turned over.

Again in the distance water splashed.

Leven stepped away from the tent and into the dark. He could feel stone against his feet as he climbed down the knoll. He flipped the hood of his weathered black robe up over his head and pulled it closed at the neck. The robe was tight against his back and shoulders and way too short, causing Leven to look like a wizard wearing floods.

Leven hiked deeper into the dark, pushing through long, ragged tree limbs and tall tangles of grass. He looked up and saw a couple of dozen stars rolling slowly as if the sky were being tilted and they were sliding backwards. With his eyes to the sky, Leven's feet faltered, and he fell forward unto his knees and palms. His hands scraped violently against a jagged rock.

"Perfect," Leven complained. "You'd think I'd know how to walk by this point in my life."

Leven moaned, stood back up, and dusted himself off. Had he been the normal Leven of a couple of weeks ago, his hands would have been bleeding profusely. But now there was no blood, and under the moonlight all he could see was a long, white scratch that was quickly fading away. Leven held his hand up and listened to the worrisome wind. He could still hear the faint sound of splashing water coming from beyond the trees.

"Worry," the wind blew.

Leven stepped out of the thick trees and looked over the ground. The half-moons covered the landscape in shadows and shine. Up and over from where he stood was a small pond, and on the edge of the pond were dozens of smaller puddles of water.

The air smelled delicious and wet.

Leven jogged to the puddles and dropped to his knees. He thrust his hands into one of the larger puddles to rinse away the dirt from his fall. As he pulled his arms out of the water, he could hear the sound of splashing. Leven looked to his left and saw a big puddle gurgling and spitting. It looked like a boiling cauldron buried beneath the soil.

He stood up and shook his hands off, stepped over to the fizzing body of water, and looked down. The puddle shot small drops of water up into the air and onto Leven. He instinctively backed up, but the water was cool and calming, like a summer rain.

Leven watched the water in the puddle settle and then grow glassy. He marveled as an image began to take shape in the liquid. There was a small, dark room with a high window and a dirty rug on the floor.

The image began to grow clearer.

Now Leven could see every thread of the rug and the texture of the walls and floor. He could hear the sound of talking coming from outside of the window. Amazed and a bit bewildered, Leven knelt down. He held his hands out over the puddle and flexed his fingers as a coolness from the water tickled his palms. Leven looked up at the moons and marveled that it wasn't their reflection he saw in the water.

He shrugged his shoulders and stuck his fingers in the water.

The image of the room and small window smeared and then returned. Leven reached in deeper and fingered the edge of the small window. He could feel the wood frame. His middle finger snagged a rough splinter and Leven instinctively tried to yank his hand out.

It wouldn't budge.

The water began to swirl around his captured arms like a toilet slowly flushing. Leven growled and pulled, but the suction of the water was too strong. The puddle pulled his arms in up to his shoulders and swirled even faster.

"Geth!" Leven yelled. "Geth!"

The right half of Leven's face began to go under.

"Clo—" he gurgled.

His head went under. Leven used his left shoulder to push up on the side of the puddle, but it was no use. The pull was too strong. Leven's shoulder slipped from the edge, and in one second his complete upper body was down in the puddle. Leven twisted and shook, but the water pulled him in to the point where there was nothing but his legs sticking out. He kicked and thrashed like a maniac, but the puddle kept drawing him in—two seconds later, nothing but feet—a second after that, nothing but nothing.

The water stopped swirling, and once again there was only the sound of the wind as it pushed through the leaves of the fantrum trees.

"Worry."

Leven flew though the air in a dream. He had reached into a puddle and now he was racing swiftly toward the ground as if he were flying. He was frightened and exhilarated all at once. Flaring out his legs, he turned to the right. He wiggled his arms and lifted up and then back down a few feet. He was falling, but with some control.

Leven could see the hulking black mountain of Morfit off in the distance. The silhouette was sprinkled with thousands of small, flickering lights. Leven witnessed the darkness in the far sky as black dreams and selfish imaginations polluted it.

Leven dropped hundreds of feet. His stomach was in his mouth and his head was in his toes. He bent his legs and his body shot over the land at an alarming rate. He felt a pull, spun wildly around in the air, and then was thrown downward.

Leven could see the Lime Sea in the distance and land rushing up to him like steam. Everywhere there were large wooden buildings with pointed towers and turrets. The buildings made a large square around a giant piece of land. The ornate structures slumped and crumbled as Leven pushed through them, coming to a stop against a hardwood floor.

Leven's body sprawled out on the floor in the shape of an x. His head spun and he found it hard to open his eyes as he lay there. He breathed in deep and tried to lift his head, but a rough voice stopped him.

"Lie still," the voice said. "Keep your face to the floor."

Leven was happy to oblige, seeing how he felt as if he had just been hit by a large truck. Even with his face to the floor he could see something walking around him, the shadow of whoever it was shifting as it moved. The shape stopped above Leven's head. It moaned as if bothered and then spoke.

"He set up so many traps," the voice said. "So many traps laid out for you, and you fell for one of the tamest."

"Traps?" Leven slurred, unable to speak clearly with his mouth pushed against the floor.

"Traps—all over Foo," the voice answered. "He needed to speak with you. Devices and gadgets designed to keep you on the course. It's interesting that you fell for such a simple one. Nobody in his right mind reaches into a puddle in Foo without testing the water."

"I did," Leven reminded him.

"I wouldn't admit that," the voice mocked.

"Why?" Leven slurred.

"Let's just say we set up many surprises designed to bring you to me."

"Who are you?"

"*Me* will do."

"What?" Leven said, lifting his head just a bit.

"Lie still," the voice said again.

"No way," Leven said, pushing himself up.

"Lie still!"

Leven jumped onto his feet. He looked around, ready for a fight, but there was nobody there. "Where are you?"

"Couldn't you have just stayed down?" the voice said, sounding disappointed.

"Who are you?" Leven asked again, still looking around.

"That's not important. You've nothing to fear from me at the moment, but that could change. I speak for one who has every interest in what you're about to do. He arranged this."

"The Dearth?" Leven asked angrily.

"Certainly not the Dearth," the voice said lightly. "The Dearth moves on his own accord and for his own purpose. Even now he's pushing through the exit. What can you do but leave him be? Foo has no need of such darkness. He no longer whispers from the soil. His thoughts are on Reality."

Read Book Five to find out more!